THE SYNDICATE MANAGER

RICHARD LAWS

First published 2018 by Five Furlongs

© Richard Laws 2018
ISBN 978-1-9164600-1-0 (Paperback)
ISBN 978-1-9164600-0-3 (EBook)

I would like to say a huge thank you to everyone at Ownaracehorse;
trainers, jockeys, stable staff, our horses and of course all our shareholders.

I'm particularly indebted to Peter McCafferty for all his hard work and
understanding, to Pat Grant for her support, editorial prowess and
encouragement and to Mike Dunn for his editorial advice, enthusiasm and
car-parking skills.

Published by Five Furlongs 2018

For Rachel

One

The roar from crowd at York was still a faint, distant buzz at the moment. It started when you came into the straight, and your horse began to tighten under you. Instead, it was the sound of the hooves pounding on the turf which was the primary sound filling Raul Garcia's head, along with the odd shout from other jockeys, jostling for positions, voices muffled by the stiff, head-on breeze.

The Ghost Machine felt good. He travelled well within himself and Raul could feel the colt's untapped reserves beneath him. In front, two horse widths out from the running rail and four lengths up, the pacemaker was starting to come back to the main body of the field, and on the rail to the left of him, Raul sensed another runner come under pressure as the jockey's mannerisms transformed from an easy sit into an exaggerated push. Raul eased his mount out slightly to the right to ensure a clean passage around the struggling competitor, his rider now pumping his fists up the neck of the horse and then pulling his whip through. 'Not yet,' said the metronome in Raul's head.

The three furlongs pole started to take shape as it rushed toward him. Raul felt a presence move up behind him on his right. He stole a glance at the almost black horse with a milky white blaze running across its forehead which seemed to drift up effortlessly onto his right flank. The last horse he wanted to see at this moment. The Ghost Machine, also aware, flicked an ear and responded by lengthening its stride momentarily. 'Not yet Ghost,' communicated Raul through a soft hand movement on the reins. The horse on his inside started to lose its pitch. The pacemaker slipped quickly past on the rail, his race over, and the three jockeys in front of him all started to row along, lined abreast for a moment, but then, within a single stride, the symmetry was broken.

The thick, blood red circle with a number two in its centre was a few strides away when the commentary on the public address system came lilting through the breeze, punctuating the slap of hooves on the grass. It was high pitched, excited. The crowd roar became audible moments later. Whips made contact with hide and their staccato cracks peppered the soundtrack. Raul felt The Ghost Machine's gears start to mesh as he was joined on his outside. 'Don't get blocked!' screamed the voice inside him, but Raul ignored it 'Keep your nerve,' he answered.

Directly in front of him a large colt started to roll around, first to the right, then back to the left, his rider pushing and then pulling him straight. To Raul's left another of the leaders, staying on dourly, came back to him. Raul was on top of them too quickly. Two sets of flashing metallic hooves fizzed through the air in front of The Ghost's nose. At his side the white blaze had gone, now a powerful black rump of rippling muscle filled that view, the public stands framed the vista. 'Go now, go now,' called the incensed inner voice 'Wait boy, wait...' Raul answered.

In front of him the two leaders were joined by the black horse. On the inside, a chestnut colt came under pressure and edged towards the rails, taking his nearest challenger with him, the two of them weakening, but continuing to stretch down the Knavesmire.

'Go! Yelled the voice,' 'Go,' screamed Raul in reply.

The Ghost Machine was given two inches of reins and needed no more. He went forward powerfully, lengthening his stride to move alongside the two horses on his inner within three strides. In front, to his right, Raul saw the jockey on the black horse change his whip hand and land a blow to the horse's left flank. A second sense told him nothing else was finishing behind him, there were no sound of snorts, shouts, or imminent hooves.

For the first time Raul pushed. He crouched lower in the saddle and felt the click of the gear change. Within two strides he was past the two horses on his inside, switched his whip to his right hand, and gave The Ghost a flick. Nostrils flared, The Ghost took a lungful of air and stretched out. Off the leash, the thoroughbred changed his leading leg and surged forwards, edging onto the running rail. On his outside, the black horse plunged its head down in response to its rider's hands pushing urgently up its neck and the two horses were suddenly nose to nose. There was a single stride of total unison, and then The Ghost opened up.

Forty five thousand people took a breath together in a split second of group awe, then let out a deafening roar which could be heard in York city centre, two miles away. The Ghost hit the furlong pole a nose up, pointed his toe and gripped the turf, pulling the winning post to him. On his outside, a whip cracked onto his rival, but was lost in the wave of noise coming from the public address system and the mass of onlookers. With the imperiousness of one who knows he has talent, the grey horse spun away from the rest of the field. Raul, caught in a microsecond of time which seemed to last longer than it should, glimpsed the big red 'O' as it become larger. The sound of hooves behind him diminished and as he met the finishing line the thrill of excitement raced through his spine and he let out a delighted 'Yes!' and punched the air with his whip-encrusted fist.

The commentary continued to babble in the background as gasps were followed by excited exclamations ringing between the watchers. Spontaneous applause broke out in the top of the stands and quickly spread into all the racecourse enclosures.

The Ghost Machine, sensing the release in the saddle, immediately flicked his ears forward and took his exertion down a notch, then another. A gloved hand slapped the grey down the neck and he responded with a snort, blowing big breaths down his inflamed nasal passage.

From the winning post the gallop became a canter, the canter a steady trot and finally the man and equine athlete came to a stop three-quarters of a minute later, almost a third of the time it had taken them to cover the previous mile from starting stalls to finishing line.

Inside the commentary booth at the top of the premier stand, an ex-jockey waited for his cue, turned away from the scene below, looked into the lens of a television camera, and delivered a shining review of horse and jockey. As the dark blue and yellow colours returned to the winners enclosure cameras whirred, clicked, and flashed.

Raul held his hand to his dark blue cap in response to the cheers from the throng of race-goers around the parade ring. York racecourse was still buzzing. He threw the reins over the colts head and slipped off the horse without fuss, immediately helping the lad undo the straps and buckles keeping his saddle in place. The result was repeated over the public address system and a sharp breeze whipped around the ring, the autumn trees still retained their leaves, producing a rustling soundtrack to the proceedings. After speaking with a dozen excited owners, Raul turned, saddle across his arm, and started his walk towards the weighing room. Television cameras and media people pressed toward him. The first four horses, all now back from the course and unsaddled, drank, stood, were led in circles and received thanking pats from various well-wishers, their energy apparently spent now. The public address struck up again, announcing that the presentations were about to take place in the winners enclosure.

It happened so quickly. Celebration turned to tragedy in a matter of moments. The reality of what a three quarter ton horse can inflict to a human being, played out in public with the event recorded, horribly, from every angle. The black horse with the milky white blaze, placed second, snorted. He junked backwards slightly. Then he lunged backward, pulling the lead rein from his stable lass's hands. The colt was onto his front legs, pushing his weight down, before his back began to rise skywards. His back legs contracted, then extended and then… connected.

A sickening, unnatural crack broke through the convivial atmosphere. The gathered crowd gasped and then fell silent. Some turned away, others stood staring, open-mouthed. A child laughed somewhere, incongruous in the increasing silence. Quiet mutterings began, and race-goers in the stands started to flood onto the balconies, some straining for a view of the scene. Thousands of faces pointed down onto the parade ring. Some turned away, shocked, others stared without comprehension. Horrified parents fled with their children, pushing through the sea of people, hoping to save their offspring from an image which would surely disturb their fragile minds.

The unmoving body of a smartly dressed woman lay unnaturally on the finely mowed carpet of grass in the winners enclosure. Her eyes were open, but unfocused, and an ever-increasing puddle of thick, dark red blood began fanning out from where her head touched the turf.

Two

'You can take your Mother on a round the world cruise. *Wouldn't she like that?*'

Olivia Dunn was left with the final phrase ringing in her head even though the telephone receiver had been dead for over a minute. It was the way he'd said it, the emphasis was just a little... wrong. He had stated these words four, maybe five times during their three minute conversation. It wasn't just the line itself; it was the tone and delivery, in a perfunctory style, almost staccato. Had there been a threat, a touch of malice or bullying in there too? She wasn't sure, but it had certainly left her feeling just a little unnerved, or perhaps insecure, despite the fact she was sitting in her favourite armchair, at home, with her eighty year old mother only in the next room.

Olivia shivered, got up from her tired, but comfortable armchair, pushing up from her knees and cursing the pain in her lower back under her breath as she first took the full weight of her body. The cold seemed to seep into her bones by the time they reached the middle of winter, something she wished she hadn't inherited from her mother. She crossed over to the large bay window and parting the curtains, peered out into their front garden, seeking inspiration. It was an uninteresting view, the cold temperatures rendering the plants inert and lifeless and she soon turned away.

What had he said on the phone? She mulled his words again, absently looking around for a pen or pencil. Six fifteen in the evening, that was it – a package... no, a letter... at six fifteen. She glanced over at the brown and grey marble fireplace which curved around an open coal fire. It lay silent, almost spent and flameless. The small carriage clock on the mantle read ten minutes past six, under which four golden balls spun relentlessly left and then right, twisting the time away.

How had he known about mother? It was strange. Very strange. Also, just a touch exhilarating. Even at sixty-three, I can get my heart thumping she thought. Olivia smiled inwardly, but then caught herself and shook her head from its reverie and focused again on the man on the phone and what was about to happen.

She pulled back the curtain again, and then a set of nets, shifting her body slightly to gain a view of the path that led to her door. There was no one there. The streetlights showed a bare city street with wet pavements. Rain that was attempting to become sleet lightly hit the window and slid down in greasy rivulets. Whilst it was a city address, there was no need to come down this Edwardian crescent unless you lived here. Most people who passed her window were known to Olivia, those she didn't recognise tended to be heading for one of two different doors whose inhabitants appeared to have a social life which extended beyond the road.

5

To all intents and purposes, Gilbride Close was a little enclave, and a fairly exclusive one at that, consisting of a small crescent of three story Victorian villas. Olivia and her mother had chosen it because it was close to the centre of Edinburgh and a safe environment for two ladies in the flush of retirement.

So why didn't she *feel* safe? It was probably his tone or the unexpected nature of the call. She recalled the conversation... no, not a conversation, a monologue. Had he been reading from a script? She pondered this for a few moments before a movement in the street distracted her thoughts.

A large, black executive car crept slowly and silently up to the front doorstep and stopped. Olivia's natural reaction was to move away from the window, but she steeled herself and stayed put, crossing her arms as she surveyed. Her Scottish boarding school training kept her there, watching the tall, thick set, dark suited man who immediately kicked open the passenger door and emerged from the vehicle. 'You stand up to threats and bullies,' she whispered involuntarily, 'you don't back down'. 'Fear is something you overcome through a clear mind,' she continued under her breath. The voice of the man on the phone sang through her head once again and her heart thumped harder in her chest.

The suited man straightened, looked into the window and caught her gaze, but only momentarily. His was a hard, worn face and she judged this man had walked up plenty of front paths in his time. He wasn't the communicator, he was the messenger.

Olivia quickly called out 'Don't worry mother, I'll get this!' The doorbell rang a second later, a single trill of the bell. Olivia was already through the door of the sitting room and opening the retaining door, looking through the stained glass panels at the shadow of the man standing behind her front door. The streetlight threw weak shards of coloured light onto the walls and floor of the porch, usually a gay, happy entrance but the black outline of the man, especially his wide, dominating shoulders, blocked out any semblance of gaiety.

Being careful to ensure the security chain was firmly in place, she unlocked the door with the key which was already sitting in the lock, cracking the tall, wood and glass door three inches and ventured 'Yes?' in a clear, soft Scottish voice.

A gruff English voice replied 'Miss Olivia Dunn?' Silence seemed to stretch out in front of her. This was all very strange and becoming more bewildering by the second. It was six fifteen, exactly as she had been told by the man on the telephone.

'Oh, Yes. Indeed...,' she responded a few seconds later.

'Good – then this is yours,' he rasped. A gloved hand appeared in the crack between the door and its frame, grasping a large white envelope.

'For you,' he indicated, waving the envelope enticingly.

Was there the slight hint of menace in his voice? Olivia wasn't sure. The white corner of the envelope now poked through the crack in the door a few inches.

She tried to take the proffered letter, with the intention of closing the door immediately, but the hand retained its grip. Also in the man's hand was a small square pad of paper and a pen attached to it.

'Sign!' he barked.

She took a look at the small pad which appeared to be a delivery docket. Olivia scribbled an unintelligible signature on the pad, whipped the letter inside and shut the door quickly, realising that she had never looked into the man's face throughout the entire exchange.

Why was her heart pounding quite so loud? It was just a phone call and a delivery… why was it all so... strange. Yet exciting. The letter was still in her hand. There were two handwritten elements: in capitals, 'Hand Delivered,' and underneath 'Three of Ten'. The second sentence made Olivia ever so slowly grit her teeth.

She took up a letter opener from the hall table and slit the missive open with a single practiced movement. The envelope paper was thick, but it opened willingly enough. It contained a sheet of folded paper and a holiday cruise brochure. Unfolding the single piece of embossed and headed paper within the envelope to a full size, it struck her as unnaturally large. It was like opening a map.

Casting her eyes quickly down the page, she noticed only one portion of the entire letter. It stood out, and was clearly meant to stand out. After all, it contained the critical element of the communication. Written in tall, red italics across the middle of the paper were the words: Pay Olivia Dunn (three of ten) the sum of forty five thousand pounds plus two all-inclusive tickets for a one month around the world cruise, see attached. In smaller type, the sentence continued 'for full and final payment for her ten percent share of the colt The Ghost Machine.'

There was another sharp rap at the front door. The fuzzy black shadow had returned and he stood with the side of his head close up to the glass paneling, as if he was listening.

'I need an answer Mrs Dunn,' he barked into the glass, his breath forming a crescent of condensation. Olivia stood looking from the shadow to the contents of the letter and then in the direction of the back room where her mother was making a pot of tea.

She straightened, took a breath and speaking slowly and clearly, without the hint of wavering in her voice, she replied sternly, 'Young man, please take yourself off my porch. These old birds are signing nothing.'

Olivia paused, adding, 'And has no one ever told you that referring to someone as a number is the height of impudence!'

Three

Ian Furlong pulled off the main road in his two-seater Mercedes and made his way down the side street which led to the underground car park below his building. The engine growl grew in volume as he passed tall, nondescript brick walls, the noise reverberating between the buildings. His headlights bounced off the single lane road, illuminating the uneven, infrequently repaired tarmac. It was cold, and the first sparkles of a frost shone back from the road surface.

Ian slowed the vehicle and feathered the throttle, taking it around the raised manhole covers that were spotted across the narrow street. This wasn't a car for being confined in the centre of a city, it cried out for the open road, but business in the city kept the sleek machine under wraps for now. Ian loved every nut, bolt and gasket.

A solitary old streetlight bounced its milky beams off the sculpted grey vehicle and when Ian shifted into the darkness at the bottom of the street a man stepped from the shadows and walked purposefully into the centre of the road. The car headlights picked out a short, possibly overweight man in an overcoat with a wide sallow face. He was completely bald and Ian noted on closer inspection that he was younger than he had at first imagined. The man stood stock still with his hands moving in a 'slow down' motion. Ian drew to a halt about ten yards away from him.

He watched as the man walked toward him, then around the front of the car and into the darkness beside it. As he walked, he produced a folded card file from the inside pocket of his overcoat. He reached the driver's door and waved his free hand in a 'window down' motion.

Ian looked through the driver door window deep into the bald man's eyes and with a look of utter disdain, engaged first gear and pulled away at speed, wheels protesting at having to leave rubber on the road. He glanced into the rear view mirror to see the man still standing in the road, open mouthed, file still in hand, his face reddening.

The automatic gate to the basement car park opened as soon as Ian descended the down ramp thirty seconds later and he pulled the car quickly into his parking space, the garage door reassuringly clicking closed behind him. He jumped lithely from the car and headed to the lifts, pressing the penthouse button. Once in his apartment he went directly over to an architect's easel which was setup in front of a large glass wall overlooking the docklands. Ian flicked his artists light on and pulled up a stool.

For the next twenty minutes he sat in silence, the only sound coming from outside as the boats and barges still working on the Thames during late evening ploughed up and down its dark waters. The only other noise to penetrate the silence was the touch of a pencil point on cartridge paper.

Ian put aside his drawing utensils and contemplated what had emerged from the paper over the last few minutes. It was a portrait of a slightly overweight, bald man.

Ian looked again and reappraised his sketch. He grimaced, accepting the fact it was a portrait of a *very* unappealing, ugly bald man.

Four

He had been winning well all night. These new lads Roger had introduced to the game were young and inexperienced and he was quietly and systematically leeching their chips from them.

His usual starting stake of five hundred pounds was securely returned to his inside pocket, and another two thousand three hundred pounds sat in front of him when two kings came his way halfway through the night. He pushed all in and watched the two newcomers follow his lead. This was a big pot for this game, and despite going up against a pair of nines and ace, ten suited, his win was confirmed when another king hit the communal cards straight on the flop.

The pit boss, Roger, had floated past as he raked in his winning chips, totaling over six thousand pounds. He whistled under his breath and David White allowed a smile to flash across his face. Tonight, he could do little wrong. He was playing tight, controlled poker and getting his reward. He flicked a ten pounds chip towards Roger who caught it and deposited it in his black velvet jacket pocket.

'To keep me lucky, Roge,' he said, following it with a dry laugh.

There was no response from Roger, and he didn't expect one. The pit boss opened his lips and bared his very white teeth. It wasn't a smile, more of a professional acknowledgement. Then he stepped back into the dark, almost disappearing from view as he exited the arc of light thrown down by the poker table.

This as what David liked about Castles. There was no pretence that customers were there to be cosseted and waited on. You were there to gamble. Everyone on the Castles payroll knew there was only one purpose to their employment: make sure every punter who walks through the door is gambling and the more they gamble, the more you focus on them. On the poker tables winners are as good as losers as the house takes its percentage no matter who wins or loses. Put simply, do everything you can to make the gambling continue relentlessly.

Another half a dozen hands were played and small sums of money were transferred around the table, consisting of six men and one woman. As well as the two new recruits, who had stayed seated and signed cheques for new stacks of chips, there were four other regulars. David had played with all of them, knew them and their game, and quietly harvested a small profit from each of them as the months ticked by. For the sort of stakes he played, with average pots growing to a couple of thousand once or twice a night, on average he cleared about ten thousand pounds a year in profit. He could lose up to two thousand in a bad night, but that was rare. He wasn't a reckless player and conserved his stack on his bimonthly visits to Castles.

He was considering leaving with close to seven thousand pounds profit for the night when he was dealt a pair of pocket queens, a strong hand if played aggressively. A couple of players dropped out even before David pushed a thousand chips into the middle of the table. The response was a few grumbles from the regulars and cards were stacked around the table. That is, until a decision was required from the first of the two new players. He was in his late twenties, short dark hair, combed violently across his scalp and liberally greased, wearing a fake retro biking jacket over a plain black t-shirt. He had been sitting at the table before David had joined.

'I call,' he whispered in a nondescript accent, and tossed ten one hundred pounds chips into the centre of the table. 'It's time to get my money back,' he added to no one in particular.

Outside the ring of light surrounding the seven players and female dealer, a soft hum of conversation started up. The bet had drawn the stirrings of interest from the table watchers. David altered his position in his heavily padded chair to look directly over to the young man. He got nothing in return. The new boy had motioned to a waitress and was quietly ordering a drink, completely oblivious to David's interest in him.

The other new punter at the table was also younger than David, probably early twenties, wearing a cashmere sweater and sunglasses which sat on a thin nose. When David came to look at the boy, for that was all he appeared to be, he had pretty, delicate, almost girlish good looks.

As two more of the regulars stacked, the good looking newcomer counted out his chips and stated 'I'm in.'

The hum outside the table light increased slightly in intensity. Three and a half thousand chips sat in the middle of the table as the dealer flipped over the first three communal cards, showing two jacks and a ten. David didn't hesitate; he thrust all his chips towards the dealer and declared 'All In.' To his amazement, both the men did exactly the same, with apparently little thought to their decision. He was convinced he must be beaten. They had to have pocket aces or kings.

With just over twenty thousand pounds at stake, the last two communal cards brought a seven and another jack. David turned over his queens, to reveal his full house, but fully expected he had lost. He swept a hand from his forehead over his bald scalp to remove the growing pinheads of sweat.

'No,' said the biker, tossing his cards, face down, towards the dealer. The pretty boy did the same, with little discernible emotion, and reached into his back pocket, removed his wallet and bought himself in again.

'Idiots,' David thought to himself, 'Never should have gone all in with less than a couple of big cards in front of them.' He scooped up the chips in front of him and considered an exit.

'Hope you're going to stay a while and give us the chance to get our cash back,' said the pretty boy. He gestured towards the large stacks of chips in front of David. There was a slightly Nordic flavour to his tongue, and David placed him as Swedish, possibly Norwegian. No, he was a Swede, he decided.

'Don't you think you've had enough for one night?' said David carefully. The biker laughed, but it ended quickly as a cackle.

'Come on old timer, play a bit more with us,' he added, adopting a slightly deliberate pronunciation when getting the 't' in timer out. 'I want to go all-in with you one more time.'

He seriously thought of standing up and leaving. But this was too good an opportunity to pass up. If they continued to play fast and loose, he knew he had them beat in the long run, and when the time was right, they'd forfeit their chips and slouch back to wherever they had come from.

'The night is still young, and so are you my friends!' David replied, 'Let's play cards.'

****

Having cantered up the casino stairs three at a time, through smoked mirrored corridors and plush sitting areas, it was almost a relief to burst through the swing doors, out into the crisp, cold early morning air of the street. David glanced at his watch and took a large lungful of London, trying to steady his heart rate and stem his self-loathing.

He hadn't just lost, he'd lost big. Between the two of them, the young, unknown players had taken his profit and a lot more with it. He pulled on his jacket and crossed the street without looking, his mind in a whirl. Mounting the opposite pavement, he stopped, found his bearings and walked two shops down and entered a small greasy spoon café. He sat down heavily into a plastic chair, ordered a coffee and tried to keep his palms off the table for fear of them sticking to the dirty plastic tablecloth.

David sat fingering his cheque stub for thirty five thousand pounds and staring through the stained off-white net curtains at the street for about twenty minutes. He eventually gave a disgruntled sigh and started to get up to leave, when he noticed one of the men he'd been playing against outside in the street. He was walking on the opposite side of the road. It was the biker, his jacket collar pulled up around his ears to stave off the biting breeze. He was looking around, as if trying to identify a landmark. He appeared to find what he was looking for, crossed the street, reached for a door handle and got into the back of a black Range Rover.

David ordered another coffee and watched as the Range Rover did nothing but sit silently at the curb for the next ten minutes. He was watching the car so intently he almost missed the second player walking right past the front of the café. David shrank back in his less than adequate seat and watched open-mouthed as the baby-faced man opened the door to the same car and also got into the back. Thirty seconds later the car engine spat into life and set off sedately up the street. As it passed the café, David looked up toward the driver's seat where a tall, thickset man sat alone in the front of the car as it whisked past.

David looked nervously around the café. It was six thirty in the morning and only he and a select group were present: a total of five people, including the proprietor, who was bustling between the back kitchen and the serving area. No one else had spoken or even looked at him, and they apparently had even less interest in two men getting into an expensive car outside. His heart rate had slowed, he was starting to get a grip, but his mind was racing.

He was staring into his weak white coffee when quite suddenly he was aware of a tall man stood over him. This awareness rocked him out of his thoughts and he tried to stand up, pushing the chair backwards in the process and scraping it against the tiled floor. One or two customers looked up with disgruntled looks on their faces, but soon looked away again when their eyes fell onto the gentleman in a knee length black coat stood over a frightened looking, small, balding man.

'Don't get up Mr White,' said the man plainly and directly, but quite softly. 'I have something for you.'

David noticed the highly polished shoes, expensive knee length coat and a faint smell of aftershave. The man produced an envelope from the inside pocket of his long black overcoat, unfolded it, and handed it to David.

'How did...,' David started, taking the envelope, but was cut short by the stranger.

'Best to take the envelope and sign here to accept it please,' the man interjected softly, holding a hand up to request silence.

David paused a few seconds but did as he was told, taking the proffered pen to scribble his large, flowery signature on a delivery docket. The man dropped the signed docket into his inside pocket, turned on his heel and quietly left the café. One of the other customers looked up with querying eyes as he left, but soon averted their gaze. The man wasn't the sort to engage with eye to eye; he oozed controlled aggression. David watched him make a clipped right turn, passing the front window of the shop. Then he unfolded the envelope to its full size and turned it over.

It read 'Five of Ten.'

Five

The young, yet definitely very bald man stood at the door to the flats buzzing incessantly on the number eight button on the stainless steel plate and then stood back and looked upwards towards the fourth floor. He wiped the drizzle from his face and winced when a trickle of water travelled down the back of his neck. Despite the cold and wet day, beads of sweat sat proud on his forehead as a result of the climb up the steps to the glass and brick building five minutes previously. He poked the intercom again with a fat fingered hand and bent his head towards the speaking grille.

'Please, Mrs Rowbottom. I just need a few minutes of your time and I think it really could be to your advantage. My name is…'
The intercom light flashed off again and he scowled, hunched his shoulders against the cold and pressed the number eight button once again. After thirty seconds of holding his forefinger to the button plate the light flashed on again.

'I've told you. Go away or I'll call the police. I don't care who you are, I have no wish to sell the share,' said a shrill, tinny female voice at the other end of the building intercom.

Again the red light blinked on and the bald man quickly barked in an equally high pitch, 'Your husband Mrs Rowbottom. Your husband?'
This time the red intercom light remained steadily illuminated.

'Your husband,' he said again. 'I can give you control!' he paused, willing the little red light to remain lit. 'I can give you control of the company.'

Again, the intercom light went dead again, but only for a second.

When it re-lit the female voice that came through the grille was slower and more deliberate. 'What. Exactly. Are you talking about?' she said in staccato fashion, an upward inflection at the end of each word.

The bald man smiled inwardly and produced a rain splashed card folder from the breast pocket of his overcoat. Glancing every now and then at the front of the plastic coated folder he spoke into the intercom for thirty seconds. The red light remained constant. Then after a pause the lock buzzed and he pushed against the thick glass door and entered the building.

Forty-five minutes later Cynthia Rowbottom parted the blades of a vertical hanging blind and watched the bald man carefully pick his way down the forty or so steps from the front of her building. He crossed the road to a badly parked Range Rover which straddled the footpath and part of the road and climbed into the back seat. A few seconds later the car pulled into the road without indicating, disappearing quickly from view.

She let the blind resume its vertical position, turning to the kitchen island upon which lay a card folder with a plastic front where the words 'Eight of Ten' were written. She plucked a bottle of Talisker whisky from an inside bottom shelf of a kitchen unit and found a tumbler into which she poured herself a few fingers and threw an ice cube in for good measure.

Taking a large mouthful of the twenty year old golden liquid, she swallowed and then started to giggle. Cynthia Rowbottom's bottom lip began to wobble. Then a grin which she would normally not allow any of her friends to see, crept uncontrollably up her well worn, but expensively cared for face. Then she let out a loud, full-bodied laugh. It was her first fit of laughter in over eighteen months.

Six

He awoke with quick, shallow breaths and immediately thrust his arms out, stiff in the still air. Lying on his back, the flat palms of his hands grasped, fingers closing on nothingness. Still shaking off the confusion of half sleep and half waking, he didn't recognise the room, but at least it was a room, which was strangely, but welcomingly reassuring.

Seconds later the white painted ceiling and pale blue walls smudged their way to recognition and his breathing became a little deeper. He rolled onto his side, pushing back the heavy, deep maroon duvet, realising he was home. A rub of his eyes and the red digital glow from his bedside clock helped confirm it was just after four thirty in the morning.

Max. Where was he? Again the tightness returned to his breathing, a hot stinging flush started around his face, then rushed to the rest of his body.

Before his brain got there, his often-repeated routine of padding across the landing to his son's bedroom was already completed. In a poster laden bedroom a small blonde lump nestled under another duvet adorned with a childrens TV comedy character, although it was hard to make it out due to the seven year olds nocturnal movements.

Ben brushed back the edge of the duvet and his son's face appeared, completely content, as only a sleeping child can be, his chest rising and falling in a shallow but constant rhythm. Replacing the duvet, he left the bedroom and paused on the landing, staring down the stairs, contemplating whether to attempt sleep again. The initial concern for his son quashed, the real reason for his waking rushed at him – the crack of sunlight between head and hoof, the hard, unnatural jerk of impact and the life in her eyes being extinguished.

He gripped the banister at the top of the stairs with both hands, his eyes shut. The dreams were vivid and still hurt. They hurt like hell, slicing their way through his head with the same unceasing venom. What was so frustrating was his lack of control; he had no way to switch them off. The release switch he could flick when he was awake simply wasn't there in his dreams – and the dream always built up to the same moment of crazed panic. He sighed, mumbled 'fool' under his breath, then made his way downstairs into the kitchen and clicked on the kettle.

The farmhouse cottage was too big for him and one child, but it was difficult to move from a place with so many memories, and besides, Max didn't need any further upheaval at the moment. Mind you, four bedrooms in a one hundred and fifty year old farmhouse, with two retired horses, four sheep, one dog plus ten acres and a mile to the nearest neighbour wasn't exactly the greatest place for him to find playmates when he needed them.

Benjamin Ramsden crossed the wooden kitchen floor again and

caught his reflection in the large oblong window which provided a view onto the back lawn. He rubbed two days of stubble on his chin and noted that it was still pitch black outside, the window rendering a decent image of him staring back at himself. His once blonde hair was now flecked with grey, which appeared from various points on the edge of his hairline, and the lines around his eyes looked deeper and more ingrained than he remembered. He could be fitter he supposed, he could probably eat a healthier diet and he could even probably cover up some of the ravages of time and experience. His self-appraisal had little in the way of vanity attached to its purpose. He must look acceptable to his clients who expected him to play the role of syndicate manager at all times. Looking himself up and down once again he conceded he was thinner than a year ago. Gaunt, he thought, I look like I need a good meal.

He sat down at the corner of the large, eight person farmhouse kitchen table which occupied the centre of the room, robotically made a strong black coffee and picked up the newspaper from the day before.

The sound of Racing Post pages being flicked filled the room. This April morning was deadly silent apart from the distant rustling of the large beech trees at the bottom of the garden and the odd creaking noise from the aged house as it settled on its timber frame and stone foundations.

He idly turned through the first few pages of news until his eye was caught by a group of winning owners caught in that iconic shot after victory, with horse, jockey and beaming connections. The dream flitted into his mind again, that image of clean air between hoof and Anna, and the tension rose in his chest, his heartbeat quickening.

Ben crumpled the paper shut, dropping it to the floor, feeling the panic rise through him. He stood and held his head with both hands, tears starting to well up in his eyes. Forcing himself to take deeper breaths, holding his hands to his chest, he could feel the beat of his heart, concentrated on it, controlled it.

He reflected miserably on his inability to control his emotions. It was probably time to take the advice of his friends and specifically his mother-in-law and head to a decent doctor.

****

Dawn broke and slowly entered Sunday proper, sending broken beams of weak sunlight across the kitchen table. With a coffee inside him Ben felt better and was scanning the day old paper, but he crumpled the Racing Post shut again when there was the sound of a floorboard flexing above his head, and the light slap of bare feet as they crossed Max's bedroom.

'Go back to bed, it's only seven o'clock Max,' Ben called towards the stairs.

17

Silence was provided in return, apart from the sounds of bathroom noises.

'Max?' more direct and increased in volume this time.

'Ummm!' came the response. A light, trill voice.

Two minutes later the seven year old emerged from the bottom of the stairs and joined his father at the kitchen table, receiving a stroke of his hair as he passed him.

'You don't sleep so I don't,' said the boy plainly but in a very low voice. He pulled a chair out and sat, head in hands, pushing his cheeks up in childish mock annoyance.

The argument was a regular one, and not one for a Sunday morning, thought Ben. His eyes returned to the Racing Post which he ruffled in response.

'Well, seeing as you're up, do you fancy going to see The Ghost?' he asked.

Max took his head out of his hands and his rumpled brow turned to his father. A small grin appeared and the light in his eyes switched back on in an instant.

'Ummm,' he agreed.

By seven o'clock the two of them were in Ben's six year old Golf, which looked, and drove, like it was much older. He kept the car well maintained, but it was rarely clean. Mojo, Ben's ludicrously small Irish Jack Russell bounced playfully on the back seat and drew nose art on the inside of the misted up car windows. She went everywhere with Ben, was obedient, loyal and could walk for miles. It was rare to find Mojo any further than hailing distance from Ben. The radio pumped out tinny piano blues which Ben hummed along to, whilst Max maintained a steady, intense gaze on his iPod.

It was only a twenty minutes drive to Joss O'Hoole's racing stables from Ben's home. One of the main reasons for choosing the farmhouse ten years ago had been its proximity to Joss's training yard. Anna had insisted Ben wasn't too far away from Joss, as it meant that most of the time her husband wouldn't be too far away from his family. Now Ben took his family pretty much everywhere with him.

Yorkshire countryside trundled past them as the small car navigated the minor roads. Every now and again a pheasant or rabbit would stare into the headlights before darting into the nearest hedge. Ben's mobile phone sat propped up in the central console between the two front seats and lit up with a text message, but he didn't pay any attention to its demands to be read. He concentrated on the winding country road, despite knowing it well, screwing his eyes up when the car turned into the morning sun.

Then a call came in from Helen, Ben's mother-in-law. He picked up immediately. Helen had been a very positive female influence for Max since Anna's death. She had excelled with her positive attitude and ensuring simple things like cooking, cleaning and running the cottage were rigidly maintained in the aftermath of Anna's death. These were things which Ben had struggled to get to grips with at first and continued to forget or ignore. Helen had been instrumental in maintaining a stable environment for Max, and indeed himself. In the process, he and Helen had spent more time together and Ben had come to recognise the same strength of character in her which he had loved in her daughter.

Ben's own parents were both long dead, as he was the product of their late decision to have a single child in their forties. Both had passed away in their sixties, leaving Ben self-reliant since his early twenties.

He often reflected that he had lost a wife and a mother for Max, while Helen had lost her only child, upon which she had doted. Helen's husband had died of cancer eighteen months previously, his health failing over a period of a few years, a situation which had placed strain on Anna and her mother. To be plunged into further grief from Anna's death had drawn Helen even closer to Ben and Max. She was a regular caller at the cottage and Ben had made an effort to build Helen into their lives as best he could, as much for her sake as their own.

There was a short pause after the call connected and then Helen asked in her broad North Yorkshire accent 'Are you in the car with Max?' Ben looked over to Max and mouthed a silent and emphatic 'Yes' to his son, which drew a smile, and Max answered 'Yes, I'm here Nana! We're in the car on the way to see Dad's horses.'

Being referred to as 'Dad' brought a grin to Ben's face. This was a new development, with the previously used 'Daddy' now being consigned to the past. Recently spending more time with older children had certainly seen his son mature in a number of ways.

'I hope you have a seat belt on Max!'

'Yes, Nana. Dad makes me.'

'And you'll be careful at the yard won't you, my love?'

'Yes Nana,' sighed Max starting to lose interest in the conversation.

'Good boy Max. I'll want to know all about the stables when I'm next across to see you!'

Max didn't reply to this immediately and Ben sensed the boy would rather return his attention to his iPod.

'We're on our way over to Joss's. We'll be there in a few minutes,' Ben said.

'Hello Ben. I was really calling to make sure you were okay? You seemed a bit pale on Friday night. You haven't had any more…' she hesitated, clearly searching for words other than 'panic attack' so as not to worry Max.

'I'm fine Helen. But you'll be happy to know that I'll be making that appointment you suggested.'

Ben placed more emphasis on the last few words, leaving it there, hoping Helen would understand. She showed she did by replying with a crisp, 'That's a big relief Ben. Thank you.'

She continued after a short pause, 'I also wondered if you'd mind me popping over on Tuesday? I was thinking I could take Max swimming after school.'

Helen lived no more than a fifteen minutes drive away, which had been a prerequisite when Anna and Ben had set up home. His wife had been close to her parents and although Ben had found the closeness a little claustrophobic at first, he learned to live with it, and in time had come to value the Grandparents' involvement, especially with Max, who thrived on the attention.

'Of course Helen. He'll be home from school at the usual time. You can collect him from the cottage,' Then he added 'Stay for dinner afterwards if you like.'

'Great. Want me to bring my special lasagne?'

Ben gave a short laugh 'I'm an open book to you aren't I?'

'Absolutely. I'll be there at five to pick him up. That okay with you, Max?'

Max shouted a positive response and Helen rang off after a number of goodbyes and 'see you soons' to them both.

Ben and Helen had fallen into a regular weekly routine following Anna's death. Ben had struggled to keep the daily chores going following the day at York. Over the course of the three weeks between Anna's death and the funeral, the cottage had descended into disarray. He and Max survived by eating boxes of cereal and when they ran out of clean clothes, they'd had no idea how to work the washer or any other appliance come to that. Helen had insisted on getting a decent meal into the both of them and helped get the cottage straight. After taking control of the household duties Helen had stayed for a few days to help develop a new regime of shopping and cleaning before leaving Ben to pick things up. However, her home cooking was something he couldn't replicate, and so it had become a standing arrangement; she would come over on a Friday, pick Max up from school, and then the three of them would eat together in the evening. She was an excellent cook and Max in particular looked forward to his Nan's meals at the end of each week, having survived on a diet of mostly frozen offerings up until then.

Helen had taken Anna's death very badly, but she bounced back much quicker than Ben and proved to be quite resilient, once she found a supporting role in Max's life. She gave them room to live, but was there whenever Ben asked and provided a constant, enduring source of love for Max, a female element to his life which could otherwise have been lacking. This was something Ben had come to value greatly, but it did help that she also made a startlingly good lasagne.

Ben's train of thought was snapped back to the moment when he turned into the entrance to the track which led down to the O'Hoole yard. He knew something wasn't quite right before he got to the bottom of the drive. The flash of blue glinted off the grey stone walls of the farmhouse despite the bright spring sunshine and as Ben straightened the nose of his VW up to swing into a parking space, he was met by an unmarked police car with internal blue lights flashing and revolving. There were two people pounding on the oak door to the farmhouse; a man and woman both in full police uniform, shouting to make someone aware of their presence and looking in through the dark, unlit windows.

The scene brought his early morning dream back into his consciousness and for a moment his world swum with light, sirens, medics, and police. He shook the cacophony away with a blink, instructed Max to stay in the car a little more stridently than he had wanted to, apologised to his son, and reassured him before getting out. The two officers, one male, one female hadn't seemed to hear the car turn into the driveway, but now that Ben's door clunked closed they both wheeled around.

The two exchanged a quick glance and a nod. Both wore body protection and the male figure, a lean, angular jawed thirty something ranged above Ben at about six feet. He took a few paces towards Ben, holding one hand up, gesturing him to halt his approach.

'Morning Sir. Do you live at these premises?' The policeman delivered the question in what Ben considered a louder than required voice. It was as if he was projecting to make a speech or address a crowd. Ben was also struck by the officer's eyes, which were a striking dark blue.

Before Ben could respond, the high wooden gate to the left of the farmhouse scraped open, the bottom sill catching on the ground and the policeman turned to see a tall, wiry man with an unkempt mop of straight brown hair push the stable gate back.

Joss O'Hoole battled with the warped wooden gate, pushing it back and forth a couple of times before it swung open. He slotted the bolt into a holding connection, turned to his visitors, and offered a generous smile.

'Good morning, officer!' he exclaimed, walking over with his hand held out in greeting. 'Has our rogue caller has been up to his tricks again, or are we of interest for another reason?' he asked rhetorically, beaming apologetically at the policeman.

'We are investigating a report of a disturbance at these premises...' the officer replied, but was promptly cut off by Joss once the basis for their visit was established. Ben smiled to himself. Joss was not a man with any time for much more than the facts. Some found him brusque, even rude, but small talk was not his forte, unless it was concerning a racehorse or his two children, and even then, probably in that order.

'Then I assume a quick tour of the yard and a cup of something hot will be in order?' Joss interjected. 'Oh, and let me introduce Benjamin Ramsden, one of our owners,' he added, waving a hand in Ben's direction.

'He'll be up here to check up on his prize possession, drink my coffee, and eat copious amounts of bacon sandwiches, so I guess today is Sunday.'

The policeman started to say something, but was immediately cut off by Joss once again. 'Speak to my wife Marion, she will sort you out.' He held the door stables gate open expectantly. The policeman paused, waiting to see if there was anything else to come from Joss. Ben noted that this guy was a quick learner, as the officer had already discovered that any attempt to talk over Joss would be fruitless, as you would simply be drowned out.

The policeman nodded at Ben and then turned to Joss, 'I'm sorry to have to do this Sir, but we have to take these reports seriously. We'll get around the yard and be out of your hair as soon as we can. Are we okay to enter your stables Mr O'Hoole?'

'Yes, yes of course. But just watch out for a couple of fillies coming out,' replied Joss, already pumping Ben's hand and waving a hand to Max who was watching the exchange from the car, his head out of an opened window.

'Come on Max out you come, you'll miss breakfast otherwise!' Joss shouted. The boy immediately threw the car door open and jumped out, followed a split second later by Mojo. The two of them sprinted over to Joss, the little dog dancing around on his back legs with excitement. Ben raised an eyebrow at Joss and nodded towards the turned backs of the two policemen.

'Oh, just a pain in the backside,' said Joss, 'They keep getting phone calls from an idiot who gives them some reason to be checking us out. So far this week it's been everything from drug trafficking to domestic violence and everything in-between. This is the second time in four days the police have turned up. It's a distraction, but they're usually gone within twenty minutes. They've not found anything – yet!' he laughed boyishly.

'Have they any idea who is making the calls?' asked Ben.

'No, it's a different guy each time apparently. And if you're wondering, it's not affecting 'The Ghost'.'

Joss bent down to Max and enthusiastically said, 'Come on, let's go and see the best horse your Dad has ever owned,' and scooping the youngster up and onto his shoulders he went through the yard gates, with Max whooping with delight.

Whilst the outside of the farmhouse was plain and functional, with nothing more than a few spaces for cars to park and a short drive leading to the road and exercise gallops beyond, once through the yard gates you entered a completely different world.

Riverside Stables had been home to three generations of O'Hoole. Everything was pristine, ordered and perfectly laid out for one single purpose – to house and train thoroughbred racehorses. It may not have been the biggest, or the most prestigious yard in the training centre of Middleham, but Ben knew Joss provided his horses with quality living quarters and some of the best training facilities in the North of England.

The farmhouse was probably the only part of the yard which hadn't been replaced or renewed over the passing of the last century, and it said something about the O'Hooles that they spent what spare cash they had on their horse's accommodation, rather than their own living quarters. The walkway passed the farmhouse on its right and then through an arched opening, revealed a forty box oval stabling block. Two stable lads led horses across the central space towards the paddocks, some stable doors were open, with muck barrows, shovels, forks and other horse related equipment leant almost regimentally against walls. Two more young lasses were stood, fork in hand, speaking with the policemen while behind them another lass gave a couple of riders legs up onto their mounts.

'Those fillies should have been out ten minutes ago,' muttered Joss, and set off towards them, Max still clinging to the trainers scalp, legs clamped in Joss's hands.

The Policewoman, seeing Ben stood alone, peeled away from her colleague, and walked over. She introduced herself to Ben as PC Wentworth, a young looking woman no more than five foot seven with a pale complexion and dark brown eyes, which Ben had completely missed a few moments earlier. She asked if she could take down a few basic details and did so with the minimum of fuss, before thanking him and moving off to speak with a stable lad.

With the fillies having departed to complete a workout on the shared gallops close to the village, Joss was back at Ben's shoulder.

'What's all this about this time?' asked Ben, waving a hand towards the two policeman and at the same time looking Joss in the eye.

'I could take the nonsense before, but the latest caller accused us of abusing horses, which isn't on. The police offered to come in and ask a few questions of the lads, just in case they know anything about it. Can't see it doing any good, but at least they are wasting their own time on a Sunday and not mine!'

'Come on, I'll show you the mare,' said Joss, gripping Ben gently by his shoulder. After twelve years of friendship the two men were relaxed with each other and although it was founded on a commercial relationship, Ben enjoyed being with Joss and his family and knew it was reciprocated by the trainer. He and Max had been drawn even closer to the O'Hoole family since Anna's death six months previously, providing the sort of support which is only available from those who share the grief. Joss was the trainer of the Ghost Machine, and both he and his wife Marion had been in the winners enclosure at York when the accident happened.

'Before you ask,' said Joss, 'Max has gone down with Rachel to feed the lambs in the bottom paddock. They'll be fine. I want to show you your newest aquisition.'

Joss led the way through the main stabling area and out to a line of six large boxes which sat against the wood tree line and were quiet, but still looked well scrubbed and fit for purpose.

'The last one on the right,' instructed Joss, pointing the way, as he skipped off and disappeared for a few moments into the bottom stable, emerging with a couple of carrots in his hand.

'Open it up, she won't be frightened,' he added.
After a quick look in to see where the occupant was, Ben kicked open the bottom swing bolt and pulled the spring-loaded central bolt. Joss caught up with him and the two men stepped into the stable.

'She arrived last night,' said Joss, 'Came across from Ireland on transport at about ten o'clock and walked off as fresh as a daisy. All she wanted to do was eat and sleep.' He paused. The mare hadn't acknowledged their presence and was happy to stand with her back to them.

'Marion brought the kids in to see her this morning and she was great with them. She's just like the breeder promised, straight forward, and easy to be with and she's settled in well,' stated Joss, moving across the stable to the sizeable animal.

The mare lifted her head from the hay she was picking through and stared dolefully at the two of them, as if somewhat irked by their presence. When Joss reached her side she didn't move but brought her head up to him and looked around, expectant. When Joss produced a big fat carrot, her mouth moved over it, ensuring she didn't have a finger as well, before she crunched down on it. Immediately, the only sound in the stable was of the mare's teeth splitting the fibres of the carrot, quickly reducing it to shreds. A few seconds later she was at Joss's hand again, searching with her lips for the rest of the vegetable.

Ben moved over and slowly ran a hand down the mare's head, starting at the top of her forehead, over her white fleck between her eyes and down to her nose. He had seen her before of course, when they had bought her at the Irish Mares' sale seven months previously. Since then, she had stayed in Ireland, having been barren for a year, but now was the start of something new and quite exciting. She would be their first broodmare.

'What are we calling her?' Ben asked.

'Well, the lads have started calling her 'Bertha' because of her size.'

'That'll do,' said Ben 'So, The Ghost's Mother is called Bertha!'
Ben had wanted to move into breeding horses for some time now,

but the basis for starting to breed, that 'foundation mare', was all-important. A racing dynasty could be founded on a single brilliant mare with the ability to pass on the right genes to her offspring. More importantly, if she could not only produce fast colts, but also fillies who could prove themselves on the racecourse and would in turn become successful broodmares, then she could have decades of her bloodlines proliferating the sport. But quality foundation mares were rare and proven ones often changed hands for more than any young two year old, no matter how well bred. This mare was Ben and Joss's stab at the breeding game and a huge gamble even though they had bought the mare before The Ghost Machine had advertised his mother's true value.

The two men chatted about their plans for her covering dates and transport arrangements, leaving the mare alone once more in her large, quiet stable. She snorted and returned to her pile of hay in the corner. Joss carefully engaged both bolts on the stable door before he became distracted by Max and Joss's children running down the yard.

'I want to see The Ghost!' demanded Max excitedly.

'He loved the lambs,' said Rachel, at fourteen years old, she was tall for her age but sometimes an unnervingly intelligent girl, the eldest of Joss's two children. Ben wondered if Joss's wife Marion had been the same as a child, and reflected that both mother and daughter were unconventional in many ways, and had a knack of seeing things as they were, thus making life simple for those around them.

'But he was most insistent that we got to see 'Ghost', so we brought him back,' Rachel rolled her eyes at Ben, but then added a little seriously, 'He can be a bit demanding can't he?'

Ben produced a broad smile and nodded theatrically. Rachel responded with a relieved smile of her own, and taking Max by the hand, led him towards the nearest barn.

The Ghost Machine's box was in the centre of the barn, so they passed half a dozen other horses before reaching his stable. They found him, lying down on a bed of wood shavings, half-asleep. When the entourage of people stopped at his stable door, the colt got to his feet and poked his head out of the stable door, much to the delight of Max, who was being held up by Rachel to pat The Ghost Machine's neck.

Max then moved his hand around and felt the horse's forehead, and his small fingers couldn't help but trace the diamond shape which sat between the grey's eyes. The Ghost Machine was a strapping, good-looking grey, but he had two very major defining features – a large diamond of dark, brown black which was placed in the very centre of his forehead and an almost white mane.

The horse stood stock still as the youngster finished joining the four sides of the diamond together. Then as Max withdrew his hand, The Ghost Machine moved backwards and into his stable again.

Ben was reminded of the first time he had seen him at the Doncaster Sales over eighteen months previously. The colt had been bred in Ireland, but shipped to the sales at Doncaster in August, the major equine sales centre in the North. He was one of four hundred horses that had gone under the hammer over two days at their 'Premier Yearling Sale'. He was the first offspring by an unraced but well related mare, and his sire was an old, well established sort, but had recently fallen out of favour, resulting in a more affordable covering fee due to a couple of years without a major winning son or daughter. There had been little to recommend him on paper, and Ben had initially discounted him when analysing the catalogue. But when he'd seen this colt swagger around the parade ring, relaxed and unperturbed, in stark contrast to many of the other juveniles, he'd called Joss over, and together they had looked him over in detail. His dark diamond on his forehead was certainly a talking point, however Ben had been impressed with his intelligent nature, and most of all, that swagger.

They had to go to eighteen thousand pounds to secure him at the auction. Not a great deal of money for a thoroughbred, and he wasn't even mentioned in the reporting on the sale, as others went for hundreds of thousands, but it was still a decent investment for Ben.

As he had hoped, syndicating him hadn't been a problem. The colt had grown well through the autumn and he had found eight other owners to take shares in him. Each held ten percent, with Joss and Ben retaining the other two ten percent shares. By April of the following year he had been ready to race.

Joss had always liked him, although from being broken through to March he had been a bit of a handful on the gallops, tending to want to muck around with his lad or lass, rather than put his head down and run. Then Raul had joined the yard. His family hailed from South America and he was an apprentice rider trying to make a name for himself in the UK. He was a first rate horseman and a neat, effective little rider who could do light weights, an ability which was valued in racing circles. The European diet and lifestyle now provided a challenge to home grown jockeys. But it was this rider's connection with the grey which had stunned Joss. The diminutive, cocoa-brushed lad had soft hands in the saddle and seemed to speak with The Ghost Machine when they worked together.

On his racing debut at Nottingham racecourse in May over six furlongs in a Maiden race, the two of them went to the front quickly and spread-eagled the field, but in the last half a furlong they were run down by a well bred colt who won by two lengths, 'The Ghost', as he had become known in the yard, finishing second. He had never shown anything like that on the gallops at home, so both the trainer and the syndicate were more than happy, having beaten thirteen other youngsters home. It had been the start of the rollercoaster ride that characterised his two year old season.

His next race came at Doncaster in June, another six furlong Maiden and still, the only talking point about The Ghost Machine was his unusual markings on his head. Held up in rear, he passed six horses down the straight and bolted clear in the closing stages to record a facile victory with Raul in the saddle once again. The jockey came back afterwards and told the half a dozen or so shareholders who were there, 'The horse needs to be passing. Always passing. He loves to pass. You don't disappoint him with nothing to pass, always *he must* be passing.'

The Ghost did the same at Newmarket in July. He was entered in a Conditions race, for two year olds at the July meeting, one of the lesser races at the meeting, but still worth over ten thousand pounds to the winner. Despite Raul being an apprentice, Joss and Ben stood firm when it was suggested that another jockey take his place in a better class event. The South American grew in self-confidence, reveling in the belief Joss placed in him and he rode the grey with style and panache – horse and rider gaining maturity. Over the same six furlongs he and a well-regarded youngster from a top Newmarket stable kicked clear, The Ghost being punched out to win by a neck, with over six lengths back to the third. That was when the racing press started to take some interest.

It was at York's Ebor meeting in August when the colt stepped up in distance to seven furlongs and faced his stiffest test. The Ghost made a mockery of the race, racing away from his opposition over a furlong and a half out and winning as he liked. He had now arrived on the scene and he started to get quotes for the following years big races like the Two Thousand Guineas, St James' Palace Stakes at Royal Ascot and The Derby. The York race was his last that season, mainly because he was growing, but also because of what happened in the winners enclosure…

In his box, The Ghost Machine tossed his head upwards quickly then turned away from the small gathering outside.

Ben snapped back to the present as a wave of sickly coldness pulsed through his body. He saw Anna, smiling, in the flush of early pregnancy, breeze ruffling her hair. Then the movement away to his right, hooves touching the sky and a crack of light between her head and the animal's feet. The sickening, inhuman position she lay in on the parade ring grass, the blood; and he couldn't reach her through the mass of people. The stable whirled, tears welled in his eyes and in a light headed daze, Ben staggered backwards until he leant against the stable opposite The Ghost Machine. Only Joss noticed, as the children were trying to coax the colt back to his stable door.

'You okay?' Joss asked, worry etched on his face.

'Yeah, I think so. It comes over me every now and again,' Ben answered uncertainly as he slid slowly to the ground, sitting with his back to the wooden stable. He placed his hands to his chest for the second time that morning, feeling the quick thump of his heart.

'Just take your time. Take short breaths,' he told himself.
Ben started to control his own breathing and the feeling of dizzy, light-headedness seemed to be subsiding. As if looking at himself from the outside in, he noticed his breathing was coming in quick hot breaths, but he was regaining control. The horizon came back into focus and the hazy out of body feeling slid away.

Joss was still staring directly at him, wearing a worried expression that Ben didn't see too often in his friend.

'I'm okay Joss. Just give me a minute.'

The children had turned around and started to ask the same questions. Joss quickly told them Ben was absolutely fine, speaking in a reassuring and simple manner, and ordered them to run to the farmhouse to collect a glass of cold water. All three of them, managing uncertain smiles, shot off like bullets on their errand.

Jake, Joss's travelling head lad, arrived at the scene, running up to see if he could help out. Jake had been with the yard for ten years and was a very good horseman. He was trustworthy, a hard worker and respected by pretty much everyone in Middleham. He had been The Ghost's stable lad since the colt had arrived at Riverside Stables.

Jake looked at Ben on the ground, who was hugging his knees and trying again to bring his breathing under control and then turned his gaze on Joss, raising a questioning eyebrow. Again, Joss was quick to quash any notion that this was anything out of the ordinary.

'If you'd gone through what he has in the last ten months I think we'd forgive you for wanting to have a sit down when you wanted!' he stated sternly to the lad.

Jake, slightly ruffled by this rebuke trotted out the pat answer, 'Of course Guv'nor,' and with a nod of apology in Ben's direction, headed to the bottom end of the barn where he grabbed a standing pitchfork and disappeared into a stable.

Ben breathed heavily, mouth open, his chest rising and falling in fast, jerked motions. Joss watched silently as Ben took three gulps of air and then looking up, held out a hand. Joss pulled Ben to his feet and kept his grip on Ben's hand for a few seconds until he was satisfied that his friend could stand unaided.

'If he brings too many bad memories back for you, then we should sell him,' Joss's voice was slightly strained, but serious.

Ben shook his head 'You have to be kidding. Between him and Max, they are the only things that are keeping me from going crazy this last year. I have my moments, that's all. I just need to catch myself before I think too hard about it, that's what brings it on. I'm okay now, you can let go of me.'

Joss stared back into Ben's face, unsure whether to believe him, but finally grunted an 'Okay' and released his grip on Ben's hand, although he positioned himself in such a way that if his friend went backwards again, he would be there to catch him.

'See the doctor will you. Please?' Joss insisted.

Ben ran his hands through his hair and blinked a few times.

'Don't worry, I'm seeing a counsellor this week. I've got to go into Leeds, my GP has set it up.'

In truth, Ben wasn't too sure a talking session with someone would be of any use. The dizzy spells came on infrequently, but when they did, they hit him regularly over the course of a couple of days before disappearing for about a week. The thought of going through the York race once again with another stranger filled him with hand clenching dread.

'Good,' said Joss quietly, 'It's time you saw someone, you can't carry on falling over all the time, people will think you're a drunk or something.'

Ben smiled uncertainly at the trainer, whom he noticed had darker rings than normal below his eyes.

'Don't preach to me, Hooley. You look like you could do with a good night's sleep yourself!' he exclaimed.

Joss let out a belly laugh, 'Yeah, a trainer's life isn't exactly conducive to a healthy lifestyle is it? I wasn't back from racing at Lingfield until midnight last night, so I didn't see my bed until two o'clock this morning. Marion was asleep with the dog when I got upstairs. I'm convinced something is going on there. He's that bloody big I thought it was another bloke in the bed with her!'

The two men shared a moment's levity with each other and Ben began to feel himself returning to something like normality.

Zippo, the family dog, was the source of much merriment in the O'Hoole household, as he was a huge Great Dane who doted on Marion, Joss's wife. Zippo loved the kids, but just about put up with Joss. Marion had arrived home with him as a pup, tucked under her arm after rescuing him from the top of the moors. Typical Marion, she had spotted him when out for a hack and befriended the shy and hungry youngster and brought him home. When an owner couldn't be found there was no discussion – Zippo stayed. He grew of course, and Ben remembered both Joss's children and Max actually riding the dog around the yard at one stage. But he simply adored Marion and would spend his entire day around her. Joss had drawn a line at the dog spending time upstairs, so Zippo slept in an old scullery he had to himself, but when the opportunity arose he would be up the stairs, bound onto the bed and be lying at Marion's feet, or more likely on them, when she woke. This rather got on Joss's nerves, as it meant that almost a stone of deadweight dog would often lie between him and his wife in bed.

'Come on,' said Joss as their laughter subsided, 'Let's see if the police have finished poking around and getting under my staff's feet. We can join the team for breakfast.'

They met the children running back to the barn with three cups of water, and a worried looking Marion in pursuit behind. She brightened considerably when she looked up and saw the two of them walking down the barn, but still greeted Ben with a hug. On the plump side, Marion was beautiful in nature and voluptuous in stature. She couldn't be bothered with anything more than simple makeup, she wore her blond hair quite short, she dressed for purpose, rather than effect, and Ben thought she was wonderful, the perfect complement to Joss's taut and sometimes stilted manner. Marion was funny, a chatterer, sentimental and fiercely protective of her family, which she took to include every lad and lass in the yard. She and Anna had immediately become solid friends when they had first met and Ben was aware that Marion had also been deeply affected by the death of her friend.

After providing assurances that he was indeed fine, and dutifully drinking two of the three glasses of water, Ben took Max's hand and the O'Hoole and Ramsden families headed down the yard to the farmhouse kitchen.

Seven

Sunday breakfast at the O'Hoole stables was the stuff of legend. The two huge ovens went on at seven thirty and by nine o'clock in the morning there were perfectly roasted sausages, crisp bacon, eggs of all descriptions, waffles, bread, toast, beans, black pudding… the list went on. Everyone pitched in, so when Ben and the children walked into the huge kitchen the table capable of seating sixteen people was laden with food.

Half a dozen stable hands and work riders had already sat down, four of five more were on their feet stirring, grilling, frying, microwaving and serving. Greetings were passed between everyone and Ben spied another two of Joss's owners already sitting down and waved a hello to them both, but only recognising one. Joss rang the yard bell, which sounded right down to the bottom paddock, and a few minutes later the last two lads appeared eager-faced at the kitchen door and took their place at the table.

'Have we lost our policeman and woman or have they been escorted from the premises?' asked Joss of the late joiners to the meal.

'Just seen them out of the yard now Guv'nor,' replied a lean teenager with a tight zip up jacket on and a pinched face.

'Did they say anything before departing our premises, which by the way, is *supposed to be secure*?' Joss questioned, placing emphasis on his last few words so that all the staff could hear.

The lad paused, mulling over his reply. Ben had seen this pause from Joss's staff many times. Anyone who worked at these stables knew that when they were talking to the boss, they made sure they gave him every piece of information, correctly and precisely. It saved time. Otherwise he would be quizzing you relentlessly until he felt he had all the information from you.

'The chap said thanks, and that everything was fine and he would hopefully not be coming back. He said he couldn't stay for breakfast and you'd be hearing from him one way or another. If they track the guy down who made the call he or his PC will be in touch. The woman just got in the car and said nothing – didn't even reply when I said goodbye,' said the stable lad, clearly disappointed the twenty-something year old policewoman had shown next to no interest in him.

'Fair enough,' replied Joss. Then after a short stare into the middle distance he added 'That WPC was wearing makeup and earrings,' he sniffed, 'Not that she needed it.'

'Yeah, she wasn't your usual policewoman,' agreed Ben.

'Oh really?' Marion called over from the other side of the kitchen.

'Sounds like you and my husband are getting smitten with good looking ladies in uniform! Either that or you're suggesting a policewoman isn't allowed to be feminine…'

'Not for one second, my love,' said Joss lightly, sensing dangerous ground, but winking conspiratorially to the table. 'Give me a woman who looks good in wellies, an old woolly jumper and is capable of bringing in the wood for the stove, that's my kind of gal. You can keep your wishy-washy officious types!'

Marion looked down at herself in the exact getup her husband had described and holding two medium sized, dusty logs in her arms.

'That's just as well then,' she announced primly and after placing one of the logs on the fire, cuffed her husband's head playfully.

At that moment more food arrived at the table, along with two towering steel urns containing tea and coffee. Conversations broke out again up and down the table.

Mojo sat herself down in the corner of the kitchen, close to Marion's Great Dane, but not quite on his vast bed, not until the bigger dog had settled. Then she covered the last few feet, aimed a quick lick at Zippo's ear and flopped down beside him. The dog's antics drew a comment from one of the owners down the table, pointing out how comical they looked together, being the two extremes, both in size and attitude.

Ben sat Max down beside him in chair which was too low and too big for him, but in the full knowledge that Max thought this was 'real'. They were in the middle of the table and Max beamed around at everyone and at the prospect of unlimited top quality pork sausages. Following a short silence for grace, provided in a stern voice by Joss, everyone tucked in.

Immediately, four discussions started, laughter punctuated the air, food was passed from person to person in many directions at once and this was all directed by Marion at the head of the table. She paid particular attention to the children, ensuring they had plenty on their plates. Max stood up on his chair, pulled a large flowery serving bowl of beautifully cooked pork sausages towards him, and carefully chose three, dropping them one at a time onto his plate. Next he squirted brown sauce on them and grinning with happiness over his choices, he settled down to spear his first sausage with his fork then munch at it between dabs in his sauce.

Joss did an introduction to a lady called Loren Plummer who he explained had just placed a young filly with him to train, her first ever racehorse. She was rather prim and upright, and turned out to be an interesting, well-educated lady of about forty. Ben asked a few questions about her two year old and she did the same about The Ghost Machine. It transpired that she had lost her father the year before and he had insisted she buy a racehorse with some of her inheritance as a way of finding her a husband from the right background. It was never explained whether her father's target man for her was another racehorse owner, or whether a bookmaker, jockey or a racecourse steward would do. Ben decided not to ask.

'My poor father always wanted me to find a husband and was forever manufacturing ways for me to meet eligible men!' Loren revealed to Ben apologetically.

'Well we'll see if it works I guess! You never know,' he managed in reply.

'I rather hope it won't work actually,' she shared quietly, 'You see, I've already got a partner, but Dad couldn't quite wrap his head around it.' Loren looked in Ben's eyes and saw the flicker of understanding there.

'Ah well, perhaps you'll fall in love with the horses instead,' Ben stated lightly, 'I find there's always something for everyone in horse racing,' he added, falling back on one of his stock replies to new Owners.

Loren seemed to appreciate this though, and smiled back generously.

'Ben, I think you've met Eleanor before?' asked Joss.

Ben looked up from his bacon and eggs and swallowed before replying 'Yes, of course, we met a few months ago at Wolverhampton when we both had a runner there. If I remember rightly, I was there watching a filly of mine finish down the field, and Eleanor was kind enough to invite me into the winning connections box when her colt won the next race doing cartwheels!'

Ben reacquainted himself with the lady's face, crusted with wrinkles. She was a larger than life character, and a very jolly type. She was a habitual racegoer and that night at Wolverhampton had been no different, with her appearing at the course with an entourage of nephews, nieces and friends who doted on her.

Eleanor Hart's face crinkled with delight, and she nodded furiously up the table at Ben.

'Yes, I remember now. It was 'Pudding's' third run and he really did well that day,' she remarked excitedly.

Ben hadn't remember the horse's name, but now placed it – a gelding which was named Elusive Hart, but had the stable name of 'Pudding' because when he'd arrived at the yard as a yearling he was as fat as a pig and had been dubbed 'The Puddin' by one of the lads. He had, of course, grown into a lovely big, strapping handicapper and won a couple of decent class races last season, but the name had stuck and was apparently approved of by his owner.

'Is he coming on well enough for the start of the flat?' Ben asked across the table.

Again, the wrinkle encrusted face started with furious nodding.

'Yes, I saw him work in the ménage this morning and he was raring to go, we can't wait. I think he's looking even better as a four year old.'

She went on to describe the horse's work in detail, obviously delighted to have an audience which was happy to listen to her. Eleanor was a respected breeder with a couple of decent mares and maintained a steady flow of a horse or two a year into the O'Hoole stable, as her mother had done to Joss's father when he had run the yard. Her horses were never going to be stars, but they were decent enough, and along the way they had managed to win a couple of nice conditions races and the odd larger handicap. Ben was aware she had other horses dotted around the midlands and south as well, usually with older, established trainers.

'We're going to run in about a week, going back to Wolverhampton actually,' Eleanor added at the end of her monologue.

Joss quickly gulped down a slug of coffee and interjected 'Ah, that's right, the gelding loves it around there doesn't he? He raised an eyebrow to encourage a response.

'Oh yes!' the old lady enthused. 'He loves the sand there, but I'm also hoping we can try and bag one of the big handicaps at York with him in summer too.'

The conversation continued, centred upon Eleanor's horses. Lads and lasses soon started to push their plates away from themselves. After clearing their plates and cutlery from the table and thanking Marion, one by one they headed off to finish their Sunday morning's work. Usually there would be fifteen stable hands in on a morning, but on Sunday that dropped to about eight or ten, as Joss would tend not to plan any gallop work unless there were horses needing preparatory work ahead of a run in midweek.

The kitchen emptied of staff and after the children and Max left to see their ponies, Marion and Joss were left with their three owners.

Eleanor, perhaps realising that she had dominated the conversation through a good proportion of the meal asked after The Ghost Machine.

'He couldn't be better. He's got the constitution of an ox and the temperament of an angel. He's the perfect racehorse,' said Joss. 'And it scares me witless, because it's all down to me not to screw it up!' he added with a smile and running a hand through his largely uncontrollable hair.

Joss ran through the start of the race plans for the colt, but Ben zoned out slightly, having heard the detail of this horse's expected route through the upcoming flat season so many times he could recite it word for word. That's what happened when you had a really good one, the best horses had their own set of races and every owner dreamed of following in the footsteps of the great and glorious through a season of race meetings at Newbury, Ascot, Newmarket, Goodwood and perhaps taking in Longchamp, or even the Breeders Cup in America.

And Joss was right, Ben reflected. A horse like this only came along once in a while, and for a trainer like Joss, perhaps once in a lifetime. It was so easy for things to go wrong and the horse not reach its potential. One knock to a knee, a false step leading to a fall on the gallops, a bug picked up at the track. All these things happened to horses all the time, you had to limit their exposure to potential problems and hope it didn't happen to you. If it did, well, there was the difference between a good horse, and a racehorse which was the leader of its generation.

For Ben, a relatively successful but low stakes syndicate manager running about a dozen horses a year, The Ghost Machine was definitely a horse of a lifetime. He didn't have the big money needed to buy really top quality bloodstock, he just bought the best he could afford. But with The Ghost Machine he had potentially hit the jackpot. Although the horse had only won a Conditions race at Newmarket and the seven furlong Group 3 Stakes race at York in his two year old season, the way he had done his winning had been impressive, and bookmakers had installed him at twelve-to-one for the first classic of the season, the Two Thousand Guineas at Newmarket in May.

Ben came back to the conversation when the attendance of the police was raised by Eleanor.

'So what's been happening here this week?' she queried. 'One of your lads told me that you've had two or three visits from the local constabulary. Is everything okay in the yard?'

Joss closed his eyes and let out a sigh. Marion looked concerned for a few moments, lightly touched his thigh under the table and fixed a reassuring gaze into her husband's eyes. He looked up at his owners. 'I really don't know why it's happening, or who is behind it, and neither do the police.'

'Since last Thursday we've had three visits, including today, and all they can do is look around the yard, ask a few questions, and then leave. They seem to have no clue who is making the accusations or why. I've even been down to the local police station to try and get to the bottom of it but they'd got nowhere tracking down whoever it is. I was given the standard sort of stuff about it being 'their duty' to follow up these accusations. They will be *making enquiries*, but I haven't had any feedback at all.'

He took a gulp of his coffee and continued, 'I guess it's probably a disgruntled stable lad who thinks it's funny to waste everyone's time, but I'm not so sure. They took the names of three or four staff I had to get rid of in the last two years because they weren't up to the job. They said they would follow up with them if they had the time, but beyond that, I don't know anything more.'

Joss's cheeks began to flush slightly as he went on 'What gets me though, is when they come in looking for horses which have been mistreated. I mean to say, what does it take for someone to throw accusations like that around? I've never mistreated a horse in my life, and neither did my Dad, he…'

'It will just be a silly youngster,' interrupted Marion, looking at her husband and placing a hand on his and squeezing lightly. 'The police have been here three times now and haven't found anything. I'm sure they won't be paying too much attention to these calls if they continue. After all, it's wasting their time too.'

'Yes, but mud sticks in this game, and it won't be long before I have hacks from the papers asking daft questions,' Joss groaned, 'It won't matter two hoots what the truth is if they get hold of a story that will fill up some space and sell a few extra papers.'

Ben was about to offer his support, but Marion got there first. Grabbing Joss's hand in hers, she told him 'Everyone who knows you at all will treat this for what it is... balderdash! And as for mistreating a horse, well, I bet your horses are healthier than the police's own horses!'

Joss laughed and thanked her with a nod and a halfhearted smile. In a brighter voice he said 'Well, hopefully that will be the end of it, but I really can't stand all this muck stirring, it wastes precious time I could be spending with the horses. Whoever has done this must really have an axe to grind, and I can't think of anyone I've dealt with who would be reduced to lying about the yard.'

Ben examined the trainer and the woman by his side and realised that Joss wasn't so much worried about the police, but more bewildered by what it took for someone to make the accusations.

'Let me tell you something,' said Ben quietly. 'You're not the easiest man to work with in racing. You're stubborn and single-minded, demanding and have ridiculously high expectations of everyone around you, which is sometimes not understood by staff when you criticise them. But, you're also the most straightforward and fairest person I know in racing, and what's more, you'd never allow a horse to suffer.'

Joss, a little taken aback by this heartfelt announcement, eyed Ben pensively. Marion on the other hand looked back to her husband and murmured her agreement.

After a short silence Joss cracked a smile, 'It's nice to have the old Ben Ramsden with us again! You haven't made one of your worldly insights like that for... well, some months. A shame it had to be about me, but hey, welcome back!'

All of them laughed, including Loren and Eleanor. Ben sat resting his head in one hand and rolled his eyes for comic effect. It had been some time since he'd got really animated about anything, and he had to admit, it felt good. His loss of Anna, and particularly in such awful circumstances, weighed heavily on him so much of the time. Any relief was welcome, and it was partly due to Joss and Marion, along with his other good friends, that he was still holding it all together.

The five of them sat at the kitchen table and chatted for another few minutes, and then Eleanor claimed she had, 'things to get further on with,' and Loren took the opportunity to excuse herself, after thanking Marion for the breakfast. Both owners offered their own support to Joss and assured him that his difficulties with the police were sure to be short-lived.

Ben offered to clear the plates and wash up but was flatly refused by Marion so he made an exit as well. Sunday was a busy day, busier than many weekdays, as there were syndicate members to call and update as well as horses to check up on and paperwork to complete. Ben had four trainers up and down the country, and he had to keep on top of race entries, declarations and runners. He had two horses running that week, and no matter what condition he was in, the work had to be done.

He went back up to the broodmare's stable one more time to spend a little more time with her, Mojo following him up there, trotting at his heels, and then the two of them walked to the bottom paddocks to pick up Max. He wasn't difficult to locate – the kids' screams of playful delight could be heard all over the yard. Ben found the three children jumping and falling all over a number of bales and rounds of straw which had been pushed together to form a platform of sorts. They were shouting pirate sayings at each other and battling each other with sticks which doubled as swords. Ben watched them from a short distance away for a few minutes. Max was totally engrossed and looked like he was defending his straw 'ship' from the two marauding pirates. Funny, Ben thought, Max is always on the side of the good guys, never the pirate, the blaggard or the invader. He always wants to seek and not hide. Ben wondered for a moment which parent had passed those particular traits to their son.

He was shaken from his thoughts by Max himself, who leapt from the bales onto the grass and came running up to him, out of breath and sporting flushed red cheeks. The boy said nothing, throwing his arms around his father's legs, giving him the tightest hug he could muster.

Finally, ten seconds later, he released him and with Mojo barking excitedly beside him, he beamed up into his fathers' face and said in a breathless voice, 'I really like it here Dad.'

Ben crouched down so that he was level with his son and then whispered 'So do I,' in his ear.

Eight

Ben slammed the phone down into its holster with such force it missed and skittered across his desk and onto the floor. He threw his biro across the room and let out a frustrated bellow. The pen bounced off the wall of the upstairs box room which constituted his office, leaving a small blue mark on the off-white paintwork. It didn't seem to Ben to deliver enough damage given the exertion in his throw and certainly didn't make him feel any better.

The whingeing tones of Graham Loote still rang in his ears. Sometimes conversations with syndicate members could be frustrating to the point of exasperation. However, in every racehorse there were always owners who believed they knew better than the trainer, the syndicate manager, and even the horse itself.

Mr Graham P. Loote was a case in point. Even when his horse won, he would find some aspect of its performance to criticise, and when there was a setback or delay in racing the horse Mr Loote would be the first to start demanding all manner of changes, some which were utterly ridiculous. But that was the job, Ben reflected as he picked up the phone and crossed the room to retrieve his pen.

This time it was a complaint about the ride a jockey had given his horse. In a tightly packed field the young apprentice had made a split second decision to go for a gap which closed up on him as he made his move. This had the effect of baulking another runner and sending the horse itself back in the field a few lengths, losing all chance of winning. The move also earned the jockey a two-day suspension for what the Stewards regarded as irresponsible riding. Graham Loote was not the sort to pass up on a glaring opportunity to berate the rider, the trainer's decision to put an apprentice on board and to ensure that Ben was made aware of all his grievances and gripes, which usually included pedantic references to previous digressions.

Ben sank back into his rotating leather chair and after sighing loudly, stared out into the cottage garden. The sharp spring breeze rustled the old brown leaves which still clung to the beech hedge and a steady drizzle beat out a rhythmic melody on the windowpane. Loote was an annoying pedant, but at least he paid his training bills, which was more than could be said for a number of his clients at the moment. He switched his attention back to the computer on the desk and the list of clients marked with red sums attached to their names.

Sunday afternoon was his catch-up time. When nine to fivers would be out with their family or friends, Sunday afternoon was paperwork day in the lives of most racing people. Chasing owners for payment was a regular job, but a very necessary one. Ben could list dozens of trainers he knew who at any one time were owed many thousands of pounds by owners with less than stringent payment schedules. In some cases these debts could build up to incredible sums, simply because the trainer didn't want to lose a good horse. It could easily take a trainer's businesses to the wall. Being a dedicated and successful racehorse trainer didn't make you a good businessman, which many young trainers lacking business acumen found out to their cost.

Ben scanned down the list of defaulted clients and chose the biggest minus figure on the list and reached for his phone. But before he could pick the handset up it rang out, the small screen pulsing Joss O'Hoole's name.

Clicking the accept call button on the phone he said 'Missing me already are you?' into the receiver.

There was a pause at the other end, and then a serious sounding voice said 'Ben, its Joss. Have you had a visit from anyone today?'

Ben snapped into a more serious mode. He could hear a hint of suppressed rage in the trainer's voice. 'No. No one's been here all afternoon Joss,' he replied, under the impression that Joss wanted him to be succinct.

There was a pause on the line as Joss related this answer to someone in a hushed tone. Ben assumed it must be Marion. Outside the wind whistled round the roof tiles and the rain splashed against the window in short bursts. Joss was not prone to long silences, so the sound of crackling white sound from the earpiece made Ben tense his face and press the phone closer to his ear.

'You'd better get over here Ben. You can bring Max with you and make sure you have your mobile phone with you. We need to talk about this face to face.'

'Uh, sure,' replied Ben, perplexed, 'But tell me what on earth is going on? Is one of the horses ill?'

'No, absolutely not, I'm sorry, I should have said. Nothing like that,' said Joss, but Ben sensed the irritation rising in his friend.

'I was going to wait until you got here, so you could see it for yourself, but I may as well tell you now. Someone is trying to buy out your owner's shares in The Ghost.'

****

Crunching his tyres on the entrance to Joss's stables for the second time that day, Ben hurriedly jumped out of his car, undid his son's seatbelts and picking Mojo up, tucked her under an arm and carried her up to the house. Sensing his father's mood, Max grabbed Mojo shouted a, 'See you later,' and immediately skipped off up the yard to find his playmates from earlier in the day.

Joss was already at the front door and greeted Ben with a

39

perfunctory nod.

'Come on in, we're in the kitchen. You had any calls from the Ghost's shareholders yet?' asked Joss.

'No. Nothing from any of them, as far as I'm aware. Why?'

'The paperwork says we have to sign the agreement and not inform anyone else. I guess we may have lost a few of them already. You need to check,' instructed Joss.

Ben located his mobile phone in his coat pocket and realised he had three missed calls already showing. 'Damn the phone reception around here,' he said under his breath.

Sitting down at the kitchen table with Joss and a concerned looking Marion, it only took a few minutes for Ben to grasp what was going on. A hand delivered letter and contract had sat on their kitchen table waiting for his attention as soon as he'd walked in. Twenty minutes later, after six phone calls, four left messages and a certain amount of cursing, not so much under his breath this time, he leant back from the table, tucked his hands behind his head and delivered a synopsis of the situation.

'We've lost two owners in The Ghost, got another one thinking about it and I can't get hold of the other four at the moment. That's twenty percent of the colt gone and forty percent not accounted for...'

'Well I gave the chap who came to the door with this little lot short shrift,' said Marion indicating the paperwork on the table.

The knock on the front door had come midway through the O'Hoole's Sunday afternoon and after handing them an envelope marked 'One of Ten' the caller had insisted on waiting at the open door until he received an answer from Joss himself. When the refusal had been made, the man had walked to a Range Rover with tinted windows and had been driven off by someone else who had never left the vehicle.

'If they think they can just waltz in here and take the best horse we've ever trained from us for a paltry forty thousand pounds then they are very much mistaken!' Marion said, simultaneously busying herself with her iPad at the end of the table.

Ben sighed expressively, 'It didn't take too much persuasion to make the first two shareholders sign,' he groaned, trailing his finger down the list in front of him.

'David White took twenty five. He sounded relieved when I spoke with him, as if the money would make a big difference to him. I guess everyone has a sum of money where it becomes too tempting.'

Joss was pouring everyone another cup of coffee but hesitated, slopping the black liquid from the spout of the jug.

'Was it the same name on each contract, this solicitor?' he pointed to the papers on the table.

'Yes, the elusive Mr A. Armitage,' Ben replied. 'There's no answer on his number at the moment. Anything on the web Marion?'

She looked up from the iPad 'I'm on a website now. It looks like he's an equine specialist solicitor with a firm called Langland's, based in Newmarket.'

'I've heard of them. I think they sponsor a race or two, a couple of the big handicaps at the July meeting,' Joss remarked.

'Do you think it's this chap behind all of the offers to The Ghost's owners?'

'I doubt it. I think he will just be a front man for a client. It's hardly surprising really,' replied Ben, 'If I wanted to remain behind the scenes and make offers to pick off a controlling interest in a valuable racehorse, going through a law firm makes a lot of sense. It makes everything seem to be above board and you preserve your anonymity.'

Marion brought the iPad over to the two men and placed it down between them. 'Look at this. I've got a picture and some information about this chap here.'

Ben looked down at the digital representation of Mr A. Armitage on his company's website. Even though the photo was only down to the top of his chest, he appeared to be a small, thick-set man, possibly in his late twenties, although a completely bald head didn't help him hold back the years. He could have passed for forty on a bad day. The short resume confirmed his age was twenty-eight and he was a partner in the Newmarket based Langlands practise, having qualified in Edinburgh.

There was no denying it, Mr Armitage was pretty ugly. The photographer had obviously tried his best by turning his subjects body away from the camera, tilted his head back at an angle towards the lens (presumably to stop his shiny baldness from blinding the shot), however it still wasn't a pretty sight. Armitage wore an ill-fitting grey pinstriped suit and white shirt, both of which appeared extremely tight and pulled at his neck and he stared out at the camera unsmiling, with a large, wide grey face.

'Well, he's a real looker isn't he,' remarked Joss playfully. 'I assume he's a decent solicitor because he isn't going to win any beauty contests.'

Ben and Marion chuckled and the atmosphere in the kitchen relaxed a little. Ben reflected that it was quite true. There wasn't any light under which Mr A. Armitage was going to present himself as pleasing to the eye. His nose was bulbous and there was the start of a double chin, even at this age, which provided his jawbone with a creased ring which underlined it from ear to ear.

There was a short précis of the man to the left of the photo, with nothing of note apart from what Marion had already pointed out: he specialised in 'client management', which resulted in two sets of shrugs when Ben asked what that could entail.

Ben turned away and thought hard for a few moments. 'It seems we have found our man, but we need to determine his client. But right now I need to get back on the phone and try and track down everyone in The Ghost. As long as we have fifty-percent of him accounted for, he's going nowhere.'

Ben opened a pristine new page in his A4 sized notebook, which accompanied him pretty much everywhere, took out an artist B2 pencil with a half worn rubber at the end and sketched out the names of the shareholders in The Ghost Machine, writing in their share and whether he had spoken to them. Even as a small child he had realised he worked best on any problem when he could look write it down and view the whole picture on paper, and usually one single page, mapping out a solution and making the issues fall into place. Somehow the act of getting everything onto paper seemed to help him separate the fact from fiction, and often gave him the answer to whatever he was trying to solve.

He often analysed a pedigree of a thoroughbred the same way, linking previous winners, any negative or positive character traits in the family and attempting to determine the potential in the un-raced yearling. Anna had often referred to his jumble of words, pictures, stars, graphs, arrows and flows as his 'Matchstick Men', as there would inevitably be a stick man somewhere on the page. Joss had enjoyed pointing fun at Ben's hand drawn, almost childlike pictures, but he soon came to realise that Ben's Matchstick Men could be valuable. Indeed, the reason they had ended up buying The Ghost Machine was in part to Ben's scribbles.

As Ben's picture started to take shape, Joss and Marion waited patiently in the background, sipping tea, passing behind Ben's shoulder as he worked intently on the page in front of him. He started with a group of figures with percentages above their heads, then ruled a line to one area of the page and added tick marks and more percentages. Another area was labeled with a large question mark. Then a group of arrows, short questions in speech bubbles and some smaller pictures.

From time to time Ben would stop, lean back in his chair, and apply the rubber, brushing the resulting shards of blackened debris off the paper. Then after staring off into the distance he would moments later return to the page, editing, highlighting, and adding emphasis with bold strokes of the pencil.

Finally he pushed the page away and stood up.

'Damn they have been clever,' Ben exclaimed. 'The time, the day, and they knew where I would be and more or less where the rest of the owners were. It's been executed with almost military precision. Say what you like about our mysterious Mr Armitage, he has orchestrated a near perfect coup.'

Joss, looking fearful, brow furrowed, started to ask a question, but stopped himself, knowing Ben well enough to realise the answer was probably already on its way. He held up a hand and instead said, 'But you have an answer or a plan? So we can stop him taking control of The Ghost?'

Ben recognised the pent up fear and frustration in his friend and answered quickly.

'Yes. I need to speak with those owners I haven't got hold of yet. Then we can make sure that we still hold the controlling percentage in the horse. What our unknown foe has hopefully forgotten is that the heart plays a big part of any ownership of a racehorse and that, thank goodness, is rarely able to be bought, if all you offer is money.'

Ben knew how important The Ghost was to Joss. If The Ghost maintained his upward curve he could be a contender in the most important three year old races through summer. Winning more races at group level would attract more owners and their horses to Joss's yard – it was the ultimate method of advertising for a racehorse trainer.

'I need to use your landline, if that's okay?' Ben asked. Even before he had received a nod of approval from Marion he'd jumped to his feet and was striding purposefully out of the open kitchen door, his face a mask of concern.

Joss fixed on Marion's eyes and saw his own fears reflected in them. He walked a few paces over to the large kitchen table where Ben's complex, hand drawn pencil picture showed a large heart shape in one corner, boldly outlined and underlined three times. Marion joined him.

Among pictures of phones, pound notes, think bubbles, cars, palms and fists and much more, there were names, matchstick men and women. Joss's eyes scanned the whole piece of paper, but finally he was drawn to a small section at the bottom of the page where two shareholder's names had been placed, and which Joss recognised. These matchstick representations of their owners had been transplanted to an area all of their own. Drawn above these two owners were several small hearts which grew larger, seemingly ballooning up and hovering over their heads.

Joss leaned over the page and rubbed his chin.

'Well. I hope this makes sense to him. It's all Greek to me.'

'It will. That's why you're the trainer and he's the syndicate manager,' Marion replied, lightly placing a hand on her husband's back and rubbing it reassuringly.

Ben retrieved his notebook from the car and returned to the house, sitting himself down at the large, aged desk in a ground floor room off the hall which doubled as a racing office and somewhere private for Joss to offer owners a tea or coffee and discuss their horses. He opened his notebook and quickly found a handwritten page entitled 'The Ghost Machine'. Each of the twelve owners were listed with names and addresses, telephone numbers of all descriptions: home, mobile, holiday homes all penciled in around or below each address. He ran a pen down the names, striking out those he knew had already sold their share to Mr

43

Armitage. Seven owner's names remained, with Ben's own making a total of eight.

Ben picked up the receiver from the top of the old-fashioned phone which sat on the desk. A bell tinkled inside and the dial tone could immediately be heard once it was removed. This was an item Joss steadfastly refused to upgrade, as he claimed the handset and coiled chord fit perfectly to his shoulder and ear without the need to hold his hand there for long periods. However Ben was pretty sure the real reason was that Joss's father had used the same phone when he was alive. Joss had a framed photo of the man himself on the wall of his office which showed Nick O'Hoole, handset clamped to his ear and shoulder, writing on a copy of The Sporting Life at the same desk in the seventies.

The yard long loop of coiled plastic felt a little strange to Ben, being attached to the end of the handset and bouncing between the phone's base and its large handset. Within minutes of his first call Ben was playing with the coils and realising he was perhaps missing something by using hands free phones.

Half an hour passed, during which time Joss and Marion remained in the kitchen and heard the phone's bell chime half a dozen times. Ben replaced the handset and returned to the kitchen and sat back down at the huge table. Joss joined him and after placing new steaming cups of coffee in front of them, Marion pulled up a chair.

'Right, this is where we are,' Ben sighed. 'The Ghost's shareholders are ten people... or at least they were until last night. Each of them holds a ten percent share. When they bought into The Ghost a ten percent share cost them two thousand pounds and each of the owners are registered as owners with Weatherby's, racing's bank, which means they have to confirm the transaction with them before the sale is complete.'

'You and I,' Ben nodded towards Joss, 'We both have ten percent each. Then there's Duncan who has ten percent as well. I've spoken to him and as you would expect, he knows the score and he's not going anywhere with his share.'

The yard blacksmith, Duncan Jones, lived less than a mile away from Ben and similarly, was bringing up his family in a remote cottage. The same age as Ben, the two of them were good friends and neighbours who had become even closer since Anna's accident. Ben was slightly embarrassed at how much he relied on Duncan's wife, Nancy, to help with Max's school runs as well as general advice around the house. Duncan and Nancy had been wonderful since the accident and totally supportive towards Ben and Max.

'If you add Olivia and Janet Dunn's share, that's forty percent still with us and...'

'Olivia?' cut in Marion.

'Oh right. Yes, you know, the Scottish ladies... Olivia always comes racing with her eighty year old Mother Janet,' explained Ben.

Marion nodded her understanding. 'Oh yes!' she exclaimed, 'She's lovely, well, they both are. They wouldn't sell would they? They love The Ghost to bits.'

'No they haven't sold their share. It sounded like they were pretty shaken up when they got their envelope, and I had three voice messages on my mobile from them by the time I got here. I've called them back and they are fine. We can count on them; Olivia's made of stern stuff and her Mother is as sharp as a tack. Some sort of hefty bouncer type turned up at the door and offered Olivia money and a cruise around the world for a month but she gave him a definitively Scottish answer from what I can make out,' replied Ben with a half smile.

Something appeared to cross Ben's mind and he frowned. 'What's a bit strange is how Armitage knew that the two of them always take cruising holidays…'

Ben went quiet, appearing to Marion and Joss as if he was trying to make a connection. Marion nodded a further assurance Ben's way and he returned a quick smile and his attention to the list of shareholders.

'Rob Bawtry hasn't sold, so we're up to the important fifty percent which means the horse can't be taken to another trainer. He called me and he wasn't having any of it. Apparently they called at the pub early this morning and got him out of bed so he wasn't in the best of moods when the envelope was slid under the front door.'

Ben continued, 'He opened it and gave them a mouth full. I got the impression he was more agitated about being knocked out of bed early after a long night of work, rather than the fact they wanted his share of the horse. They wouldn't leave until he'd opened the letter and signed their delivery receipt.'

Ben consulted his notes, 'The offer was different again. Enough to pay for his Mother's care for the next three years. Almost sixty thousand pounds. Whoever is behind this has certainly done their homework. They've tried to make every offer as tempting as possible for each shareholder, which is a little worrying.'

'Is Rob's Mother in a care home then?' asked Joss.

'No, at the moment she's living in the cottage next door to Rob. She had an accident a couple of years ago, a head injury which left her pretty confused and prone to wandering off. She needs a lot of supervision, but Rob works next door, so he can pop in to check on her when the pub isn't too busy. She also has a carer who is there four days a week, which I would imagine is pretty expensive. I think the pub's profits are eaten up with the costs of his mum's care one way or another.'

Ben pinched the bridge of his nose and added, 'Rob has enough spare cash for the share in his horse, but little else, by all accounts.'

He looked up from his pen and paper to see Marion hugging

herself and Joss leaning against the wall, head down. Marion released the grip on herself self-consciously, 'It must have been tempting then,' she said flatly. Then thoughtfully, 'I didn't realise he had all that to contend with, he is so much fun and interesting to be around at the races.'

'He's good at running the pub, I know that. He's built it into a really decent business with good food and a chef who's getting a name for himself, but I think it takes up all his time. I guess the horse is a sort of release. There's a host of reasons for owning something as frivolous as a racehorse, but for him it's an indulgence which gets him away from the day to day realities,' Ben explained.

The air of gloom held for a few moments, but then its dreary magic was broken by the entrance of a wiry young lad wearing riding gear and with a helmet tucked under his arm. A shock of blonde hair was plastered to one side of his head and he was halfway through the room before the quietness of his surroundings caught up with him.

'Oh, sorry boss,' he said apologetically, coming to a halt. 'I just needed to know what you wanted doing with that grey filly in the bottom yard today, y'know the one which is coming back from the tendon injury?'

Ben looked up with immediate recognition and smiled at the young apprentice jockey, 'Hi Robert, you okay?'

'Yeah, good thanks Mr Ramsden. Can't wait for the season to get going properly, the boss's got some nice horses again this year.'

He indicated Joss who was now sitting at the kitchen table, 'One or two of yours are interesting too!' he added with a cheeky smile.

Ben was about to reply, but Joss cut in.

'Okay Robert, just take her down to the river at a walk and trot her up the smaller hill, nothing too difficult. Make sure she doesn't mess you about, she can take a grip. She had her lass off her the other day by dropping her shoulder when she wasn't concentrating.'

'Yeah, but Pam spends more time on her backside looking up at the sky than in a saddle,' said Jake winking and turning on his heel to head back out, 'Don't worry boss, I know she can be a monkey, I'll keep her straight.'

'And give her a pick of grass up at the top of the hill,' Joss called after him as Jake's steps receded on the York stone floor and crunched away on the pea gravel once he stepped outside.

'That one's got a quick tongue, so it's a pretty good job he has a quick brain too,' Joss said light heartedly. 'Only seventeen and thinks he knows it all, but then I guess they all do at that age... He would kill for the ride on the Ghost, he...'

'You were just the same you know,' interrupted Marion, tapping her husband on his backside with the flat of her hand. 'And I seem to remember you were far less sensible than Robert as well,' she added, winking conspiratorially at Ben.

Catching the lift in the atmosphere, Marion moved and leaned over the notebook scribbles in front of Ben.

'Look, from what you two have worked out, it looks like we are still holding onto enough of the Ghost at the moment. Even if this mysterious solicitor has forty percent, he can't force us into anything can he? We've still got control and nothing we do tonight will change anything.'

Ben grimaced, but nodded his agreement. Joss shrugged his shoulders and put his arm around his wife. 'Once again, the reason I married you comes into sharp relief when some commonsense is required.'

'Ben, why don't you and Max stay with us tonight? We're going to have a picnic tea down by in the River House with the kids this evening, and you can both stay in the guest room in the main house,' suggested Marion.

Joss chipped in, 'Sounds like an excellent plan to me. Then you can come to Ripon with us tomorrow and help me deal with my owners. I may even throw in one of my famous 'stick to your ribs' breakfasts as well if you can cope with it.' He paused, thoughtful for a second, and then pointed out: 'Besides, I've two runners tomorrow, and I'm short of someone to lead up.'

Ben relaxed his frame a little and then slowly and purposefully closed the notebook and pushed it away across the table. He ran a hand slowly through his hair and finally nodded his approval.

'That would be... very welcome,' he said warmly, 'If only because I think Max would be devastated if he found out your kids were down at the river tonight without him. As for Ripon, its time you had a winner, and you know what good luck I am. Our conniving lawyer man from Newmarket can wait until tomorrow.'

****

The evening had passed quickly, with a cold meat and pickle sandwich supper down in the rickety old boathouse which Joss had restored a few years back. The restoration had consisted of Joss directing pretty much the entire riding and stable staff to sweep, clean, saw and nail every plank of wood in the place until he was satisfied that it was safe for everyone to sit under. Then he brought in an industrial sized gas heater, tables and a variety of chairs, which meant you could sit out there even in the middle of January and still be fairly comfortable. But in the summer months it was idyllic, sitting out where the rowing boats used to be moored, looking over the silent running river as the sun beat down.

They'd retreated to the farmhouse when it started to get dark, and after hot chocolates, Max and Ben said their goodnights and went up to the spare room in the attic which consisted of a pitched ceiling, two single beds, a few mirrors on the whitewashed walls and a small en-suite washroom. A tired Max had peeled his clothes off, jumped into bed and fallen asleep immediately, and Ben was not long after him. Mojo curled up at the bottom of Max's bed, exhaled contentedly and closed her eyes, the last of the three to fall asleep.

Ben was woken by the slamming of doors and muffled voices. It was dark, and picking up his phone, its sudden bright glow confirmed it was still the middle of the night. Max stirred and sat up on his elbows in bed, looking uncomprehendingly at his Father. Mojo's head was pointed to the door and she growled quietly.

'It's Ok Max, I'll find out what's going on,' Ben whispered. 'Go back to sleep.'

Max turned over obediently, eyes shutting before his head touched the pillow. Ben jumped out of bed, instructed Mojo to stay and, careful to be quiet, he opened the bedroom door and headed down to the first floor.

Standing at the top of the stairs in his borrowed robe, Ben could hear the sound of voices becoming clearer. Joss was at the back door to the farmhouse, having an animated discussion with someone. Snatches of conversation rose up the stairs to Ben, with Joss clearly exasperated by something. Ben's immediate thought was concern for one of the horses, possibly one of his own, and he continued down the stairs. He reached the bottom just as Joss closed the door and turned around.

He was clearly irritated, and rubbed his eyes when he saw Ben.

'Police again!' he hissed. The rings around his eyes looked even deeper than they had been a few hours before.

'More phone calls and now they are crawling around the paddocks and yard looking for someone.'

The two of them spent the next hour with flashlights, touring two policemen, completely different to those from earlier in the day, around the perimeter of the stables and farmhouse buildings. Apart from disturbing the horses, dogs, poultry and stable staff sleeping in their own onsite private flats at the other side of the yard, their ramblings around the six acre site yielded nothing.

Ben and Joss watched the two constables crackle up the pebble drive in their squad car afterwards, before heading back to bed. Ben climbed the stairs and found Max in virtually the same position he'd left him, fast asleep. Mojo looked up from her self-styled bed in the mess of the boys' bedclothes and, content it was Ben who had walked in the bedroom, resumed her watch over her young master.

Nine

'That was pretty surreal last night,' Ben commented at breakfast only a few hours later.

Marion and the children, plus a smattering of stable staff chattered, moved around the table, helping themselves to a mass of toast, fried eggs, bacon and sausages which kept being replenished in the middle of the table. Coffees and teas were being produced and Ben reflected on how friendly and homely the whole setup was with the O'Hoole's.

Joss nodded his agreement, standing over the kitchen oven where he was poking a spatula at frying eggs and bacon.'I don't know about you, but with what's gone on with The Ghost and these damned police visits, it starts to make you think someone is messing with us. It's been three days since I last had a full night of sleep.'

The comment was stated conversationally, but a pang of worry crept over Ben as he ate. Could the mysterious caller who kept sending policeman on missions to the yard be linked into what was happening with The Ghost syndicate? He considered the thuggish callers on the syndicate members, and their link to the Newmarket solicitor, Mr Armitage. Ben had been approached to sell horses many times before, but never like this. It must have taken time to work out who everyone was, and what would motivate them to sell their share in what could turn out to be a racehorse of a lifetime. He considered how quickly forty percent of the horse's shareholders had been persuaded to sell, and wondered with growing unease whether this Armitage man would resort to more direct means in order to acquire the rest of the shares.

Racing always attracted a wide variety of people wishing to own racehorses and among them were the incorrigible gamblers, the crooked and even worse, those who combined both traits. In Ben's experience they were easy to spot. They would ask about the odds first and had no interest in the horse beyond whether it would win or not. These people rarely visited the yard, and if they did, it would be to press the trainer into revealing what they might consider 'inside information'. Feeding a carrot to their horse would appear alien to this sort of owner, but they would be the first on the phone to Ben or the trainer when any horse in the yard was running. The fact they didn't own the horse would be of no consequence, they would see it as their right to receive valuable knowledge from the stable, in order to beat their bookie. It would be a call which started with 'Hi, how are you? But quickly it would move on to 'So, what are your chances today?'

Live in a crooked world, and you think crooked thoughts, Ben reflected. He cringed at the recollection of a few past owners who if a horse had performed badly, would be the first on the phone (they would rarely go racing), with assumptions which started with 'What a terrible ride, the jockey's bent.' and would finish with 'Why didn't you tell me he wasn't trying?' Of course neither would be true. Horses have bad days, bad races, can be badly handicapped and on the odd occasion, receive poor rides. There doesn't always have to be a conspiracy, and yet when you are motivated solely by the money in your pocket and a view that the whole of the sport is somehow fixed, conspiracies are everywhere. It was almost part of the attraction to horseracing for some, but Ben had little time for these people. He recognised that gambling and bookmakers were an important component of the sport, but he would not allow the state of an owners wallet determine the race plans or decisions on a horse's wellbeing.

Joss took a more compromised view, always reminded Ben that if it wasn't for the gamblers, there wouldn't be the money in the sport, crowds at the races and such a strong market for the top class horses.

'Racing allows them to stick it to the man, and we give them the dream of doing so! Get used to it!' was one of Joss's more memorable responses to Ben's complaints about the constant calls he was getting from one particular gambling owner. Ben had giggled at Joss's 'School Of Rock' reference and eventually realised the pointlessness of his agitation over serious gamblers owning racehorses. But it did rankle when he had to be accepting of owners who were only pleased with his service when they were getting one up on their bookmaker.

Looking up from his frying duties, and noticing Ben's faraway look, Joss recognised Ben's state of mind and continued his upbeat morning tone, upping its volume.

'Thank goodness we're racing today, it's a chance to get away from this madhouse. We can have a normal day out at the races with my two runners today. You still coming Ben?'

Ben, lifted from his thoughts of policemen, thugs, horses and all the swirling questions between them, snapped back into the room.

'Oh, I, er, need to drop Max off at school, and then I'll get over to Ripon and help you lead up if you want,' he responded while trying to clear his mouth of sausage.

'I'm also going to drop in at Duncan's as well so I can make sure he's up to speed on what's happening with this solicitor down in Newmarket. I'll be at Ripon well before the first race, I've not been racing for weeks so it will be like a day off for me, without a runner of my own.'

At a quarter to eight in the morning Ben was sitting in his car, ready to set off. Max was hanging out of a window, waving goodbye to a long line of work riders walking their mounts down the yard entrance on their way to the gallops. Ben felt slightly bloated, but strangely happier with a larger than necessary cooked breakfast inside him. It was the most he'd eaten at one sitting for well over eight months. Max on the other hand, wasn't happy at all with having to leave the stables for school. He and Mojo watched all the fun and excitement evaporate from their day as the line of horses headed off in a different direction to their own.

Back home half an hour later and after a change of clothes, Ben took Max around to Duncan's cottage. In effect, Duncan was his next door neighbour, but he and his wife Nancy and their three children were about a quarter of a mile away down a single lane country track. As they rolled into the entrance to the their eighteenth century cottage, Nancy was already outside loading her kids into the family's fourteen year old convertible. Max immediately brightened, seeing the three children bundling into the ancient runaround. He jumped out of the Volkswagen once he'd been freed from his car seat and ran over to the Jones family.

'Hello there Ben! Am I taking this one to school this morning?' Nancy asked brightly. Her soft plump cheeks had a reddish pinched tinge from the sharp, cool morning, and she smiled warmly at Ben as he approached.

'I was rather hoping you would,' he answered with mock astonishment, and an exaggerated wink. The two of them hugged, and behind them a male voice shouted 'Oy, put her down you!' from over towards the large garage that doubled up as Duncan's workshop.

Already in heavily marked overalls despite the time of day, Duncan gestured with a half wave for Ben to join him. Nancy squeezed Ben's hand, and dropping her voice so the children couldn't listen said quietly 'Duncan has told me about the horse. I hope everything's okay?'

'It's not great, but we've still got control, and I should find out more later today if I can get hold of this solicitor. It's really why I've come to speak to Duncan, as I thought he might know him from his time down at Newmarket.'

Nancy nodded, dropped Ben's hand and shooed the children into the car, 'Come on everyone, we're late. Into the car. Now!'

Kids, coats, hats, car seat buckles and schoolbags were stuffed in every crevice of the car's interior, Ben and Nancy helping the four children in. Josh, the oldest at fourteen, sat with his knees up to his chest, with the passenger seat as far forward as it could go. He was a strapping lad, only a fraction off six feet and looked mournfully out of the window as his younger sisters clambered into the back of the aged Peugeot. It was still cold enough for the kids to require winter coats, and they struggled to get strapped into their safety belts. The three in the backseat fought for room, but after a few sharp words from Nancy the disgruntled trio settled uncomfortably into the rear seat, belts firmly in place.

A few minutes later, Nancy finally pulled out of the drive. Ben watched them go, with Duncan by his side, the two fathers smiling and waving.

'I really should get Nancy a new car shouldn't I?' said Duncan rhetorically in his thick Welsh accent as the packed car finally disappeared from view. 'She doesn't complain though, she just continues to jemmy the kids into it and off they all go as happy as ever. When it's warm she puts the roof down and the kids think it's the best car in the world.'

'A sight which makes you happy to be alive I bet,' snorted Ben, breaking into a laugh. 'As the three of them are carted off and out of your hair for the day…'

'They offered me a new car you know,' said Duncan, turning and walking back over to the garage with Ben, 'A new people carrier worth thirty grand and twenty thousand in cash for my ten percent in The Ghost.' he added.

Ben examined Duncan's chiseled face. In his early thirties, Duncan was lean and fit. He was also good looking, but didn't have a clue that he was, with thick, dark curly hair and brown eyes which lit up a boyish smile, revealing a perfect set of crisp, white teeth. He was totally disarming and yet one of the most genuine people Ben had ever met.

'And your reply was…,' prompted Ben enthusiastically.

Duncan paused, as if trying to conjure up the exact phase he'd used, then whilst scratching his forehead replied 'I think it was something along the lines of 'Sod the people carrier, go get me a Bugatti and a hundred grand and I'll think about it boyo,' turning his lilting Welsh drawl into an over the top accent from the valleys.

'Unfortunately, they weren't too interested in my terms and they beggared off sharpish after that,' he added back in his own accent.

'Proper big, almost nasty sorts, they were too. I had to get the kids away inside when they rolled up in their big blacked out limo. Didn't like them at all, sort of rough, even though they had suits on, you know what I mean?'

Ben nodded agreement and related to Duncan the other owners' encounters with who he could only assume were Mr Armitage's associates.

The truth of the matter was that Duncan could ill afford to turn down that sort of offer for The Ghost. His blacksmithing business gave his family enough to live on, but with three young children, everything was tight. The Jones's were a happy bunch, Nancy, being from an arts background, worked part time at the local library and when she wasn't running the kids everywhere, she painted. She sold a few of her canvasses of stylised cattle, horses, hares and other assorted animals at local galleries from time to time. Duncan ensured they were never without the basics, but brand new cars were the last thing on his list of affordable requirements. If anything, his company van containing all his blacksmith equipment was the most valuable thing the family owned. Their cottage was rented and there was little else of real value around the place.

Ben had told Duncan to get into The Ghost after he'd seen the colt work for the first time as a two year old. As Joss used Duncan as his stable farrier, he worked off the cost of his ten percent and his monthly training fees by doing extra work around the stables, an arrangement which both

Ben and Joss were more than happy with. Duncan was good with his hands, and knew how to make a shoe help a horse to get balanced and grab the earth when it was running at speed. He was particularly adept with the nervous or excitable young horses. With horses he was amiable, gentle and was able to soothe and calm them. With people, Duncan spoke his mind and had a wicked sense of humour.

Duncan continued to pack away tools into the back of his small van, commenting, 'I wouldn't have sold unless you'd told me to. You must know that. I know he's valuable, but I'm not in it for the money. Mind you, I think Nancy might have a different view, she was a bit taken aback when I told her what they offered. I don't think she realised that he was worth that sort of cash.'

Ben clapped his friend on his back, 'I knew you wouldn't sell. Besides, if The Ghost can build on his form from last season he'll be worth a hell of a lot more than Armitage is offering. Then Nancy will have no arguments when we sell him for a career at stud as a stallion. She'll have enough for a new car and then some.'

'Enough for a Bugatti?' asked Duncan, shooting Ben an incredulous glance.

'Yeah, alright, so he won't be making us all millionaires, but we'll still be racing in some pretty decent races with him, if he's trained on.'

'And do we think he has?'

Ben smiled and sucked his breath in over his teeth, 'Joss thinks so. He's still only done a couple of proper gallops so far, but apparently he feels good and he's certainly filled out over winter.'

Duncan picked up a large box of tools and plonked them noisily into the back of his van, closed the doors and turned, 'No worries Ben, I'm just glad to be involved. Nancy and I had a great time with him last season. I won enough on his last run to cover all his winter fees. You can't ask for much more than that.'

Duncan and Nancy were there that day at York, as had eight out of the ten shareholders. Nancy was standing beside Anna in the paddock when she received her fatal kick, and had returned home with Anna's blood all over her, as she had been the first to rush over. Ben could see her now, kneeling over Anna on the manicured grass in the parade ring, smudges of blood on her hands, face and down the sides of her dress, tears washing translucent lines between the red smears.

Ben had thought that Duncan was a sensitive soul, as he had simply frozen to his spot in the parade ring, but he understood many days later that although Duncan was the last to move, he was the one to keep his head. Ben decided he must have been taking stock, working out what needed to be done. He had been the strong one that day. Duncan had a way with horses, and, it appeared, with people too. In the most stressful of situations he had been calm, straightforward, and reliable, all in one. He had ensured the other horses were quickly out of the way, and had rapidly assembled a group of people facing outwards to form a barrier from the onlookers around the winners enclosure until the Red Cross, and eventually the ambulance crew arrived. Duncan had maintained a serious, workmanlike reaction to the accident when others were unable to cope and in the fullness of time Ben had come to reflect that the day could have been much worse had it not been for Duncan's ability to cope with that sort of pressure. He, on the other hand, had wilted almost immediately.

Inside Duncan's warm little cottage, Ben grasped the coffee proffered, and sat at their kitchen table. It turned out that Duncan had done some research but knew precious little about Langlands, the solicitors in Newmarket. There was nothing to go on beyond what could be found by searching the internet.

'I called a few people I could trust to give me a straight answer in Newmarket, but there wasn't a great deal to learn about the firm or the man. The practice is based in the high street and I spoke to one of the smaller trainers who had used them for a bit of work concerning a land dispute, simply because they were the cheapest, but he didn't deal with this chap,' Duncan explained between sips of his tea.

'It looks like they have been around a while, but not a large practice or particularly known for dealing with the racing people in the area.'

Ben sucked air over his teeth and rocked back in his chair, 'I can't see why they haven't approached us direct,' he said with some exasperation, 'It's really underhand the way this has happened, but I still think the other sixty percent is solid.'

Duncan asked 'So who have you got left? Your Scottish girls haven't sold have they?

'No, they are fine, although they didn't like the way they were asked one bit,' replied Ben, shooting a glance at Duncan and raising an eyebrow.

Ben produced his notepad and flicked to the page of the latest entry, 'At the moment there's yourself, Joss, the Scots girls, Rob and Ian and of course myself. We all have ten percent in Ghost. But if anyone else were to crack it would make things very difficult, especially if whoever is really behind this decides they want to move the horse to another trainer or even taken him abroad.'

'This chap can't force anything with fifty percent though, could he?' queried Duncan.

'It would be difficult, but managing The Ghost could get complicated. Owning a controlling percentage is the only sure way you have of directing what happens to a racehorse. If Armitage got fifty percent he could, for example, force a sale or insist on a change of trainer which would really muck up the plans we have for the horse.'

Ben rubbed his forehead between thumb and forefinger. Duncan recognised agitation and tiredness in his friend as he answered.

'I think Rob will be okay, but Ian could be a problem. He doesn't strike me as someone who would turn down the right sort of approach. He works in the city and that usual means money is a big motivator.' suggested Duncan.

'I'm not so sure. Ian was good on the phone last night. I think he's intelligent enough to realise that The Ghost could be special. He's also got enough cash for the offer he got to be of no consequence to him,' Ben pointed out.

'I think your best bet is to get yourself into this Armitage bloke's face pretty quickly and find out what the score is, before you lose another ten percent or more in the horse.'

Ben nodded his agreement and produced his mobile phone from his inside pocket. After checking the Newmarket number again, he dialled. It took several rings and it seemed as if there was plenty of clicking on the line but eventually a man's voice answered and after asking for Mr Andrew Armitage, Ben was momentarily placed on hold.

Duncan picked up the empty mugs and started rinsing them in the background. Condensation was building on the kitchen windows and outside in the yard Ben could see the rain creating rivulets as it cascaded off the red clay tiles on the roof of the garage. It struck him how badly Duncan could have done with the cash from The Ghost, and what strength of character it may have taken to turn it down.

The voice on the phone shook Ben out of his thoughts and he responded, only to discover that Mr Armitage was not in the office, so could he leave a number? Ben did so, and spent another half a minute trying to impress upon the man to whom he was speaking that a speedy reply was a big part of the request.

Pocketing the phone again, Ben stood and went over to where Duncan, shirt sleeves pushed up over his elbows, and head bowed, was at the sink busily clearing what was left of the family's breakfast utensils.

'You could take the cash you know, I wouldn't blame you,' said Ben.

Duncan turned and caught the intense gaze from his friend. He smiled in response and held Bens gaze, 'I'm not selling to anyone,' he said in a slow and deliberate tone. His smile broadened, 'Besides, by the end of the season he's going to be worth ten times what those idiots offered! Joss will work his magic on him and I'll be able to buy this place and get it sorted.'

Ben smiled, and watched Duncan's good looking face crumple into a smile. But there were the worry lines apparent too in his face, and guilt wafted over Ben like a warm breeze. He had really needed his friends over the last year. Duncan and Nancy had been so supportive, and continued to be. But this, this was as if Duncan was placing friendship before the wellbeing of his family.

Ben turned away and looked out into the front yard again, the rain shower continuing to make everything glisten outside when the sun poked through the clouds. He watched as a spider whipped across its web on the outside of the window, mistaking a drop of rain for a potential meal. The insect showed huge dexterity to clamber the few inches to the outskirts of the web before pausing and then retreating up one of the primary cables to crouch under a curled up leaf. Ben was lucky to have people around him like Duncan and Joss, but he had a consuming feeling of guilt over just *how much* he'd needed both of them. They continued to give his day-to-day life that veneer of stability. Ben hoped it wasn't just pity or misguided loyalty from having been at York that day which drew these two families to him. However, he reminded himself that he'd known both men for many years before the accident. Even so, how much could he take from them? Duncan was forfeiting a life-changing amount of money for him. This mess with The Ghost Machine was happening at the wrong time. He would like to curl up in a dark place, but most of all he'd like to forget.

Duncan interrupted Ben's train of thought, clapping his hand on his friend's back and stating he had work to get on with. Ben muttered his agreement and follow Duncan outside. The shower was light now, the spring sunshine evident behind quickly fading rain clouds, and the two men walked over to their vehicles.

'So I can't interest you in a day at Ripon races then?' Ben called over.

'I'm afraid not, I've got about fifteen horses to see to today at three different yards.'

Duncan continued with a question of his own 'So you got a runner today then?'

'No, no runners of my own, but I'll be seeing some of my owners. I'm really there for a day out with Joss and to help him with his runners. He's got a couple going there today and I know the owners fairly well, so I'll help out and do a few meet and greets.'

Duncan nodded his understanding and jumped into his van. 'Just remember to chase that Armitage bloke, I'd like to find out what he's up to. Let me know if you get hold of him. You can tell him from me that sending two big bruisers to my door in the hope of intimidating me and my family won't get him what he wants.'

Ten

By the time Ben reached Ripon racecourse it was just after midday and although the public car parks were only just starting to fill up, the trainers and stable staff areas were a hive of activity.

Having left Mojo to chase and snap at the mayflies around Ben's overgrown acre of back garden at the cottage and use the 'dog flap' as he wished, and Nancy offering to pick up and mind Max after school, Ben effectively had a free afternoon. With both members of his family safely accounted for Ben was looking forward to Ripon races, a track he'd been lucky at in the past and a thoroughly nice place to be on a weekday afternoon. This was their first meeting of their season and apart from his stabling duties for Joss, which he enjoyed anyway, these few hours were his own.

Without a runner of his own he would not be needed to meet and greet Owners. However this was his workplace, so it wouldn't be like attending as a member of the public, there would be plenty of owners, trainers, jockeys and race day staff who would be demanding of his time. Also, a day at the races with Joss usually meant mucking in somehow and sometimes mucking out. He entered through the stable staff area, showing his stable pass, having already bumped into three different sets of racing connections with which he shared a few comments and pleasantries about the start of the season.

The tribe of race-goers which fell into the 'Owners' bracket were generally pleasant, especially at this, one of his local racecourses. But since last summer it seemed everyone, including those only tenuously connected with racing knew about Anna, who he was, and what had happened at York. Of course, the industry was small and had supported him through it all. He'd been stunned by the avalanche of well-wishing cards, emails and text messages. But meeting people still had that element of 'He's the one who...' attached to most encounters at the races. Ben regarding this treatment as inevitable and forgave people sharing their gossip behind the back of their hands, but he still wouldn't bring Max to the races. The nods in his direction and quick looks away when he walked into an owners and trainers bar were too obvious, even a child couldn't miss them.

Despite the first race not being off until after two o'clock, there was a hubbub of noise from the stabling area, which at Ripon was situated well away from the main stands. It meant stable hands were required to lead their horse around the back of the course in order to enter the pre-parade ring.

Horses were being led in and around the stables, some for picks of grass others on their way to their racecourse stables. Brays, whinnies, and the constant gabble of trainers, stable hands and the odd jockey gave the scene a sound all of its own. Ben curled his face into a smile as the sound of hooves on the concrete areas of the stables greeted him. The hollow echo of metal plated feet on ramps of horseboxes was incessant, a standard background noise as runners arrived or departed. It lit Ben's enthusiasm. He had been at racetracks all over the world, and that few hours before a race meeting took place were always his favourite, where the anticipation and expectation was so palpable you could taste and smell it all around you. Ben moved through the stables and allowed the fresh spring day to draw him into the new turf season.

He ran into Joss and his two stable staff at the far end of the stables, seeing to their two charges. The trainer looked up from a water bucket and smiled to himself as Ben walked up.

'Don't be thinking that you've any excuse! For being late you're leading up in the second!' he exclaimed with a mischievous growl.

'I expect my stable staff to here on time and not roll up with a suit on, an hour late and wandering around like they own the place. Oh yes, I forgot, you do own the place...'

'Fine!' Ben cut in with mock anger, 'I'll lead up, and when we win best turned out I'll still split the prize between Ruth and Jo here! Never let it be said I don't pull my weight...'

'Ah Ruth,' interjected Ben. 'You heard the man. We have an owner here who is willing to lead up Iron Balls for you!'

Ben looked a little sheepish all of a sudden and the two young stable lasses started to giggle and looked for a response from Ben. The Iron Duke was a seventeen hand gelding who had a mind of his own and was renowned in the yard for being a difficult sort who would bully his way through the day and find it terribly funny to leave a young rider on the floor by rearing up and spinning at the same time before he set off up the gallop.

Joss winked at Ben, 'You up for it then?'

The two fresh faced stable lasses beamed encouragement and Ben also saw a hint of hope in the eyes of Ruth, an eighteen year old that looked about sixteen.

'Go on then,' muttered Ben, rolling his eyes at Ruth and receiving a smile in return.

Joss disappeared into a stable with his bucket of water and came straight back out into the sunlight, head collar in hand and traded a large wink with his staff.

'A pantomime Dame would have been delighted with that,' remarked Ben, 'Should I be feeling I've been done over, or is there something in your eye there Joss?'

Joss shot his hand out and clicked his fingers in triumph.

'What did I tell you two! You have to know your owners and this one does guilt better than any. Nice pleading look by the way Ruth, you'll go far my girl. Now get yourselves off and get some lunch for yourselves and something for the two of us before he changes his mind!'

With the two young girls despatched to get a sandwich from the stables canteen the two men looked over the stable door at The Iron Duke.

The gelding was a decent sprinter, but often threw his chance away in his races with slow starts or general monkeying around when coming with his run in the closing stages. But as a result of not winning on many occasions, he stayed strangely competitive as his handicap mark never wavered that much. He was running in a competitive little six furlong handicap in the second race on the seven race card.

Joss's other runner was a better sort, and held a decent enough chance in the fifth if he could make a seasonal debut at the same standard as he finished the last season. He was a four year old gelding called Silvery Sun and had managed to get into the feature race off a low weight. But with this being April, and on seasonal debut, his race fitness might find him out. Ben was good friends with the three Owners, who also shared in one of his other syndicate horses trained by Joss. They were retired pals who loved their day out at the races and been lucky to land on Silvery Sun, a cheap buy who had just about paid his way for them over the last two years with a win each season.

Once the two girls were out of earshot, Joss peered around the end of the stables and looked over one or two boxes close to them. When he was sure there wasn't a stable lad or lass who could overhear their conversation he turned to Ben.

'Sorry to bring the mood down, but I wondered if you'd got in touch with our mysterious forty percent owner of The Ghost?' asked Joss in a much lower tone than the one used previously.

Ben tensed his jaw and pushed his bottom lip upwards, 'I've pretty much spent all morning on the phone. You, me, and Duncan are solid, Olivia and Janet Dunn are their normal rock-like selves, and Rob and Ian are okay, but a bit shaken up. Not necessarily by the offers, but the way in which they were approached.'

'And the Mr Forty percent?' Joss persisted.

'No headway. I've called that solicitors office in Newmarket three times and got the distinct feeling that I was being sidelined. Half the time there's no answer. No calls back, and there's been no contact with Weatherby's yet. I'll probably have to go down there and find out what's going on.'

Joss was silent for a moment and Ben waited, sensing there was something else to come. Sure enough, Joss's forehead creased.

'I've had another call this morning. It was Armitage himself this time. He was quite abrupt but basically I've been offered seventy grand for my ten percent and a guarantee that The Ghost would be kept in training with me for at least this season.'

Ben turned his back to the stable door, shielding his eyes from the spring sun. He whistled under his breath and exclaimed, 'Wow, they really want the fifty percent badly…,' his voice trailed off as he processed the new information.

The two men said nothing for half a minute. Then finally Joss said nervously 'In the end, I'm running a business, and that's good money for the horse Ben.'

'So what did you tell Armitage?' replied Ben with a sigh.

'Nothing much, said I would think about it. I've got a mobile number for him.'

Ben paused and looked down the stable yard, deep in thought. Finally he turned back to Joss.

'Giving you the guarantee of training The Ghost is at least encouraging, and in the end, everything has its price. If you want to take the offer, I'd understand. It's a good offer and at least the rest of us would know the horse is staying with you.'

Joss nodded, 'I haven't decided to sell. I'd need to talk to Marion first. You are the first person I've told. But it's a lot of money, and will come in handy for the breeze up sales. If The Ghost fulfils his potential on the track this season he would be worth more, but anything could happen between now and the end of summer.'

Ben gave another resigned sigh, 'At least when he goes and wins he'll do so with your name against him as trainer. It's probably too good an offer for you to refuse – I know that – but it's a weird way for Armitage to be going about things, it just feels, well, underhand somehow with all this cloak and dagger stuff.'

'He sounded like he doesn't know too much about racing either,' said Joss. 'He referred to Ghost as a mare at one stage, and was far more interested in getting my email address so he could send over a copy of a sale contract. I did ask him who he was working for and he clammed up and said it would 'become apparent in the fullness of time'. He sounded like a bit of an idiot to be honest, but I've had plenty of owners who play the big 'I Am'. I'm actually more worried about where it would leave you.'

Ben sniffed. He had to remain philosophical about the sale of The Ghost.

'Oh don't worry, I'd understand if you sell your share. Both of us have to make a living from what we do, I'm not going to get upset about it, that's for sure, but it will be a shame. I think the quicker I can get hold of the elusive Mr Armitage the better, so we can get this whole thing sorted before The Ghost runs his first race this season. That's only a fortnight away now.'

The conversation halted abruptly when the two stable lasses reemerged around the corner of the boxes, carrying several bacon sandwiches wrapped in tin foil. Ben gave Joss's arm a friendly slap and the two of them walked over to intercept them.

****

An hour later Ben was in the owners and trainers bar talking to a few of his owners, there to enjoy the start of the turf season. He shared a coffee and a chat with them regarding their respective horses before excusing himself to renew his acquaintance with the retirees who owned Silvery Sun. Again, he smiled, shook hands, and caught up with a snapshot of what each of them had got up to over the winter, but it was difficult for him to keep his mind from wandering to the situation with The Ghost Machine.

Ben had both bought and sold a large number of horses, and was professional when it came to selling them. He recognised that every horse had a value, and becoming too personally attached to a racehorse was not always too good for your wealth. But The Ghost had become more than just a Guineas hope, as it was the horse which had brought Anna to the races that day, and the horse she had stood stroking before the runner-up had lashed out and killed her. No goodbye, just an abrupt loss. Selling his own share in the horse would be... difficult.

The table of owners continued their convivial conversation about the days' racing ahead of them and the chances of their gelding, but Ben could not maintain his attention, allowing the potential loss of The Ghost to overwhelm his thoughts. He became aware of his heart starting to dip, missing beats and his neck muscles started to sag. Forcing the vision of Anna and the day at York from his mind Ben snapped back, regaining control, and his attention moved to the racecard he held in his hands. He realised he was gripping it fiercely, sweat from his hands smudging the black print.

One of the retirees looked closely at Ben, but relaxed when Ben returned the look with a sheepish smile.

'Sorry, I zoned out there for a moment,' he said uncertainly, 'I can't imagine what they are putting in this coffee.'

This weak attempt at an explanation was grudgingly accepted by the enquirer, but the concern wasn't wiped from his face. Ben took up his cup to sip the rapidly cooling black liquid, breathed deeply and was aware of his heart starting to hit a steadying rhythm.

Ten minutes later, after wishing the Silvery Sun owners the best of luck, he was on his mobile phone speaking with a receptionist for the bereavement counsellor in Leeds, confirming an appointment date for later in the week. Whatever happened with his business, and more specifically The Ghost Machine, Ben knew he had to be around to look after Max. These panic attacks, heart issues, or whatever they were, had to get sorted. He'd always been in good health, and the feeling of not quite being in control was disconcerting.

He wandered around the racecourse as the first race started to draw closer, trying to simply enjoy the atmosphere. He put the situation with The Ghost out of his mind, stopping to watch the young two year old runners for the first race enter the parade ring. The crowd was a good one for this opening meeting of Ripon's season and the decent spring sunshine had probably brought out a few extra hundred people. Ben watched the race, which developed into a good finish between two horses trained locally, to the partisan crowd's delight, and straight afterwards he headed back to the stables along with the beaten horses.

Joss and Ruth were both at The Iron Duke's box but they quickly disappeared once Ben was set up to attend to the gelding. Joss offered Ruth to help with the lead up, but Ben waved them both away. He had done this many times before – as a teenager he had spend three years as an apprentice with a small jumps trainer near his home town, but his increasing weight and the fact that he really wasn't a great rider combined to place him down a different path, although still within racing. But he'd done his fair share of leading up and it was rather nice to be doing it again.

The gelding was already tacked up inside his box and he snorted as Ben unbolted the stable door. He removed his jacket and rolled up his sleeves then ran a hand down the four year olds neck and gave him a friendly pat before checking him over and leading him out of the box. The Iron Duke was fine around the relatively quiet stabling area, but as they walked down the long white railed walkway towards the back of the stands, Ben became increasingly aware that the gelding was starting to get excited. However, a couple of firm tugs on his head collar had the big lad behaving once again.

Ben was one of the first runners into the racecourse proper for the second race. After walking around the pre-parade ring a couple of times, which became increasingly busy as the twelve runners started to stack up, Ben was directed into the much bigger and tree shadowed parade ring. A crowd about three deep in places stood watching the horses circle around. The owners, trainers and connections were milling around the parade ring under the mature trees, whose young green leaves only enhanced the feeling of renewal.

The first round of the parade ring with The Iron Duke was enjoyable enough, with the gelding showing his temperament, insisting on shouldering into Ben at regular intervals. This 'hurry up' was the brute telling Ben he wanted to get on with it, but Ben simply tightened his grip and walked back across the gelding's chest to keep him straight. The two of them strutted jauntily around the ring with Joss, Ruth and connections looking on with smiles and the odd giggle as well.

He hadn't noticed them on the first circuit, but on the second, he saw them.

Two men stood on the top tier of the small three step viewing area at the exit closest to the chute leading to the course itself. You really couldn't miss them, they stood out. Race-goers look up and down at their paper or form guide, they size up the horses, or watch the connections in the middle of the paddock. What they don't do is seize upon a stable lad or lass and concentrate solely on them as they walk around the perimeter of the parade ring.

Ben could only see the two when he was walking towards them, and it didn't help that the gelding was making things difficult. But for a full fifteen seconds he could see them both standing, hands in the pockets of their almost matching leather jackets, staring down at him. He passed them, no more than a few yards away each time he came to the bottom sweep of the ring. They stood slightly apart from the rest of the crowd, both large men in their forties with short, and in one case, shaved hair, and oozing tamed aggression. As his circuits of the paddock mounted up, Ben realised that the men were clearly more than happy for Ben to notice them. Their faces were slabs of unsmiling greyness, and Ben remembered the description Olivia Dunn had provided for her 'visitors' a few days before. These two fitted perfectly.

The racecourse public address system announced that jockeys were to mount and Ben passed the two again, their eyes not flinching contact from his. He felt like screaming 'What?' at them to force a response but suppressed the urge.

Raul was riding The Iron Duke and peeled away from the connections. Ben gave the jockey a leg up on the far side of the parade ring and came round to the chute. The men had disappeared. With relief, Ben headed down the chute to the course entrance before allowing the gelding to be released from his lead rope.

The rest of the pre-race activity went to plan, although the slightly excitable gelding did try to whip round a couple of times before setting off down the course. By the time his young jockey was at the six furlong start Ben was standing with Joss in the stands. He said nothing to the trainer about the two men at the parade ring as Joss was concentrating on the starting stalls, so Ben scanned the crowd from his position halfway up the Owners gallery in the stands, but saw no sign of the two leather-clad bouncer types. He was sure they had to be the same two who had turned up at Olivia's and also Duncan's home, the coincidence and their mode of operating was simply too similar. But why would they be so overt?

Before Ben could consider this question further the commentator announced 'They're off,' and the race was underway.

Raul got the gelding out of the stalls sharply enough and into a decent enough position on the heels of the two disputing the lead. Over two out he edged the gelding out and travelled up nicely on the outside as one of the prominent horses started to weaken. When the field hit the furlong pole Raul asked The Iron Duke to quicken and he found enough to nose ahead, but holding his head high, he allowed the horse on his inside to fight back. In the last hundred yards he was passed on his outside by another competitor and in a bobbing finish the Iron Duke's number was called by the public address as one of the horses contesting a photo for second. With a job still to do, Ben headed straight down trackside in order to collect and lead the gelding into the winners enclosure.

With the run over, and having a decent blow, 'Iron Balls' was a much easier horse to handle after the race, happy to be led into the winners enclosure and take up his position in the third placing spot following the result of the photo. Raul jumped off and the owner, a diminutive middle aged chap with laughter lines traversing his face, along with his equally beaming wife bobbing around behind him, came over and happily gave the gelding a pat on its neck. With Ben eying the gelding warily, The Iron Duke thankfully decided not to take a chunk out of either of them and Joss skillfully steered the two of them and Raul up the weighing room steps and out of harms way in order to discuss the run.

Ben proffered the gelding a bucket of water which he noisily gurgled through for a few seconds before throwing his head up and showering a few bystanders with drops of icy cold water. The horse seemed to be making sure that he could see into the four deep crowd which had formed around the small semicircular winners paddock and also scare the life out of them as well. If the two mystery men were there, Ben thought, he was not going to see them as he had his hands full with the gelding. He settled on walking the gelding around in circles in order to keep him occupied and more or less under control in the confined space.

In truth Ben was quite relieved when after only a few minutes the 'Horses Away' announcement came through the public address. He nodded a goodbye to the connections and was the first of the three handlers out of the winners enclosure. He headed off to the racecourse stables with The Iron Duke who was far happier now he was on his way. Away from the crowd, the gelding calmed down again and walked without bumping into his handler this time. They made it back onto the racecourse and over to the manned walkway gate which opened as the first three finishers in the race approached in single file.

As Ben walked through the gate he saw the two leather jacketed men leaning on the white plastic rails which created the horse walkway outside the racecourse. The other side of the walkway was a grass verge, and then a line of parked cars which denoted the start of the public car park. They stared fixedly at him as he led The Iron Duke onto the walkway and fell in about three yards behind Ben and the horse, albeit the other side of the rails.

Ben glanced over his shoulder and after checking they were keeping pace with him, he took a few moments to decide how to play things. There was no outward aggression from the two of them, although

Ben would argue there was plenty of intimidation. Given he had over half of a ton of bristling horse in his hand, he was going to find it difficult to turn around and face them and inexplicably they seemed happy enough to say nothing and simply follow him. In a hundred yards time the walkway finished and twenty feet later he would enter the gate to the stabling area and they wouldn't be able to follow the horse in there without a stable pass. Part of him actually wanted to face them down and discover exactly who they were and what they wanted, while on the other hand his thumping heart told him he was just as well to keep walking. The two horses behind had a young lass and a senior lad walking them, but there wouldn't be much aid coming from them if things went badly.

Ben overheard a murmur from one of the two men, but resisted the temptation to shoot a look in their direction. However, with the end of the walkway approaching in thirty yards time he slowed his pace a little, effectively stacking up the two horses behind him. Then he set off at a quicker pace.

'Ramsden. Benjamin Ramsden?' the nearest man asked in a growling voice.

Ben feigned deafness and continued to walk at the same, quick pace and said nothing. He stole a glance across at the two men who were now quickening their walk in an attempt to come alongside and match his speed on the other side of the rails. Ben noticed the smaller man on the outside was being forced to skip a little to keep up, getting caught out by the undulations on the verge, much to his annoyance and Ben's delight.

'Hey, you. You are Ramsden aren't you?' said the man, raising his voice to almost a snarl. The sound of the crowd and the public address system presenting the prizes for the last race coming over the racecourse walls cut across the man's protestations.

Ben waited another few steps and then provided the age old response to an unwanted confirmation request of your identity.

'Who wants to know?' he shouted back, eyes set straight ahead.

This sounded clichéd to Ben as soon as it left his lips, but he wanted to keep the two of them upsides him a few more seconds.

The man shouted louder this time with annoyance flaring in his tone 'Are you Ben Ramsden?' he demanded.

Ben looked across to the two men, now trotting alongside him. They were close enough for him to see where the man's eyelids were saggy and ringed with dark shadows. The man with the gruff voice was close up to the fence now and looking towards the gate to the stables only twenty yards away, then back to Ben, aware he might lose his quarry.

Ben put on a final short spurt of speed, which the two men immediately matched. The Iron Duke was trotting now and then as the white rails finished, Ben leaned into the geldings chest as he reached the end of the walkway and whipped the gelding around, sharp left so that

'Iron Balls' spun around the end of the railing. The two men, who were at jogging pace, suddenly saw a wall of muscular bay horse bearing down on them. Momentum took them both straight into the side of The Iron Duke. A satisfying yelp came from the silent man on the outside as he ended up almost underneath the gelding, whilst the talkative one was sent sprawling on top of his partner voicing a number of expletives.

Ben let out a few feet of The Iron Duke's lead rope and the four year old half reared and then backed off, snorting his discontent but otherwise without a blemish on him. Both men cowered on the floor and tried to kick away from the hunk of horseflesh which must have seemed to have been of monstrous proportions to them, given he was such a tall, muscular gelding. This left one man on his backside on the grass, and the other trying to spin away from the tangle of arms and legs. The other horses on the walkway had halted a few yards away and the two handlers were watching open mouthed.

With his heart continuing to pound in his chest, Ben gripped The Iron Duke's lead rope tightly and said a few calming words to him. Then he spun round to face the prone men.

Clearing his throat theatrically, Ben stared down at the two men who were still trying to get to their feet and said in a purposefully clipped tone 'You really must watch where you are going on a racecourse as accidents can, ahem… happen.' Then with a little less sarcasm he added 'Who are you and who sent you?'

Among a tirade of expletives the first man up was the talker. He brushed himself down, but only succeeded in smearing the worm cast mud and grass stains further into his jacket and trousers. He finally straightened, standing taller than Ben, breathing heavily and clearly not in a mood for further levity. Ben said nothing, instead he raised a questioning eyebrow to the man and continued patted The Iron Duke's neck. The gelding snorted, as if to order, and the standing man took half a step back.

He reached into his jacket and Ben tensed. However, all he produced was a thin wad of folded papers. He took a step closer and threw the papers to Ben's feet, accompanying them with more swearing to help them on their way.

'Who we are is none of your business,' the man hissed, adding a few more grumbled complaints under his breath while continuing to brush himself down with his grass stained hands.

The other helped his comrade up, and the two men then turned to glare one more time at Ben, whilst switching eye contact nervously between him and 'Iron Balls'. For his part, The Iron Duke did an excellent job of simply looming over the two of them and flared his nostrils. The two men turned to walk away, still watching Ben and the gelding for a few steps, before turning and shambling off towards the other end of the car park.

Ben watched them go, his chest still thumping. He wanted to shout after them, wanted more answers, but that chance was gone. In fact, he wanted to intimidate the men further, wanted to… He questioned just what he wanted to do. This whole incident could not have taken more than a minute, but yet he felt positively alive, tingling with a kind of buzzing. He looked after the men, who were disappearing into the sea of cars in the public car park and he took a few bigger breaths. It was obvious that a rematch wasn't going to happen today, not while he had half a ton of horse in his hand.

He scooped the papers up from the grass and managed to grab a few more deep breaths as he corrected the orientation of the sheets. He quickly folded them up as the other two stable hands brought their charges closer, making anxious enquiries about Ben's wellbeing. After thanking and assuring them that he and The Iron Duke were both quite alright, he waved the offers of help away and bid them to carry on to the course stables. Once they had led their charges away, he unfolded the four sheets. The first page was entitled 'One of Ten'.

****

'It's a contract of sale for my ten percent,' Ben told Joss as the two of them stood together in the stands ahead of the feature race of the day. 'I think I've been offered the same deal as you.'

Joss had been busy preparing and then looking after the owners of Silvery Sun, who were grouped behind the trainer further up the stands. Ben hadn't had time to go through things in detail and could see that Joss was engrossed with the stalls loading process which was showing on the huge television screen in the centre of the racecourse.

'Oh right,' Joss replied distractedly. He was never too responsive before a race so Ben took no notice of this apparently lack of interest from his friend, and settled in to watch the race.

Ben had sat and read the contract in the stable tearoom once he had sorted The Iron Duke out with a wash down and plenty of water in his box manger. Without having seen Joss's version, it did appear his offer was identical to Joss's and indeed, the contract was very similar to the one Duncan had showed him.

Ben reflected that the offer of seventy five thousand pounds for his ten percent was realistic, but he had no intention of taking profit on The Ghost just yet. The colt had his three year old season almost upon him, and within two races the youngster could be worth plenty more, if things went his way. He could also be worth much less, but that was a chance Ben was more than willing to take.

He tried to put the contract out of his mind and instead concentrated on the video screen in the middle of the track, remembering that this was the feature race of the day and his trainer had a horse in the race with a real chance.

'Only one to go in,' Ben said, nodding toward the massive TV screen.

Silvery Sun broke well enough from his mid-stall's draw and with Raul once again in the saddle, he settled the gelding into mid-division. In a tightly packed field, the mud was spraying up behind the runners, but all seemed to be going well up to about two furlongs out. As a few jockeys started to row along, Raul switched the three year old to the inside rail and made progress to sit in around sixth, and riding his luck, a space opened up in front of him and he surged through just under a furlong out to level up with the two leading the race.

The line of three thoroughbreds pulled about a length and a half clear of the rest of the runners, settling down to fight out the honours between them. In the last fifty yards Silvery Sun, with the rail to guide him, stuck his grey head down really pleasingly. Much to his Owners whooping delight, Silvery Sun came home the winner by a longish looking head at the post.

The retirees, Joss and Ben all immediately bustled out of the stands, and pushed as politely as possible through the crowd towards the back of the course where the winners enclosure awaited. The gelding came in to a decent reception, winning the race as third favourite and a popular local winner, as Joss only trained about thirty miles away from the course. Beating a Newmarket based trainer into second place was always greeted with enthusiasm from the very partisan Yorkshire crowd.

Ben congratulated the owners, who were clearly ecstatic about the win. Silvery Sun had won a maiden the previous year, but struggled with a handicap mark a little too high through to the end of the previous season. He had then run on some unwelcome fast ground in September and as a result finally dropped back down to a decent mark for the new season. Joss had convinced the owners to let him have the winter off, and come back fit and ready for the spring, and the plan had paid off with a win in this Class Three race worth fifteen thousand pounds to the winning connections.

Leaving the owners and Joss to their champagne and a re-run of the race in the winning connections room, Ben set off with the horse and Ruth prior to the trophy presentation in order to help with the gelding in the dope box. The stewards can ask for a test whenever they wish, and had decided today was the day for Silvery Sun. So, they headed to the 'dope box', a special stable which would collect a urine sample after a run. Ben had thought he'd keep Ruth company as Joss was a master at entertaining winning owners. Besides, he was quite happy being in an area that needed permits to enter, just in case the two beefy delivery boys decided to return for a second time today. Ben thought it was unlikely though, as the two of them had seemed surprisingly cowed by being decked by his gelding. He reflected that despite their tough and thinly veiled aggressive demeanour, the two of them had quickly crumpled and while they were undoubtedly unpleasant, their air of intimidation had evaporated too.

Ben walked over to the stabling area alongside Ruth and the two of them chatted, reliving the race again as they went through the after-race process with Silvery Sun. Half an hour later, Joss appeared wearing a broad smile on his face and carrying his trainer's prize for the win, an unopened bottle of champagne. That would be greeted with some enthusiasm back at the yard this evening, thought Ben.

****

After agreeing to speak again in the morning about the offers from Armitage, Joss and Ben made their own way home before the rest of the Ripon card was finished, Ben to pick up Max from Duncan's and Joss with his two human helpers and two equine athletes safely loaded into the back of his dual horsebox.

Once Ben jumped in his car he realised he had a few missed calls and two messages, and, after he had travelled the few miles down the B roads from the racecourse, he pointed the car up the motorway and started listening to his messages with his hands free set. The first was from the office of the Bereavement Counsellor confirming his visit later in the week, and then a high pitched man's voice came through.

'Mr Ramsden, this is Mr Armitage,' said an affected nasal voice with a certain amount of vibrato in there too, which gave the sentence a singsong quality.

'I believe you have been trying to contact me,' he lamented, 'But I expect you have the documentation by now.' There was a pause and the hint of a sniff. He went on 'I understand it to be a *very* favourable offer and look forward to you returning the signed document so that the transaction may be completed.'

He rolled the 'r' in the word very and finished the sentence on a higher note, as if asking a question. Ben immediately wondered whether he was from somewhere like Australia or New Zealand, but it was the word 'transaction' which left him with gritted teeth. The solicitor's words dripped with a snarky cockiness that reminded Ben of a bully he'd run into at secondary school. Armitage seemed to view his relentless pursuit of Ben's clients as a mere trifle and The Ghost Machine's ownership as a simple matter of how much money it would take to purchase him.

The message stopped abruptly there and ten minutes later Ben realised he was breaking the speed limit and gripping the wheel of his Volkswagen with both fists and with rapidly reddening knuckles.

His mind was still spinning with his dislike for the whole situation by the time he reached home with Max, having picked him up from

Duncan's. The seven year old sat quietly hugging his school bag in the passenger seat as they drew up to the house. Mojo appeared at the front room window from between the curtains in a frenetic hysteria as the two of them decamped from the car and entered the house, the little dog running rings around the two of them as they moved around the hall and then into the kitchen, dropping bags and kicking off shoes as they went. Ben walked over to the kitchen sink with the dog's water bowl in his hand and was quickly joined by Mojo running around his feet, the dog anticipating a meal and quite beside himself with glee.

Max spoke, but Ben didn't hear, still deep in thought. He turned the tap on and only realised when the water was cascading over the edge of the bowl that his son was trying to speak with him again.

'Is everything okay Dad?' asked the young boy, moving over to lean against his father's legs.

Shaken from his introspection, Ben looked down and cupped the boys face in both hands and bent down to his son's eye level.

'Yes of course. It's just work at the moment. It's...' Ben searched for the right words. He finally settled upon, 'It's just a bit busy at the moment, that's all.'

'You're not talking too much to me,' the boy said with a concerned look on his small face. 'We all used to sing in the car and make jokes and play games.'

Max paused and gave a weak smile.

Ben returned the smile with a grin, moving his hands to the boy's hips and starting to tickle him.

'Oh, so we don't have fun anymore eh?' said Ben in pretend anger, eliciting a giggle from Max as he wriggled to get away from his father's hands.

The next ten minutes were spent with Ben pursuing his son through the house and finally into the garden, attempting to catch him. Each time he was caught, the boy would be tickled mercilessly whilst Mojo bounced around between the two of them. Finally Ben tackled the boy to the ground in the back garden and they rolled around in what turned out to be fairly muddy rain soaked grass until they were both breathless, chests heaving from the physical exertion, but mostly as a result of the laughing. The little dog had been barking excitedly and jumped over the two of them as they rolled around, and he continued to do so for a few more seconds.

The two of them lay on their backs staring at the early evening sky, getting their breath back. Eventually Max started to shiver, and the two of them pulled each other up and headed inside the house for a hot shower and dinner. Ben forgot about work for the rest of the evening, waiting for Max to go to bed before returning to the issues concerning The Ghost and Armitage.

He tried to consider the contract but found he couldn't concentrate on it, putting it to one side and instead caught up on some alternative syndicate work. He was about to switch his computer off and make his way upstairs to check on Max, when his mobile phone started to ring. Joss's name appeared on the answer screen.

Ben took a deep breath. It was hardly ever good news when any trainer called in the late evening or early morning. Joss was no different in that respect. After a long days work, the evening was the only opportunity for a trainer to kick back and relax, so to be calling owners at this time usually meant it was important, and usually regarding a problem with a horse. Ben answered hoping it was just a further conversation about the offer for The Ghost.

'Enjoying that champagne I hope,' he remarked as a greeting, hoping his upbeat tone would be reciprocated.

'No, not really,' came the reply from Joss in a flat voice.
Ben bit the inside of his lip and said 'Is it one of the horses?'

'Joss paused and then replied 'Oh, no, no. It's not one of yours, but I thought you should know that I've had some bad news tonight. In fact, I wanted to see what you thought about it. Well, Marion thought I needed to let you know.'

Ben picked up a note of anger in Joss's voice, which was rare for the man. He considered a reply, but in the end said nothing and Joss continued, 'I got a call from the Clerk of the course at Ripon about half an hour ago. He knows me pretty well, as he's moved around the Yorkshire courses quite a bit, and he was just giving me a bit of warning.'

Joss sighed and in a broken voice added, 'The dope test for Silvery Sun has come back positive.'

Eleven

Ben was numb for over an hour after Joss had hung up the call. A positive test for any racehorse was a rare occurrence, and with the stringency of the racecourse testing, no trainer took any chances with anything they put into a racehorse's system, least of all Joss, who maintained a strict regime at the yard. He had a complete ban on the stable hands bringing any substance or food into the yard which could affect a horse's performance, no matter how small.

The positive test of Silvery Sun would mean the horse losing the race and its prizemoney. There would be an investigation by the authorities with fines at best and the loss of Joss's training license at worst, but just as importantly the reputation of the yard would be tarnished for a long time. Owners would potentially remove horses, staff could be lost, and it would all be industry news within a few days.

Ben reflected that mud sticks, and especially mud which suggests the racehorses you're in charge of are competing with an unfair advantage. The racing press would rally around some trainers, and put the boot in for others. Ben was pretty sure that Joss would get their support on this one, as it had to be a mistake of some sort, but social media would soon be full of the bile those websites thrive on. Even if the yard was exonerated in the end it would take many months for that to happen, as the gears at the racing authority turned slowly and the stigma of being a 'bent trainer' would manifest itself much quicker and wider than the truth.

A very upset Joss and an incandescent Marion (who had been raging in the background about how honest the yard was throughout their telephone conversation) were currently ringing around all their owners to ensure they heard it from the stables, rather than the press or the racing grapevine. However Joss had scant information; it would be a day or two before the authorities would determine the exact cause of the failed test and then officially charge him and inform the press.

Later in the evening Ben settled into his favourite armchair in front of the television, aiming to watch the late news. He found he couldn't concentrate on any of it, or the comedy show which followed, as his mind was still alive with the situation with Joss. He stayed away from any alcohol; his thoughts were too full of the day at the races, the Armitage phone call, the situation with the other owners of The Ghost, and now the ramifications of Joss's yard having the shadow of a doping scandal hanging over it. Syndicating racehorse was not a straightforward business at the best of times, but Ben had never had to deal with such a complex set of issues all at the same time. To cap things off, the news on the positive test was already starting to make its way around the great and good of the racing world. Ben's mobile chirped every few minutes with text messages and app alerts from friends, business partners, shareholders in Joss's horses and even one from a race commentator.

Given the late hour, Ben sent a text message to all his owners with shares in the five horses he had with Joss and most responded with disbelief and plenty of support. Ben had asked for them not to contact Joss just for now, but he was sure the trainer would be deluged with people wishing to show support or simply wanting more information. There were also bound to be a few owners who wanted to remove their horses from the yard.

It wasn't until well into the night when Ben got up from the armchair to check on Max, that he noticed the Armitage agreement was still on the kitchen units where he'd thrown it before playing with his son. The three pages of paper seemed far less important all of a sudden. He was halfway up the cottage stairs when a thought struck him. He bounded up the last half dozen steps and poked his head around Max's bedroom door to find him fast asleep and with half his duvet dripping off the bed. Ben quickly pulled it back over the sleeping boy and went back downstairs, grabbing the papers. He flicked on his table light on his desk and it cast a long shadow over the room as he sat down to read through the agreement. He knew what he was looking for and speed-read the first page, seeking and quickly locating the clause named 'Termination'.

He read through the three paragraphs twice before he leant back in his chair and pushed it away from the desk.

'The little sods,' Ben said under his breath, aware of the youngster sleeping above him. He considered his next action, stared into the distance, then picked up his mobile phone and called Joss. It was only after it had rung out three times that he considered the time – it was 11-30pm – Joss would most likely be in bed on a normal weekday, but then this wasn't by any stretch of the imagination a normal day.

An unexpectedly gruff, tired voice answered the phone after only two rings with a simple, 'O'Hoole'.

'Joss, its Ben. Have you signed and sent those sale documents for The Ghost Machine yet?'

'To be honest Ben, I've had bigger things on my mind this evening.'

'I know, but have you? You know, signed that contract of sale or done anything with it?'

There was a pause and then Joss responded, 'No Ben. It's not even crossed my mind.' A mixture of anxiety, stress, and a tinge of irritation all mixed into the tone of his reply.

'Good, well don't,' Ben instructed, 'I know it might sound unlikely, but I think that positive dope test could be linked to that contract.'

There was no reply from Joss, so Ben went on, 'Listen. You know the positive test is either a mistake, or a cock-up in the stables. You'd never knowingly send a horse to the races with a banned substance inside them. But there is another possibility, and it's buried in the small print in that contract you were handed today.'

Again there was no reply from the trainer. Ben waited, and after another few seconds Joss finally cleared his throat and answered.

'I've been running around the yard trying to find out what could have produced a positive dope test, and you're telling me someone's done this *on purpose*? I can't believe any of my staff would knowingly do such a thing, even the ones I've had to let go.'

He sounded confused and exasperated. Ben could hear Marion saying something in the background.

'Look, it's late and you've had a hell of a day. Just promise me you won't sign that document, at least for now?'

'Ok Ben,' Joss responded in a tired, resigned voice, 'But tell me why this is so important will you?'

'Sure. I know this will sound crazy, but I've been looking through the contract that Armitage had delivered to me at Ripon today. There is a clause buried in the small print that basically says that should you, as trainer of The Ghost, be found to be using any illegal methods or substances, a change of trainer can be forced if fifty percent or more of the owners agree by vote.'

Again Ben allowed a short pause for this information to settle on Joss.

He continued, 'It means that if Armitage can get another ten percent from somewhere he can take The Ghost elsewhere. This positive test means that if you sell your ten percent to Armitage's client the colt could leave the yard the next day, even though the contract appears to guarantee The Ghost stays with you if you sell. He has the right to enforce a change of trainer because of this positive dope test, so if you sign, you lose the horse.'

'Oh, for heaven's sake,' exclaimed Joss, anger taking over from frustration.

There were mutterings in the background and Ben guessed that this news was being relayed to Marion.

Joss came back clearly again, 'So you're telling me that Armitage has managed to dope one or more of my horses just so he can get his hands on The Ghost?'

'It looks like that, but we'll have to see exactly what the positive test was for before we can reach any hard and fast conclusions.'

'Well I can tell you that,' replied Joss quickly. 'I've had the industry doping squad in the yard this evening already; taking blood samples and making a nuisance of themselves. Can you believe my own vet found enough anabolic steroid in Silvery Sun for him to be so far off the scale that they retested the samples three times to make sure their equipment was working right! It's just bloody ridiculous. Even if you were

74

going to use steroids, the amount in his blood was way over a dose to enhance his performance, besides, it was long acting, not short acting.'

Ben asked for an explanation, not understanding this new detail.

'There are two different type of equine steroid, short and long acting. You'd tend to give racehorses short acting, otherwise it would never come out of their systems in time for them to race, as you need about one hundred and twenty days for it to work through their bodies. Long acting can take twice as long to come out of their systems,' explained Joss.

'Basically, Silvery Sun was given so much long acting steroid he won't be able to race for around six months. If I could get my hands on who did this to him I'd wring their necks,' he added angrily, losing his temper again for a few seconds.

'Have the investigators or your vets any ideas where and when it might have been done?' asked Ben.

'They can't be certain, but we think fairly recently. The Racing Authority lot has looked all over him and they found an unexplained syringe puncture in his neck. It was under his mane and unless you were looking for it there's no way you could have picked it up.'

Ben considered this and said, 'I suppose if that's how it was administered, it could have been done at any point up to the start of the race.'

'Yeah, for what it's worth, the Racing Authority vets said they thought it had all the hallmarks of tampering, but that won't pacify plenty of my owners, or the press. I've already had a few calls from nervous owners looking to move if it gets widely reported. The Silvery Sun lot are good owners and pretty understanding, but a season on the sidelines isn't going to go down well, especially after a win which will certainly be taken away from them.

Joss added, 'And we don't know yet if any of the other horses have been hit with the same thing. So far we're clear, but we're only halfway around the rest of the yard. Before you ask, I had The Ghost tested first and he came back negative.'

Joss was sounding a little more positive, but still very downcast.

'Well that's a relief anyway, albeit a small one,' Ben said, trying to be supportive and displaying his own relief at the same time. But a moment later he realised this was exactly what he should have expected. If you are going to frame a trainer for doping in order to release a horse into your custody, you don't go doping your own horse – you do it to others in the yard. That was a really dirty trick and took what Armitage and his cronies were doing to another level.

'If it's okay with you, I want to get the remaining shareholders in The Ghost together before we do anything else. I have things to do tomorrow, so is Friday late afternoon okay with you – I don't think you have a runner?'

There was another short pause to the sound of paperwork shuffling as Joss checked a diary.

'That's fine Ben. The owners are welcome to come over here to the yard and they can view the horse at the same time. He's looking great and we'll be working him tomorrow morning in his last piece of proper hard work before his seasonal debut, as he's already got his entry for the Greenham meeting, so let's get them together and we'll thrash out what's to be done.'

Ben finished the call by thanking his friend and reassuring him again. He almost put the phone down, but the mare Bertha came into his head for some reason.

'Joss, how many people know about Bertha?'

'All the lads know we have a pregnant mare in the bottom barn, but only Marion and I, and I suppose Jake are aware of her pedigree. There was no need to bring any attention to her.'

'Good,' said Ben, relieved. 'Do me a favour, can we keep this between us for now – maybe have a quiet word with Jake as well?' Joss came straight back without hesitation, 'Sure thing Ben. You have my word.'

Ben rang off a few seconds later and then called around the other four remaining members of the syndicate; Duncan, Rob Bawtry, Ian Furlong and Olivia Dunn. It was getting on for midnight now, so he left messages for a couple, but managed to get hold of Duncan and Rob.

It was well past midnight when he replaced the phone on its cradle, switched his office light off and dragged his tired mind upstairs to bed. He was half-way up the stairs, attempting to pick his way up them to stop the floorboards squeaking and waking Max, when a new thought struck him; when there was a serious crime the police always looked to the close family or relatives first. Ben contemplated each of the remaining people left in The Ghost syndicate for a few moments. After only a few seconds he was forced to pinch the bridge of his nose as a throbbing had started in his temple. It had been a long day. He discarded the notion that any of these people could be involved and slowly climbed the last few stairs to bed.

Twelve

Ben was experiencing a strangely euphoric light-headedness following his appointment with his bereavement counsellor in Leeds. His day had started well enough with the usual school run drop-off for Max at Duncan's, visiting another of his trainers in Malton to see some morning workouts, and then responding to some of his messages from the night before as he drove into the city after lunch. There was even some better news from Joss, who had been told by the Racing Authority that they would be able to give him an interim indication of the reason for the failed drugs test later in the day. It appeared they were just as keen as the yard to get to the bottom of the issue. It was in their interests too, Ben thought, as he followed the traffic through one pretty village after another. The Racing Authority didn't want cheaters in their sport, but they also didn't want a fairly high profile trainer to start getting the wrong sort of coverage in the press if it could be avoided.

After parking at the back of a long terrace of substantial Victorian town houses, Ben had found his counsellor's name last on the list of six bell buttons available on the outside of the building. Without any speaking a buzzer released the steel and glass reinforced door. She had been standing waiting for him on the top landing as he ascended the three storeys and six flights of stairs.

'Mr Ramsden?' questioned a motherly middle-aged lady who couldn't have been more than five feet tall, including the bun of whisked brown hair perched on the top of her head. She resembled an English teacher Ben had once been taught by in Middle School, and wore a thin v-necked camel coloured jumper, which had both sleeves pushed up to reveal two freckled forearms.

'Um, yes, that's me,' said Ben uncertainly, extending a hand to her.

As they shook, the dim light on the landing shaded the lady's face somewhat but Ben had picked out a pleasant smile enhanced by an array of straight teeth. A small pair of perfectly round horn-rimmed glasses sat three-quarters of the way down the lady's thin, straight nose.

'Yes, you'll probably have guessed already, but just to be certain, I'm Esme Trent. I'm pleased to meet you Ben, please come in,' she said, gesturing to the open door at the end of the landing.

The room Ben entered was in stark contrast to the rather glum, poorly lit public areas of the old building. This was a bright space which looked recently painted in a chalky purple, with three large sash windows that reached up to a tall ceiling and benefited from an ornate white rose in its centre. There was a work desk with a laptop in one corner, and an understated open fire with coal bucket and irons close by. The rest of the room was dominated by expensive looking weathered leather lounge furniture, which all faced towards the windows and the view of the city rooftops beyond.

Ben indicated a two-seater sofa and received a nod from the counsellor in return.

The next hour seemed to take no time at all to Ben and he emerged into the weak spring sunshine only a few steps from elation. He knew he had changed as a result of the accident, and not for the better. Over the eight months since York, he had encountered a host of difficult emotions and it had affected his life in a shattering way, both mentally and physically. But the overarching feeling which filled him with self-loathing and dread was simple – he was angry. Not just a raised voice or the pounding of a fist into an open hand; there were times when Ben believed he could rip rooms apart, smash everything and, more worryingly, everyone in his path.

Ms Trent, or Esme, as she had asked to be addressed by Ben, had explained that particularly in men, it was common for a violent reaction, or at least a suppression of anger leading to very high levels of stress when being reminded or contemplating the circumstances of a death.

After Ben had explained how he felt an anger growing within him over the last few months, she had asked, 'So have you become angry and become physically violent?'

'Absolutely not,' he had replied immediately, but then pictured the scene at Ripon two days before and wondered whether that was altogether true. He hadn't thrown any punches as such, but he had manufactured a situation which had seen two grown men being taken off their feet and intimidated by half a ton of racehorse. He had also experienced a release of sorts afterwards.

'Well, perhaps I have had a tendency to be more aggressive in certain circumstances,' he modified. As soon as the words left his mouth he reflected this last statement had perhaps been delivered a little too quickly for it to sound altogether true.

Esme had also written a note, but then continued, 'And do you think you are able to manage these aggressive tendencies at the moment?'

Ben paused, considering his answer. He did feel he could trust this woman, which was odd, as he tended to need all sorts of verification before truly trusting anyone. But his natural protectiveness won over and he finally shrugged and replied, 'I think I've coped.' They then fell into what Ben felt was an uneasy silence.

Esme had waited a good ten seconds, as if Ben was about to continue, but finally made a short note on her pad on her lap, looked down her spectacles at Ben and said 'You have the classic symptoms of a traumatised bereavement. The difficulty sleeping, sudden violent thoughts or tendencies and a wish to suppress them are quite normal Ben. The fact that you were there at the time your wife had her accident could also be causing you to reevaluate your conduct that day, and feelings of guilt and anger will be mixed in there too.'

Ben realised that this was the longest statement the counsellor had made during the entire session. However, it was also a great relief to hear that he was behaving like any other person who had seen their spouse die in an instant in front of them... He ran that thought through his head again and marveled on how utterly alien this whole situation was to him.

For the rest of the hour-long session Esme discussed some basic coping strategies and asked Ben about his son, friends and work. She had closed the session with a final question, asking Ben whether he had come to see her today of his own volition.

'No,' he admitted, 'I have a good friend called Duncan, and it was his wife Nancy who made the appointment. Well, I have to be honest, this was about the third time she's made this appointment, I just...'

'Weren't ready, by any chance?' interjected Esme with a smile and roll of her eyes.

Ben allowed himself a rueful smile of his own and nodded his head.

'Hmm. I guess I just needed things to get to the stage where I accepted I needed a bit of help.'

Esme looked to her watch, but didn't move from her perch on the edge of her seat, 'You know Ben, I can tell you have had some of your fears or perhaps misconceptions allayed today. But it will take time. You can see me as you wish, but don't expect the anger and the stress to disappear overnight. You'll need to work on it every day for some time to come. Use the suggestions I've made and still take things one day at a time.'

Later, as Ben had set off down the stairs after thanking the counselor, she had called after him, saying, 'And please pass on my thanks to Nancy on my behalf, for the recommendation. She does sound like a very good friend indeed!'

Ben sat in his car for ten minutes after the session without switching the engine on, simply enjoying a level of contentment he hadn't felt since the day Anna had died. He had been hoping this session would not work out, but as Duncan and Nancy had suggested, talking to someone outside his circle of friends and work had proved to be liberating. He allowed the warm feeling to wash over him a little longer before being interrupted by the chirp of his mobile phone.

The caller ID revealed that it was Graham P. Loote and Ben scowled. He realised that the declarations for Saturday's races would have just been announced, and Graham P (he insisted on the middle initial) would be no doubt be complaining about some element of the arrangements for the race, be it jockey, headgear, owners badges or even the time of the race being utterly inconvenient for him. Ben pushed the call to voicemail and tried to recapture the settled feeling from moments before, but after a few seconds the phone rang again and Graham P. Loote's name blinked at him again from the face of his mobile. He ignored the chirrup of the call tone, turned the ignition key and headed for Max's school.

****

An hour and a half later Max, Duncan's two girls and Josh jumped into his Golf outside school for the twenty minutes journey back to Duncan's cottage. Ben pulled into Duncan's dirt and gravel drive to see a Range Rover blocking his path into the cottage. This wasn't unusual, as Duncan was visited by riding or country types on a regular basis, asking for his help with shoeing or booking him for a visit to their hack or pet pony. Nancy could be selling a painting or some of her leatherwork she completed in her spare time, repairing anything from reins and head collars through to complete saddles.

Ben reversed his car back onto the road and parked it on the verge. He jumped out to start sorting the kids with their school bags when he heard Duncan's raised voice. Bobbing his head back into the car he asked the four children to stay where they were for a moment, and walked back into the driveway.

Duncan was standing legs apart, arms crossed and had the stance of an irritated man. A very large chap with a shaved head was standing, stock still in front of the blacksmith. Ben thought it best to announce his arrival, as it didn't appear the conversation was that friendly.

'Hi Duncan, everything okay?'

Duncan acknowledged Ben with a nod but didn't take his eyes off the man in front of him.

As Ben got within a few yards, the man turned and gazed down at Ben. He must have been well over six foot five, as he towered over Duncan as well.

Duncan indicated the man with a pointed finger saying, 'Meet Demetri. He's here to buy my share in The Ghost. He thought he'd try and let himself into the house, which I took as a sign that I shouldn't sell. What do you think?'

The man had a wide smile which he flashed in Duncan's direction, but quickly returned to Ben.

'Ah, this must be Mr Ramsden,' he said in a deliberate, heavy Eastern European accent, extending the vowels in Ben's surname.

He continued, 'As I was trying to explain to Mr Jones, I am here to provide you with a good offer for your shares in your wonderful racehorse – you are Mr Ben Ramsden?'

'And you are?'

'Forgive me,' he returned in a measured tone, 'I am Demetri Krzysztof. I represent the party who owns forty percent of the animal, and who wishes to make very good offers for the remaining shares.' He offered a large hand which Ben ignored.

Ben toyed with the notion of not admitting his identity, but the idea of this ogre of a man pitching up at his own house later in the day didn't sit well with him, especially with Max around the house.

'Yes, I'm Mr Ramsden, but we're not selling. Besides, I would never sell to someone I don't know and have never met. I would also never sell in the driveway of my friend's house,' said Ben, sizing the man up as he spoke.

He was certainly big and muscular and appeared to be the sort who could handle himself if the need arose. He was in a different league altogether to the two would-be bad boys at Ripon. This one wore a shirt and tie, an expensive looking overcoat and appeared to have a diamond earring in one ear.

'So who do you work for Mr Krzysztof?' asked Ben.

Demetri smiled his broad smile once again, 'I'm not able to share that with you at this time, but I can assure you his money is good. He reached into an inside pocket and pulled out a plastic wad which was unmistakably fifty pound notes.

'I am able to sweeten the deal with a small upfront payment to show good faith to both of you,' he said, turning to make sure Duncan could see the hunk of cash too.

'In fact, this could be a tax free bonus perhaps...'

'Forget the pitch, I've heard it all before from your other trained monkeys and neither of us is interested,' Duncan interrupted.

'You're attempting to get us to sign the same document we've already got, for the same money and with a touch of intimidation added on top for good measure. Which isn't working by the way,' he added, spitting out the last few words.

'He's right,' Ben responded, 'If it's the same offer that your two idiots at the races offered, then you can get back in your car. Go back to whoever is behind all of this chicanery and tell them we're never going to sell, especially after that last stunt you pulled.'

'There is five thousand pounds here, the same for you both. That's on top of the offer within this document,' said Demetri calmly, although Ben had to concentrate hard this time to catch all the words through the thick Eastern European accent.

Duncan laughed and shook his head, crossing his arms again in a clear statement of defiance.

'Just get back into your drug pushing car and go back to your boss and tell him he's not going to buy us,' barked Duncan.

Ben thought for a moment the large man was going to react badly to Duncan's outburst, but instead he pushed his bottom lip up and shrugged. Tucking the bundle of cash back into his pocket he turned and walked a few paces before stopping and spinning around and gazing into both men's eyes for a few seconds. In a slower, more deliberate voice he said 'Thank you for your time gentlemen, I'm sure we will be in touch again soon.'

Then the giant of a man jumped into the driving seat of his Range Rover, fired it into life, spun it around Duncan's drive, and out onto the single-track road followed by a light shower of dust.

Ben and Duncan watched him leave, with Ben not altogether sure that there wasn't someone else in the back seat. There had been the hint of movement as the car had broadsided them. However, the blacked out windows were impenetrable. If there was someone in there, they made sure they couldn't be seen.

'Can you believe I found him dickering with the lock to the front door,' Duncan exclaimed as soon as the car disappeared out of sight.

'He didn't realise I was working in the garage and he'd have walked right in the house if I hadn't caught him. Nancy's in there, and god knows what would have happened if she'd been here on her own. I'm pretty glad you turned up when you did as well.'

Hearing her name, Nancy appeared from behind the door to the cottage.

'I heard you arguing, but stayed inside,' she said, joining her husband and putting an arm around him.

'I heard someone trying to post something through the door. Are you both okay?' she asked in a quiet voice, squeezing her husband's waist against her.

'Trying to *post* something?' Ben repeated, ignoring Nancy's question.

'Yes, he...'

'Where are the kids?' Duncan interrupted suddenly, alert once again.

Ben held two hands up and started to set off down the drive. 'They are fine,' he called behind him, 'I'll get them. I told them to stay in the car – it's parked on the verge, just the other side of the hedge.'

He jogged to the end of the hedge, and realised his heart was thumping. Not from physical exertion, this was stress. He'd left the kids in the car. Was there someone else in that Range Rover that he hadn't seen? No horse was worth... He rounded the hedge and a wave of relief washed over him when he saw Max, Josh and the two girls looking up at him expectantly from inside the car. He knew why he was relieved. The stakes had just increased and that thought unsettled him.

Thirteen

The following day Ben was at Joss's yard a good hour before The Ghost Machine's syndicate was due to have their meeting. He had Max and Mojo in tow, but the two of them soon disappeared down into the lower stables in search of Joss's daughters, Zippo the dog, and further adventure.

Ben thought Joss's forehead wrinkles had a deeper edge to them when he walked up to him outside the farmhouse. Assuming the current pressure was taking its toll, he tried to keep things light, but Joss had seemed distracted and after telling Ben he had things to do, broke off to see to some feeding in the top barn. He'd not spoken to Joss in detail about Silvery Sun, or received an update on the doping allegation, but put this down to the trainer being busy with runners, the stress of the racing papers having picked up the news and the disruption of having Racing Authority officials crawling over the yard with swabs and medical kits. He himself had syndicates with runners over the weekend, and had been tied up most of the day sorting out a couple of jumpers set to race at Uttoxeter at the weekend.

The doping case hadn't been headline news in the Racing Post, but there had been a fairly detailed report from their Northern correspondent relaying as many of the facts that they had, which wasn't a great deal. A few of the online racing news websites had posted the news, but no more than a few lines, so Ben was hopeful that it wouldn't be newsworthy enough to make it into the Nationals. Ben had a quick word with one of the stable lads about one of his two-year-olds before making his way up to the farmhouse and settled into a seat at the kitchen table and started to prepare the meeting.

Joss joined him half an hour later, coming in through the back door and crossing to wash his hands at the kitchen sink.
'You ready for this evening then?' he asked as he turned the taps.
Ben looked up from his seat at the kitchen table. 'Yes, but it's a strange position to be in. An unwanted takeover bid to contend with and espionage - anyone would think we were running a business empire – it's all a bit unreal.

Joss leant back on the kitchen sink and rubbed his forehead. 'I suppose The Ghost could be worth millions if he was to train on as a three year old and win a couple of Group One's, and then we'd have a significant asset on our hands as a stallion, but we're still a long way from that. I know he's the best I've ever had, but is he Group One material? I really couldn't tell you. He could be injured tomorrow and be worth next to nothing.'

'You're talking like a man who wants to sell his share.' Ben pointed out.

'Maybe. I'd only sell if we can keep him here though. This could be the only chance I get to train a proper Guineas or Ascot horse. Besides, we'll know where we stand a week on Saturday. The Greenham will be a proper test for him, his biggest challenge to date.'

'He was promising as a two year old though, and that form is already in the book.'

'Yes, he won his races as a two year old at a decent level but now we're going to be sitting down at the top table. There are bound to be horses from the top yards in the South that haven't even had a debut run yet.'

The two men were silent for a while as they both contemplated the statement. Ben was aware they were stepping into the unknown with The Ghost and was under no illusions as to the enormity of the quest they were setting out on with the colt. Ten years of syndicating racehorses had seen him have good, bad, and indifferent horses. Horses with issues, horses that didn't try and horses which were bitterly disappointing despite possessing plenty of ability. What made a top class racehorse wasn't just speed, it was temperament, intelligence, heart and above all, luck. And the greatest of these was luck, something he and Joss seemed to be in desperate short supply of in the last year.

Ben broke the silence. 'I visited your local police station yesterday. They were asking about the positive test for steroids.'

'Oh great, so the police are involved now,' moaned Joss.

'No, not at all,' replied Ben quickly 'We're in a training centre, they were bound to get to know, they're being called out to stables or dealing with people in racing all the time around here. Anyway, they said that it wasn't anything they would get involved with, but said to look to those closest to home, the lads, lasses or even the syndicate itself. An 'inside job' was their take on it.'

Joss sniffed. 'I've already grilled everyone on the yard. If this has been done by anyone inside the stables I think I'd pick up on it, but they all seemed as shocked and disappointed as we are. But I'd not considered the syndicate itself... what do you think?'

Ben looked down at his notepad in front of him. 'I'm like you, I can't see anyone left in the syndicate wanting to do this. But I guess it's easy to see the best in people you only meet from time to time and let's face it, we know little of their private lives. We both need to be open minded and look for anything out of the ordinary, even from people we trust.'

'That's the worst of it,' said Joss 'Whoever is behind all of this is making us doubt the people around us. 'I'm starting to wonder whether losing a single racehorse is preferable to losing friends, colleagues, owners and my business.'

Ben opened his mouth to start protesting, but Joss held up a hand 'I know, I know. Whoever is doing this to us wants us to be thinking like this. You don't need to give me the lecture.'

Joss strode out of the back door and left Ben alone, unhappy and in a cloud of doubt.

****

An hour and a quarter later there were eight people, including Ben, seated around Joss's kitchen table. Olivia and Janet Dunn were the first to arrive, and, after greeting Ben effusively, the mother and daughter team headed up the yard to feed The Ghost a carrot or two. They always had carrots with them and delighted in sending a special supply for The Ghost at Christmas and his birthdays – on both his actual birth date in March and on January first when all horses become a year older in the formbook.

Duncan was next to pull up in his farrier van. He was on his own this evening, leaving Nancy to look after the children. Rob Bawtry and Ian Furlong walked into the yard together a few minutes later, having met outside when parking their cars. Ian had his ten year old son, Mark, with him. Ben had bobbed out of the farmhouse to greet them and they too headed off to the Ghost's stable to view the colt. Finally, Joss appeared and went to collect all The Ghost's owners from the top barn and it was a relaxed group of owners from very different backgrounds that arrived at the farmhouse to find mugs of hot chocolate and buttered scones waiting for them, courtesy of Joss's wife, Marion.

After some small talk they all found chairs around the expansive kitchen table except for Marion who stood against the kitchen units. Ben began by thanking everyone for travelling to discuss the horse. Both Olivia and Ian had driven over two hundred miles by car. Ben had offered a telephone conference option to them so they could listen in from home, but both had been insistent that they would be there in person.

'I'd like to start by just giving everyone an update of where we stand in terms of the ownership of The Ghost. I think it will help us all to know what the options are and how the events of the last few days have changed things,' Ben stated to general murmurs of agreement around the table.

'From the original ten shareholders in The Ghost, each of whom held a ten percent share, four have sold their ownership – so forty percent has gone to someone who we presume is a client of Armitage's,' Ben stated in a matter of fact tone.

'I've checked with Weatherby's and the mysterious Mr Armitage has now registered his forty percent ownership. Weatherby's have also sent out letters to the four who have sold to confirm the change of ownership, and there have been no queries or refusals from the people involved.'

Ben paused to see how this news was treated by the group, but with no particular interruptions or questions forthcoming, he went on. 'I can tell you that David White was given a cash payment which was apparently offered in rather strange circumstances. He was pretty vague when I asked him about it, but rather like the rest of us he was approached by an unknown man, only he was given a cash offer he said he couldn't refuse. Those of you who met David will know that he likes a bet, so I wouldn't be surprised if gambling was involved somewhere, as it seems Mr Armitage, or at least the people he represents, have done their homework and tried to tempt us all with what they think will tip the balance in their favour.'

Olivia and Janet nodded to each other and Duncan stated 'For sure,' quietly under his breath.

Ben continued 'I know that most of you won't have met Rory Dent, as he only turned up at Newbury last year when we were second in the Maiden there but he has also sold pretty much straight away. Again, the details are a bit sketchy, but Armitage had some information which Rory told me was of great important to him. I tried to find out whether it was simply blackmail, but Rory clammed up once I started to ask anything more than basic questions. It seems that not only does Mr Armitage have very decent information about us all, but he's managing to stay just about the right side of the law as well.'

He took a moment to take a gulp of hot chocolate and Olivia took the opportunity to speak in the few seconds of silence 'But surely this sort of behaviour is against the law, you can't go around intimidating people like this,' she stated in her soft Scottish accent.

Ben shook his head 'I've been to the police yesterday and they aren't interested. Unless there was an actual assault or a report of harassment which goes beyond turning up at our front doors and asking we sell our shares, they can't and won't do anything. The Desk Sergeant I spoke to in Leeds the other day was quite clear that unless there were specific threats or actual violence they would not investigate.'

'What about Ripon?' questioned Duncan 'They were pretty close to assaulting you weren't they?

Ben smiled ruefully 'Yes, I asked the Police about that too,' he said eyeing the rim of his hot chocolate cup. 'It seems I was more likely to have charges brought against me for using The Iron Duke as a weapon!'

He went on to explain to the table what happened with his two male trackers at Ripon. Ben gave the facts, but was careful to leave out his own aggressive emotions associated with the faceoff with the men. There were a few raised eyebrows when he explained how he had whipped the horse around to smack the men to the ground, especially from Joss, who was genuinely impressed with the ingenuity involved, although Ben recognised that the trainer also wanted to protect his professionalism when

Joss quickly interjected to inform the group that the gelding had come back in good order from the races and was none the worse for being used as an equine battering ram.

Ian now spoke, having been quiet since he had come in from the stable yard.

'If it helps at all, I made this drawing of the chap who made the mistake of trying to stop me in my car late at night.'

He produced a pencil sketch, placing it in the middle of the table. Although he was tall and could potentially loom over people of lesser stature, Ian was very poised and measured. He tended to only speak when he deemed the subject worthy of comment. He always wore thin, round gold-rimmed spectacles and was concise, neat and fiercely intelligent. Ben had a lot of time for Ian. He was the sort of person who could constantly improve a conversation, with only a few well-chosen words.

Ben recalled a particularly memorable occasion when he and Ian had been at a table in the Owners and Trainers restaurant at Newmarket racecourse, and they had been unfortunate enough to be seated close to a particularly obnoxious race-goer. This very rotund, freely sweating chap in an ill-fitting suit had been well on the way to being drunk early in the afternoon and egged on by a drinking companion had started to grope each of the waitresses as they passed their table. Ian had waited until there was no one within hearing distance, leant over to the man, grasped his hand, and whispered a single sentence in the man's ear. The effect had been astonishing, the colour had drained from the man's face immediately and with bulging eyes he had stared aghast into Ian's face and then to Ben's before muttering an excuse, grabbing his letch of a friend and never returning to his table for the remainder of the afternoon.

Ben had asked Ian what he had said to the man, glad he'd headed off so promptly, but very curious to discover what could have shocked the man so much. Ian had pointed out that the man had been wearing a Masonic tiepin, so he had shaken his hand in a 'particular' way, intimated from his words he was of high rank and warned him of the consequences of being exposed as a sex pest to his Lodge Master. Ben had asked if he was a Mason and Ian had replied 'No, never interested me. I've read a book or two...,' and with no fuss whatsoever he had gone back to perusing his racecard and sipping his coffee.

Now the group each pored over the drawing. It was an almost perfect rendition of Armitage in pencil. More up to date than his photo on the internet, as Ian had captured the increase in the size of his cheeks and chin fat, and the drawn, puffy skin under his piggy eyes.

Ian, Duncan, Joss and Rob all agreed they had met this man and been offered a combination of money and some other benefit. Ben produced a copy of the internet photo of Armitage and although there was an age difference, the two renderings of the bald man in his late twenties were a positive match.

'You're wasted as an architect,' said Duncan admiring the portrait. There was a general hum of agreement around the table. Ian inclined his head slightly in accepting the comment graciously and quietly tucked the sketch away into its folder once again.

'I can help you out with James Rowbottom's share, well, I mean his wife's share – Cynthia,' said Rob matter of factly as he leant back in his chair. 'That's if anyone is interested. I spoke with him yesterday.'

Ben raised an eyebrow, but was then reminded that Rob and James had got on well at the races the previous season. Ben's owners very often struck up strong relationships with fellow shareholders as a common interest in racing, and specifically your own racehorse was a great icebreaker.

'Sure, give us the low down,' said Ben encouragingly. 'The more we know, the better we can discover exactly what's going on.' This was met with universal agreement around the table.

Although he was a publican, Rob wasn't the type to be the life and soul of a gathering. He ran a decent, clean, and popular pub and preferred to remain in the background, allowing his staff to face the customers most of the time. An ex-military man, he had invested his pension into the business and it had worked well for him for the past fifteen years, as he had an aged mother who needed constant supervision, which didn't come cheap. He'd taken the share in The Ghost primarily to give him an outside interest which took him away from the twenty four seven existence a pub required in order to be successful.

'He called me at the pub just after closing time last night and was in a real state. You know he split from Cynthia because she found out he was seeing someone else. Well, as part of the divorce settlement, she got the share in The Ghost,' Rob explained.

'James was pretty gutted he had to give up the horse, but didn't have a choice, otherwise he'd have had to have given her a controlling share of his company.'

'What's he do again?' asked Duncan, digging into another plate of scones which had appeared on the kitchen table.

'He has a fairly big company that manufactures and sells industrial pipes. It was Cynthia's Father that started it, but James took over about five years ago. It seems that Cynthia was given a decent amount of cash for her Ghost share, but unfortunately for James, Armitage also offered three percent of the company shares. He's no idea where the shares came from. He reckons he must have made a few enemies among the board. That three percent gave Cynthia a controlling share and the ability to force an immediate directors meeting at which James was voted out.'

Duncan whistled and the news was greeted with various other exclamations by the other shareholders.

'I hate to say it, but it probably serves him right,' said Janet Dunn. Her voice wavered slightly, revealing her to be the oldest person in the room. 'A woman scorned cannot be expected to give up an opportunity like that,' she stated levelly.

There was a crackle of laughter around the table, especially from Rob who admitted he had found the whole conversation with James difficult. He had apparently asked whether Rob could get him an owners badge from him for the Ghosts' next run at Newbury.

'I had to be a bit noncommittal and told him to speak with you Ben, but I guess he was just wanting to get back into the group somehow. I did feel a bit sorry for him. He's at a loose end now of course with no job, and no horse, come to that!'

Ben sighed. 'I'll call him and see what we can do. He's been a bit of an idiot playing around behind Cynthia's back, and he's paid for it I guess. But it does show once again that Armitage knows his mark's well – Cynthia didn't need the money, but that percentage in the company was obviously worth far more to her than her horse running in some big races this season.'

'Speaking of which,' Ben continued. 'We do need to talk about Newbury and the other possible plans for the season with The Ghost, but before we do, I just need to go around the table and know where we are with Mr Armitage if that's okay.'

Ben scanned the shareholders and was greeted with nods right around the table.

'Right, firstly, you will all know that one of Joss's horses was tested positive for a banned substance a few days ago. I'm pretty sure that the doping was a ruse to ensure Armitage had complete control of the horse even with only fifty percent. I'm not sure exactly when and where it happened, but it looks like Silvery Sun was 'got at' sometime in the last few days.'

There were several comments from around the table, a couple giving support to Joss, the others protesting about the unfairness of such a thing happened and the type of people capable of such an act. Janet and Olivia, along with Marion were particularly vociferous in their condemnation of the people behind the doping, even surprising a few of the men with their 'take no prisoners' reaction.

'You're a bit of a firebrand there aren't you, Janet,' Duncan commented in jest, only to be straightened up with a cold stare from the octogenarian.

Ben took the opportunity to step things up. 'I've also spoken with all of you and pointed out that if one more of us sells, Armitage will have control of the horse. To be clear, he would be able to remove the horse if he wants to and race The Ghost when he wants and where he wants – even abroad. He could also force a sale. Are we all okay on this and understand where we stand?'

Ben was silent for a few moments and again received nods of acceptance or a quiet 'yes' from each shareholder in turn as he went around the table. This included Joss and wife Marion, who was standing leaning against the kitchen dresser behind her husband.

'What I need to know as the Manager of the syndicate is whether anyone else is expecting to sell their share to Armitage. If so, we may as well make plans to hand the horse over, or all of us sell so that we at least get a decent price by acting together. If we all decide not to sell, then we stand our ground and get on with campaigning The Ghost this season – which for him will start next Saturday at Newbury, if all goes well in his last week of training.'

Ben spread both of his hands, palms down on the kitchen table, glancing at all seven of the people in front of him, making sure they felt the gravity of the question he was about to pose.

'Before I ask the question I want you all to know that I would completely understand any of you wanting out. It's your decision and there would be no recriminations.'

He took a couple of breaths.

'So, is anyone else planning to sell and give Armitage control?' Ben felt his heart thump in his chest as he finished the question. He had been in situations like this before; sure he would get the answer he was hoping for from all concerned. But no matter how well you knew people, they could still surprise you.

Again he scanned the faces around the table and to his relief, Joss started with a 'No'. Ian shook his head smartly and stated 'No'. Janet and Olivia looked at each other and said 'No' in unison.

'He can go boil his head,' added Olivia.

It was an 'Absolutely not,' from Rob. Duncan, sitting to Ben's left was the last to speak and true to form he paused, looked serious for a moment, and then produced a toothy grin and said 'Of course its no. Let's get this racehorse to the Greenham meeting and win us a horse race!'

This was greeted with the banging of a few firsts on the table and a little whoop from the Scottish ladies. Joss looked mightily relieved and the tightness in his face was reduced markedly. Marion gripped his shoulders from behind and beamed at everyone.

When everyone had calmed a little, Ian held up a hand for silence and turning to Ben asked '*We* have all said no, and we have assumed you are a 'No' too Ben.'

Ben went to start a reply, but was hushed by Ian's hand once more.

'I would like to know that the decision to continue with The Ghost is really what you want Ben. After all, the offers we have received are not insignificant. But I'm also aware that this horse may hold some deeply sad memories for you after last season. I can't imagine how you must still feel about the day at York, but I'm sure I speak for everyone around this table in saying that if you wished to sell, we would go along with you.'

The kitchen changed from convivial, to a sudden deadly quiet. From outside, the sound of a whinny from a distant stable broke the silence, but no one moved a muscle. All eyes were on Ben.

'I don't know what to say,' said Ben, initially bewildered, but he quickly cleared the fog as that day at York flashed through his mind once again. He pushed it backwards as far as it would go, cleared his throat, and continued 'Thanks Ian, it's good of you to be concerned, and I'm touched, but what happened was simply an accident. I admit I'm still working hard to come to terms with the fact that Anna isn't here anymore, but it makes me even more dedicated to the horse. Anna loved The Ghost and I want to be leading him in when we win a group race with him!'

'Steady on!' exclaimed Joss 'No pressure then!'

The tension in the room evaporated a little as people appreciated their trainer's reaction, but Ian's expression remained stoic and he watched Ben carefully.

'You do know that we will be racing against Panama this season? I would expect to bump into Billy Bentham's colt at least a couple of times if The Ghost continues to improve,' he pointed out.

Ben could see Olivia, head tilted and with a hand over her mouth, obviously explaining to her mother that 'Panama' was the horse which had produced the fatal kick at York.

He looked straight back at Ian and replied steadily 'I know. And I will be fine. I admit I'm still a little raw around the edges, but I'm much improved lately, getting professional assistance and feeling very positive. I want so badly for The Ghost to go well this season, and Billy's horse will be one of the many we will hopefully beat at the races.'

'Thanks Ben,' said Ian, offering a handshake. 'I'm sorry I had to bring it up. I'm sure you understand that I didn't want the rest of us to be pushing you down a path you didn't want to tread?'

Ben grasped Ian's hand in both of his own and swallowed down the urge to shed a tear. Ian's words could get to the heart of things with rapier like accuracy he thought once again, God love him.

Ben was relieved when Marion produced a pot jug for further top ups of hot chocolate, along with a large plate of chocolate biscuits which Duncan tucked into with relish, explaining that he'd only had a small sandwich for his lunch after he loaded up with three of the freshly baked cookies on his opening attack on the plate. The way Duncan managed to remain stick thin despite eating like a racehorse was something Ben could never quite wrap his head around.

The group broke into several conversations as they poured the thick chocolate liquid into their mugs. The pause also allowed Ben to centre himself once more. Once they had replenished their drinks and were crunching through the homemade cookies, Ben handed over to Joss and he ran through his plans for the next few months for The Ghost.

'He is still the best horse in my yard by a country mile,' Joss confirmed 'And he is in great shape. Given the issues we've had in the last few days, I have moved his stable again, and we'll probably do so every few days, at least leading up to the Greenham next Saturday. He will also have a stable hand with him all night. I can give you a cast iron guarantee that only my most trusted staff will be handling him and we will be watching him like a hawk.'

He continued 'If the ground stays at 'Good or Good to Soft', I think he will go there with every chance, though we wouldn't want it any softer really. Looking through the entries at the moment, there are eighteen in there and the ones I fear are the unexposed ones, simply because you don't know how good they are going to be. There are a few without wins, and one or two with very good breeding from the top flat yards, but we've got the form already in the book, which counts for a lot...'

There was a sharp rap at the backdoor to the farmhouse. This was rare, as virtually every person who came to the yard would go to the front door. If you were entering the kitchen from the yard, it was usually staff or the family, so a knock would be superfluous.

Joss shot a look of annoyance toward the door and then craned his neck backwards to see out of the window. The door then opened a small way.

'Er... Guvnor?' said an Irish voice through the crack in the door. 'I've two fella's here saying they are here to see The Ghost's syndicate. Can they come in?'

Joss indicated to everyone to stay seated and he and Marion went to the door, opened it and stepped outside.

Around the table no one paid a blind bit of notice to Joss, everyone standing as soon as he and Marion went through the door. Duncan and Rob walked over to the window to peer through, though at a desperate angle.

'It's Armitage, I'm sure of it. And he's got that Polish thug with him,' whispered Duncan.

Outside, Joss was met by an embarrassed stable lad, who was relieved to be sent on an errand that meant he could dart away. Two men stood in the yard, one small and bald and the other extremely large with a closely shaved head.

'Mr Armitage,' said Joss levelly, staring down into two small slits which indicated where the man's eyes lay. Even in mid April the evening air had a serious nip to it and Armitage wore a bulky overcoat which was drawn up to its lapels. His bald head was inflamed, pinched by the cold, and the excess fat around his chin popped out of the top of his coat as if squeezed from a tube like toothpaste. His companion hung behind, eyes fixed on Joss, but with a lithe balance which intimated that his body could leap into immediate action should it be called upon to do so.

'Ah, Mr O'Hoole, it's a pleasure to be here tonight in your workplace,' Armitage said in his high-pitched squeaky voice Joss recognised from their telephone conversation. He noticed that Armitage's face fat wobbled slightly when he spoke and the man had a white speck of spittle which rolled constantly around the right-hand side of his mouth. It appeared the man had a crooked mouth, which could account for his affected mode of speech.

'I um, believe there is a meeting of the syndicate here this evening?' Armitage asked, the end of his enquiry rising in note as he reached the end of his question.

Joss looked at the two men again and said nothing. Marion put her hand on her husband's back in reassurance.

Looking slightly perplexed, Armitage started to say something but Joss cut in before he could get his first word finished.

'How did you get into my yard?' he asked firmly.

Armitage gave a wonky half smile. 'We knocked on the door and were let in Mr O'Hoole. Erm, well, your stable person was kind enough to engage with us.' He indicated a small leather gloved digit in the direction the lad had disappeared off in.

Joss sniffed 'I *bet* you engaged him.'

Armitage, showing a flash of impatience, replied 'Yes, well I am here to engage, er, speak with you and the other members of the syndicate.'

Joss started to speak, but Armitage held up a hand and referring to a small pad produced from his inside pocket, continued to talk over him.

'As the named authority owning forty percent of the animal known as, er, The Ghost Machine, I believe I have the right to speak with the other members of the syndicate and indeed as I will be paying your bills for our share of the keep of the animal, you should treat me as you would any other owner.'

'Not when that owner interferes with my business,' Joss retorted, simmering rage shining through the words.

Demetri, still standing behind Armitage, twitched slightly but relaxed a little when Marion took hold of Joss's arm and pulled his ear close to her mouth. He listened for a few seconds; head bowed slightly, and then blew a short burst of air through a rounded mouth.

'Okay, my wife will ask them,' Joss conceded through gritted teeth. 'But you'll stay out here with me.'

As Joss finished his sentence, two of his bigger, beefier stable lads came around the corner of the stable yard at a run, with the smaller, out of breath lad who had met the two visitors following up behind. Joss acknowledged the two newcomers and nodded a direction. They followed the instruction, crossing the yard to stand a half a dozen yards away from the two men, both with arms crossed, eying up the large silent man behind

Armitage. Demetri turned his head slowly to take in the new arrivals at the other side of the yard.

Armitage put away his notebook and with both hands palms up said 'Look, this is a business call. I wish to speak with the syndicate and once that is completed we will depart. We are no threat. In fact, I have a very healthy proposition for you all.'

His voice sounded sickly sweet and made Joss feel sick and yet Armitage seemed incapable of producing a smile on his face. What with the messing around with The Ghost, the Racing Authority crawling over his yard and the barrage of concerned owners calling the yard, he was in no mood to cut a deal with the people who had caused it all.

Marion came back out of the house, closely followed by all the members of the syndicate. Ben first made sure the two elderly Scottish ladies were in earshot, but well hidden behind the men and then skirted around the rest to take up a position on Joss's right-hand side facing Armitage. With a crescent of seven people now standing outside the back entrance to the house Armitage and Demetri took a few steps back.

'Well?' demanded Ben.

'Ah, er, Benjamin…'

'Ben Ramsden,' said Ben in a much more controlled voice than he was anticipating. His heart was drumming in his chest and he could feel the anger pulsing through him. He exhaled slowly and felt the tension in his breathing dissipate a notch.

Armitage became businesslike, fishing for his notepad again and Ben was reminded of a wet behind the ears office clerk. If it hadn't been for the Polish giant at his side it could almost have been comical.

'I er, would like to know a little about The Ghost and also to make your syndicate a final offer,' said Armitage, stumbling slightly over the last few words.

Joss snorted 'Well it is customary to make an appointment when viewing your racehorse you know.'

'I apologise if this time is inconvenient but I see you do have all the syndicate members present… apart from us.' Armitage replied with an air of expectation.

Joss sighed. 'You seem to know a lot about me and my business, including how to access a private area. So you will no doubt know that we have had someone tampering with my horses.'

Armitage blinked nervously and said nothing, so Joss continued.

'I've never had a positive dope test before until now, and it's perhaps coincidence that you decide to turn up now in front of my owners and my yard. We know absolutely nothing about you or who you are working for. In such circumstances I'm sure you can understand I'm not too interested in showing you around the place!' Joss said, his anger bubbling under his words.

It was probably one of the longest speeches Ben had ever heard from Joss and he looked towards the trainer and then to the two men in front of the small crowd of owners.

Armitage also appeared to be somewhat taken aback and muttered something under his breath.

'Again, my apologies,' He spat from his lopsided mouth. 'But as owner of two fifths of the racehorse I demand to view the animal.'

'You demand do you?' barked Joss stepping forward and poking an index finger into Amitage's chest. He may not have been quite the size of Demetri and certainly not the same width, but he towered over the bald man and Armitage shuffled backwards, a red flush rising from his neck up his face.

Demetri stepped in front of his partner, held out two large hands in placatory manner, and spoke for the first time.

'We are here for two reasons, first to make an offer, and second to inspect the racehorse. We wish to conclude this quickly and without further bad feeling.'

Demetri had scanned the group as he spoke, but landed his gaze onto Ben as he finished.

'Okay, then. Make your offer,' nodded Ben to the giant of a man.

Armitage started to make his way forward but Demetri stuck an arm out and held the man back.

'We would like to provide a final offer of one hundred thousand pounds to each of you in return for your shares,' he said flatly.

A small gasp came from the back of the group and the one of the stable lads swore and whistled quietly which elicited a glare in his direction from Joss.

Demetri added 'Of course we would pay you a quarter now in cash and the rest would be forwarded to your bank accounts within three hours. I would need your signature on the contracts Mr Armitage has with him...'

'Not interested!'

It was a shrill ladies voice from the back of the huddle of owners, and heads turned to Olivia Dunn.

'I am not interested in anything you have to say or your money and neither is my Mother,' she added defiantly.

Duncan laughed. 'Aye, and that goes for me too, bucko.'

Ian and Joss also added their own agreement to Olivia's outburst.

Demetri didn't react. Instead he slowly transferred his gaze to the last two men. Armitage behind him was rolling his eyes as the syndicate stood solid. The only two to have said nothing were Ben and Rob Bawtry. Rob looked away from Demetri and turned to Ben.

'As far as I'm concerned, I've already given my word we are staying put. This is your business Ben, what do you say?' he asked.

Ben winked conspiratorially at Rob and then turned again to

Demetri and Armitage.

'We will sell,' he said quietly. There were gasps and mutterings from behind him.

Armitage started to extract more paper from another inside pocket and shuffled forwards again, clicking a ballpoint pen as he went.

When Armitage was in front of Ben, proffering a pen he thrust a single finger out 'But the price is three million pounds. Each,' he said, prodded Amitage's chest as he spoke each of the last few words. The man's face once again flowered with colour as Ben rapped on his ribcage.

Ben caught the glimmer of a smile waft across Demetri's face but then the big man sighed and he stepped forward to pull Armitage back once again. The solicitor was spluttering about how ridiculous Ben was being.

'I'm sure your offer will be considered,' Demetri said demurely, gripping his colleagues arm tightly. 'However, I would be grateful if we could now view the racehorse Mr O'Hoole. Perhaps with an escort? We would not need to touch the animal, we simply wish to ensure his wellbeing and photograph him.'

Ben ignored the request and returned with 'So who is actually buying these shares. Who's your paymaster Armitage?'

Armitage sneered back at Ben and licked his lips. He appeared ready to reply, but seemed to think better of it and remained silent.

Demetri shook his head by means of warning towards Armitage and replied 'We are unable to confirm that information Mr Ramsden. But I do believe we have the right to view the horse as Mr Armitage here…,' he gestured to the restrained Armitage with a sharp flick of his eyes '…is listed as the owner with the authorities.'

Joss looked towards Ben who shrugged and said 'I suppose they do own a leg.'

Joss sighed again and instructed the two stable lads to come across with a smart jerk of his head. Then he turned to the syndicate and his wife

'I'll go with them. We'll be back in ten minutes,' and then to the two men 'I'll be watching you two like a hawk.'

Marion had a few quick words with her husband and then Joss set his two lads off up the yard in the lead. They were followed by Demetri, still directing an agitated Armitage by the arm, and then Joss followed a few paces behind.

Once the five of them had disappeared from view, Ben ushered the remaining group back into the kitchen. As soon as the door closed everyone wanted to speak at once and several conversations struck up immediately.

Olivia was first over to Ben, asking why he had made an offer. Once he started speaking, the others became quiet and listened in.
'I don't want to sell, I just needed to gauge their reaction,' explained Ben.

'Whoever is behind all this chicanery seems to be getting more desperate and whilst they concentrate on money they might just leave Joss's horses alone.'

'But three million pounds?' Olivia questioned wearily.

'Look, they knew we were all meeting, they managed to get into the back yard even though Joss has this place on lockdown. Despite Armitage acting like an ass, everything else points to them being very well informed and planning every move.'

'In fact, they have a worryingly high volume of detailed information about us,' said Ian thoughtfully.

Ben took two breaths and continued. His heart had been pounding again, but slowed with the deeper breaths he took. 'At least the spotlight will fall on me rather than any of you, and more importantly, keep Joss out of this mess. He needs to concentrate on getting the colt to Newbury in one piece for the next week.'

The content of the conversation spiraled around the kitchen. Who is behind the buyouts? How will the positive dope test affect Joss? Could The Ghost's run next week be affected by the change in ownership? Ben confirmed the answer to the last question was a definite no, as any shareholder with forty percent would not be able to control the running and racing of the horse.

Fifteen minutes ticked by and Ben was considering going to find Joss when the front door of the farmhouse opened and then closed and he walked into the kitchen to an expectant audience.

'They're gone. I watched them walk down the drive and then get into a Range Rover that was parked the other side of the front paddock. I think they went over the paddock fence, walked across the field and round the ménage in order to get into the yard without coming to the front door.'

'What did they do when they saw The Ghost?' asked Marion.

'Nothing really,' Joss replied 'The Polish one asked a few questions, mainly about how well he was working, they took some photos and that was it. They never got anywhere near the horse, I made sure of that.'

Marion started to pull a sweater on, talking at the same time. 'Is someone with The Ghost now?'

'Yes, don't worry I've got Jake with him and I've also moved him to a new stable already. He's in the side barn now in the corner. That whole area of the yard has cameras so you don't need to go up there now. It's not ideal to be moving him around the yard like this, but I think we have to be careful with what's going on.'

Marion unperturbed, headed to the kitchen door. 'I'm going anyway. Anyone else like to come with me?' she offered to the room. Olivia and Janet jumped straight to their feet followed by Ian and Rob.

Duncan smiled and said 'I'm always up for a pat of my racehorse, count me in.'

Joss turned to Ben with a boyish grin on his face 'Come on mister big shot thirty million pound horse, we may as well join them with The Ghost, then I can tell everyone about the plans for next Saturday together.'

'They didn't say no to the three million each,' Ben pointed out lightly.

'They didn't say yes either,' Joss replied.

The syndicate grabbed their coats and hats and made for the back door. Ben was trying to make sense of the visit from Armitage and Demetri and was running the conversation through his head. There were a number of things that really made no sense and a lot of questions remained unanswered. How did they know the syndicate was meeting at that moment? How did they circumvent the locked front door and yard doors? And most of all, who on earth was really playing this game with them?

He forgot all these questions immediately when he put a foot out of the back door into the backyard and was accosted by Max, Mojo, Zippo and Ian's son Mark who were skimming around the yard like fighter planes, arms out wide and making screeching noises. The two dogs skittered around after the boys, enjoying the game as well, jumping up when they stopped and barking at their heels when the planes wheeled around.

'Boys!' Ben called. 'Land your plane, we're going to see The Ghost. Want to come along?'

Mark stopped in his tracks and dropped his arms but Max continued to circle the adults, arms perpendicular to his body, making machine gun fire sounds. He wheeled around the group once more until he reached Mark and then challenged him to a race to The Ghost and the two boys promptly charged off, to the amusement of everyone.

'Good to see you have everything under control Ben,' Duncan teased.

Ben produced a smile which turned into a grimace, replying. 'If only.'

Fourteen

The next week flew by as Ben was kept busy in the home office, visiting another trainer in the South and going racing with three of his syndicate horses. They had enjoyed variable success on the track, but at the start of the season it was to be expected as horses needed their first runs after the winter break. The home phone and his mobile phone were constantly busy as the flat season starting to get into full swing and the turf meetings became more numerous. He was pleased to see that Joss managed to saddle another winner in a Class Five handicap up at Redcar in midweek.

No one in The Ghost's syndicate had heard anything else from Armitage and it seemed that everything on that front had gone quiet. Looking back at the confrontation, he was relatively pleased with the way it had gone. It was clear to Ben that Armitage and the group of men attempting to intimidate the syndicate was responsible for the doping. But with no hard evidence pointing to them the racing authorities and the police were not going to pursue the possibility.

He'd spoken with Joss a couple of times and learnt that the horseracing authority would still be holding an enquiry despite the findings pointing to foul play and most likely fining him for the positive dope test, but thankfully he had been advised that a loss of his license was unlikely. Joss had found himself a decent solicitor with experience representing trainers and it was now a case of being patient. High profile cases of this kind took an age to process before a hearing would be held. Joss had been instructed by his counsel to expect that his visit to London to stand in front of the authority would be at least another two months away. In the meantime he was able to continue training and racing the horses in his care, but should expect testing of his horses, both at the racecourse and at home, on a regular basis.

Joss had also discovered something of interest and perhaps importance during his conversations with the lead investigator from the Racing Authority, quizzing him while he worked at the yard. It emerged that the dope test carried out at Ripon on Silvery Sun had come about because of an anonymous call into the head office of the Racing Authority the afternoon of the race. The caller could not be traced and no record of the phone call was made, other than the fact that the caller insisted that Joss O'Hoole's horses should be tested. This sort of information was always taken seriously and had been passed on to the Ripon Stewards who had acted upon it.

Joss had explained that the stewards at any racecourse would only consider testing a horse when the circumstances warranted such action. This was usually when a horse had underperformed or shown marked improvement on the track. It wasn't standard practice to test the winner of a race as a matter of course unless the stewards on the day believed there was a good reason to do so. Joss had been buoyed by this news. The Racing Authority investigator had drawn attention to the call and hinted that given the evidence he had amassed, it probably helped Joss's case. It seemed likely that whoever had got the steroids into Silvery Sun had also ensured they would be discovered.

Ben woke on the Thursday, two days before the Greenham Stakes at Newbury and waited nervously for the final declarations to be announced. He sat at his computer at 10-00am and clicked through into the declarations page, returning every minute or so to see if they had been posted to the Weatherby's website. Finally at 10-15am a list of horses names appeared with the phrase 'Final Declarations' written alongside.

There were twelve declarations in total and looking down the runners Ben saw that The Ghost Machine was listed fourth in order of his official rating. This meant that in the handicapper's view The Ghost hadn't achieved as much on pure form as some of the others. A couple of the unexposed horses Ben had feared were thankfully not in the final lineup, but there were another five horses from top trainers still in there with limited experience, but obviously well thought of by their connections.

Panama was declared as well. Ben shuddered upon reading the same name which had been plastered all over the press – as the 'Guineas hopeful that had killed with his kick'. Ben felt no malice towards the horse, a well-bred colt with a respected trainer, but he could feel the twinge of anger building in his chest. Panama's name in the line-up was a reminder he could do without and he flicked over it as quickly as possible to concentrate on the other runners. Besides, he knew Panama's background and ability in minute detail.

Ben concluded his analysis of the race an hour later. As expected, it would be a very competitive contest, but then the Greenham was worth thirty thousand pounds to the winner and classed as a Group race – one of the highest grades. Run over seven furlongs it was the first race of the season for quality three year old colts. In past years this race had set the scene for the young colts and would provide an indicator of the sort of quality to be expected from the new generation. They were pitching The Ghost Machine in at the top level for the first time and the prospect both thrilled and daunted Ben.

Joss was in touch later in the morning to discuss the race, and ran through his plans for getting the horse down there on the day, a four hundred mile round trip. The Ghost Machine was to travel on Friday afternoon and stay overnight at a yard in Lambourn, a major training centre close to the racecourse. The three year old would be attended by Jake, Joss's travelling head lad and another trusted stable hand. All the colt's meals would be taken with them and at least one person would stay with him every minute of the day and night. They would then set off from

Lambourn to make the short journey to Newbury on Saturday morning and, again, stay with him right up to race time in the middle of the afternoon. Joss had left nothing to chance. He and Ben would be travelling down on Saturday morning along with Duncan and be waiting at Newbury to meet his staff and the Ghost Machine when they arrived.

Ben decided to leave Max at home for this race. There were good reasons for leaving him in the care of Nancy once again, uppermost in his mind being a potential run-in with Armitage and his hired muscle. All of the syndicate would be there, including the Scottish ladies who were travelling by train and taxi to reach the course by late morning. Everything was set.

Joss appeared to be hopeful, but not confident, and the early betting shows on the race reflected this position. The Ghost Machine was a 12/1 shot, with six other horses ahead of him in the betting and sharing the same price with Panama who had received glowing gallop reports from the Racing Post in recent days. The favourite with the bookmakers was a Newmarket based colt from a powerful stable and owned by one of the major worldwide owners based in Saudi Arabia. Priced at 5/2, Heading South was a worthy favourite having won his only race to date; a very hot Newmarket Maiden over seven furlongs at the end of the previous season. He had achieved this by an impressive four lengths. Both the runner-up and the fourth placed horse in the same Maiden were also represented in the race, albeit at much longer odds.

Ben had enjoyed success with his horses, with a number of good winners over the course of the last five years, but the best to date had come in a Class Two handicap. Even contesting a Group race with one of his racehorses was a tremendous achievement, given the sort of budget he was forced to work with. He checked the sales prices of the other contenders and found to his satisfaction that The Ghost Machine was by far the cheapest colt of the twelve. Heading south had cost his owner an eye-watering one and a quarter million dollars at the Keenland sales over in America as a yearling, and there were others boasting six figure price tags in the field. At eighteen thousand guineas The Ghost Machine had exceeded expectations and was already proving to be great value.

The big question was whether the colt had trained on. Had he been at his very best as a two year old in his first season, or was there more to come? Ben had quizzed Joss relentlessly on this topic, to be returned with assurances that the colt was showing all the signs of being even better as a three year old, but he was also aware that only racing against the best of his generation would provide the definitive answer. The Greenham was the first staging post for the colt's season and would shape everything to come.

That afternoon Ben visited Esme Trent in Leeds and again enjoyed a great sense of release following the visit. She had given him a few more coping techniques to work on and instructed him to return in two weeks time, happy with his progress.

Early on Friday morning Ben dropped Max at school along with Duncan's kids and on a whim headed to Joss's yard. He spent half an hour at The Ghost's box with the impressive grey horse, fed him a couple of carrots, gave him a tickle behind the ears and wished him good luck, much to the stable lad's amusement, before returning home to do a day of distracted work in the office.

Helen arrived with Max in the late afternoon and the three of them enjoyed one of Max's grandmother's fabulous Lasagne. Helen was her normal buoyant self and as she worked for a florist, brought with her a large armful of cut daffodils which hadn't sold that day. Ben had to admit the addition of a dozen bright yellow daffodils in each room, flowerheads dazzling in contrast to their dark green stalks, gave the cottage a new appeal. Anna had brought flowers into the house most days, often picked by herself from the local hedgerows or meadows and Ben realised it was another trait she had inherited from her mother. Helen settled into a chair in front of the fire and spent the evening, needle in hand, mending various clothes she had found in Max's bedroom. Ben had asked her to stay overnight to look after Max and allow Ben to head to the races early the next day and she leapt at the opportunity. He spent the evening in his armchair beside Helen, looking through the Greenham runners on his tablet and tried, unsuccessfully, to control his nervous anticipation for the day to come.

Fifteen

When Joss edged into a space in the Owners and Trainers parking area at Newbury racecourse and finally brought his ten year old Land Rover Defender to a stop, none of its three occupants moved to exit the vehicle. The four hour journey had started with a wakeup call at five o'clock, care of Duncan hammering on Ben's door with shouts of 'Today's the day Benny Boy, get your suit on!' followed by a tedious stop start trip down the M1 Motorway, interspersed by a couple of quick breaks at service stations, one of which included a takeaway breakfast Ben wished he hadn't eaten very soon afterwards.

Ben observed that the idealised version of racehorse owners and trainers travelling everywhere in helicopters and living the high life was laughably way off the mark. Ben had shared the driving with Joss and all three had dozed on and off, spending the rest of the journey reading The Racing Post or sharing the odd conversation. Nervous excitement built with every mile closer they got to Newbury. Joss was quiet, while Duncan was talkative, which could have caused friction on a long journey, however Ben was adept at being a buffer between the two.

The Owner car park was thick with cars at eleven o'clock in the morning even though the start of racing was more than three hours away. It was turning into a decent enough spring day for the end of April, with plenty of cloud scudding across the sky on a stiff breeze. The sunlight shone through in small bursts which brightened everything considerably and brought a welcome tingling of warmth to the skin before quickly disappearing again.

Ben and Duncan pushed their doors open and spent a few moments stretching and yawning before starting to pull on their ties. Joss had already checked on The Ghost on the way down, satisfied with the response from Jake and the crew in Lambourn, and was waiting for a call to say they were on their way. The call came while Joss was still in the driving seat. Ben could tell there was something wrong even before Joss started talking, as the trainer's brow had wrinkled in an unmistakable sign of tension.

'What?' Ben asked, and was waved away by Joss. 'What is it?' Ben tried again through the driver window.

Joss held up a hand to mute Ben and a few seconds later wound his window down to report. Each second felt like a minute to Ben.

'The horse is fine, it's the bloody transport. They have two flat tyres.'

'The horse box?' questioned Duncan 'But it's almost brand new. How did they manage two flats at the same time?'

'They don't know exactly. They loaded The Ghost up about twenty minutes ago, got to the end of the lane leading from the overnight stop and suddenly the box lurches to the left and both nearside tyres are flat. They're sitting on the outskirts of Lambourn and have had to call for a rescue because they only carry one spare wheel,' Joss said despairingly.

Ben picked at his teeth, trying to work out the logistics. 'It could take an hour and a half to get a recovery van there and then get the tyres changed. It's going to be cutting it tight to get here in time for the race.' There was a short silence. Then Duncan put out an open hand and demanded the keys to the Defender.

'Keys!' he barked again when his request was met with no response from Joss, who was still sitting in the driver's seat looking bewildered.

'The box is your new one isn't it? The two horse smaller box that you don't need a special license to drive?' Duncan questioned in a slow, slightly irritated tone. He received a positive response from Joss.

'Well then. Your spare tyre on this...,' he tapped the roof of the Defender. '...will also fit the horsebox. I'll drive over to Lambourn which will take, what... forty five minutes, get the tyres changed and the box will be here by one o'clock. The race is due off at three o'clock, so we'll have The Ghost here is good time. If we wait for a recovery truck, we could miss it. What's the latest the horse can get here before being classed a non-runner?'

Duncan looked between Joss and Ben expectantly, almost jigging on the spot, keen to get going.

'It's supposed to be two hours before race time and we're racing at three o'clock, but I can go to the clerk of the course and ask for an extension. He's a decent chap. I think he'd give us a bit extra if we needed it, especially given the fact we're running in the feature race,' answered Ben.

Duncan turned to Joss. 'Is there someone in Lambourn we could get to help?'

Joss now seemed to catch up and grasp the situation and what Duncan intended. He jumped down from the Defender to stand beside Duncan.

'There's a couple of trainers I know who could possibly help out, but they might all be either on the gallops or on the way to a race meeting themselves at this time on a Saturday. I think we go with Duncan's idea and I'll see if I can get help at the same time.'

'No point you two coming,' instructed Duncan as he relieved Joss of the keys and climbed into the Defender. 'You have my mobile. Tell the guys in the horsebox to have it jacked up ready for when I arrive and have that first wheel changed with their own spare if they can.'

Ben had thought of jumping in beside Duncan, but his friend was way ahead of him. Joss would be needed here to speak to the Clerk if needed and Ben was better off supporting him and explaining things to the other members of the syndicate. Duncan was a decent mechanic as well as a blacksmith and changing a wheel would be child's play for him.

Joss was obviously thinking the same thing, as he was grabbing overcoats from the back seat. He slammed the door and stepped back to allow Duncan to pull away. The two of them stood together, coats over their arms in a vast car park, both feeling anxious as they watched the vehicle shoot directly across the steadily filling car park to the traffic free exit.

'All we need now is for your ten year old Defender to break down,' Ben noted sarcastically as the two of them turned towards the racecourse entrance.

In the Defender, Duncan tapped Lambourn into the satnav and was relieved to see that it quoted thirty five minutes for the journey down the B4000 rather than the forty-five he was expecting.

Joss spent the next twenty minutes speaking to Jake in the horse box, then to the yard boss where his staff had over-nighted. The Ghost had been taken out of the box and led back to his overnight box, only a few hundred yards down the road. Then he called a couple of trainers in Lambourn, one of whom said he would pop over to help if he could. His other trainer contact was, as Joss feared, in a horsebox on his way up to Nottingham races with a runner.

They found a table in the Owners and Trainers bar and Ben had spent Joss's time on his phone with paper and pen, constructing one of his information pictures.

'Do you think the flats where intentional?' Ben enquired when Joss finally hung up on his last call.

'I hadn't even considered it,' admitted Joss distractedly, checking for messages on mobile. 'What would anyone have to gain?'

Ben sighed 'I know, I'm struggling to see any reason for Armitage not wanting The Ghost to run today. Although if he did have a reason, I'm sure he would happily stop at nothing to prevent the horse getting here in one piece.'

With crossed arms, Ben stared miserably out of the ceiling to floor plate-glass window onto the finishing furlong of the racecourse. The more he looked at the scene, the deeper his depression became. Nothing about this horse and syndicate was working out well. It was stress from morning until night, and if he'd never bought the colt, there would be no Armitage, no stress and Anna would... Ben's attention snapped back to the bare table. Joss continued to poke a finger at his phone's screen. Ben rubbed his face with both hands and became aware of the clammy warmth under his palms, perspiration being transferred from his forehead. It came like a wave, swamping his senses. He rode the panic attack, taking a few short breaths, picking up his racecard and attempting to concentrate on the runners and riders in the first race. But Anna's face flooded into his thoughts and he shivered and suddenly felt hollow in his chest. Then a shudder and anger started to well up inside him, a stark, hot rage that fizzed and threatened to push its way out of him.

Desperately, he tried to strike up a conversation with Joss, who was still engrossed in his phone, but Ben's mouth was dry, lips engorged. Before he could issue a word his vision began to cloud and the owners and trainers bar spun away in a distorted rainbow of colours.

Joss heard the thump of Ben's forehead hitting the table before he realised anything was amiss and was straight out of his chair and beside his friend, pulling him back off the wooden surface and leaning him backwards. He looked into Ben's face and saw he was barely conscious with eyes unfocused and mouth askew. Ben panted short sharp breaths and his arms flopped by his sides. Joss shouted over to the bar for water and, supporting Ben's upper half, pulled him away from the table and then thrust his friends head towards the floor and between his legs.

What had she said? I need to do something to stop this, I need to focus, focus on... Damn it, what do I focus on? The top of Ben's head felt strange and the tip of his forehead ached. Esme. It was Esme and she wanted him to focus on... Max. Max, and his smell, his smile, his laugh...

Ben swam uneasily back to full consciousness. He blinked tears from his eyes and viewed a wall of Royal Axminster carpet in purple and red with white outlines. His head was being forced between his knees by an unseen hand. A glass of water held by a man's hand resolved into focus to his left-hand side and suddenly his throat felt so dry it hurt. Cupping the glass in both hands he took a small sip and then a deeper draft, raising his head as he did so. A concerned face peered at him. There appeared to be another person standing close by. He could see a pair of shiny black shoes.

It took another half a minute for Ben to recover. A half minute spent sipping more water, plenty of measured breathing and rubbing of a sore forehead. Joss's concern was still written in the furrows across his forehead, but there was evidence of relief there too. He was speaking as he offered Ben more water and eventually Ben replied.

'Thanks. Thanks, I'm better,' he managed to croak. It took another minute for Joss to be satisfied enough to return to his seat across the table and leave Ben nursing a refilled half pint glass of tap water and a growing red lump on the centre of his forehead. A couple of members of the Newbury staff were placated by Joss and moved away, but noticeably stayed nearby and continued to shoot concerned glances their way.

'I'm sorry,' Ben repeated for the third time and Joss waved his apology away again.

'I'm fine now. It's just these weird dizzy spells...,' Ben started.

'That was no dizzy spell. You were out cold for a few seconds. Keep drinking the water,' Joss instructed from across the table.

'Guess I was lucky to have you to catch me then.'

'Lucky nothing,' Joss snorted. 'You've almost head butted the table in two and got a lump the size of a goose egg to show for it. I caught nothing.'

Ben's fingers moved up and stroked the angry swelling on his forehead. It stung and didn't feel part of him when he touched it, so he tried to leave the throbbing lump alone.

The minutes passed and the colour came back to Ben's face. As he went through recovery, the bar started to fill up with more owners. Within another ten minutes he was back in control and Joss asked the question Ben had been waiting for.

'We know why you get these panic attacks and we know what brings them on. So why don't we sell the blasted shares in The Ghost and get rid of the problem,' blurted Joss a little more loudly and severely than he had intended. The bar was now dotted with people and a couple close by peered towards the table with raised eyebrows.

'It's not the horse,' Ben replied casually in a soft voice. 'I appreciate the offer, but I'd be having these dizzy spells, horse or no horse.' He rubbed his forehead again in irritation and was rewarded with a spear of pain through his temple.

Joss slowly shook his head from side to side. 'Well, you're an ungrateful little sod. That's the last time I stick your head between your legs to stop you passing out.' He stuck his chin out in mock admonishment and Ben returned a smile to his friend.

A vibrating mobile on the table made both men flick their eyes to it and Joss scooped it up quickly with both hands. 'It's Duncan. He must be at Lambourn by now.'

Ben watched his friend's face closely as he took the call. Joss focused out of the window as he listened, adding his agreement or instruction from time to time. Ben could only just hear Duncan's Welsh inflections but gave up trying to understand what was going on as the noise from the bar was growing in volume. He pushed aside his mild irritation at not being part of the conversation and took another few sips of water. He was feeling much better now, although the throbbing on his forehead was quickly developing into a full-blown headache. The phone conversation looked like it would continue for some time so he set off to the bar in search of some painkillers.

He returned to the table feeling a little better for having been on his feet, and took the paracetamol tablets begrudgingly sourced by the barman.

Joss hung up the call and turned to Ben 'You're not going to believe this.'

He paused a few seconds, placing the mobile onto the table carefully, but focusing elsewhere as he searched for the best way to impart the new information.

'Okay. So Duncan gets to Lambourn and finds Jake with the horsebox. He's busy changing one of the flat tyres. Duncan gets on with

107

the second one using my spare. They eventually get the tyres sorted and Duncan heads off to the overnight yard to get Courtney, the lass with The Ghost. Jake stays with the box.'

Ben nodded his understanding and gestured for Joss to continue.

'On the way to the yard Duncan found a huge patch of inch long tacks on the road just outside the entrance. We've been lucky, as they must have pulled out wide to get out of the yard, otherwise we'd have four flats. Thing is, Duncan said that if he had to call it, he thinks the tacks have been deliberately placed there.'

'Why does he think that?'

'He said something about them being new and too many of them. It didn't look right. But get this. They collected The Ghost and walked him back up the lane to the horsebox and when they got there the other two tyres are flat. Only this time they've been let down.'

'Bloody hell, what next?' exclaimed Ben. He checked his watch. It was five to twelve. The Ghost needed to be booked into the racecourse in just over an hour.

Ben pursed his lips. 'So do we need to declare as a non-runner?'

'No, not yet. Duncan is taking two more wheels off the Defender and leaving it on bricks. Whoever did this to the box didn't think to let the tyres down on the car. They are on with it now and Jake is helping him along with Jeff, the trainer I called earlier.'

'Doesn't he have a box we could borrow?'

'No, I'm afraid not, it's out collecting a horse, but he's been helping with the wheels,' responded Joss getting to his feet.

'You stay here, do your job and keep calm. I'll go and find the clerk and warn them we could be late booking in. We still have enough time as long as there aren't any more setbacks.

'Oh, and you could call Duncan and tell him to have someone watching the box and the horse just in case someone tries anything else.' called Joss as he made off into the growing throng of people in the bar.

Over the next half an hour, Olivia and Janet arrived and listened dumbstruck as Ben explained the situation. Ian turned up fifteen minutes later and took the news in his usual cool, measured style. Both asked him about the angry looking bump to his forehead for which Ben found a benign excuse which seemed to placate them. Sharing his personal issues with the syndicate at the moment would be too much to bear.

Ben called Rob Bawtry to warn him before he got to the track. He was in his car with James Rowbottom, the ex-owner of The Ghost. Ben had managed to acquire an Owners Badge for him. For a moment, Ben considered contacting Armitage, but quickly dismissed the idea. The last thing he wanted was to be explaining this morning's events to someone who had probably organised the entire debacle. Come to that, he wondered whether Armitage would turn up at the races today, but dismissed this as highly unlikely. He was guessing that the only interest the mystery man or woman behind the buying up of The Ghost shares was their investment value. Actually turning up to speak with the trainer in the parade ring and meet with the owners they had tried to intimidate was superfluous to that requirement.

Joss returned at just after one o'clock, checking his watch nervously as he pushed through the bar, now bustling with owners and trainers. He managed to locate a spare chair and dragged it over to the table and after taking a moment to compose himself, greeted the syndicate and started updating the group.

'The clerk will allow us to go right up to the wire, which is quarter past two. Any later than that and he can't guarantee anything. I've just got off the phone with Duncan and he's almost finished getting the last wheel in place. That gives him three quarters of an hour to get here in proper time, and then another twenty minutes on top which we will hopefully get from the racecourse.'

Joss looked around the table and through gritted teeth continued 'The Ghost seems to be taking all the messing around in his stride and it will take another ten minutes to get him loaded. But if everything goes to plan, they'll be here by two o'clock. All this rush won't help him though... I wish we'd brought him here really early.'

This comment drew a reaction of wholesale support from the group, all of whom made it clear they felt Joss had done everything to ensure the colt would get to the course in fine condition. Ben wondered if the same support would be there if the horse didn't actually arrive in time...

The next few minutes was taken up with a variety of questions which Joss and Ben did their best to answer. However, as Ian pointed out, whatever the cause, the transport was now heading to the racecourse and all they could do is wait for it to arrive. Joss called Duncan again and to his relief he was able to report that they had The Ghost on board and were on their way. All three of them had squeezed into the cab of the box and were back on the road to Newbury. The traffic was okay so far and they hoped to arrive just after two o'clock, an hour before the race.

Duncan had ended his phone conversation with Joss in his own inimitable style. 'Of course we are all out of tyres now, so if we get a proper flat in the next thirty minutes we're going to be royally buggered.'

Joss decided not to relate this to the syndicate even though he'd strangely enjoyed the Welshman's parting quip.

In the background there was a muted cheer from outside the bar as the first race of the day, a Juvenile Maiden, went off on time and the stands swelled with race-goers. That made it half past one. Once the race finished Joss waited for the general excitement to calm down around him and then excused himself.

'They should be here in about half an hour. I'm going to the horsebox parking area to meet them and help get the horse ready. I'll see you in the parade ring,' he told Ben anxiously. Joss unconsciously rolled a racecard around in his hands as he spoke and then with a tight smile headed off through the bustling post race crowd.

Ben spent the next half an hour checking his phone and battling with a headache, either from the table bashing it had received, or simply caused by the tension resulting from The Ghost's upcoming race. Ben would always become nervous with anticipation before one of his horses ran, and particularly so when it was a better grade race. Today was a double whammy, it being a Group Three race, the first time Ben had fielded a runner in such a classy event, plus the continuing uncertainty over whether The Ghost would actually arrive in time to race. He told himself that he had a right to feel nervous but in truth the tension was making his heart thump worryingly loud in his breast.

Rob and ex-shareholder James turned up together after the first race and, after going through the entire story once again, Ben made his own excuses and went for what he hoped would be a calming stroll around the back of the stands. It was now two o'clock and, according to latest text message from Joss, there was still no sign of Duncan.

The second race of the day went off while Ben was wandering, deep in thought behind the stands. He watched the runners for the third race at two thirty starting to emerge from the stabling block while a badly distorted version of the race commentary echoed around the buildings. He heard the public address commentator start to increase his volume and pitch and the excitement transferred to the crowd's volume as the race reached its climax, finishing with a cheer as the favourite crossed the line in first place.

Ben paced across the manicured lawns wracking his brain for answers. Why wouldn't Armitage want the horse to race? Why try to delay the horsebox? Then it came to him, well sort of came to him, but it was still fuzzy in places. As a non-runner, it would mean Armitage was able to negotiate a price for the horse as The Ghost's form currently stood, whereas if he were to win, or even get placed in the first three home in the Greenham The Ghost's value would automatically shoot up. Ben quickly realised this was a weak argument. Armitage had just as much reason to want the horse to race, in order to increase the value of the shares he already held. As he strode along his mind swam with the reasons, outcomes and possible reactions the syndicate would have to what would transpire over the next hour.

Ben stopped walking and just stood. He could feel his pulse throbbing across his forehead, each beat of his heart a spear of pain through his brow. He was confused and couldn't focus on anything for a second. He stopped trying to work everything out and instead paid attention to his physical condition. Every heartbeat pushed more pressure upwards into his throat until each thump rang in his ears. He halted and stood stock still, having arrived close to a set of white plastic rails which indicated the lead-in chute from the racecourse. The back of the stands was filling up with people now, all jostling to get a glimpse of the winner of the race and soon Ben was surrounded by excited, bustling race-goers. He was oblivious to them.

He remembered Esme's words again. 'Think of the people you love. Those still with you and add colour to your life. Then bring them to the front of your mind and push the rest to the recesses of your conscious thoughts. Concentrate on breathing, not huge gulps; take short, positive breaths to bring your heart rate down.'

Ben closed his eyes and concentrated, and succeeded in clearing the worries and anxiety from the here and now. He took several shortened breaths, thankfully feeling his heart rate slow as he did. He thought of Max and Mojo and, flicking his eyes open again, looked to the sky as he took another short gulp of air into his lungs. He recalled the three of them playing in the back garden at home. Things settled, he relaxed a little and the drumming in his chest became less strident. He brought his gaze down from the heavens and they came to rest on the winner of the two o'clock race being led in by a stable hand, jockey still on board, acknowledging the applause and calls of congratulations from the crowd. The horse was flanked by two prim sponsorship women wearing gaudy red sashes with the sponsor's name emblazed across them and dressed like out of place air hostesses complete with the small pointless hats. The whole entourage made its jaunty way towards Ben.

He never understood why including female models draped in sponsorship regalia was a requirement for important races on the flat. Placing them to walk in high heels on grass in front of tired racehorses was frankly ludicrous as all they ever did was getting in the way. Ben accepted it was simply an insidious ploy to get the sponsor's name into the television coverage, but watching them approach it struck him as dated and faintly ridiculous. He looked over the rails at the two models as they walked by, having to comically increase pace to a trot every fifth or sixth step in order to ensure they kept far enough ahead of the winning horse without getting their stilettos stuck in the soft turf.

The mare, stable lad and jockey preceded by the two tottering models continued onwards, being lost from Ben's view as the crowd pushed further towards the winners enclosure. He turned to fight away from the rails as some sort of clouded memory struck him. Something about that winning group was gnawing at him. But his head pulsed with pain when he tried to dredge the memory up, and an answer wasn't forthcoming. He let the annoying lost memory fade from his thoughts and pushed away from the walkway, eventually coming to the edge of the crowd and to an area less congested.

His mobile buzzed in his pocket and retrieving it from his inside pocket, he saw a text message from Joss. It simply stated 'The eagle has landed.' Relieved, he was about to set off back to the owners bar to round up the syndicate, but a hand appeared under his elbow and Ben turned to look into one of the most recognisable faces in racing.

In a silky smooth Middle Eastern accent Sheikh Abu Kamsun said 'I do apologise Mr Ramsden, I didn't intend to startle you.'

Swarthy and immaculately dressed, the member of the Saudi Arabian royal family held out a hand in greeting and his eyes sparkled as Ben shook a warm dry hand.

Still a little star struck, Ben replied 'That's fine. I was… elsewhere for a moment.'

Abu Kamsun smiled broadly 'I can imagine. You have a wonderful colt on your hands Mr Ramsden and I am sure you will want to concentrate on the race. I merely wished to congratulate you on finding such a talented horse and wish luck to you and your trainer, Mr O'Hoole I believe?'

'Yes that's correct,' said Ben uncertainly, but after a few seconds recovered. 'I'm delighted you like our horse and I'm sure your own will give us a run for our money.'

'Oh, you can be certain of that!' replied Kamsun with another broad grin.

Kamsun was probably the wealthiest owner in the world, with over a thousand horses in training in three different continents and a multibillion dollar interest in bloodstock. Ben spied Kamsun's trainer in Newmarket over his shoulder, catching his eye and receiving a smile and a nod in return. Kamsun was well known for his bottomless pockets, his affable nature and his penchant for buying up progressive horses. Ben was expecting his approach was a pre-cursor to a conversation about selling The Ghost, but was disarmed when the Sheikh enquired after Max.

Momentarily taken aback Ben stared vacantly into the Arab's face, but recovered once again to reply 'Thank you for asking, Sir, he is very well considering...'

'Please, Abu will do fine, Mr Ramsden.' interrupted Kamsun waving away the title.

'Well, he is fine, I'm sure you are aware he lost his Mother...'

'Yes, I was abroad at the time when watching the race and was shocked. I hope you do not mind the suddenness of my introduction, but I have been wanting to wish you well and tell you I am impressed with your fortitude in the face of such a calamity, but also you ability to locate good quality horses for such little outlay.'

Somewhat floored for the second time, Ben thanked the Sheikh again.

'Well, I see you may have other well-wishers. The race awaits Mr

Ramsden. May the best horse win.'

And with that Kamsun nodded, turned and was immediately joined by his trainer and two bodyguards whom Ben had only just noticed, and the group headed off towards the parade ring.

Before he could follow, another voice called his name from over his shoulder, female this time. 'Ben, good to see you, I'm soooo… excited for you.'

He spun around to be greeted with a beaming Eleanor Hart in full flow. She had a gaggle of about a dozen people around her who she started to introduce at a terrifying rate. They included friends, relatives and from what Ben could make out, a number of other breeders and the odd trainer or two, including the trainer and connections of two of the other runners in the Greenham.

After a chaotic round of hand pumping, he was asked a few banal questions about the horses chances which he answered quickly, while Eleanor smiled beatifically, holding his left arm linked tightly in hers. She could be a bit of a snob at times and Ben felt he may have unwittingly become a pawn in a game of 'I know more people than you', a racecourse pastime in which Eleanor was an expert. It was only after he had thanked the group and excused himself to join his own syndicate that he realised the trainer of Panama had been among the Hart entourage, albeit on the periphery. The poor man must have been snagged earlier by the force of nature that was Eleanor Hart, thought Ben as he hurried over to the parade ring entrance.

There were another few handshakes and calls of 'Good Luck' before he entered the parade ring. As he crossed the grass to his own group of owners he realised he was feeling much better. His headache had subsided. Kamsun and Eleanor must have kept me busy long enough to forget my woes he reasoned before joining his gaggle of owners.

Ben was aware of the heavy media presence and the interest concerning the 'horse that killed an owner' which surrounded this race. The Racing Post had run a leader that morning highlighting the rematch of The Ghost Machine and Panama and drawn comparisons with the York race – the last time both horses had run last season. However, such was the public interest even they had devoted a number of paragraphs to retelling the York incident. Ben had already spotted two different sets of television crews roving around the parade ring.

Duncan was there with Ian, Rob, the Dunn's, busy regaling them with the story of the journey to the racecourse. When Duncan saw Ben he gave him a strong handshake and pointed out that they had only just got the colt to the track in time.

'Joss was tacking him up as we took him out of the box.' said Duncan gasping for breath. 'I've just legged it from the car park to get in.' He confirmed the colt was fine and shook his head when asked about the flat tyres stating 'Long story, I'll tell after the race and over a stiff drink.'

All of the runners were now parading with their stable hands around the circuit with large crowds of about four deep watching on behind the rails. Inside the parade ring the different groups of connections huddled together in discussion. Ben looked around the turf ring and located the trainer of Panama, Billy Bentham, who must have extricated himself from the company of Eleanor. Sheikh Kamsun stood in deep conversation with his trainer, his suited entourage ringing the two of them. Ben also counted off three or four more trainers he recognised with fancied runners.

He also caught a glimpse of Kurt Wildman, the trainer of the only foreign runner in the race, an unbeaten three-year-old called Gutenberg. There was no sign of The Ghost, and every eye from Ben's group was focused nervously on the pre-parade ring gate from which the colt should appear.

'Here he is,' said Duncan, the first to spot the big grey with his signature brown black diamond on his forehead and white mane. His well combed mane was being caught and flicked by the breeze as Joss and Jake led the colt through the gate, across the walkway and into the parade ring. Joss said a few words to Jake and then looked up to locate his owners.

A shout and a number of hand waves saw Joss jog across the paddock to be greeted warmly by everyone. Everyone that is, apart from two of their number.

As Joss reached the syndicate, Armitage and Demetri, who had appeared at the parade ring gate without being noticed, joined the back of the six owners. Demetri stood across from Ben with hands held together in front of him in a purposeful pose, legs apart, face serious and unsmiling. Meanwhile Armitage held out a hand to Joss who took it gingerly and gave it a halfhearted shake. Both men wore dark grey tailored suits with black ties, Armitage having clearly made an effort compared to his usual shabby garb. When Ben examined the man closely he was curious. Armitage was clean shaven, had more colour in his face and he also seemed to have lost some weight from his neck and chin. Ben was transfixed for a few seconds.

'As an owner of this animal, we have the right to...,' Armitage started in his high pitched smarm.

'Yes, yes,' Ben interjected irritably.

'You're at a racecourse not in a court of law. Just be civil and don't embarrass yourself in front of the cameras.' Ben gestured toward the three man television crew which were moving closer to them, trying to get sound bites from trainers and connections.

He left the two men to have a stilted conversation with Joss, Armitage asking the questions, Demetri looking on.

Duncan and the two Dunn ladies turned their backs to Armitage and started a separate conversation and Ben noticed Ian quietly sidling around the group and edging towards the two men as they concentrated on what Joss was saying. He was then turning to view the stands which faced the back of the course and the parade ring.

Ben caught the back end of a question Armitage was asking, something about the way The Ghost Machine was walking around the ring. Ian suddenly interrupted Armitage, stating in a stern voice 'I see your boss isn't too happy with you!' he then flicked his eyes to the stand.

Armitage, momentarily lost for words, shot a glance to the right-hand end of the stand and then quickly looked back to Ian with both brows furrowed.

'Too late,' Ian murmured and broke into a wide smile.

He turned to Ben and called Duncan and the rest of the syndicate across.

'The person responsible for forty percent of The Ghost machine is here. He, or she, is in the stands to the top right. Do you see – with the binoculars and the phone to their ear.'

They have listening, and most probably, communication devices on them,' explained Ian gesturing to Armitage and Demetri. 'You can see the buds in their ears.'

As one, the entire syndicate turned and looked up towards the stand and focused on the right-hand side of the viewing gantry and the distant figure standing on its own. It was almost certainly a man, casually dressed and leaning against the rail, looking down on the parade ring from about seventy feet away.

Duncan had whipped out a small pair of fold up binoculars from his suit pocket and squinted up.

'He's seen us looking at him and he's off,' reported Duncan. 'That's it, he's disappeared inside the stand.'

Ben turned back to face Demetri and Armitage and found their backs were receding quickly out of the parade ring. He considered for one moment whether to follow them and demand explanations, or even to run over to the stands and find the man who had been watching them, but he quickly dismissed this idea. The jockeys were starting to come down the steps of the weighing room and out into the parade ring, and there were definitely more pressing issues in the next few minutes.

Joss had been collared by one of the TV reporters and was giving an interview when Raul walked up wearing the syndicate's distinctive white silks with a black star on his chest and back. He gave a nervous smile and shook all seven hands, with each syndicate member in turn greeting and wishing him well. Meanwhile, the horses continued to be led around the parade ring.

Joss made his excuses and rejoined the group, now huddled closer together. He nodded to Raul and then quickly ran over the riding plans which every member there had heard at least twice before, but it seemed only right to repeat them now.

'Slow and steady to the start, don't let him stride out or he might get excited and bolt. We're in stall 12 on the outside, so we'll go in towards the end, so keep him away from them and out to the back until you're called,' Joss instructed Raul to a series of rapid nods from the young pilot.

'It's essential he gets a decent start today. It's only seven furlongs and we need to make plenty of use of him, so get him out and up into a share of fourth or fifth. We don't want him out the front; we need to get a lead. Hopefully there will be plenty of pace in the race as I think seven is probably his minimum trip now – we could do with it being run at a really decent clip and it to become a bit of a test of stamina. But get him within a couple of lengths throughout.'

Raul, his eyes locked with Joss's was nodding to each instruction.

'I'll be just off the pace and ride him just like we did over seven at York last year. He loved passing them that day.'

Joss added 'Yes, that's fine, but it's a wide track here, so make sure you keep him concentrated on what's going on in front of him, don't allow him to come off that inside rail if you can. Then if you're in the right position and you've still got horse under you, ask him to go win his race well over a furlong out. He'll need time to pick up.'

'I know, boss,' confirmed Raul. 'There was a bit of turbo lag last time, but when he got going, he flew.'

The mounting up bell was rung at the other end of the parade ring and Raul tipped the brim of his cap to everyone and walked towards the big grey horse to further calls of good luck from his owners. Ben watched Joss give Raul a leg up and then turned back to the syndicate and said he would see them back at the unsaddling area afterwards and again wished them all the best of luck.

'You watching it on your own?' Duncan asked as they walked towards the parade ring exit.

'Yes. I'm far too nervous to be with other people while he's racing, you can go and stand with Joss in the stands. Is that ok?'

'Just as I would expect,' replied Duncan, slapping Ben on the shoulder playfully. He disappeared into the crowd once they got to the stands and Ben made his way to a spot on the rails just behind the winning post so that he could watch the race on the big public television screen, but also be close enough to the unsaddling area to ensure he could get there quickly afterwards.

Once he had his pitch on the rails, Ben looked back at the stands, nervously waiting for the race to start. There was a familiar knot of apprehension in the pit if his stomach and he could feel a couple of beads of sweat pricking on his forehead. He took out a white handkerchief and dabbed them away. He was feeling much better now, but the bump on his forehead was still sore, although considerably reduced in size. The huge

TV screen showed the last of the twelve runners making their way to the start. A number of them had already got there and were milling around in front of the starting stalls.

Ben turned and looked back at the crowd in the stands. It was cool for April, but there was still a close to capacity crowd and the stands were almost full. No one was paying any attention to him and he seemed to be surrounded by other owners and a few stable lads who were there to watch the race and then sprint to collect their charges straight afterwards. He cast his eyes over the crowd, wondering where Armitage, Demetri and the other mystery owner might be, hoping to perhaps catch a glimpse of them. But the volume of positions to watch the race were too numerous, and Ben quickly realised the chances of picking them out of the fifteen thousand people present was highly unlikely. After running over countless rows of race-goers he turned back to the rails and raised his head to the TV screen. The public address announced the horses were going into the stalls and Ben gripped his racecard harder.

Down at the seven furlong pole Raul sat quietly on The Ghost, the two of them stood motionless about thirty yards from the stalls. He gave his stirrups a small push with his feet, a nervous tick he'd never really lost since learning to ride at the age of five. He adjusted his position in the saddle, happy with the firmness of the girth strap. The big grey stood stock still and looked over towards the mass of trees and bushes which surrounded the start, the breeze picking up his white mane and flicking tufts one way then the other. The starter called the first few horses in and so Raul coaxed the grey to walk a little closer to the starting stalls.

Raul had never ridden in a Group race, and this was a Group Three, worth over thirty thousand pounds. He had joined The O'Hoole stable at sixteen, after spending most of the previous five years working, rather than studying for his GCSE's, at a small riding stables in West Yorkshire. On his sixteenth birthday his Father had taken him on a bus to Middleham and one by one, had walked to every single racing stable and been turned away until one of the trainers had given them directions to the O'Hoole's, which was some way out of the main town. They had walked the two and a half miles to the stable down country roads, by which time it was late evening, and knocked on the yard gates. Joss himself had come to the gate, met his father and Raul had been at the yard ever since.

He had come through the apprentice ranks at the O'Hoole stable, but it was only last summer that he started to get regular daily rides. With a fifteen percent strike rate he'd ridden twenty-two winners in the last two months of the summer season, but with limited rides through the winter, he was still on less than fifty winners and therefore claiming his five pounds allowance, given to young riders who had yet to reach the fifty winner mark. Whilst this was an important ride today, probably the most important of his riding career to date, Raul never felt more relaxed that when on the back of a horse.

The Ghost Machine gave a nervous snort as they watched another three horses being led forward and installed and Raul looked beyond the stalls down the seven furlongs of the straight course at Newbury which terminated with the cluster of stands. It was a wide track, built for a galloping horse like The Ghost, and Raul's first job would be to get him out of the stalls quickly and to find the horse some cover.

The starter called another two runners forward and a stalls handler strode over to the horse and rider and placed his lead rope through The Ghost's bit and stood waiting for the last few to load ahead of him. Raul saw the gate close behind the second last horse and gave The Ghost the instruction to walk forward and the two of them slid quickly and quietly into their stall on the far outside of the field. The gates clicked into position behind them and Raul felt the horse tense under him as the starter raised his flag.

The first impact came before the gates opened. It was a sharp ping which rocked his helmet and sent his centre of balance over to the left of the stall. The second, only a second later made a dull thumping noise into the top of his neck and a spear of crushing pain seared down Raul's right–hand side as the starting gates opened. Off balance and touching a hand to his ear in reaction to the pain, Raul lurched dangerously to the left as The Ghost propelled himself forward through the gate. Raul bounced off the inside of the gate and was sent rocking backwards and out of the saddle.

On his inside, Raul caught a blurred glimpse of the rest of the field, an indistinct mass of horses and riders. He held tightly to the reins with his left hand and tried to lever himself back over the rim of the saddle as The Ghost fought him, wanting to go forward. In a moment which commentators later described as 'defying gravity' The Ghost gave a staccato buck once he was free of the stalls. The upward motion sent Raul up off the horse's rump and threw him forward through the air, arms flailing, landing halfway up the horse's neck. He instantly scrabbled wildly for balance, whip spiralling away beneath the thrashing hooves, grasping the reins with one, then the other hand while the horse took a few more steps forward.

Raul managed to slide painfully back down and into the saddle while still desperately trying to get control of the reins, both feet desperately gripping the flanks of the horse, stirrups flapping loose. In the meantime The Ghost still went forward, although each stride also took him sideways towards the outside rail. Raul fought to get into a racing position on the horse, his balance starting to feel right again. The pain now seemed to be centering on right ear, fanning out in stinging hot ripples. He pushed the pain away, concentrating on regaining full control and was relieved when his toe found his left stirrup. He dug his toe into place and finally adopted some semblance of a racing crouch and pushed The Ghost forward. A stride later he angled the colt's white head to the left and gunned him towards the back of the pack, now many lengths in front of him.

Ben's heart folded within him as he watched Raul struggling to stay in contact with The Ghost. The initial anxiety for the safety of the horse and rider was replaced by a hollow acceptance of the situation. When Raul regained control of the colt the TV angle changed to show the effect of the extraordinary exit from the stalls and the nervous tension ebbed away from Ben as realisation dawned. The Ghost's chance of getting competitive in the race had been dashed already. By the time Raul had found a foot in a stirrup he was ten lengths behind the field and a further four lengths away from the leading horse. Over a seven furlong straight trip the chance of making up that sort of ground in a top class race was negligible.

The on course commentator boomed The Ghost Machine's name over the public address system, reporting on the great recovery from Raul but ruling him out of contention.

Ten strides into the race Raul found his second stirrup and collected himself, crouching low and allowing the Ghost Machine to simply bowl along at his own speed. As he bent over the horses' mane, holding the reins softly in his hands the six furlong pole flashed past. He considered throwing everything at the horse to achieve a position where he could tag onto the back of the pack. But that would almost certainly leave him with no finishing speed, but there was a small chance that if the pace was quick, he could perhaps pick off a few in the latter stages of the race. With the finishing line still indistinguishable in the distance Raul made the decision to allow The Ghost to dictate his own pace and let the race unfold as the horse wished.

The five furlong pole scudded by and Raul crouched lower as the grey horse pounded behind the field, the odd clod of turf being thrown in his way by the ruck of horses in front of him. There was the noise of the horses' hooves hitting the ground, the expiration of air from the horses' lungs in regular snorts and the wind whipping through The Ghost's mane, through which Raul looked straight ahead and worked in concert with the animal. Motionless, apart from the faintest of rubs to The Ghost's withers, Raul could sense the horses at the back of the pack inching closer to him. The four furlong marker flashed past and ahead one of the back markers had his pilot working hard, the jockey animated as he urged his mount forward. Raul edged The Ghost to the right, drew alongside the opponent and left him behind within three strides.

Raul felt a sting of pain to the right-hand side of his neck as he moved the horse over, but pushed it away again, concentrating on what was happening ahead of him through the horses' ears. Another two started to come under pressure and The Ghost reeled them in, doing his own work, still in the same rhythm he'd been in since his fifth stride of the race, Raul still sitting motionless. There seemed to him to be many lengths still between himself and the horses at the head of the race but The Ghost now had other horses to spur him on and he went between two runners as the red and white three furlong pole disappeared in Raul's peripheral vision.

Another furlong and another two horses fell behind The Ghost. Cries of encouragement from riders flicked through the air and then were lost. A sharp crack of a whip just in front of him made The Ghost change legs and move around the flailing arms and legs of a spent force. In front of him Raul counted five horses and riders, three only two lengths in front and another two runners with four lengths on them. The final furlong pole could now be distinguished, emerging from the inside rail and suddenly the green fields were no longer alongside the track as instead, a sea of people and buildings became the backdrop.

For the first time in the race, Raul started to ask the colt for more. He pushed his hands up the horse's neck in time to his stride. As if flicking a switch, The Ghost's nose dipped lower and the horse stretched towards the three horses in front of him. They came to him far quicker than Raul was expecting and suddenly there was a three length gap to the horse in second place and another three or four to the last horse to pass, with the fourth, fifth and sixth horses receding quickly behind.

Now Raul heard a burst of excitement from the crowd and he was dimly aware of The Ghost Machine's name bouncing around the stands. The horse responded, pushing harder from his hind legs and finding more for him. The finishing pole was only a hundred yards in front of him and he pushed the grey forward with more urgency. The leading horse was well in front, but the second placed colt was possibly within striking distance. The horse in second place edged right but The Ghost compensated, following the same trajectory, every stride brought him closer as the horse in front started to wobble and founder as his internal fuel dissipated and its stride shortened with every step. The finishing line was now only strides away and still Raul pushed. The Ghost found further stamina for him, nostrils flaring, the once rhythmic snorts now closer together. They were on the opposing horses' flanks, on its shoulder, alongside. Both horses flashed past the winning post together, both riders lunging desperately in that final stride.

Raul caught his breath, extended his knees, and pulled back on the reins softly to bring The Ghost's head up. Then he noticed the spots of blood which flecked the horse's mane and ran down the hairs, some already congealing. He looked down at his silks which were much the same, thin red rivulets of wet and drying blood peppered the white areas and disappeared into the star on his chest. Instinctively his right hand went up to his ear and he winced at the pain his probing fingers created

Bringing his hand back down Raul found himself rubbing a sticky red treacle of blood between forefinger and thumb.

He'd seen his own blood before, a life in a racing stable had meant Raul had fallen off, been kicked, bitten, and bashed by horses on a daily basis for the last six years. But hell's teeth, he thought, there seemed to be a lot of it on him.

The Ghost Machine finally came to a halt about a furlong and a half past the post and Raul allowed the colt to just stand and catch his breath. He gave the three year old a pat down the neck, turned and hacked back towards the stands. After only a couple of cantered strides Raul could see Joss, Ben and Jake running down the track towards him, so he slowed the colt to a walk again.

Joss was first to the colt, shouting up at Raul 'You okay son?'

'Yes, I think so. I don't really know what happened,' he shouted back.

Jake arrived and put a lead on The Ghost and stood him, rubbing the grey's forehead and slapping his neck. Ben was last there, also asking Raul if he was okay. Joss indicated for Raul to drop off the horse and once he was on the ground Joss held the jockey's head carefully in one hand and removed his helmet with the other, tossing it to Ben.

'Look at that,' he said, indicating a large welt on Raul's neck. 'Someone has had a go at you with an air rifle by the look of it. One of the pellets hit your neck; the other has ripped your earlobe. You might need a stitch in that.'

Ben produced a handkerchief and told Raul to remain steady, carefully folding the cotton square so it curled around the bottom of his ear, then put some pressure on it.

'Hold still, we'll just try and stem the flow. We'll get you to the course doctor. Oh, and by the way, bloody good ride. Who needs a whip eh!'

Raul nodded his appreciation but winced at the flower of pain the motion created.

Joss looked up and as he expected, the ambulance crew, media, and racecourse officials were making their way over the track to them. He quickly went around the colt to make sure he was well and swore when he got to the other side of The Ghost.

'Jake. Give me his sweat sheet,' demanded Joss, indicating the sponsor's sheet the stable hand had tucked under his arm. He took it and threw it over the grey and quickly pulled it over at both sides and tied it under him.

'What's wrong?' asked Ben.

'I thought there was something not right when he bunny hopped and launched Raul backwards after the stalls opened. They've shot him in his flank. The pellet is still in him – I can see it,' replied Joss angrily.

'We've enough going on with the positive dope test without this hitting the headlines. There's no lasting harm, both of them will be fine, but we can do without the exposure – agreed?'

Ben nodded. The ambulance was pulling up to them now and Joss bowed his head close to Raul.

'Listen lad, you'll be fine. And by the way, Ben was right; you rode a lovely race on him in the circumstances. But you tell this lot that you jumped from the stalls awkwardly and must have caught yourself somehow. Okay? We don't want this coming out just yet.'

Raul gave a single positive nod before two ambulance staff arrived and started asking questions. Satisfied that he was lucid and in no immediate danger, they walked Raul slowly towards the ambulance and he disappeared into the back before being driven away.

Joss turned his attention to Jake who was leading the horse around in circles, but before he could say anything a public address system announcement boomed across the racecourse.

'Here is the result of the photo for second place,' said the male voice followed by a dramatic pause. 'There is a dead heat for second place.' And again a pause.

'Here is the official result of the Greenham Stakes. First, number eight, Panama. Second in a dead-heat is number six, Landing Lucky and number twelve, The Ghost Machine. SP's are…'

Several people now milled around the colt, far more than usual for a runner up in a Group Three race. Joss gave several instructions to Jake and the stable hand immediately set off to the winners enclosure with The Ghost Machine.

Ben knew one thing: He had to get over to the seven furlong start and see what he could find. Whoever was over there firing pellets at Raul might still be there.

Joss found the clerk of the course hurrying over to him and so took him aside and gave him a quick explanation after which the various Newbury staff members started to disperse. The TV were next and again, Joss gave a short few comments to the effect that Raul was fine apart from a minor cut which had been caused by the horse exiting the stalls awkwardly. Yes, the horse had returned sound and yes, he was aware that given the problems at the start The Ghost Machine had run a very credible race.

With the TV crew making off to interview the winning connections, Joss and Ben followed The Ghost back to the chute and through to into the winners enclosure. The Ghost was the last to enter, and took a long drink of water when it was offered to him.

The rest of the syndicate found their way into the winner and placed horse unsaddling ring and huddled round Joss and Ben, with questions being fired in from all angles.

Ben peeled off from the group and looked over to the other side of the enclosure where the winning connections were camped out in front of the first placing signage along with Panama. Trainer Billy Bentham was being interviewed for television, a large microphone being held to his heavily bearded face by one of the racing channel correspondents.

Bentham looked as unkempt as always, perhaps even more so today in a Tweed suit which appeared to be at least a size too small, displaying an inch of grey sock at the bottom of his trousers. But the man could train a racehorse Ben thought to himself. He was less prolific now, but a decade ago he had been the leading trainer in the country with horses being sent by leading owners from around the world. Now he had another potential champion on his hands.

Panama's owner, James Corrigan, beamed expansively as he held the horse's reins for photographs. In his late forties, with a pronounced jaw line and known for a modicum of self-promotion, he had made a small fortune from suspended ceilings of all things. As the photographers parted, Corrigan caught Ben's eye and flushed slightly, but recovered to tip his Panama hat to him. Ben was caught unawares and awkwardly gave a half wave back to the other side of the winners enclosure. There had been anxious apologies offered on the day, a letter of condolence sent to the house and plenty of column inches in the sporting press about how horrified Corrigan and Bentham were regarding the accident with their racehorse, but today was the first time he'd seen them both since that day last summer.

Panama himself looked to be calm and at no risk of any repeat of his deadly actions from the previous summer. Ben noted with grim realisation that while Corrigan held the leather straps around colt's head, smiling and answering reporter's questions, there was also the same stable lass who had also been at York, gripping tightly onto the colts head collar, as well as his lead rein. A Newbury steward stood to the side of the group, ensuring a few yards of space was being maintained behind the colt, waving a few people away as the colt moved around the winners enclosure.

The television crew wrapped up their interview with Bentham and moved onto Corrigan. As the personnel in front of the camera changed, Ben's eye was caught by the woman standing in the background on the steps of the weighing room. It was the promotions girl he had noticed earlier in the day, standing with a colleague. Ben glanced at his racecard and realised that the Greenham and the race before were both sponsored by the same company, so she must have led Panama in after his win. Ben looked more closely at her, moving a few yards to the left to get a better view. There was something about her which was gnawing at him for some reason, and it wasn't just her looks.

She was certainly model material. Ben guessed she was in her early twenties and about five ten, although her heels might add an inch or two. Then there were the striking brown eyes and chestnut hair which ran in ringlets down to just over her shoulders. She wore a plain white dress which was quite conservative, and the sponsor's silk sash ran from her shoulder to her hip. A perfectly symmetrical face and a stance which Ben supposed was classic model's 'way to stand', with one leg just in front of the other to accentuate her curves. But that wasn't it. There was something about her face which he couldn't quite place.

The girl was smiling and scanning the winners enclosure, standing alongside another promotions girl in an identical outfit. Her gaze passed over Ben, but then suddenly flicked back and she locked eyes with him for a long few seconds, her plastic smile fading into uncertainty for a few moments. Awkwardly, she broke the connection to Ben, looked down, composed herself, and then resurrected the smile again. She returned to scanning the audience, but to a higher level this time, which excluded Ben.

He started to make a move towards her but as he took his first step the 'horses away' public announcement was made and the winners enclosure started to clear for the presentations. Ben cursed and filed out of the enclosure with the rest of his syndicate and other connections of the placed horses and was soon got caught up in another conversation about Raul's injury and subsequent excellent ride with Janet and Olivia Dunn. Joss offered his apologies, which was accepted by everyone, and then sprinted off to oversee The Ghost being washed down. Ben assumed the trainer was also aiming to ensure the pellet was removed from the horse's flank.

Now caught in the seething mass of race-goers straining to find an unobscured view, Ben watched the presentations for the Greenham. But his mind was elsewhere, flicking through the thoroughly weird set of events which had led to this moment.

First it looks like the horsebox has been sabotaged, then Armitage turns up in the parade ring as if butter wouldn't melt, along with his boss, who himself melts into the stands when he's spotted. Then we've got someone at the seven furlong seemingly taking potshots at Raul and The Ghost Machine, and even so he runs an incredible race to finish four lengths behind a horse that kicked and killed his wife eight months ago. Ben's head spun with conflicting ideas and impossible links between the incidents.

One by one, the owner, trainer, and then jockey of Panama were presented with various mementoes or bottles of champagne with applause from the onlookers in the crowd when they were announced. However Ben was concentrating on the promotions girl. She now flanked the host and the sponsor, radiating her plastered on smile for the photographers.

The faintest of smells of cooking sausages from one of the on course eateries wafted across on the breeze, that unmistakable combination of hot fat and sizzling sausage meat… and a memory burst into Ben's thoughts. That day at Joss's yard, when the two police officers had called around, they'd been eating Sunday brunch. Ben dug deeper and a realisation surfaced. It was the WPC, she'd had the same face, the same... eyes. Different hair, in fact, no hair, she'd had it bunched up behind her cap. But the same makeup, yes, those pretty-doll looks. She'd had similar make-up and earrings. Could it really be her?

Ben checked himself. How could this be right? A promotions girl at the races at Newbury is also a police officer up in North Yorkshire? He supposed it could be possible, but surely he had this all wrong.

He looked over at the girl again, straining to make a positive identification when a large, firm hand dropped onto his shoulder and a deep eastern European voice said his name. He turned and wasn't too surprised to find Demetri staring down at him. A momentary parting of the clouds allowed the sun to suddenly beat down, backlighting the man's shaved head. Ben found himself shading his eyes with a hand as he looked up into a face which gave absolutely nothing away.

'Mr Ramsden,' Demetri repeated dolefully. 'It is time for you to meet Mr Pod.

Sixteen

Ivan Podogrocki stood on the balcony of his private suite, leaning with both arms on the viewing rail at the top of the Berkshire Stand. He disdainfully took in the vista of over ten thousand race-goers spread over the enclosures below. They talked, shouted, read, watched, noted, walked, ate, and gambled. However, they were of no real interest to him. They were Ants. Ants, which crawled busily and ineffectively over each other. They achieved very little, if anything at all. He held a thumb and index finger close to each other, closed one eye and idly imagined how many could be crushed between the two.

Ivan wasn't relaxed in an environment like this, with so many people moving, touching, crammed into enclosures like cattle. He'd learnt from an early age that crowds of people provided plenty of cover for the one individual who may want to get close to you and inflict harm. It was one of the many drawbacks to having an oligarch for a father – a ready supply of people who would rather see you dead than alive, even if it was just by association. He drew back from the balcony, having enjoyed the sun playing on his face, but wary of the exposure it provided.

He pulled the glass doors apart and reentered the suite, being careful to close them behind him and cast an eye over the various period pieces of furniture which were scattered almost randomly around the room. Settling for a red velvet sofa against the wall he picked his way through the strange mixture of tables and chairs and carefully sat down, crossed his legs, placed his hands in his lap and waited.

About a minute later there was a single sharp knock at the door. Armitage, who had been sat silently in an armchair set back against the far wall, rose, unlocked the door to the suite, and after a cursory glance, allowed first Ben and then Demetri to enter.

Ben took in the room, which had antique furniture wall to wall, and a huge number of paintings, originals if he wasn't mistaken, seemingly on every suitable wall space the suite could offer. A number of Victorian style lamps provided the only lighting, with most of the room being lit by sunlight which filtered through the floor to ceiling glass wall at the far end of the suite. It reminded Ben of a London Men's club. The room had that tired, fusty tang of threadbare tradition.

'Ah, Mr Ramsden, the syndicate manager of our racehorse,' said Ivan, accentuating the first letter of Ben's surname in an accent which seemed to mangle some sort of Eastern European dialect with Glaswegian. Ben stared across the room to where the speaker sat, bolt upright on a hideous red velvet sofa tucked against the right-hand wall. He'd not even noticed the man when he'd first scanned the room, there was such a mash up of decor.

'According to Weatherby's, its Mr Armitage's racehorse,' Ben spat back, indicating the small bald man now standing beside him. He'd answered rather more cockily than he'd intended and took a few seconds to steady himself. The man on the sofa didn't move and stared back at him, looking Ben up and down with a critical eye.

'You are correct. But that will alter when the time is… suitable. I am Ivan Podogrocki and along with these gentlemen I own forty percent of the horse which lost its race today.'

Demetri touched Ben's elbow and guided him over to a sofa opposite Ivan and gestured for him to sit down.

'I can imagine that you may feel somewhat intimidated by the presence of all of us, so they will be leaving us,' Ivan said, waving a stiff two fingers towards his men and both Armitage and Demetri quietly left the room.

Ben was amazed at how young the man was. He was mid twenties, slim but muscular, with short straight hair parted rigidly. He wore a pale coloured linen suit and an unbuttoned silk shirt and Ben somehow got the sense the man was sitting uncomfortably.

Once the door had clicked shut, Ivan crossed his legs to display a pair of expensive rider-like boots. He switched his attention directly into Ben's eyes and continued abruptly. 'I wish to discuss The Ghost Machine with you. But first, I want know a few more things about you, Ben.'

'Mr Ramsden will do fine, you're not a friend. I've one of two questions for you too.'

'As you wish, Mr Ramsden,' Ivan replied curtly.

'Given I know nothing about you, and you have been attempting to sabotage my syndicate and The Ghost himself I don't see any need for me to explain anything about myself,' Ben exploded. He could feel his heart pumping and the first strands of anger working their way up from his chest towards his neck. He took a steadying few short breaths.

'I am not the one who has been hiding behind other people for the last fortnight. I am easily contacted and even have a website with a full description of who I am and what I do. That's information enough for you. I want to know who the hell you are and more importantly why you're trying to wreck my horse's chances.'

Ivan remained stoic and unmoved by the outburst. Ben's irritation was fanned further by the unflinching set of hard blue eyes set into a face that was far too skull like to rate as beautiful.

Now I see where Demetri gets his social skills from thought Ben as Ivan maintained his stare for an uncomfortable few more seconds.

Finally he opened his thin lips, licked them, looked towards the glass doors to the balcony, and in a measured tone said 'I deal in information Mr Ramsden. Information is my business and I am successful at acquiring it and using it to its full potential. I already know every recorded piece of information about you, your business and your family.'

Ben's pulse jumped on the mention of his family. Ivan must have read his reaction in his face as before Ben could reply he held up a wiry hand in a hushing motion.

'Your family and friends are not of interest to me. But sometimes in order to fully understand an individual, conversation is required. I wish it wasn't, as I find such a requirement tedious in the extreme,' Ivan said, looking away into the distance again.

'However, I need to understand you Mr Ramsden, as it appears there are many more complications to owning The Ghost Machine than I envisaged. You've become an important component in our involvement in bloodstock.'

'I don't know how you work that out,' Ben said, truly confused by what Ivan was saying. 'You've bought a percentage of a racehorse. I happen to run the syndicate which owns the controlling share and that's it – that's where our involvement ends.'

Ivan adjusted his position on the sofa slightly, issuing a small sigh as he did so. He examined the ceiling of the suite for a few seconds and then directed his steely gaze back at Ben.

'You should know that I rarely have to wait for information Mr Ramsden. Your profile suggested you would not release the information I require without some sort of explanation. So, I will provide it. Please relax yourself and listen to what I have to say. When I have finished I will ask my questions and hopefully you will give me the answers I require.'

Bewildered once again, Ben was unsure how to reply and instead found himself simply nodding his acceptance.

Ivan leant back on the sofa, still very upright with legs crossed, but with a slightly less alertness about him, as if the diatribe he was about to provide, although necessary, was a tedious exercise.

'You will find all of this information by doing a very simple internet search on my name. I am Ivan, my father is also named Ivan Podogrocki. Google him. He is a Polish industrialist but what the internet will not tell you explicitly is that his considerable wealth was mainly amassed through deeply illegitimate activities through the eighties and nineties. In a nutshell, my Father prospered in a country which favoured those entrepreneurs who were adept at bribery and corruption.'

Ben listened impassively, but he sensed distain in Ivan's voice as he spoke.

'My Father packed me off to Scotland to an expensive boarding school at the age of eight, his idea was to keep me out of the way as several attempts had been made on his life and other members of my family. Again, all of this is available online if you're interested. No doubt you have noted that I speak with a Scottish accent, this is because I remained in the highlands after completing my education. Scotland is also where I was first exposed to horseracing, at tracks such as Hamilton, Musselburgh and on the odd occasion, Ayr.'

Ivan sighed again, patently finding the act of explanation a joyless experience. Ben considered for a brief moment whether to ask a question, but thought better of it.

'Now we come to the part which is not freely available Mr Ramsden,' said Ivan fixing his hard, blue-eyed stare onto Ben once again.

'I have a skill. It involves the understanding of technology, the internet, and its architecture. In short, I am able to access information about people, companies, and countries which is highly valuable if you know how it must be leveraged. My resources are considerable. I do not hurt people, neither do my associates, and would certainly not harm an asset of my own.'

Ben was about to point out pumping drugs into a racehorse and the intimidation of owners blew his statement well out of the water, but Ivan anticipated his comment before he could get his first word out.

'I know, for example, that you will feel that some of the methods I have adopted in order to acquire our percentages in The Ghost Machine bordered on underhand. Your own psychological profile is interesting in this respect. You have a high requirement for being in a stimulating and unpredictable environment, which I presume horse racing offers, but yet you have virtually no appetite for bending the rules to your own advantage.'

A crooked grin swept across the thin lips and for the first time Ivan outwardly showed a modicum of enjoyment from the situation.

'That must be terribly trying for you,' Ivan stated mirthlessly.

Ben was at a loss as to what to say in reply. He leaned back on his sofa and considered the man who sat directly across from him, taking his time. Ivan was watching him carefully, Ben could see his eyes twitching as he took in changes in mannerisms and movement.

'I'm not interested in what you think of me,' Ben said with unconcealed contempt. 'You also failed in your attempt to buy The Ghost.'

'We own forty percent of a horse, which despite today's setback, which we will come to later, is now worth far more than I paid.'

Ben couldn't argue with that. Today's performance had been nothing short of incredible, and it now must place the horse as a leading contender for the Two Thousand Guineas.

'Now to the reason I have shared this information with you,' said Ivan, uncrossing and then crossing his legs again.

'There are currently two major bloodstock powers in Europe. There is room for one more and I intend to move into that space. The Ghost is the first of a number of colts and mares I wish to acquire in order to establish a breeding business. Until now I have been doing all of this through my associates, Mr Armitage and Mr McDonald.'

Ben's forehead creased 'Mr McDonald?' he questioned.

Ivan looked a little bemused and then the hint of a genuine smile spread over his face. 'Ah, I see. Demetri has been using his Mother's accent again has he? You will need to take that up with him. He really is incorrigible.'

'He's Scottish?'

'Oh yes, I thought that would be clear. We all are. And that's where the stud will be based and where The Ghost will stand as our first Group winning sire. This is why you are here Mr Ramsden, I don't meet with anyone face to face unless it is absolutely necessary.'

Ben was at a loss for words at the sheer cheek of the man. He stared over at Ivan, eyes wide, unable to stop his mouth dropping open. The whole day had been unreal since their arrival at the track, but now it had taken him into another even more jaundiced direction.

Finally he swallowed and managed to blurt out 'You'll need exceptionally deep pockets to make that happen.'

'Oh please Mr Ramsden,' Ivan responded levelly. 'Your aggression is becoming tiresome. You have managed to thwart my efforts to secure a controlling stake in the horse, and for that I congratulate you. However, we must now work together, and I'm sure our goals can be reached amicably.'

'Work together?' Ben exploded. 'After what you have done to The Ghost, the members of the syndicate and to Joss's livelihood you expect me to trust you and work with you?'

'But of course,' responded Ivan calmly. 'How else are you going to find out who is trying to derail your horse's season?'

Ben's heart missed a beat and silence descended on the room. A shaft of late afternoon sunlight streamed through the windows as the clouds parted outside and motes of dust were suddenly visible in the room, dancing in the air between the men.

He desperately tried to make sense of what he's just heard. 'You're a liar. You broke the law when you drugged those horses in an attempt to gain control of The Ghost.'

Ivan's eyes narrowed and Ben's confidence jumped a little. He had apparently touched a nerve.

'I drugged horses,' said Ivan slowly. He uncrossed his legs, stood and silently walked around the sofa. Ben felt the hairs on the back of his neck stiffen as he fought the intense need to twist his head around and follow the man's movements as he walked behind him. Ivan crossed the suite and stopped a foot away from the glass wall and looked out onto the racecourse, his back to Ben.

After thirty seconds of complete silence, where only the muffled sound of the public address system could be heard announcing runners, Ivan asked 'What colour are the racehorses which were drugged?'

'What?' replied Ben incredulously.

'Humour me, Mr Ramsden. Tell me colour of the drugged horses,'

Ivan insisted.

Ben, still sitting on the sofa but now facing the windows, let out a gasp of exasperation. Gripping the bridge of his nose between two fingers he tried to bring the horses concerned into focus.

Finally he answered 'Silvery Sun is a grey and the other is a roan mare.'

'The roan mare, describe her to me.'

Ben tried to visualise the mare. 'She's not a horse I know well, but she is very light coloured over her mane and back, almost ginger in places with flecks of grey around her neck and chest.'

'Her head?'

'I think she has a fairly wide white blaze and a snip of white on her nose.'

Ivan turned around, now stroking his bony chin between three long fingers on one hand. 'You believe it was I who introduced a drug into the O'Hoole training stables in order to force a change of trainer?'

Ben raised his eyebrows and opened his palms in a shrug. 'It looks that way doesn't it? You're certainly capable of it, you've already demonstrated that,' he added sardonically.

'If Joss had sold his ten percent you could now force him to forfeit his training and my syndicate could lose control of The Ghost. That's according to your own contract Armitage produced for Joss to sign.'

Ivan seemed suddenly invigorated and a grin returned to his face

'So Mr O'Hoole was ready to sign was he?'

Ben cursed to himself for being so open and responded 'Well he won't be signing now, or in the future,' in a catty rebuke.

Ivan snorted an unkind laugh and returned to the velvet sofa 'You really are one dimensional in your thinking Mr Ramsden. The colour of the horses is the key.'

Ivan continued to grin at Ben, his eyes blazing. He thought it was a more of a grimace the longer he looked at the man.

After a short pause Ivan burst out with another condescending cackle. 'Whoever did this got the wrong racehorse!' he exclaimed. 'They were after The Ghost.'

Unnerved, Ben tried to piece things together. But his confusion had obviously registered on his face as Ivan sniggered again and then continued.

'Given what happened to The Ghost out there on the racecourse, even a 'play it by the book' type like yourself should recognise what's happening. Someone is trying to stop The Ghost competing. I'm flattered that you thought it was me, but look at the evidence – I have nothing to gain from what happened today.'

Ivan paused, raising a thin black eyebrow, goading Ben to catch up.

Ben felt like the walls of his mind had suddenly crumbled and a new realisation took hold.

Still trying to piece things together he said 'You're saying someone was searching for a grey horse to dope at the yard because they were searching for The Ghost?'

Ben's mind rushed through this new possibility. Up until the day before Silvery Sun had been doped, The Ghost had been stabled in the same barn. He followed the logic to its conclusion and felt a little sick. Ivan said nothing and was staring wide-eyed, twirling a single finger in an annoying, childish 'come on, hurry up' fashion, so Ben continued.

'In that barn they find two grey horses beside each other, at least they look grey over the stable doors to someone who doesn't know the horse. I guess they think one must be The Ghost and administer the drug by syringe straight over the stable door, divided between the two greys to make sure they get the right one. But in fact neither is The Ghost...' Ben's voice tailed off.

Ivan greeted Ben's findings by raised both his hands and splaying his fingers wide like a magician; all that was missing was a 'tadaa!'

'It was a very lucky escape for The Ghost, as the vets report stated the level of drug in the horses affected was so high it may have had a negative impact to performance. If he'd been given the full dose I presume it may have killed him.'

'No, it wouldn't have killed him,' Ben corrected. 'But it would have lasted long enough in his system to be picked up a full two weeks later for today's race. Besides, how did you get hold of that report?'

Ivan sniffed 'As I said earlier Mr Ramsden, I have a skill which allows me to access virtually any electronically held information. I might add that the security systems Mr O'Hoole's vets employ are not worth the three thousand pounds a year it costs them according to their accounts.'

Ben only half listened to the reply, as he was feverishly working through the implications of what Ivan was suggesting.

'So you've investigated every member of my syndicate and determined what would motivate them to sell their shares?' Ben asked.

'We all have a digital footprint,' replied Ivan succinctly; clearly assuming this was enough of an answer.

When Ben shook his head in disbelief Ivan added 'Your car enthusiast was the easiest, we simply turned up with a Jenson Interceptor and Mr Maxwell couldn't wait to swap his share.'

Ivan, warming to his subject continued 'I was particularly pleased with Mrs Rowbottom and her philandering husband. We didn't even need to access anything particularly onerous, all the information was there in Companies House. Finding a shareholder willing to take a profit on enough shares to tip the balance of power was challenging, but again, you find the need and fulfill it. In that case it was the location of an estranged wife of all things!' He sounded gleeful, for the first time showing the exuberance of his age.

Ben started to ask a question but was halted before he could get his first word out. Ivan, on a roll, rattled through how he had tracked David White down and then set him up with two world-class poker players from Sweden. 'I play a few hands with them online every now again,' he explained.

'But gamblers are so predictable; there really wasn't any great joy in taking his share from him,' he opined.

It was the Rory Dent story which took Ben by surprise, not for its ingenuity, but the unlikely delicacy of its execution. Rory was gay, but you would never have known, as he was not overtly camp and was never seen out in public with a partner of either sex. He lived alone in Worcestershire and Ben had suspected he was homosexual but never broached the subject in conversation with him – it was none of his business.

'He wasn't a happy chap from an early age you know,' Ivan informed Ben as he stood, then walked casually over to a cabinet and poured himself a sparkling mineral water. He didn't offering Ben anything.

'He's stayed around Worcester all his life, so accessed his school reports from 1962 was easy enough. We found a few references in there which pointed us in the right direction. Then we contacted a few people that were friends at school. Did you know he's written three books of published poetry?'

Ben shook his head in response.

'His parents disowned him and threw him out of their rather up market home at the age of eighteen when his first book was published. The penny must have dropped, as some of the poems were obviously expressions of love for another man. We checked, and we're pretty certain it was for specific man he lived with for two years. It seems his partner walked out after a row of some sort when Rory was twenty and has never been seen since. Rory stopped writing, moved into an apartment in Worcester and became a librarian, eventually running all the libraries in the county,' said Ivan, sipping at his glass of water.

'I noticed from his bank account records that he took a flight once every autumn to Canada for a week. But he never stayed at the same places and seemed to move around erratically before heading back home. He did this for twenty-two years, can you imagine, twenty-two years of searching?'

'You hacked into his bank accounts? Ben interjected.

'I've told you Mr Ramsden, I never hurt anyone, I simply leverage the information,' replied Ivan, waving a couple of fingers derisively in Ben's direction.

'I'm guessing you found him?'

'Yes, we found the love of his life, in a small town called Watrous in Saskatchewan. He'd taken assisted passage as a schoolteacher to Ontario but then moved about and also changed his name until finally settling in a small town in the middle of the wheat belt. The change of name is was what caught Mr Dent out in his own search.'

'So you sold Rory the name and address of an ex-partner for the share in The Ghost?'

'I suppose you could look at it that way,' replied Ivan, looking thoughtful for a moment. 'He didn't want money for the share even though we offered it on top of the information from the outset. He was overcome when we told him his ex-partner was still alive and had been living happily with another man for over fifteen years. When he signed the share over to us we gave him the full name and address, but to my knowledge he's done nothing with it. Odd really. We had to assume that it was enough for him to know the love of his youth had enjoyed a good life.'

Ivan paused and looked at Ben, still sitting on the sofa. His face hardened.

'As I said earlier Mr Ramsden, we do no harm.'

'What happens if Rory actually wanted to track his ex down simply to kill him. How does that sit in your world of no consequences?'

'Ah, the rule book according to Mr Ramsden surfaces again,' said Ivan mockingly.

He continued 'The information we source is always true and correct. We do not deceive. What Mr Dent does with his information is his, and only his concern.'

Ben scowled and crossed his arms testily. This conversation was getting him nowhere. He was arguing with a zealot. Opposite him Ivan produced a thin phone from the inside pocket of his jacket and poked at the screen for a few seconds before slipping it back.

'So, are we up to speed in regard to the case of mistaken equine identity and doping of horses Mr Ramsden?'

It really chewed him up to agree, but Ben had to admit that Ivan's view of events made sense.

Ivan continued 'Someone has attempted to dope our racehorse, halt its progress to the racecourse and also shot at our jockey...'

'And the horse,' Ben muttered.

'Really? You managed to keep that under wraps.'

'Joss's idea. He thought there was enough bad press without adding petrol to the flames.'

Ivan nodded 'I agree. It would add unnecessary attention. I assume the horse is sound after his run?'

'Yes, he'll have a small wound from the air rifle pellet but nothing which will affect him ongoing. He'll have a few days out in the paddocks and should be fine. Joss removed the pellet and the course vet said nothing when he did a quick look-over after the race. It was the pellet that caused him to buck after he left the stalls.'

There was silence in the room again. Ivan refilled his glass with mineral water and the sounds of pre-race crowds and public address systems started to permeate the suite once again.

'Will you persist in attempting to control The Ghost?' Ben ventured.

Ivan produced another thin smile 'Oh yes. I understand they are called 'foundation' horses in breeding terms. He will be our foundation sire, or at least one of them.' He paused. 'But given we have this new issue of protecting our investment, I will desist from any acquisition activity for now.'

'You'll leave my syndicate alone?'

Ivan grinned again. 'Your book of rules must be a weighty tome Mr Ramsden. I will not approach your syndicate members any further until this matter is concluded. In return I expect you and you're syndicate to be available to me to aid my investigation. I expect to deal with the issue of who is perpetrating the attacks on The Ghost Machine and then we may continue his season without these distractions.'

Ivan's inside pocket quietly vibrated and he stood with a hand outstretched, indicating the meeting was at an end.

Ben hesitated, but eventually grasped Ivan's bony hand and shook it grudgingly. The sudden end to the conversation had set his mind whirling once again as he tried to place his experiences from today and the previous fortnight into some sort of logical shape, given the revelations from the last ten minutes.

While Ivan was a new age rogue, he really didn't benefit from any of the efforts to derail The Ghost Machine's racing season. The colt's value as a sire would be seriously adversely affected if he didn't compete. Ben wondered for a moment whether this could be a bluff, and Ivan was in fact trying to reduce the colt's value by stopping him running. He discounted this immediately. Ivan's shameless gloating over how he'd solved the doping riddle had been annoyingly genuine. It did look as if he was driven to enter the bloodstock business and unfortunately Ben and his syndicate were caught up in Ivan's plans. So there was still someone out there who for whatever reason, wanted to ruin The Ghost Machine's season.

'I've asked Mr O'Hoole to join me for a discussion. That should be him now,' said Ivan, checking his phone once again.

A few seconds later there was a single sharp rap at the door to the suite and Demetri pushed the door open and a rather flustered looking Joss walked in. Ben imagined this was how he himself had looked when he entered a few minutes ago.

'Oh, you've been ordered up here too have you? Everything okay?' asked Joss.

Ben rolled his eyes 'Sort of. We've a lot to discuss, but I guess

Ivan here will fill you in on most of it. I'm being released and you're next up.'

Behind him, Ivan shook his head.

Joss looked even more concerned at this statement, but Ben patted his arm and assured him. 'I'll see you after the last race down in the stables.' He said quietly before being ushered towards the door by Demetri.'

'Mr Ramsden,' called Ivan.

'I'm guessing that you're now on your way to the scene of the crime?'

Damn he was sharp thought Ben and tried desperately not to give anything away, putting as much of a poker face on as he could muster before turning to answer. But before he could open his mouth Ivan's eyes had pierced him.

'I thought so,' he said theatrically, switching his gaze.

'Demetri, please escort Mr Ramsden to the seven furlong start and let's see if there's anything there we can use,' said Ivan before the door clicked closed.

Seventeen

'How did it go with Mr Pod?' asked Demetri conversationally as he and Ben travelled side by side in the stand lift down to the racecourse concourse.

'You can drop the Polish accent now Mr McDonald,' Ben said ruefully.

'Och no. I rather like my Mother's tongue,' he replied in a gruff Highlands accent.

Ben looked up at the Scotsman to be met with a warm grin.

'Now you've met with Ivan I can drop the act,' he said, maintaining the Scottish twang, but now in a far softer voice.

'So the Polish accent is for when you are busy intimidating people?' Ben surprised himself with how angry this came out. He took a breath and tried to calm himself. The interview with Ivan had put him seriously on edge.

Demetri regarded Ben with a sallow expression. 'We're not crooks. I thought you'd worked that out by now. We never forced anyone to sell to us, we simply offered them what they wanted. That's all we ever do. We offer people what they want in return for what we want.'

That was the longest sentence he'd heard Demetri speak. Up to now he'd simply loomed in the background. Ben thought back, and to be fair, no violence had occurred in any meetings with them.

'There was an implication of intimidation,' he replied weakly and immediately wished he hadn't said anything.

Demetri laughed out loud now, holding his hand over his mouth as he guffawed deeply.

'What about those two at Ripon races then, I'm guessing they were the same ones who knocked on Olivia and Janet Dunn's door. They scared the ladies,' Ben barked back. He was starting to get the feeling that Demetri's character was insanely at odds with how he had originally appeared.

Demetri composed himself 'Ah *yes!*' he said, accentuating his last word. 'That's right, if I remember correctly it was you who attacked them... with a horse.'

The lift reached the bottom of the stand and the two men headed away from the crowds and out to the stabling block. Ben took the lead and the two of them made good progress towards the stables, but then crossed the track itself and onto the inside of the circuit. Ben was challenged by a member of the Newbury security, but after flashing his stabling badge was given access along with the excuse that the two of them were off to retrieve Raul's lost whip. There was only one more race to run before the meeting finished, over five furlongs, so there would be no horses or traffic up at the seven furlong start.

As they headed off on the inside of the course on the track which usually followed the race with judges and ambulances, Demetri drew up alongside Ben. They walked in silence for about half a furlong, Ben feeling he was taking two paces for every one of the big man beside him.

'How long you worked for Pod?' asked Ben.

'I don't work for him. We are a team and we all take equal shares in everything.'

'What, Armitage too?' Ben asked, somewhat taken aback. He'd been certain Ivan was the kingpin in the operation.

Demetri stopped walking. 'I know it's been a confusing time to this point, but now we've set you straight, you have to start trusting us. The three of us are equal partners and we have been for many years. Pod does his stuff, Armitage does his and I do mine.'

'But Armitage is a solicitor based in Newmarket. How does that fit?'

Demetri grinned warmly again. 'You must have visited the website, eh? As you've been told, Pod can access virtually anything which is held electronically. We needed a solicitor, so we created one. The owners of the firm in Newmarket aren't even aware that we've added a page on their website.'

'So you've added him to their business without them knowing?'

Demetri looked down reproachfully at Ben 'Be honest, how many times a month do you check every single page on your website. Would you really know if we'd changed anything on a hardly used page which once it's been written never gets looked at or updated from one year to the next?'

'But I called the office to speak with Armitage.'

'Did you ever get hold of him?'

Ben paused, trying to remember.

'Let me help you. The answer is no.' said Demetri. 'You won't have got hold of him because he doesn't work there. It was simply a tactic to ensure the shareholders would assume they were selling via a solicitor. Misdirection? Absolutely, but it's not illegal.'

The two of them started walking again. Ben said nothing, trying in vain to place everything into a logical order once again. Demetri allowed the silence to run on for another two furlongs before he put a hand on Ben's arm and stopped him again.

'Listen. I like you, you've got something about you, and what happened to your wife was, well…,' his voice tailed off for a few seconds.

'But as far as we're concerned we just want to beat the best at what we do. We've done that with stocks and shares and now we're going to do it with bloodstock.'

Ben held both arms straight out from his hips in frustration. 'But you know nothing about bloodstock, any of you – that's clear from how you've gone about this is a cockeyed way.'

'Ivan is the technical brain, Armitage gets things done, and I make things happen as they should. That's how it works,' said Demetri, setting off walking again. 'We've been together since school, the three of us, looking after each other.'

'What?'

'The three of us met at boarding school when we were eight years old, became friends, and discovered we work well together. We would steal out of school to go to racing and decided a long time ago that we'd start a stud in Scotland and make it the very best it could be – that meant acquiring the very best racehorses. We all decided that The Ghost Machine was the best available from his generation of two year olds.'

'But why not just go to the horse sales and buy what you need?'

Demetri looked sideways at Ben. 'Are the best stallions ever available at the sales?'

Ben had to admit that they weren't. The top three breeding operations in the world tended to retain their top class stock in order to maintain their dominance in the market.

'Although we're well set in terms of investment capital, even we can't acquire some things. And the very top class sires would be… difficult. However, a private syndicate with ten people in it, each with their own needs and foibles, well, that's a different matter. That was more our bag, and what's more, you owned a horse with exactly the right sort of profile.'

Ben walked on, not saying anything, aware that any small talk could be used against him. Whatever Demetri said, he had to remember how the three of them had swept forty percent of The Ghost away from his syndicate, and it would have been more if they could have made the deals. But it was difficult to maintain an aloof demeanour around Demetri. Begrudgingly, Ben was beginning to warm to the gently spoken Scottish giant.

As they passed the six furlong pole, the grass track running on their left, Ben pointed to the trees on the far side of the course. 'We need to cross the track, as the stalls were on the left-hand side today. There's no clear shot for anyone from the inside of the course, they must have been over there.'

Demetri nodded his assent and after a quick look over their shoulders they dipped under the white plastic rails and jogged over the lush grass to the other side of the track.

The starting stalls had disappeared, having been hauled off to start the later races further around the track, but Ben pointed out where they would have stood, easily referenced by the way the white rails came apart close to a white seven furlong marker and the indents in the grass where the wheels had been seated.

'What are you thinking? Two shots taken?' asked Demetri.

'No, Raul said he heard a ping off his helmet before the stalls opened. I think there were three shots, or maybe more.'

'Most air rifles are single shot, but you can get dual muzzles and they could have had two or more guns loaded up ready. The shot on The Ghost's flank managed to penetrate his skin so it must have been relatively close and probably a high powered gun,' said Demetri, looking around on the ground.

'So you know about guns then?' Ben ventured.

'I grew up on an estate in the highlands of Scotland with a Polish Father who loved hunting, what do you think?' Demetri said without looking up.

Feeling slightly chastised, Ben mumbled a half apology and started scanning the rough grassland beside the track. There was a swathe of long cut grass about twenty-five yards wide which ended in a ribbon of woodland. The trees were mature and already laden with newly sprouted fresh leaves, perfect cover for a hiding sniper.

Demetri continued to walk around, head-down.

'What are you looking for. Surely they shot from the trees over there?'

'Too far away. They'd need to be much closer. We're looking for a hollow or small ridge,' replied Demetri.

They found the spot a few minutes later. Ben noticed a small depression in the earth where the grass had been flattened, although someone had tried to tempt the seven inch long stems to stand upright again before they had left. There were twigs propping up some of the longer tufts of grass.

Demetri bent carefully to his knees and scoured the entire three yards square, poking odd bits of grass or turf with the end of a pen. Then he went down further. Ben watched transfixed as the big man almost bent double with his face centimetres from the ground.

'He or she smoked,' he reported, sniffing the grass in short, then long drafts. Then he started to gently tease a small area of grass stems apart and a few seconds later he pinched some soil between two fingers and stood up.

'Roll-ups. Look, some of the tobacco fell out when they were making it.'

He held a single wisp of tobacco and sniffed it again before placing it delicately into the upturned cap on his pen. The ballpoint was then reunited with the cap and secreted back in Demetri's inside pocket.

'Can I?' asked Ben, casting his eyes to the flattened grass.

'Sure,' replied Demetri. 'I'll go and see whether I can see you from where the stalls would have been.'

Ben removed his jacket and then hunkered down in the impression in the grass, looking up to where he thought the stalls would have stood two hours before. He couldn't see anything except cloudy sky. Then he stood up and saw Demetri standing looking directly at him no more than fifteen yards away – he'd been unaware the big man was there, right in front of him.

He rejoined Demetri who pointed back to where Ben had come from. 'There's a nice little ridge there, I couldn't see you at all, so no one would have been able to see someone lying there, but if I was sat on a horse you'd have a perfect view because of the elevated height. A high-powered rifle with a 0.77 pellet would cause the right sort of damage. I think our shooter took two shots in the stalls and one or two more when The Ghost came out.'

So he turns up a few minutes before the horses get to the start, shoots and then heads off?' Ben postulated.

Demetri shook his head. 'No, they would have been there for at an hour beforehand, and probably at least fifteen minutes afterwards. Whoever was there couldn't afford to be seen out in the open arriving or departing, they'd have to make sure everything was clear of stalls handlers, the starter and don't forget the television cameras.'

The two men surveyed the land in silence, imagining the scene from only an hour previously.

Demetri continued 'They would need to be a decent shot, know their air rifles and I'm sure they'd have needed to scout the land before the day. To be so far out in the open, unseen, but also have line of sight for their shots would take some planning.'

Demetri looked down to Ben for a reaction, but saw he was holding the bridge of his nose and had his eyes shut.

'Long day, eh?'

Ben released his grip on the base of his temple. 'Oh, er… yes. Sorry, I'm okay. Just a bit of a headache.'

'Not going to have a dizzy spell?' Demetri enquired.

Ben looked up into a face laced with concern, which rather curbed his reaction.

'You know about my medical condition? For heaven's sake, what don't you three know about me?' he demanded.

'You're obviously fine,' Demetri responded dryly and he turned on his heel and strode off across the racecourse and back onto the single track road, leaving Ben feeling thoroughly wretched.

He caught up with Demetri a few minutes later at the three furlong pole, panting a little after having to jog to catch up.

'Okay, I'm sorry Demetri,' he said between gasps. 'I find it difficult to change my view of people. It's something Anna always used to pull me up about all the time. I'm just coming to terms with, well, all this.' He threw out an arm to indicate a wide arc.

'It's already been a long day, and knowing that someone is able to access pretty much every single bit of information about you is quite… unnerving.'

Demetri stopped and put his hands on his hips, observing Ben closely.

'You know when we pull all the information together about someone you can get an overall feeling about them. You weigh their positive and their negative points. You've plenty of positives going on and I'm pleased you're getting help with some of the negative ones.'

Ben grimaced, realising Demetri was referring to his counsellor, but reluctantly he let it go. Demetri was watching his reaction very carefully again and smiled when Ben tried to wipe the grimace from his face.

'Tell you what,' said Demetri, holding out a large palm expectantly. 'Let's start again. I'm Demetri Krzysztof McDonald and I'm pleased to meet you.'

What the hell, Ben thought. Anna always said I was far too judgmental and lost potential friends as a result. Besides, the way this day was going, shaking the Scotsman's hand would be just as weird as the rest of it, so why not go with the flow…

As Ben prepared to hold out his hand, the thump of hooves hitting turf distracted them both. Looking back down the racecourse the final race runners were a thundering wall of horseflesh hurling themselves towards the last four hundred yards. On the trackside road Ben and Demetri were only three yards from the nearside racing rail. The slapping of hoof on grass became louder and the first crash of crowd roar hit them from the other direction. A flash of colours, whip cracks, shouts for room lost on the wind or screams of encouragement and an ever so small movement of the ground and the sixteen runners had passed them. A few seconds later the two men had to jump backwards onto the grass verge as two cars and an ambulance chased the equine and human competitors' home.

'Now *that's* why we want to be involved in bloodstock!' exclaimed Demetri as he watched the jockey's backsides disappear towards the stands. Just for a moment there was a childish look of awe upon the big man's face.

Ben smiled, took up Demetri's hand and shook it firmly.

Eighteen

Ben sat behind the wheel of his stationary Volkswagen Golf in the mammoth Birmingham National Exhibition Centre car park and checked the time on his mobile phone for the third time in ten minutes. It was almost a week after The Ghost's run in the Greenham and Ivan had been true to his word, as he and his two partners had backed off Ben's owners immediately and set about helping to track down who was behind the shooting incident at Newbury. Even though they made it clear they were protecting their investment, Ben was quietly pleased that for the time being at least, they were apparently on his side and not working against him.

Demetri had been in touch to give an update on Ivan's electronic investigations into the shooting, travel issues and doping at Joss's stables but so far there was no real progress. One lead had looked promising; Armitage had tracked down a couple of fourteen year old boys in Lambourn who had admitted to planting the tacks and letting down the tyres on The Ghost Machines' horsebox after being approached and offered fifty pounds by a mystery man. The boys had been bragging on a social media site about their touch and Ivan had unearthed their location. Subsequently Armitage had dropped in on them for an uninvited visit. The information had been supplied after the boys had accepted another fifty pounds, and the description of the man had been pretty generic: thirty to forty with mousey hair, blue eyes, and a thin nose. They'd apparently accepted the cash and the tacks and got on with the job. They had no idea what car he drove, his clothes, or his accent. It was pretty much a dead end.

Joss's discussion with Ivan had been far more productive than Ben's. Ivan had suggested improvements to Joss's security in order to preserve the safety of The Ghost and also insisted on paying for them. Now the yard had a secure buzzer on the front entrance and a gate operated remotely from the house. CCTV cameras now covered all the major areas around the yard, including a number actually inside the boxes which were spotted around the yard so that the Ghost could be moved, but still monitored. Demetri had also arranged for their own clever sidestep entrance around the perimeter of the stables to be fenced off, again with cameras to deter any entry. The yard had become a Fort Knox of training stables. What amazed Ben was that all this work had been completed in two days – Ivan and his two partners certainly got things done.

They had also drawn up a list of people who would potentially either benefit, or be seeking revenge on Joss, the yard, the syndicate or indeed the horse. Ben couldn't help laughing when the list arrived in his hands, pointing out the ludicrous nature of the exercise when he saw the first page of names. It ran to over five hundred individuals, and included every owner with Joss, every owner with a potential Guineas horse in training, every person who had worked for Joss over the last five years, plus their families, as well as all the current syndicate members in all of Ben's fifteen horses in training and past syndicates. Ben had playfully suggested adding every punter who had ever lost money backing Joss's horses, which had been received with lukewarm enthusiasm and a perhaps touch of embarrassed realisation.

The rest of The Ghost syndicate had been given chapter and verse of what had happened at Newbury and Joss and Ben's phones hadn't stopped ringing with Ian, Duncan, Rob and the Dunn ladies eager to learn more about what happened at the top of the stands. Ben had been quite relieved that he'd had no more dizzy spells or panic attacks since the day, and had been for another session of counselling which had helped him get things back into some sort of perspective again.

Another big relief was that Joss had given the colt a clean bill of health the following day. The pellet wound had all but disappeared within a couple of days and the three year old had worked nicely on the local gallops, doing some breezing work the following Tuesday. He was now a potential multimillion pound asset, which made Ben nervous in the extreme, as each syndicate member made their own decision about equine insurance. With premiums so high on racehorses he didn't have insurance and doubted Duncan, Joss or Rob would either. He'd checked, and only the very top category of insurance would cover an injury or death caused by a third party conducted on purpose. In The Ghost Machine's case, that premium was now into the tens of thousands of pounds for each shareholder. Owning a racehorse with such a life changing value created more complications than he had ever imagined.

The racing press had been all over the Greenham result at the weekend and into the next week with endless praise for Panama's win, but also for The Ghost's performance from both horse and rider. The main question being asked was whether The Ghost Machine would have beaten Panama if he'd not lost the ground at the start of the race, with opinion divided. However, everyone with any sort of link to racing were all talking about the Two Thousand Guineas in a few weeks time, for which both horses had already been entered as two year olds.

The Newbury race had been uploaded to YouTube and trended for days under the title 'Greatest recovery by horse and jockey ever.' Although a copycat posting had also done well with 'Jockey's ear gets ripped open and he still finishes second'. Ben had been amazed to discover that the race had been watched over a million times online. He and Joss had been inundated with interview requests from all sorts of publications, as the link with 'The Parade Ring Killing' made the story even more media friendly. Ben had given one interview to the Racing Post, limited to comments regarding the horse and jockey only. He had politely refused all the others. Joss and Raul had provided a joint statement which stuck to the story that Raul got unbalanced in the stalls and which had been less widely reported upon. Raul himself had needed a couple of stitches in his earlobe, but was riding out the next day and recorded two more winners for Joss within a few days. His ride on The Ghost seemed to be working out pretty well for the young apprentice.

Ben fiddled irritably with the car radio, trying to get a better reception on the aging device. He was killing time, as he didn't need to be into the vast National Exhibition Centre until four in the afternoon. With TalkSport stubbornly refusing to be found, he eventually put a collar around Mojo's neck and the two of them went for a walk around the huge tarmac jungle of cars for forty minutes. At three forty five he left Mojo sleeping happily in the back of the car, checked two of the windows were cracked open and set off towards the main exhibition hall.

He felt a little guilty that he hadn't shared this information with Demetri, but then he hadn't told Joss or any of the syndicate either. This was his own hunch, and if he got it wrong, they could all remain happily in the dark. On the Monday after the race, he'd called Newbury on the pretence of thanking them for the day at the races, but also managed to cajole the Marketing Manager into giving him the name of the agency that supplied her promotions staff.

It turned out to be one of the biggest agencies in London with thousands of people on their books, from stage actors to voice over people, models and even people with good-looking hands. Ben had been boggled by what was available; if you wanted a photo of a single foot for your advert, there were people with good-looking feet ready and willing to do the foot work.

The name he'd been given was Jade, and no surname. The Marketing Manager had told him that these promotional girls rarely used their real names, instead tending to use stage names instead. Ben had spent an entire evening sifting through hundreds of photos on the agency's internet site before he came across a photo of a very much younger version of Jade. According to her work profile, Jade Morrison was apparently available for adverts, small acting roles, hand, face and body doubles. She also did promotional work at major sporting occasions and corporate events.

Today at Birmingham NEC Jade Morrison was doing promotional work at the Coffee and Hot Beverages Show which the agency sales office had described as 'Social Interaction Selling'. Ben had no idea what this was, but when he'd shown interest in booking her, but insisted he met with the lady concerned first, the agency salesman on the other end of the phone had been quite happy to quote Jades' work schedule for the next week, which included three days at the soulless wasteland of brick and tarmac which was Birmingham NEC.

Ben had chosen a Friday afternoon to meet Jade, as he had a runner at Wolverhampton in the evening. He had also calculated that after three days of work at the NEC she would hopefully be happy to spend time answering a few of his questions. As it turned out, his gamble paid off.

He'd found her quite easily and had almost walked straight into her as she trudged around the floor of the vast NEC building. She was wandering aimlessly between the huge corporate displays with an old-fashioned cigarette tray lashed around her neck, giving out small bulbs of coffee tasters in return for delegates' email addresses. She wore a pair of ludicrously high black stiletto shoes, fishnet stockings and a 1920's kinky maid's dress and cap. Ben watched her surreptitiously for a few minutes and it only took a few minutes for him to feel pretty sorry for her as she fielded the advances of one businessman after another. She'd looked a little uneasy when he first approached, but after he introduced himself and offered to buy her a coffee she had quickly become grateful for the opportunity to sit down for a few minutes.

According to Jade's own request, they found a table at the very back of the delegate café and she ordered a black coffee with no sugar but then stared longingly at the fresh cream cakes during the two minutes it took Ben to be served. He sat down with the coffee and she immediately warmed her hands around the cup.

'I'm blummin' freezing,' she exclaimed quietly in a Liverpool accent. 'Three days I've been walking around this blummin' cave with no windows and all they give me to wear is an outfit with two hankies and a strap!' she indicated the maid's uniform and he tried to smile and cast his eyes over the lack of her clothing without appearing to be a letch. He was struggling to find the words and eventually offered 'I guess that would be quite, er, cold.'

'You're from the races the other day aren't you,' she stated, pulling the white cap off her head and pushing her tied up hair backwards.

'I saw you with one of the horses didn't I?

Before Ben could answer, she continued 'I like the racing gigs, as everyone's so happy and there are plenty of clothes to wear. Oh God, I'm sorry, I always do that, just talk over people without stopping to let them answer.'

Ben waved the apology away, but dived in with his first question. She seemed a bit flakey and he needed to get as much information as possible before she realised he wasn't a proper meal ticket.

'Do you remember doing a job for someone about three weeks ago up in Yorkshire at a racing yard. You were dressed as a policewoman?'

'Oh yeah,' she said, nodding furiously. 'That was cool, my first acting job for *ages*.' She accentuated the last word, rolling it around her mouth and smiled a real smile for the first time that afternoon, instead of the plastic smiles for the businessmen. Then her expression changed to disappointment.

'You were there weren't you! Oh bum. You're not here to book me are you? Did the surprise not work then? I knew it was too good to be true; Derek must have got it wrong, did he? What a twit he was. All he had to do was...'

At this, she raised a long nailed hand to her mouth and apologised for her language inaudibly through her fingers.

'That's okay. So it was Derek who played the part of the inspector?' asked Ben, making scribbled notes. 'So what was the surprise?'

The girl sipped her coffee thoughtfully 'Well you must have seen the big bow?'

Ben looked at the girl with what he hoped was benign concern.

'No, I'm afraid not.'

Balancing the coffee cup in one finger of her right hand Jade mimed what Ben could only assume was what the girl believed a huge bow shape to be.

'It was huge and he was supposed to put it around this grey horse so that when the chap's girlfriend turned up he could give her the horse as a gift. I guess it must have fallen off or something?'

'I had to distract a few people by walking around and asking questions and writing stuff down so that twit Derek could set up the surprise,' she explained.

Ben considered his options and decided to play along. This girl was very pretty, but wasn't too quick on the uptake. So he couldn't see her being the brains behind the doping. However, Derek was of great interest.

'No, no. It all went fine, I just wanted to contact Derek so that I could thank him for setting everything up, it worked perfectly and the, er, lady was really pleased with her present,' he assured the girl and smiled as brightly as he could.

Jade visibly relaxed and took another few sips of her coffee.

'Can I get you another one?' Ben asked, nodding at the cup in her hand.

'No thanks, I should be getting back out there. I get paid according to the number of email addresses I collect, so I'm losing money, well, sort of,' she said before draining her cup.

Afraid she would head off before he had the information about her accomplice, Ben said quickly and as casually as possible 'Well the reason I'm here is because I've lost the contact details for Derek – you wouldn't have them would you?

The girl looked at Ben for a moment. 'No, and if you're going to ask me to work with him again, I won't.'

'Really? Why's that?'

The girl's face started to pink at the cheeks and within a few seconds she was scratching a reddening patch below her ear.

'Look, thanks for the coffee, but I really have to go back to work,' she said quickly and started to push her chair away from the table, bending down to pick up her tray of black coffee bulbs.

'Please Jade, it's quite important I track Derek down. You were fine that day. I don't know if you remember, but I was at the stables that day. You spoke with me.'

She returned to an upright position, and was obviously trying to process this new information and was getting nowhere quickly.

'I was with my son and a small black Jack Russell called Mojo?'

Her face lit up like a pinball machine. 'Oh, yes, the little black dog that was bouncing around everywhere, he was lush!' she said, now beaming back at Ben. But her face fell again and she added 'Truth be told, that was probably the best part for the whole day. I know I shouldn't say it, but that Derek was horrible. I spent the whole day with him and all he did was letch over me, it was disgusting. And he left me to walk to the station on the outskirts of Doncaster; I had to pay for a taxi in the end. Said he hadn't got time to drop me back in the centre and just left me there.'

Ben suddenly felt a wave of sympathy for this nice, quite uncomplicated girl. She'd got herself mixed up in something far more complex than she would ever comprehend.

Ben made his decision and in as soft a voice as he could muster he whispered 'I'm sorry you had a bad day, but you would be really helping me if you could tell me all about Derek. You were dead right before, the surprise didn't go well at all, and I need to find him.'

The girl looked uncertain, so Ben smiled and went on. 'Listen, this trade show closes in an hour or two. I guess you are going back to London tonight, how about I give you a lift into Birmingham for the train, and I'll also pay you for your last two hours. How does fifty pounds sound?

The offer of the cash seemed to help, but then Ben remembered and added 'I've got Mojo, you know, my little back dog? She's with me today. I'm on my way to Wolverhampton races, so it's no bother. I'm sure he'd love to see you again and I could find out a bit more about Derek.'

Twenty minutes later Mojo was in seventh heaven on the lap of Ms Jade Morrison, being scratched behind her ears, stroked, and fussed over. Jade had cheered up immensely, having thrown a large overcoat over her costume, pocketed the fifty pounds and waltzed out of the NEC with Ben without looking back. She was happily regaling him with the full story of what happened on her acting trip up to North Yorkshire between adoring looks at Mojo. By the time he dropped her off at Birmingham central station Ben, Jade and Mojo were all on first name terms.

Nineteen

'She's actually called Courtney,' Ben was telling the people around Joss's kitchen table the following Friday evening. 'I felt a bit sorry for her. She thought it was her first proper acting job for months, and all she was doing was acting as a stooge for our doper.'

Ben reflected that the job Courtney had been doing on Friday wasn't much better.

Demetri nodded. 'Ivan has done a full profile of her and she checks out. Born in Liverpool, she registered with agencies across London about eight years ago and has been doing minor extra work, the odd non speaking part in adverts and lots of promo work ever since. She lives with a girlfriend in a shared flat in North London. She has no links to racing other than appearing as a promo girl at a few London area tracks now and then. That's probably where she was noticed by our doper.'

Joss, Duncan and Rob had listened in silence as Ben and Demetri ran them through what they had found at the seven furlong start at Newbury, and the information from Ben's time with Courtney. Demetri's metamorphosis from looming intimidator to trusted confidante had taken less time than Ben had expected. Some detailed explaining to the four remaining members of the syndicate had to be undertaken, but Demetri had spent Sunday and Monday visiting each of them in turn, from Scotland to London via North Yorkshire. The same charm which had won over Ben had been greeted with skepticism at first, but grudging acceptance quickly followed afterwards.

Ben continued 'He called himself Derek, but Jade thought there was something funny about that, as there was a couple of times he didn't respond when she called him that name. He never used a surname and paid her in cash before he kicked her out for the car on the outskirts of Doncaster.'

Duncan whistled. 'So he's not bothered about leaving a girl on her own on a Saturday night to fend for herself.'

'No, but I think it was more likely because she wouldn't let him touch her. He'd been making pretty lewd suggestions to her all day apparently.'

'And what about the car?' asked Rob. 'How did they get hold of a police car?'

'It wasn't a marked car,' Ben replied. 'It just had the flashing blue lights inside it. It was actually a pretty ordinary Vauxhall, I didn't give it a second look when I saw it, as they were both walking down the drive at the time. Courtney said it was filthy inside. I'd guess it only took him a few minutes to pop some flashing blue light onto the dashboard. He parked a little way up the drive, so no one would look too closely inside. I had to drive around his car when I arrived.'

'So what did he look like? Is there anything which could help us to identify our doper?' Duncan asked.

Joss stared down, placing both palms face down on the table. 'I can't believe I actually spoke with him, offered the little sod a coffee, and pointed him in the direction of The Ghost. But I can't remember hardly anything about him, too busy with other things I guess. I'd like to...'

Demetri broke in, 'I'm sure we'd all like to join you in giving him a good pasting, but we need to catch him first,' which elicited universal agreement, but Demetri prompted Ben to continue with the evidence.

'He's about six foot, thin with brown hair. Probably in his mid-thirties,' reported Ben from his notes. 'Courtney said he had striking blue eyes that she reckoned were too far apart and a thin, pointed nose. I think we have to go with her description, as I'm like Joss, I didn't really take him in, I remembered Courtney more because of her earrings and makeup.'

'Are you sure that's the only reason you remembered her?' said Duncan grinning his best waspish grin.

Ben shot his friend a withering look. 'And before he got changed into the police uniforms he was wearing faded black jeans, a cheap jumper with holes in it and a pair of black boots.'

Ben continued 'She thought he was an actor, and they were here to wrap up a horse ready for someone's birthday, but she was actually a lookout for him. I've spoken to the police in the town and they don't have any record of any calls into them. They'd all stopped a day or two beforehand. So he must have been calling for about a week before in order to set up his own visit.'

Joss nodded agreement and through gritted teeth said 'Marion and I got several calls from the police, but I'm guessing the ones the day before they arrived were this Derek, or 'Denton' as he called himself, setting up his visit.'

'That's about it I'm afraid,' Ben said, checking his notebook again.

'Courtney told me he didn't say much in the car. There wasn't much small talk apart from him making crass passes at her. His instructions to her were to make sure no one followed him when he went into the second barn. Afterwards they got changed at a service station on the A1 and he got a couple of calls on his mobile on the way back down.'

Joss sighed 'I'm wondering if our midnight visit by the police was our man calling once he got home, just to finish the job off. It was the same day our doper was here.'

'It would fit,' agreed Demetri.

'There is one more thing,' added Ben. 'Courtney remembers our man Derek had a cigarette in the car. She was quite adamant that it was a roll-up, as she said her clothes needed washing when she got back home as they stank of tobacco.'

'Which is probably the best link we have with our shooter at

Newbury,' chimed Demetri in his Scottish tones.

Ben closed his notebook and a thoughtful silence descended upon the kitchen table as the five men contemplated the new information.

Rob broke the silence 'Just remind me again,' he said rubbing the back of his neck. Ben noted this and decided Rob was looking tired.

'Why can't we pass all this information over to the police and let them get on with it. I thought impersonating a police offer was some sort of offence?'

'You're right,' Demetri cut in. 'They might be interested in the impersonation, but what we're talking about here is protection of The Ghost, and they won't provide that. Besides, we get the police involved the media will have a feeding frenzy which I'm sure Joss would rather avoid. A couple of photographers from the tabloids were hanging around the yard gates when I arrived this afternoon and I had to convince them they needed to leave.' He winked conspiratorially at Joss across the table.

'Really?' said Ben. Duncan shook his head once again.

'You are newsworthy, gentlemen,' said Demetri flicking his eyes around the table. 'Unfortunately it has a lot to do with the death of your wife last year, Ben, the doping accusation hanging over you Joss, and the ensuing 'battle' of the same two horses on the racetrack. Any further intrigue involving a potential plot to derail The Ghost will, I fear, send the press into overdrive.'

Joss leant back in his chair. He was feeling a little jaded following a busy week of runners. 'Everything will settle down after the Guineas,' he remarked in a hopeful voice. 'Then I can get on with being a racehorse trainer.'

Demetri cut in again 'Ivan, Armitage and I will be working exclusively to ensure we neutralise whoever has got it in for The Ghost. Thanks to Ben's information, we're a lot further forward now.'

'Neutralise?' queried Duncan with a worried expression.

'Ah, my apologies, some business slang does tend to creep into my language,' assured Demetri smoothly. 'We will be passing the relevant information to the authorities once we have our man. We deal in information, not violence.'

Duncan relaxed a little, but the memory of Demetri at his front door only a week previously still stung. 'Are we leaving everything to the 'Forties' then?'

Ben grinned over the table. The 'Forties' was Duncan's new name for Ivan, Armitage and Demetri which neatly pointed a gibing finger at the fact they still only owned forty percent of The Ghost.

Ben saw that Demetri, to his credit, got the reference straight away, but didn't provide any sort of reaction other than a congratulatory nod in Duncan's direction.

'Well, they seem to be best placed,' said Ben carefully. He too had been busy since the Newbury race with runners, selling shares in syndicates and juggling all that with making sure he had time for Max. However, he was also aware that the Forties amnesty on approaching his syndicate only had another week to run.

Ben added 'I'll be speaking regularly with Demetri and Joss. If anything new pops up, I'll be straight in touch with everyone, including Ian and the Dunn's. The really important thing now is that The Ghost gets to Newmarket for the Two Thousand Guineas fit and well. In the end, he's a racehorse and we've got to make sure he can race, so if...,' he paused, looking over to Demetri. '...the Forties can help that happen, then we'll take that additional help.'

This received nods of approval, although Ben was aware that Rob seemed to be barely able to keep his eyes open in the warm kitchen. It seemed practically everyone in the syndicate was suffering from lack of sleep at the moment.

Demetri then ran through the various security changes he had agreed with Joss earlier, and the plans to get The Ghost down to Newmarket in just under one weeks time. The Two Thousand Guineas would be another step up in class, with a bigger field likely and challengers who had decided to miss the Greenham and go straight for the first Group One race of the season for colts. Winning the Two Thousand Guineas could potentially guarantee a stallion's future as a sire and bring a weighty price tag to his covering fees as well. Ben zoned out from the conversation for a few moments and considered whether the Forties would actually be able to afford the other sixty percent if The Ghost were to win at Newmarket. He only considered it for a moment. You had to assume they would have those sorts of resources, based on his experience of them so far. He had got the distinct impression that money was no longer their motivation – being at the pinnacle of achievement in their chosen discipline seemed to be more of a priority.

Demetri finished off by going through the plans for the following weekend and these were greeted with the same general agreement and the meeting broke up.

Ben caught Rob before he headed out the door and asked him if everything was okay. Rob smiled, yawned and thanked Ben for his enquiry, but claimed he'd had a few busy nights recently in the pub. Ben wished him well but got the feeling there was more to Rob's current bout of tiredness than work alone. He kept himself incredibly fit having been ex-forces, and Ben had never seen the landlord looking so run down.

Eventually Ben was left alone with Joss in the kitchen.

'Another drink of something before you go?' offered Joss. 'I can boil the kettle again or even stretch to a beer if you wanted.'

Ben said he would pass, but sat down at the kitchen table again and indicated for Joss to do the same.

'I'm glad to have got you alone for a few minutes,' Ben said conspiratorially. 'I need to know what you think of the Forties and also whether you'll be selling your share in The Ghost to them.'

Joss sat down with his hands on his knees and slapped them before answering 'I can't make head or tail of them. One minute I think they are just what we need, the next I'm counting my fingers after we shake hands. They certainly have money, and they're not afraid to spend it, but I can't see them accepting anything other than success, and you and I know that owners like that don't tend to last long in this sport.'

'I know what you mean, Ivan scares the hell out of me,' admitted Ben.

'Demetri is far easier to deal with, and I've not seen Armitage since the Newbury race, and even then he was in the background and hardly spoke.'

'Ah, that's because he's on special duties in my stable office.'

Joss held up a hand before Ben could question him 'I'm sworn to secrecy, even you are exempt. However, I can tell you that it's an extra level of protection for The Ghost.'

Ben wasn't so sure he liked being kept in the dark, but let it go. There were probably many things the Forties got up to of which he had no knowledge. One more wouldn't hurt, and might just help if someone tried to get to The Ghost again.

'I think they will eventually pay enough to secure fifty percent or more, so I'm trying to convince everyone to hold out so we can get the most possible from them. The Ghost is already valuable now, but if he won the Guineas his price would increase a hundredfold.'

'Bit scary eh!' said Joss with a cheeky grin.

Ben put both hands to his face and feigned a scream 'I have to say that you're taking all of this incredibly well.'

Joss scraped his chair closer to Ben and bowed his head 'I could only tell you this, but I really don't know if I'm coming or going. I've so much going on I really haven't got time to worry about anything for more than a minute. We've had eight runners this week and four winners and I'm getting four of my two year olds ready for their debuts next week, along with another ten or more runners. What's more I've the doping hearing in four weeks time and I know for certain The Ghost's race hasn't sunk in yet.'

Joss looked directly into Ben's eyes and continued in almost a whisper 'But what I do know is that I worked The Ghost with a six year old ninety five rated handicapper off level weights this morning over six furlongs. He just stretched away from him. I've never seen a horse travel like he does; he seems to cover more ground every stride than anything he works with, but then he finds that finishing burst, its heart stopping.'

Joss was now shaking slightly. He was excited and his eyes danced. 'Raul rode him in the work and came back afterwards and was speechless. He couldn't explain what he'd felt under him. I've had to tell him not to report the workout to anyone; otherwise I'd jock him off for the Guineas. Seriously, The Ghost hasn't just trained on from last season, he's a different horse altogether.'

Ben could feel beads of sweat forming under his armpits and his shirt starting to stick. It was his standard reaction to this sort of unexpected big news. Joss spoke his mind, and wasn't someone who would use superlatives, especially when describing his horses. For him to say a horse was talented was indeed a rare occurrence. This sort of reaction to a horse's homework from Joss was... Ben couldn't find the words.

'He's good enough for the Guineas?'

'Yes, I'm pretty sure he is. I'm almost certain we have the beating of Panama, and the Sheik's horse, with a decent break from the stalls. The only question is whether there is something else in the lineup which hasn't shown its hand yet.'

'Well the declarations are out on Monday. We'll find out!' exclaimed Ben, now almost as excited as Joss. Without any warning, Ben felt a tickle start in his stomach and travel up his throat. He started to laugh, almost maniacally. The sheer weirdness and joy of the moment set off Joss. Within seconds there were tears rolling down their faces, the tension of the last fortnight falling away as they gasped for air between belly laughs.

The two of them were calmer, but still giggling like small children a minute later when Marion came in the kitchen door. She took one look at the two of them, shook her head, turned and left the way she came muttering 'Boys!' under her breath. As she walked away into the yard another peel of riotous laughter rang through from the kitchen.

Wiping their faces and trying to recapture their composure, Ben and Joss rocked back on their chairs once again.

'Oh, I didn't get the chance to congratulate you,' said Ben, reddening streaks from wiped tears appearing across his cheeks. 'That win for Puddin' at Wolverhampton in midweek. I trust Eleanor was full of the joys of spring?'

'Oh yes!' Joss said, his eyes widening and shooting a frozen stare of exclamation at Ben. 'She had her little entourage with her of course and was like the cat that'd got the cream when the mare managed to get up on the line. No one was safe from her overflowing enthusiasm afterwards,' said Joss.

'Good stuff. And well done for getting my own little winner this week. Grade six handicap, but they all count and it will keep my greatest fan, Mr P Loote, quiet for at least a week, for which I am eternally grateful.'

'All part of the service, Sir.' Joss barked back theatrically, pretending to doff an imaginary hat.

'Right. Time to rescue Max from your daughters, feed The Ghost a carrot, and then head home for Friday night lasagne with my Mother in Law,' announced Ben, getting up from his chair.

They found Max and Mojo jumping between bales of straw at the back of the second barn. They collected the two of them and then walked round to the latest stable to house The Ghost.

Ben gave Max a carrot and the youngster trotted up to feed the colt. 'He must feel like he's on a merry-go-round with all these changes of stables,' observed Ben.

'It's not ideal, but we've got to be careful. We're taking every precaution,' said Joss, indicating a stable hand who stood close by and whose only job was to tend The Ghost's stable.

'Speaking of going around in a circle, how's your dizzy spells? Anything since last Saturday?'

Ben shook his head, smiling as The Ghost bit off a chunk of the carrot Max was holding up to the colt. The loud crunch made Max cackle and giggle with delight.

'Nope. Nothing. It's linked to stress and pent-up anger so my Councellor advised me. To be fair, the Greenham day was fairly stressful, but no sign of a repeat since, so I'm hoping I might be through the worst.'

Max fed The Ghost the last of the carrot and Ben went up to the colt to give him a scratch behind his ear, before the three of them walked back to the top of the yard with Mojo taking her time behind them, investigating every smell.

****

Max greeted his Grandma with open arms, throwing his schoolbag into the corner of the kitchen as he entered the cottage and embracing the sixty six year old in a vice like grip. Helen was still bent over making the most of her grandson's welcome when Ben entered still humming the tune they'd been singing in the car on their way back from Joss's.

'Well you two certainly seem to be a pair of happy bunnies this evening!'

'Ah Helen, it couldn't get much better... All is well in the world, and what's more it's lasagne night!'

Ben turned to Max and with a big wink he asked his son 'What night is our favourite night?'

Max took a deep breath and at the top of his shrill eight year old voice he bellowed 'Friday night!'

'And why is that?'

Max pumped his fists towards the ceiling and screamed 'It's

lasagne night!'

Helen laughed and then said in a stage whisper 'It's a good job I didn't make spaghetti for a change then!'

The three of them enjoyed one of the best meals they had had for a long time, Ben answering Helen's questions about The Ghost's run, the Forties and their plans. Helen told them about the first flower-arranging lesson she'd attended that week and Max was delighted to show his Grandma and Dad the painting he'd done of The Ghost in class earlier in the day. They laughed, joked and all three of them were still sitting at the table long after the meal had finished.

After a couple of board games, which Max won hands down he enjoyed his second treat of lasagne night, as he was allowed to sit up late and sip a hot chocolate in front of the open fire before heading to bed. Helen took Max to bed upstairs and rejoined Ben who was slouching in his favourite armchair, desperately trying to keep his eyes from closing in front of the coal fire.

Helen settled into her own armchair and then looked over to Ben, a single tear rolling over her cheek. Ben sat up, worried there was something wrong, but she quickly wiped away the wetness.

'I'm crying because I'm happy,' she said between laughs.

Twenty

It had taken an hour to walk the four miles to the Joss O'Hoole yard. He had been over several windswept fields, where the young winter wheat sprouted its grass like leaves in perfect rows. The two woods had been more difficult, with fallen trees and inexplicable thickets appearing suddenly in front of him. A sharp spring shower made everything smell musty and stringy brambles had whipped at his boots and trousers. He hadn't met a soul during the entire route march. Finally, he'd gone through the small wood on the edge of the O'Hoole land, careful not to be spotted, moving swiftly from tree to tree and listening for anything other than the sounds of the wood.

It was half past seven in the evening and the sun was fading behind grey, low level clouds. The man cursed as a drop of rain pattered onto the hood of his Barbour jacket. He would have to wait.

Ten minutes later the shower stopped and the greyness had become a few shades darker. He squatted, pushed up against the base of a large ash tree, watching the final few drips of the shower hit a small pool which had formed in a knot at its root. He waited for the pool to lose its raindrop ripples. At least the wind had dropped. He could cope with the breeze, as long as it stayed like this.

The tall, thin figure checked behind the tree again, unfolding a set of binoculars to scan the long grassed paddocks in front of him and finally focused on the row of three barns at the top of the gently sloping hill. Content no one was moving behind the barns he swung the backpack off his shoulders and started to build the drone.

A few minutes later he emerged from behind the towering tree and slipped through the wood, again moving from tree to tree and checking after every few paces. He scowled when he realised his boots had left an imprint in the mud and made a mental note to bin them afterwards. Reaching a rough farm track he looked for somewhere to squat once again, choosing another broad based tree. This pitch would give him quick access to the lane and the ability to vault into the next field, or head up or down the lane if he needed to exit quickly. Always know your escape route before a sortie into enemy territory, he knew. He grimaced, the words prompting a memory full of regret and he quickly shook it from his head.

Placing his backpack to one side, he removed a set of drone goggles and after smoothing down his rain soaked hair, placed them on his head and sat on a broad root at the base of the yard wide ash tree.

A few feet from the base of the ash tree, a small red light which had been blinking red, altered colour to green and a sharp beam of white light shot out of the front of the drone. There was a short whirr of electric motors as four small angled propellers fired up. The drone hung in the semi light like an outsized bluebottle. It twitched and then lifted smoothly into the air.

The man licked his lips and chewed at the inside of his mouth nervously as he became the drone. He viewed the wood, the gate in the distance and the surrounding trees from the drone's cockpit. His fingerless gloves allowed the thumbs to move levers and fingers to press buttons around the ergonomically crafted control. Each delicate micro movement being interpreted by the drone, twitching as the instructions were sent to its silicon brain.

He cleared the edge of the wood and lifted over the wooden three bar fence. As he dropped as far down as he dared he could feel his heart quicken in his chest and smiled at a personal irony. He sped over the grass and reached the first of the barns, lifting ten metres in height so that he was hovering over the apex of the roof. Spinning to alter his view, he headed for the third barn, tapping the controls to bank left and follow the ridges on the barn roof until they ran out, and then he rotated again to take in his position. He saw two people, one going into the second barn, the other walking away from the third. It was time to go.

He spun the drone over, inducing a weird sense of vertigo for a split second and then gunned the device into the third barn. He had practiced this, now he had to deliver a flawless copy of his best run. He tried to instruct his fingers to caress the controls, rather than force them.

The drone whipped above the rafters in the barn and levelled off, spinning three hundred and sixty degrees as he searched for his quarry. No luck. He moved another ten yards up the barn and did the same manoeuvre. Still there was no sign of the grey horse.

From his next rotation he saw someone pointing at him, and another person started running. He ignored them, moving further up the barn and scanning the horses again. Some of the horses were getting agitated, he could see them pacing around their boxes. One reared when he got too close. Another person, a girl it looked like, was with a horse in a box when he whipped the camera lens around. She looked up with an open mouth, only for her expression to turn to one of shock and then pain as the horse backed away from the wailing motors and pushed the girl against the stable wall.

It's not here. Only eight boxes left. It *had* to be here.

The next burst of speed took him too far; he had to reverse and backtrack to check. Was that box empty? Where was the horse? He flicked the controls backwards once again and his heart jumped. The grey was on its knees against the side of the box. It looked around and he caught a view of the horse head on. It displayed a dark diamond in the centre of its forehead. The sight of his quarry sent a thrill through the drone pilot. He flicked another button and the perspective altered and a silver nail appeared in the bottom of his viewfinder. With the nail lined up he went down into the box.

The Ghost Machine got ungainly to his feet and snorted as the drone's buzzing got louder. The inmate of the next box whinnied and The Ghost backed away from the drone, kicking out at the back wall of the box in irritation.

He swore and darted at the grey horse, trying to avoid contact with the walls of the box, still using the silver nail as his guide. The horse's head. He had to get to the head. The grey suddenly reared before his assault could strike, hooves coming dangerously close. He jerked his head back convulsively as the horse seemed to claw at him. He darted the drone in and the grey whipped around and moved under him and out of sight. As he gained height and tried to target his quarry again, several fine metal prongs flashed across his screen. He withdrew higher, caught the grey in his cross hairs once again, and dived, silver nail centred on his equine bull's-eye. He tilted the controls downwards and the drone shot forward at its maximum speed.

Nothingness for a second. The blackness was interrupted a few seconds later with a single line of system information but before it could finish its full search for the drone the headset was ripped off the man's head, the controller deactivated and both pieces of equipment stuffed into his backpack. The man leapt out of the wood and set off at a dead sprint down the unlit track, his boots slapping against the compacted mud and splashing through the puddles, leaving them to reform and ripple silver in the moonlight.

Twenty-One

Ben stared sullenly out of the thick goose egg window onto the wing of the plane. He was tired, and not in the best of moods. He'd been staring at the same scene for over an hour now. He leant his elbow on the armrest, and buried half his face in a hand.

He wanted to sleep, but couldn't. There was too much circling his mind, too many negatives associated with every thought. It was 5-45am at Leeds Bradford airport and he was on the runway – the same runway he'd been sat on for the last hour and a half waiting for the conveyance which had been due to take him to Germany two hours ago to finally get permission to take off and gets its sorry backside into the air. He closed his eyes but a minute later Duncan's index finger was prodding his shoulder.

'What?' he moaned miserably.

'Stop twitching,' Duncan hissed under his breath. 'You're twitching and rocking and, well, mumbling.'

Ben turned to the seat to his left and tried hard to not roll his eyes

'I told you we should have gone with Joss in the horsebox, this is bloody purgatory. I hate flying – there, I admit it, it's worse than waiting to have a tooth out.'

Ben met Duncan's gaze. The Welshman looked relaxed, even laid back. He was reading The Racing Post with his seat reclined and showed no signs of the nausea, anxiety and downright fear Ben was battling with right now.

'Here… read the form for the Guineas and forget about everything else.' Duncan said, pulling a couple of pages of the newspaper out and thrusting them at Ben. 'We'll be in Cologne within an hour. And for heaven's sake stop moaning will you, you're like a little kid.' He paused a few seconds then added, 'Actually you're not – I think Max would be enjoying this, you're just being obtuse.'

'And you've been watching the Shawshank Redemption again haven't you,' replied Ben sarcastically.

The two middle-aged German ladies who sat on the opposite side of the gangway looked over, tutting to each other and then helped themselves to another boiled sweet from a packet which rustled enthusiastically every three and a half minutes. Ben knew this, because he's timed it. That last crinkle was the tenth sweet each in the last thirty five minutes.

Ben groaned inwardly, recognising his own obsession. He detested flying at the best of times and really shouldn't be on this blasted plane anyway. He shook away the thoughts of the thin metal tube he was about to entrust with his life and attempted to focus on the runners and riders in the Guineas. 'European Races. The 2,000 Guineas in Cologne, Germany, 1600 metres' was the headline on the form page. There was fourteen runners, four from the UK, two from Ireland and the rest a mixture of French or German trained three year old colts. Ben scanned down the runners and riders and started to read the form for the first German bred runner but couldn't maintain his concentration and soon gave up. He turned his head and his nose almost touched the window, inspecting the wing of the plane for even the slightest movement. Rain started to plink onto his smooth surface, but Ben wasn't really watching; he'd resumed turning the events of the last few weeks over in his mind.

The week after the Greenham had been decent enough, a fairly standard few days apart from reporters pursuing him, and one turning up at the cottage door. But after the meeting with most of the syndicate at Joss's, he'd been positive about things. That had been a big mistake.
He'd been so dizzy the next day he'd had to spend an afternoon in bed, and only surfaced mid-Sunday morning, missing his usual trip to Joss's with Max. The following week had been no better. He'd been at Catterick and one of his two year olds had broken down on debut and was subsequently found to have a bone chip in her knee which possibly ruled the filly out for the rest of the season. On its own, it wouldn't have been so bad, as there were always injuries to horses, just like human athletes, and pushing a body to be its best sometimes meets with failure. But the 'Drone Attack' as The Forties had called it, caused injuries that had nothing to do with exertions on the racetrack.

It was Thursday evening when Ben had received a call on his mobile from Armitage, of all people, when he was driving back from a Wolverhampton afternoon meeting. He'd been in better spirits, as a three year old with one of his Southern based trainers had run a very promising second on seasonal debut, only being caught in the last stride. So he had happy syndicate members, his horse was well and he had a happy southern based trainer. The news he received had made the next ten miles on the M6 Motorway go by without Ben having any memory of what flashed past.

Someone remotely controlling a drone had flown the device into the barn where The Ghost Machine was stabled. It had sought out the grey and then buzzed him before diving directly for the poor animal in order to blind him. Sat in the plane Ben couldn't help shaking his head at the memory of the drone in Armitage's hands with a strange projection sticking out four inches from its body. It had appeared almost translucent and Armitage explained that it was actually cone shaped, finishing in a needle sharp point, built from a lightweight plastic resin. The last two inches of this spike had been coated in metal. It had looked vicious.

Armitage had explained 'Homemade by the look of it, but whoever created it knew their stuff. It is light enough not to affect the control of the drone, but strong enough to embed up to a couple of inches in pretty much anything.'

He had then given an all too graphic demonstration to Joss, Ben and Demetri by thrusting the spike into the wooden wall of a stable. The spike easily pierced the inch thick plank and protruded out the other side, leaving the drone hanging in the air as if in silent flight.

Demetri's words from that night kept bouncing around Ben's head 'Letting down tyres, pretending to be a policeman and even using an air rifle may be categorised as kid's games, but this drone signals a whole new level to his activity. If the same man is responsible for this drone his intention is clear; he intended to maim or kill the horse.'

The hero of the piece had been Armitage. He'd been in the stable office, watching several CCTV monitors which had been set up earlier in the week and according to Marion, who'd been in there at the same time, he'd jumped from his chair, shouted to 'Get Joss. Barn three!' before running full tilt out into the main yard as fast as his stumpy little legs would carry him. He had reached the barn to find the stable lad outside The Ghost's box staring uncomprehendingly at the buzzing coming from the ceiling, grabbed a straw rake which was leaning against a nearby box and tried to swat the drone which kept swooping down at the horse.

Partly due to his diminutive height he had been unsuccessful until the drone came down to make its final lunge at The Ghost, when it had paused to line up what could have been the killing blow. Armitage had managed to unbolt the stable door and as the deadly spike had started its final descent he'd swung the rake down and managed to clip the drone with one of the tines of his rake. He subsequently admitted it was a lucky shot, as the drone had moved at eye-popping speed, caught on the CCTV replay they'd watched later that evening. Armitage's blow had been just enough to send the drone diving into the six inches of woodchip on the floor of the box, right in front of a highly anxious and very agitated Ghost. Armitage had immediately pounced on the wounded device, which had almost immediately become immobile.

Armitage hadn't only been lucky to despatch the flying spike. He'd ignored the fact that he was in a fifteen square yard wooden box with a three-quarter ton colt who was not at all pleased with his evening being ruined by flying buzzy things, men shouting and then invading his private space. As he lay there on top of the drone The Ghost had been kicking the walls of the box, snorting discontent and nowhere near his normal laidback self.

Joss had arrived moments later to find a disheveled, woodchip covered Armitage breathing heavily, but outside the box in the barn walkway with the broken drone in his hands and three members of staff staring down at it. Jake was at the door to the stable trying to say soothing things to The Ghost and it hadn't taken long for him spot the fact that the colt was lame behind.

Whether it was the jumping around the box when trying to avoid the drone, or kicking the walls of his box in frustration, The Ghost had managed to knock the joint in his right-hand hock. Immediately afterwards Joss felt heat in the joint and first thing the following day the vet was called. The next three days had been spent scanning and then treating the hock with the colt being confined to his box for full rest. The scans had shown a minor dislocation which would be treated with a short course of anti-inflammatory medication. Normally this sort of minor setback would have been nothing of note, the horse would fully recover, and he would be able to race again within a couple of weeks. Unfortunately, the Guineas meeting was only a week away. The drone attacker's probable objective had been achieved.

The Ghost missed the Two Thousand Guineas. This reminder crushed Ben from within once again. Even the rumble of the plane as it started to taxi towards the runway didn't raise the cloud of depression he felt pushing down on him. The colt hadn't time to be clear of the anti-inflammatories or indeed the ability to regain full fitness for the following Saturday. Three days after the Guineas he had been a hundred percent fit and ready to race, but by that time Panama had already won the race at Newmarket by two and a half lengths.

Ben winced as the plane's engines thrust the small jet down the runway and into the sky. It wasn't the action of leaving terra firma, although it didn't help, it was the replaying of the final furlong of the straight mile at Newmarket through his mind. Panama and sixteen others had set off in the Guineas on good to soft ground and split into two groups of six and ten. The smaller group had headed to the far rail, the rest had huddled together in the middle and then drifted to the nearside rail as the race reached its conclusion.

It had been a wide-open race with a 5/1 favourite and the first three horses in the betting being horses from the big, highly successful, and usually all dominant stables supported by wildly rich owners such as Sheikh Kamsun. It was obvious to race watchers that well over a furlong and a half out jockeys riding the ten horses on the nearside had got their tactics wrong. The far side was the place to be. All of the fancied horses, save one, had been on the nearside and were a good ten lengths behind the closely packed far side group.

Into the final furlong many of the nearside jockeys had already accepted defeat and the camera crew also gave up trying to keep the entire field in a single frame. They had moved to where the action was: Panama and Impressionist, a colt trained by the top Irish trainer and the favourite for the race, quickly took two lengths out of their rivals. Then about a hundred yards out Panama's jockey had flicked his whip once at the bay colt and started to ride him with some vigour. The response had been electric. They stretched out to win the half a million pounds prize with consummate ease by two and half-lengths.

Panama's trainer, Billy Bentham, along with a joyous owner,

James Corrigan, bobbing around beside him, was interviewed by an over enthusiastic correspondent after the race. After the asinine 'How does it feel?' question it emerged that the next target for the colt would be The St. James's Palace Stakes, a Group One contest over a mile at Royal Ascot. Ben hadn't been surprised. Even as early as January Joss had let it be known that the same race would be earmarked as the primary goal for The Ghost's three year old season.

He had watched the Guineas at home on television that Saturday, turning down an offer to go to Duncan's for the afternoon. He'd had another sickening bout of dizzying vertigo in the morning which wasn't helped by how he'd felt after watching the race. He'd turned the television off in disgust when the host of the show had started to eulogize about Panama's performance for the third time.

Ben had to catch himself later that day and examine where the bitterness he was experiencing came from, and where it was directed. He's spoken sharply to Max over a minor matter and pulled himself up when halfway through his tirade. He realised it wasn't the winning racehorse which bugged him. It only struck him hours after the race that Panama was the horse that had dealt the fatal blow to Anna. That hadn't mattered. What wound him up and made his blood pressure start to fizz was simply the injustice of the situation. He and his syndicate played fair, and someone else out there was cheating.

Being beaten on the racecourse, even soundly beaten, was quite acceptable in Ben's mind, but being robbed of the ability to compete was unfair. He apologised to Max and tried to push the Guineas result to the back of his mind, however that winning margin and the accolades being piled on the winner had gnawed at him for many days after the race.

Joss had accepted they couldn't run in the race with a similar sense of injustice but had displayed his frustration in a far more physical manner. His outrage at the attack had spilled over into an argument with The Forties about getting the Police involved which had ended with Armitage and Demetri leaving the yard warning Joss not to make the call. His easily provoked bad temper was unfortunately also aimed at some members of his staff. Marion had finally taken him aside and managed to snap him out of it following a very un-Joss like dressing down of a young stable lass for a minor stabling misdemeanour which had left the girl in tears. Temper in check and apologies accepted, Joss had then disappeared for a day before getting The Forties and as many people from the syndicate together to outline his backup plan; to take The Ghost abroad and attempt to win the German Two Thousand Guineas.

This race was the German equivalent of the British race, but it was rated as a lesser standard in the Pattern, the European rankings of such races. The British race was classed as a Group One, whereas the German copy was only a Group Three. However, the German race fitted in perfectly with Joss's timetable for The Ghost and looked to be the best stepping-stone to Royal Ascot. The Ghost could run in Cologne and then come back and race at Royal Ascot in the middle of June, the target being the St. James's Palace Stakes, the same race Panama and several of the other Guineas runners would be aiming for next.

The Forties hadn't been so sure when it was first discussed, but were won over when Joss pointed out that a win in a Group Three race would add significant stallion value to The Ghost. It was also agreed that The Forties would control all the security for the colt, from the travel over to Cologne, to ensuring The Ghost had someone close to him around the clock, even at the start of the race. Joss had organised things so he could be down at the starting post. It was practically a military operation to be certain Raul and The Ghost would break from the starting stalls free of any third-party intervention.

The drone incident and its fallout had been a shock, but Ben was still reeling from the way Joss had been treated at his hearing for the doping offences down in London at the Racing Authority headquarters. Joss's solicitor and barrister had assured him that it would be a lenient conclusion to the episode, but Joss had called Ben in a funk as soon as he'd emerged from the hearing.

Ben recalled the conversation. He had listened to Joss explaining the arguments which had surrounded the discussion of the findings with growing disbelief and anger. When Joss outlined the punishment which had been meted out, the details had caught in his throat and he'd gone silent on the phone for a long time before being able to get everything out. It had crushed him.

The horses involved had been stripped of all prizemoney and couldn't run for three months. Joss had also been fined fifteen thousand pounds for allowing a horse to run using a banned substance, even though it was stated at the hearing that the horse concerned, Silvery Sun, had almost certainly been compromised by the drug, rather than having his chances enhanced. It was the last punishment which had caught everyone by surprise: Joss was banned from having any runners from the yard for an entire month. The Racing Authority had chosen July, the busiest month of the summer season for the ban to be served. With no solid evidence pointing to who perpetrated the crime, the blame was laid at Joss's door by default.

Joss and Marion had been devastated; spending long days trying to shore up their business with calls and visits coming in thick and fast from nervous owners. Coming only a week ahead of the Cologne race, it threw the yard into disarray, as a raft of owners immediately withdrew their horses and sent them to alternative trainers. Joss lost fifteen percent of his horses overnight. The topic had featured in every corner of the racing press for the next few days, drawing comments from virtually every industry commentator, some of whom even questioned whether Joss should be training The Ghost. There was the inevitable 'no smoke without fire' type views expressed, but they were heavily outnumbered by messages of support. Nevertheless, the sentence from the Racing Authority hit the O'Hoole yard hard.

Ben had been in touch with dozens of his own syndicate owners to assure them that the loss of July from their racehorse's campaign would not critically effect the overall season, but there were those who wouldn't listen to reason and wanted Ben to pull their horse out of the yard. As with all his syndicates, he put the decision to a vote, and managed to have enough support to keep all five of his horses in the yard.

Now he was participating in his least favourite activity and doing so on a plane which was even smaller than he had anticipated. Described as a 'Bombardier' in the blurb on the well flicked magazine in the pouch in front of him, the fifty seat plane pitched a little as it cleared land and headed out into the North Sea. A patch of turbulence jolted the cabin to the left and then downwards and Ben felt his stomach turn a back flip. He turned worriedly to Duncan, feeling a little giddy, only to find his friend fast asleep.

Ben pushed away the urge to wake Duncan and instead closed his eyes and decided to occupy his mind with the same conundrum which had filled virtually every waking minute since The Ghost had hurt himself. He tried to picture the six-foot policeman from the yard over six weeks ago, the elements of his face, his chest, then working down to his feet, the way he walked, how he expressed himself in those few sentences. But there wasn't enough of each for Ben to create that overall image. There was too much of the face and his outline he couldn't seem to pull together to create an entire image and it fell apart every time he tried. It was infuriating.

The Forties weren't having much luck with it either. They'd got everyone from the yard together who had spoken, or even seen the policeman that day and tried to create a composite, but it had proved impossible. Most people were trying to ignore the policeman, or get rid of him as soon as they could, as Ben and Joss had done. He'd chosen his disguise well. He'd become a person who you didn't want to speak with and whom you wanted out of your way as soon as possible. No one wanted to catch his eye, so you didn't look at him. You gave him a wide berth, let him get on with whatever he wanted and bent over backwards when he requested something. Finally, you were glad when he left.

Demetri had given Ben an update on their investigations. It consisted of very little, as the trail went cold after each act of aggression upon The Ghost. They had retrieved a foot print from the wood at the bottom of the turnout paddock the day after the drone had flown – a military type boot manufactured in its thousands. The drone itself was a midrange racing drone, available all over the country and of course there were no distinguishing marks. There had been hope that the buyer may have been traced via the serial numbers on the drone, however they had been well scratched off, even from the internal compartment where the motor sat. Demetri had noted that the drone was never intended to return to its controller, its final act was supposed to see it impale the razor-sharp spike into The Ghost.

Ben shivered unhappily at the recollection and gazed out of the window of the plane. Dawn had broken and grey clouds scudded past as the small jet started to make its final descent.

At least The Ghost was already here and in safe keeping. The Forties had made sure of that. The colt had travelled over with Joss two days previously by sea from Hull and then travelled the rest of the way from Zeebrugge in a rented horsebox. Every step of the way The Ghost had never been left alone and both Armitage and Demetri had travelled with him, along with two extra men they had brought in to add 'weight' to the security. Ivan, as ever, had stayed at home. Ben imagined him sat in front of his group of super computers, monitoring the colt's every move from hundreds of miles away.

Joss had called, describing the four of them as 'scary, and not in a fun way.' But he'd been pleased to report that there hadn't been any moments of worry. The Ghost had arrived at the racecourse stables in good order, relaxed and happy. It seemed the Forties had successfully delivered The Ghost to Cologne racecourse without a hair out of place.

So far, so good Ben thought as the planes wheels came to a stop outside a small terminal building. We've all arrived in one piece; let's hope we get home in a similar condition.

Twenty-Two

He was seated straight-backed on one of the round, rotating stools at the bar and wasn't enjoying the experience. Mirrors with adverts for American beers were plastered all over the back of the bar, and the same statement décor continued sporadically right around the pub until it reached a bank of four large flat screens against the wall furthest from the entrance. The place smelled of stale beer mixed with a whiff of cannabis. There was also an annoying source of patchouli oil carried on a draught which came wafting towards the bar each time a customer opened the pub door. He curled his lip as he caught another reflection of himself in one of the smoky mirrors placed at strange angles. He looked away, instead staring fixedly at the thick steel watch around his left wrist.

Over in the other corner and directly behind him, a group of five students in t-shirt and jeans were playing a noisy game of pool, the other two green baize tables being empty. It was late afternoon and the bar was slowly starting to wake. However, he couldn't stay too much longer in here otherwise he'd have to smack one or two of those loudmouthed, spoilt rich kids with their pool cues. He spun his rotating seat round by forty-five degrees and glanced in their direction, fixing his gaze on the nearest teenage girl. Their incessant upper-class whining was giving him a headache, besides, looking at the rest of the lowlifes in this bar he could probably snap all their necks, walk onto the street and disappear in the flow of people heading home after work and no one would even notice. The girl locked eyes with him and then quickly looked away and turned her back. He produced a satisfied nasal grunt and turned back to the untouched double vodka in front of him.

He checked his watch again, then checked the screens and gestured with a single bent index finger which beckoned to a barmaid who was having a whispered conversation with a girlfriend at the other end of the bar. She looked irritated for a couple of seconds until noticing the man's expression, and specifically his eyes, then made her apologies to the girlfriend and walked the thirty feet to where the man was still wiggling a single thin finger annoyingly at her.

He glanced at the screens and growled at the approaching young girl 'This is supposed to be a sports bar isn't it?'

The girl shrugged and came to a stop far enough away to be out of range of a swipe from the man. He raised both eyebrows in unison and fixed her with an intense stare.

'S'pose so,' she muttered, arms crossed but careful not to display too much distain for her customer.

'So where's the horse racing?'

The girl started to roll her eyes but caught herself, thinking better of the attitude. This one looked slightly unhinged even though he'd not even had a sip of his drink. It was all in his eyes she decided, they were hard, cobalt blue and unflinching when directed at you and they screamed 'Go on, mess with me if you dare. I'd enjoy it.'

'Which channel do you want then?' she asked carefully.

'Horse racing from Germany. The German guineas,' He checked his watch, only flicking his eyes away from her for a moment. 'It starts in four minutes and according to your website you show international racing which is why...' His voice tailed off as if he'd become bored with his own sentence. '..I'm here.' he added sarcastically, his eyes still unmoving from the girl.

'No problem,' she answered succinctly and turned on her heel to stride down the bar, muttering something under her breath. It sounded like a couple of expletives, but he wasn't bothered. He liked the fact he'd got to her.

At the other end of the bar the barmaid opened a small cabinet and started to press buttons and the three huge flat screens which had been blank started to run through a setup procedure and come to life. Thirty seconds later there were four sporting events per screen, making the mirrors around the bar dance with reflected football, rugby and basketball pitches intermingled with golf courses, athletics tracks, and racetracks. He cleared his throat in the direction of the girl and she returned to the cabinet and a few seconds later the central screen transformed into one very large single transmission showing several racehorses milling around behind a set of starting stalls. A commentary from the track increased in volume.

He grunted something purposefully inaudible to the girl and slowly spun around in his seat. He could feel his black canvas trousers sticking to the seat as he came round to face the central screen. God this was a dive. He couldn't wait to get out of it.

The horses were slowly loading into the stalls one by one, and he took specific interest when a showy grey horse was led into its position on the outside of the track. Not long after, the stalls crashed open and the entire field jumped forward and the race commentary started.

Being the only grey horse in the field, it was easy for him to follow its progress. It sat at the rear of the field, about ten to fifteen yards away from the leaders and looked to be too far behind. He was therefore irritated when the grey horse picked off two and then another three horses in front of him just as the commentator informed his audience that there was a quarter of a mile to run.

The camera angle changed and the grey horse fell out of the shot as the coverage focused on the three leaders, all of whom were being pushed vigorously by their pilots. He winced as the side on camera panned out and the grey horse came into full view, shooting around the outside of the leaders with its jockey sat motionless. As the pole with a large white

169

number two flashed past the grey horse seemed to his eye to stretch for a few strides and suddenly it was five lengths clear of his rivals. At the number one pole the jockey pushed the horse ever so tenderly and it extended its lead by another three lengths.

He looked back to the horses behind the grey. There were three of them being pushed relentlessly, whips flailing, participating in a separate battle without the leader. Before the grey reached the finishing line he spun his seat back to face the bar and looked down at his drink, still untouched. Then, he waited.

A few seconds later there was a small buzz from the inside pocket of his black cloth jacket. He patiently unzipped the first four inches of the jacket and removed a small, cheap plastic phone, only pausing momentarily to glance at the caller.

'Yes. I watched the race,' he said in answering the call.

He ran an index finger around the rim of his glass as he listened impassively to what was being said, aware that the barmaid and her friend were showing a little too much curiosity, looking over at him and appearing to share a joke. He kept the phone clamped to his ear and directed another cobalt blue stare in their direction. It achieved its goal; they turned back to each other, heads close together.

Two minutes later he said 'I understand.' and hung up the call.

He was glad the bloody grey had won. Now things could happen his way. He grimaced after throwing the entire contents of the glass to the back of his throat but was satisfied with the kick it provided as it travelled into his stomach. He tried to slide off his bar stool but it was too sticky and ended up levering himself up and off the leatherette surface. Scowling, he headed to the pub door, raising a smirk when he ensured he caught the end of one of the student's pool cues as they were aiming. He slowed his progress enough to measure their response, which never came. He'd have loved a faceoff with one of these softheaded little rich kids.

He stopped a few yards before the door, thinking. Then he took out his mobile phone, removed, and snapped the SIM, carelessly tossing it onto the filthy bar floor. Then he took out his wallet, found a replacement and slotted the new SIM into the phone before he pushed his way through the salon type doors. There was no way he could be contacted direct now. He had his instructions and liked their simplicity. If they wanted to stop him they'd have to do it in person. He sneered down at the pavement. As if *that* would ever happen.

This could be good, he thought, taking a lungful of the early evening air. This could be very good. The gloves were off now and he had plenty of options open to him. He wondered for a moment whether this meant he was worth more, but quickly dismissed this line of thought. It was of little interest. He had permission to kill. He liked how that sounded and couldn't help allowing a crooked smile to bend his thin lips.

Twenty-Three

Duncan took another long draft of champagne and said the word again, although he had trouble pronouncing it successfully.

'Enochlophobia?'

Demetri sipped his mineral water and nodded back amiably at the Welshman for the third time in less than a minute.

Duncan whistled. The champagne was starting to make him slightly lightheaded and his lips didn't quite meet properly, making the whistle end in a wet splutter, but he soldiered on 'So Ivan is Enochlophobic? He can't stand a crowd eh! That must really make going racing bloody difficult.'

Demetri sucked in one side of his mouth as he considered this.

'Well, it adds one or two complications to a day at the races, but it's not insurmountable.'

'I guess he gets there early and leaves late?' suggested Ben.

The three of them stood in front of a large open fire in one of the function rooms in Rob's pub, the Crown and Mitre, each with a champagne flute in their hand which had been deposited there by Rob as they entered the pub.

'Let's just say that Ivan is well worth the effort to accommodate his little foibles,' replied Demetri diplomatically.

Buoyed by the rush of alcohol and a lack of a decent lunch, Duncan tried to dig a little deeper. Raising an eyebrow he enquired 'So he's the leader of your little trio?'

'Demetri produced a raffish smile and decided to humour the Welshman. 'I suppose you could say that,' then added in a deliberate tone 'But we three are as one.'

Duncan nodded knowingly, but then turned and shot Ben a look which indicated he didn't have the first clue what this meant.

'We were at school together,' Demetri continued 'We met at the age of eight and found that our... personalities and personal qualities gelled very well. We've been acting as a unit ever since.'

Ben suppressed a smile as he watched Duncan trying to comprehend whether Demetri had made things clearer or muddier for him.

His face went through several stages of understanding through to bewilderment before settling on confused.

'I tell you what Duncan, why don't you ask Ivan yourself,' said Ben, indicating the figure that had just entered the other end of the room.

Ivan walked in through the open door and stopped to look around the room. He carried a soft leather briefcase and seemed oblivious to the three men stood twenty yards away, concentrating instead on a large table with ten chairs which was set up against the back wall. His eyes travelled around the room, taking in the vaulted wooden ceiling, white plaster walls hung with a variety of well known commercial prints and finally the large semicircular mirror adorning the huge chimney breast. He looked back to the two windows bisected by a set of French doors to his left which led into a garden and then walked purposefully to the table.

Demetri nodded towards his colleague and then said quietly to Ben and Duncan 'Leave him to find his seat and get settled.'

Ben brought the conversation back to The Ghost's latest performance. Even though the race in Germany had been almost two weeks ago, it was still very fresh for the three of them, who had witnessed the victory together at the track. The quality of The Ghost's performance kept raising the three men back to the same level of euphoria they had felt in Cologne, and by the time Ian, Olivia and Janet had joined them there was an atmosphere of convivial high spirits as each Owner's experience of the race was shared, fuelled by a glass or two of champagne.

Olivia was lamenting the fact that she and her mother couldn't be there for the race but Duncan pointed out that they were about to get the chance to go to Royal Ascot, a feat dreamed of by all owners and achieved by the select few. This made Janet smile toothily and exclaim 'You won't believe the dress I'm going to wear!' which received a round of wolf whistles and giggles from the girls in response.

Ian appeared to be in good form, having made the trip up from London in the afternoon with his son who was currently playing with Max and Mojo out in the pub garden. Rob's pub had plenty of land with it and the lawns behind the buildings stretched for fifty yards and finished at a small stream with a homemade swing over it. Ian came over to stand with Ben and asked him confidentially whether Ivan would be introducing himself. Ben shook his head 'He's over at the table, his head buried in his laptop. I doubt he'll even speak unless he thinks it's beneficial to his objectives.'

Finally Rob came into the room with Joss and Marion. Armitage followed and after checking outside the double doors, closed them behind him. Ben noted that Armitage wore jeans, a plain shirt and what appeared to be steel toe capped working boots, the first time he'd seen him without a suit and tie. He had been camped out at Joss's stables for the last few weeks which Ben presumed accounted for the change in clothing. Armitage appeared to be more at home in this attire, moving fluidly across the whalebone wooden floor, although Ben noted his serious expression still produced that air of understated persistence around the man. Similar to Ivan, Armitage ignored the ring of Owners near the fire and crossed the floor to the table, selecting a seat to the right of his colleague.

Demetri had requested the meeting through Ben, so when he caught the big man's gaze and eyes were flicked to the table, Ben accepted the prompt and suggested everyone moved across. He was quite clear now that the Forties each had their roles to play, and Demetri, an adept conversationalist was also able to effortlessly manufacture actions from the people around him. Ben recognised his previous character, as the looming partner to Armitage, had just been another role he was playing at the time. In the last few weeks even Armitage had revealed abilities no one could have guessed at following those first few interactions at the yard. Joss and Marion were very complimentary about their houseguest, as he'd become, as they'd offered him a room after the first few days of having him around the stables.

It turned out Armitage, whilst a quiet man, was physically very active and had turned his hand to anything Joss threw at him, in between his racehorse security duties. As well as drilling the staff to ensure the safety of The Ghost, Armitage had displayed abilities as a carpenter, plumber and also, to Joss's surprise he was a natural with the horses, which had turned out to be extremely useful when they took The Ghost to Germany. Armitage had travelled with the horse and been quite unperturbed when asked if he could remain with The Ghost in his travelling crate during the entire voyage from Hull to Zeebrugge. Whether it was intentional or not, Armitage was also looking slimmer and healthier. His double chin was far less pronounced and the excessive sweating had disappeared.

All in all, the Forties had turned out to be one surprise after another, not all of which were positive, but their involvement had become an accepted and in some cases, valued addition to the syndicate. It was Ivan who remained the largely unknown factor. Ben was hopeful he might learn more about him this evening.

Everyone settled into their seats, with Ivan behind his laptop, eyes staring at the screen as the syndicate looked towards Ben. Armitage remained upright and stoic beside his colleague with Demetri choosing a chair diagonally opposite them in the far corner of the thick, wooden table. Ian had bagged the seat to the left of Ivan and was stealing glances at both the man and his computer screen.

Olivia and Janet sat together, nursing their champagne which had hardly been sipped. Beside them were Joss and Marion looking slightly nervous, but Ben decided that was positive, rather than negative.

Rob had offered to hold the meeting at his pub after The Forties had suggested it would be better to stay clear of the stables for now. They hadn't given a reason, but everyone seemed happy with the suggestion as Rob was known for being a very decent host and it also meant they could eat supper at the pub afterwards. The room Rob had set aside for the syndicate meeting was used for christenings, the odd wedding and also as a meeting place for various village committees and local social events. Sitting at a table full of people in early evening at the end of May with the sun casting weak shadows through the windows onto the well worn floor and the faint smell of wood smoke on the air, Ben was suddenly reminded of the debating room in the film Twelve Angry Men. He then imagined the ten people sat around the table arguing and countering each point and he quickly tried to push the comparison from his thoughts. He was hoping this was going to be far more conciliatory.

After thanking everyone and doing a few introductions and reintroductions, Ben and Joss provided a full debrief on how the colt had coped with the race abroad and his current condition. The Ghost Machine had won by an official distance of twelve lengths without being extended. His race time had been a new course record for the mile even though he'd not been fully pushed out by Raul. Joss was delighted with the way he'd been working at home since the journey back to North Yorkshire and it seemed the enforced sojourn to the continent had been a success all round. It was a shame that only a few of the syndicate had been able to be there, but as a stepping stone to the big race for him at Royal Ascot in June, Joss admitted it could not have gone better.

Ben then moved onto the primary reason for the meeting.

'We are here at Rob's to discuss Royal Ascot; the race is the St James' Palace Stakes worth two hundred and twenty five thousand pounds to the winner...,' he paused for the obligatory ooh's, table slaps and whistle from Duncan before continuing '...and how we will ensure that The Ghost gets to the track and into the race without any mishaps. We don't want a repeat of Newbury.'

Ben gestured towards the other side of the table. 'Demetri has some news for us on what the Forties have been working on.'

The big man appeared a little thrown by being referred to as 'The Forties', and Ben realised he'd not used their nickname in their presence before. He looked over to Ivan who didn't appear to be listening, still transfixed by his laptop, and Armitage who looked singularly unimpressed. Duncan smirked from behind his hand and Ben considered saying something to repair his faux pas, but Demetri took over at the bottom of the table and the moment passed.

As Demetri started to speak, Ivan pushed his laptop into the middle of the table and then stood and walked quietly to the other side of the room, drawing the curtains closed on both windows and the doors. As the light was extinguished in stages the reason for the table being close the wall became evident. A small cylinder beside the computer projected its contents onto the pale white plaster of the wall, producing an aerial photograph of Ascot Racecourse.

After a short introduction Demetri paused, now in a half-light, he sat forward and fixed his gaze into the eyes of each person as he systematically went around the table. When he was satisfied he had everyone's attention, he stated. 'We, or should I say 'The Forties'...,' at which point he shot a glance towards Ben with a raised eyebrow. '... have been working hard to ensure The Ghost is able to race successfully and unimpeded. To this end, we have left no stone unturned to identify the bogus Policeman, the shooter at Newbury and the controller of the drone. We believe they are all one man who we have started to refer to as 'The Blue Eyed Man' as the four people who have had contact with him all drew attention to the colour of his eyes and how striking they were.'

He paused again, placing his hands flat to the table. 'We also believe we have identified an individual who may lead us to this man.'

There were several intakes of breath and the convivial atmosphere in the room evaporated, being replaced with a tense bewilderment among the syndicate members not a part of The Forties.

'Who?' demanded Joss irritably, unable to maintain his silence.

Unfazed by the interruption, Demetri turned to Joss beside him and said in a voice loud enough that everyone could not be mistaken 'Billy Bentham'.

This declaration led to a stunned silence for a few seconds but the consternation around the table was palpable and suddenly three different conversations to broke out. Most of them were directed at Demetri. Ben stayed silent and looked over to Ivan who was quietly returning to his seat. He had a slight smirk on his face and once seated he crossed his legs and leaned back with his head bent down like a petulant schoolboy.

Demetri held up both hands and waved a hushing gesture at the table. Eventually the voices dropped low again, giving Duncan the opportunity to speak alone.

'Billy Bentham,' he chortled. 'Billy Bentham, the trainer of the Guineas winner this season, Champion Flat trainer three times and a corner stone of the racing fraternity. So you reckon Billy Bentham shot The Ghost with an air rifle while he was in the stands at Newbury?' he said sarcastically. 'How did he manage that then?'

Demetri nodded sagely at Duncan, his patience seemingly inexhaustible. 'If you will indulge us for a few minutes I will reveal what we have discovered and how we will be able to expose the persons responsible for this campaign of cessation against The Ghost.'

Duncan silently mouthed the words 'campaign of cessation?' and shook his head in resignation.

'You may decide for yourselves, but let us take you through what we have unearthed. I think you will all find the information very interesting, if not compelling.' added Demetri levelly to the table before meeting Ivan's gaze.

Duncan rolled his eyes irritably and the rest of the syndicate looked on with their individual reservations written on their faces. Ivan took over from his seat in front of his laptop.

'I will not bore you with the systematic analysis we have adopted to reach this conclusion. Instead I'm providing you with the highlights.' He soundlessly pushed a key on the device in front of him.

A new slide appeared on the plaster wall, one of Billy Bentham looking disheveled, his uneven and unkempt beard doing him no favours, and alongside him was black cut out image of a man with a question mark placed on top of it.

'Please forgive the image. We...ahem, thought it was appropriate,' started Ivan, looking in Armitage's direction. He continued 'We believe there are at least two people involved in a campaign to stop The Ghost from becoming the top rated three year old miler in Europe this season. The first is Billy Bentham and the second is our unknown policeman impersonator, shooter and possibly drone pilot as well.'

Ivan got up from his seat and continuing to speak, pacing around the table with his head down, hands held behind his back. Ben got the impression Ivan thought he was alone and was speaking out loud to himself.

'There are certain groups who would benefit from The Ghost not racing to his true ability. The first has to be anyone with a racehorse capable of running in the Guineas or at Royal Ascot. That draws in all the owners and trainers.'

The slide on the wall changed to a huge pie chart showing both sets of people as slices. Then Ivan immediately added another two.

'There are professional gamblers and bookmakers. Both could potentially benefit from having access to inside knowledge. The opportunity to lay horses to lose could be a potent motivator on major races which have high liquidity...'

Olivia and Janet looked confused and Ben interjected with an explanation. 'If a bookmaker or big gambler knew The Ghost wasn't going to win they could bet on the horse to lose,' he explained.

'Indeed,' Ivan said with a hint of impatience. 'Then we have the retribution group. This slice of the pie is made up of anyone who could be seeking revenge, attempting to blackmail or to extort money.' He paused and stopped pacing for a moment, then added 'Or all three.'

'There are of course the lunatics to consider,' Ivan said, setting off on his circular amble again. Ben watched Ivan's back receding and couldn't get the image of one of his old schoolteachers out of his head.

'Someone mentally unstable and with no sane reason for targeting The Ghost, such as the normal things: money, power or glory, but given the evidence so far I believe this group can be ignored. The policeman was too convincing and the drone attack far too contrived.'

Setting off again on another circuit of the table the final piece of pie slipped into his animation on the wall. Its title was 'Ourselves'.

'This brings us to a group we cannot ignore. Take a good, long look around this table. In these situations there is a high probability that the person behind this campaign is sitting with us,' said Ivan holding his index finger up and twirling it as he walked.

'Rather like every good police drama, we should look to the family first, and in this case the family is our syndicate. We each have much to win or possibly lose. And before anyone asks, I include myself and my associates in this group,' Ivan said in a matter of fact fashion.

Duncan, who had looked fit to burst with indignation a second or two earlier, swallowed his objection in the dying moments of Ivan's last line. The syndicate looked around the table at each other and then back to Ivan who had started making a ticking noise with his tongue against the roof of his mouth. He had moved into the centre of the room and was standing with his back to the table, looking towards the drawn curtains.

'So, which one of you is the most likely to be the person behind the blue eyed man?' he said, lifting both arms aloft like a boxer accepting victory in the ring.

'Oh, for heaven's sake Ivan,' said Ian leaning one elbow on the table. He held his forehead in his hand and looked sideways with tired eyes at Ivan. 'Can we please get on and discuss whatever it is you have discovered. This is not a murder mystery and I don't think any of us are too impressed with your amateur dramatics. Given you suffer from enochlophobia you sure like playing to the crowd.'

This received a battery of smiles around the table and even a little snort of laughter from Olivia.

Ivan turned smartly around and fixed on Armitage 'Too much?' he asked, as if Armitage was the only other person in the room. Armitage pursed his thin lips and then gave a shy shrug. Ivan peered into the far corner of the room for a second, as if making a mental note and then walked back around the table and took his seat.

He stared at his laptop screen and then in much quieter tone he stated 'After extensive research I can tell you that none of you fit the profile of Mr X or have tangible connections to someone with the skills to carry out such activities.'

Ivan continued 'Of course as you would expect, Mr Bawtry is the most high profile of all of you but even he would not have much to gain. All heads turned to Rob who was staring openmouthed at Ivan.

'Ah, I see you are not aware of Mr Bawtry's background,' said Ivan in mock surprise, but quickly added 'I merely wished to demonstrate that our ability to investigate people is well beyond... well, virtually any other organisation, and that includes the authorities. I apologise, er,... Rob. There is no need for us to dwell on this further.'

Rob still said nothing, but had regained his composure and flicked his eyes around the table. Finally he sighed resignedly and said 'I was SAS when I was in the forces. That's it really, but I guess this information geek will want to tell you more.'

'On the contrary!' exclaimed Ivan, appearing hurt that anyone could even consider he would reveal such personal information. 'I would simply wish to thank you for your service on behalf of everyone here.'

Rob studied Ivan's face carefully across the table, the two of them locking eyes and eventually, satisfied the man was being serious, he grunted 'You're welcome,' managing to muster a modicum of warmth.

'This is turning into a fascinating evening,' admitted Duncan, effectively removing a good chunk of the tension which had filled the room once again.

'You're going to tell me next that Janet here was one of the highest paid hookers in Glasgow and Ben is Lord Lucan's lovechild, are you?' he added sardonically. 'Can't we just get on and find out why the hell you think a seventy-year-old Billy Bentham would want to dope our horse?'

'Yes, I think we could probably do with moving on,' agreed Ben quickly, slightly worried that Janet might take offence. But she was sharing a smile with her daughter when Ben looked over to check.

Demetri nodded to Ivan and the plaster screen behind them flickered as they found the slide they were looking for. It was a simple list of bullet pointed items entitled 'Billy Bentham Evidence.'

The table fell silent once again and Demetri's smooth and calm voice took up the narrative.

'Billy Bentham,' he said slowly, consulting the single sheet of paper in front of him. 'Trainer of Panama, winner of the 2,000 Guineas and the Greenham. Seventy-one years old and married for the last fifty years, was highly successful in the eighties and nineties with over twenty group winners, but since then has struggled to maintain the quality of horses. His yard size has reduced considerably from over one hundred and eighty horses in 1995 down to thirty-five at present. Apart from Panama he doesn't train any other racehorses of note.'

'He leases his fifty acre yard in Berkshire, but also has a large debt with three different horse sales companies.'

'How big?' asked Joss.

'Altogether, just over one point two million pounds.' replied Demetri.

There was an intake of breath from around the table. It could be expected that most trainers would owe sales companies a certain amount of money at any time, as they needed the horses to be in their yards in order to sell them to new owners. At times, the racehorse sales company's role in the industry was as a credit broker for trainers.

'That's a lot of money,' Joss said in surprise. 'He really will need Panama to do well for him.'

'Exactly,' agreed Demetri. 'It seems he tried to upgrade the quality of his horses when his results started to dip in the late nineties and it didn't work. Owners with serious cash behind them started to leave him around fifteen years ago and since then he's been buying expensive yearlings but not finding owners for them.'

'Did he buy Panama?' asked Ian.

'No. His owner…,' Demetri ran a finger down his notes.

'James Corrigan,' prompted Ben. 'He tends to select his own horses from the sales or breeds them himself and then places them with a group of about four different trainers. Billy had no input to the Panama's selection, but he has trained it from being a yearling.'

Duncan chimed 'Lucky Billy. Can't buy a good horse himself, but an owner produces one for him to train just as things are getting tight.'

A quiet voice asked 'How do you know about his debts. Surely that's not public is it?' Everyone looked over to where Janet was sitting.

The oldest person in the room was gazing watery eyed at Demetri.

'Well… madam,' Demetri started, but was cut off by Ivan.

'We are able to access information from all manner of sources Ms Dunn. Some of it is from public sources but if we need to dig a little deeper we are able to access personal digital data if we need to,' he stated with a casualness which clearly irritated the old lady.

'So you stole it?' she corrected, now leaning forward towards Ivan's side of the table.

'No. We accessed it,' Ivan replied, meeting her gaze. 'We have merely accessed the truth in order to determine whether it affects our situation.'

Janet shot a look at her daughter. 'I want to know that we aren't going to hurt anyone because of what…,' she pointed a thin bony finger at the other end of the table. '…this bunch get up to with their computers.'

There was a murmur of agreement and Ben felt he needed to step in.

'I have spoken with Ivan at length on this point, as I know there are a few of us who don't fully understand or agree wholly with his methods. However he has convinced me that his…,' he searched for the right word for a moment. 'Err… his *investigation* of The Ghost's attacker will not harm anyone or any organisation.'

A few mutterings started up and Ian cleared his throat. 'I think all of us from the original syndicate find it difficult to fully trust three people who cleverly inveigled their way into ownership of The Ghost.'

Ivan bridled at this and was about to protest but Ian placed a gentle but unmoving hand on his arm and he remained silent.

'I can tell you that I've already sounded out the police, and I know Ben has done the same,' he added, nodding at Ben. 'Given the evidence we have at the moment, I'm afraid the police would not pursue our case. I took the opportunity to speak off the record with a Detective Inspector friend of mine in London a few days ago. She advised that whilst the police would record our complaint and suspicions in case things escalated, there currently isn't enough evidence or a crime serious enough for them to launch a proper investigation. And she was certain there would be no resources made available to protect the colt. I also doubt the racing authorities will have the resources either. We are on our own until the attacker breaks enough laws for the authorities to take note. As such, I do think we need to allow Ivan to continue helping to protect our horse, but only within the tight remit Ben has negotiated.'

Ben studied Ian anew. The man really was as sharp as a tack.

'Many thanks for that Ian,' Ben managed. Ivan and Demetri indicated the same.

At the other end of the table Janet said in her soft Scottish accent 'Okay, boys, you've won me over, but I'll be watching you closely, mark my words.'

Olivia cast a look apologetically around the table and received a few smiles in return.

'You do that Janet,' said Duncan turning to Demetri and waving an erect index finger in the man's face. 'These boys better play fair or we'll set you on them!'

The old lady cracked a smile. 'I have been known to kick a few shins in my time,' she added before rolling her false teeth around her mouth.

Olivia shook her head and then looked pleadingly along the table to Ben in hope that the spotlight could shift from her mother.

Ben took the hint 'So Demetri, please continue.'

Demetri settled back again and held up a hand towards the plaster projection. 'We have Billy Bentham owing plenty of money, with little in assets. He discovers in the May of the colt's two year old season that Panama is very decent indeed, in fact he is potentially a world class racehorse, so what does Billy do?'

'You place a very large bet with several bookmakers,' he added, immediately answering himself.

A new slide appeared on the wall with four bullet points with odds and numbers against them and a six-figure total at the bottom.

'We thought it would be worthwhile looking at bookmakers and seeing if anyone would benefit from The Ghost losing his races. What we found is that Billy placed four bets of five hundred pounds each with different bookmakers in May last year. The bet was that he would train the top three year old in Europe this year. He managed to get odds varying from 400/1 up to 750/1 and stands to win almost two million pounds if Panama continues to dominate the three year old colts division this season.'

Demetri stopped for a few seconds to let this information sink in before adding. 'I think this is a pretty good reason to stop The Ghost beating Panama.'

'How did you get this information about his bets?' said Ben but immediately wished he'd never asked the question. 'Oh hold on, I don't want to know,' he added sheepishly.

'Online bookmaker's websites are a joke,' Ivan responded in a derogatory tone.

'But Billy can't have done all these things himself,' Joss pointed out. 'For one, he stood in the stands only a few yards away from me when The Ghost got shot at Newbury.'

Demetri took a sip of water and placed the glass carefully back onto the table 'We're not suggesting he actually carried out the various acts against our horse himself, but he does have the strongest motive we have found, and by some way...'

'We have looked through bank accounts, bookmakers accounts, Weatherby's ownership records and cross referenced every owner, trainer and yard employee. That's a total of over five thousand people we have investigated.'

We have factored in the use of a .77 calibre pellet with the type of air rifle with those bought across the country in the last six months. We have read the report on the exact makeup of the drug used to dope Joss's winner at Ripon and then looked at where supplies of the drug could have come from, again referencing every person on our list with purchases of the materials. We've done exactly the same with the drone Andrew managed to capture.'

There were a couple of furrowed brows which threw Demetri for a moment. Then he realised.

'Ah, I should explain. My colleague Mr Armitage does in fact have a first name, but as school friends we always referred to him using his surname. It sort of stuck when we left college.'

Armitage, who had been totally silent up to this point, now turned to the table 'Armitage or Andrew is fine. I'm both to my friends and enemies alike.'

Ben did a double take. Had Armitage just spoken in a lower register? His annoying high-pitched southern twang wasn't there anymore. It shouldn't surprise him he thought, Demetri had used an act to produce results, and in his own way, Armitage may have been doing the same. Coming across as a wholly disagreeable solicitor with a pedantic nature and an annoying personality was perhaps perfect for the job. Armitage's comment received a rather muted response. Perhaps the others were thinking similar thoughts.

'Anyway,' Demetri quickly interjected 'We drew a blank on the gun, pellet, and drone. They sell in their thousands and although we know the drone was bought recently because it's a model which only became available ten months ago, we were unable to discover a link to any of our five thousand suspects. It would have been nice to find Billy had bought the same model drone online a few months ago, but the likelihood is that our bogus policeman did all his own dirty work, including the sourcing of his materials.'

'Can you hack into phone companies?' Ian queried.

'I don't hack anything,' Ivan retorted.

'I caress and persuade technology to bend to my will without the need for strong-arm tactics. Hackers just throw mud at the wall. But yes, I can access phone records.'

Ian cast Ivan's words aside with a flick of his wrist 'So have we got Billy making any calls which would be incriminating over the last few months?'

'No, not that we could discover,' admitted Ivan. 'Although he does order a worryingly large volume of fast food takeaways.' he added sarcastically.

Rob sighed irritably and received a few questioning looks. 'I'm sorry, but it seems to me that all we have is a trainer of a damned fine horse placing a few bets to try and pay off his debts. Is it just me that thinks this is all a bit tenuous? There is nothing which links him to the rest of the stuff which has gone on.'

Demetri was the first to jump in with a reply. 'We don't have a definitive lead on the man, or woman, who has been attacking The Ghost. Billy Bentham is our number one suspect on the list. I could name the next ten if you wish, but that's not the point.'

He swiveled in his seat to speak directly to Rob. 'Armed with this information we will be able to plan how we can protect our horse and we might even be able to catch our 'blue eyed man' in the process. Ivan is certain that our man will attempt to stop the colt running his race at Royal Ascot.'

'All the data points to some sort of attack before or during the race,' Ivan confirmed. 'Our man is ingenious, bold and although he hasn't been one hundred percent successful, he is well informed. In fact, he appears to have only one weakness. He is not a horseman.'

'What makes you say that?' asked Ben.

Ivan started to count off his reasoning on his fingers. 'He couldn't identify the right horse when he was in Joss's yard. He had the perfect opportunity to ruin the colt's entire season and he got the horses mixed up.

He also shot the colt in its rump, when he could have gone for an eye, and finally he tried to blind The Ghost with a lightweight nail. Anyone who knows racehorses would have worked out that simply buzzing the animal with the drone until it ended up hurting itself in its box was a far better strategy. Horses are their own worst enemy – look what happened anyway – we had to miss the Guineas because of one small knock. The Ghost only survived that assault because our man tried to over complicate his attack...'

Ivan was still holding up three digits when Demetri spoke.

'We have planned the entire three days of the colt's travel, overnight stay and day of the race activities at Ascot so that the Ghost will always be safe and protected. That way he gets his chance to race. If, as we suspect, our blue eyed man will try to get to The Ghost at the races, then we will spring a trap to catch him.'

'Now that's more like it!' exclaimed Duncan.

Demetri clapped a large hand on the Welshman's back 'I'm glad you like it so much, as you're going to help us make sure we catch him.'

Duncan's eyes grew large and a smile crept over his face.

'In fact, we need all of you to help us,' Demetri announced, opening up his arms to the entire table.

'You all have a valid reason for being at the races, as owners of a fancied horse in the most important Group One race of that days racing. We may need to call on all of you to play your part on the day. What I want to do now is take you through those plans for the day of the race.'

There was genuine astonishment around the table, and it was Joss who was first to verbalise his support.

'Well anyone who thinks it's okay to injure my horses and try to ruin my business needs to look out. I'm in.'

Marion grasped her husband's hand and said 'Me too.' determinedly.

Ian and Rob both nodded their approval and Oliva burst out with 'Och, absolutely,' excitedly.

Duncan caught Janet's eye and asked 'Come on Janet, you going to help us kick some shins?'

She responded with a throaty laugh and nodded back vigorously.

'What about it, Ben?' asked Demetri.

The table waited for a reply, but Ben was deep in thought. He quickly glanced around the nine other people and tried to pull together the various strands in his head in order to produce a coherent statement. It was important he got this right. Placing both hands palms down, arms outstretched on the rugged wood table he started to speak.

'I know we all want to see The Ghost run his race at Ascot, but our own safety has to come first. Are we sure this blue eyed man isn't going to attack one of us?'

There was silence around the table.

'His actions have become more brutal each time,' he continued. 'And if he does go for one of us instead of The Ghost, how will we protect ourselves? It's all very well being gung ho and wanting to trap him, but trapped animals tend to fight back.'

He let out a small sigh. 'Some of you here, like me, have witnessed a death on a racecourse, albeit accidental. I really don't want to go through another, accidental, or otherwise.'

Ben could feel his voice started to crack, but swallowed down the lump that had suddenly appeared at the base of his throat.

'If we do this, I want to be absolutely certain that everyone is going to be safe,' he said shakily. 'I'm probably just being over cautious...' He croaked to a stop, suddenly dry and reached for his drink. There were a few worried glances between the syndicate.

Unexpectedly, it was Ivan who then spoke and he did so in a tone which was very different to his usual brusque, arrogant manner. He closed his laptop so that he could meet Ben's eyes.

'I can assure you Ben that we will be placing no one in harm's way. Once you hear what we have planned I think you and the rest of your partners will go to Ascot safe in the knowledge that there will always be someone watching and ready to act at all times. We will find the culprit, deal with him properly and no one will be placed in any danger in doing so, you have my word on this.'

Ben looked back at Ivan and felt he'd just seen a new side to the man. He had wondered more than once over the last two months why Demetri, in particular, held Ivan in such high regard. This band of brothers thing they had going on, was certainly intriguing.

There was agreement with Ivan right around the table. Ben also received personal commitments from both Armitage and Demetri regarding the safety of everyone, including themselves and the Ghost.

Demetri suggested that it was perhaps the right time for a short break, after which The Forties would go through the plans for the two days at Ascot. This went down well with everyone apart from Ivan, who remained resignedly behind his reopened laptop until everyone returned a few minutes later. There were definitely times when the petulant schoolboy comes out to play, thought Ben, as he sat back down, having watched Ivan roll his eyes at everyone as they returned to the table. It must be exhausting for him.

'It's lovely to see your boys playing together in the garden,' commented Olivia when she came back to the room with her mother. There was a waft of cigar smoke as they sat down and Ben made a mental note that one of them, probably Janet, must smoke. That was why they'd been in the garden, as Rob had a smokers' gazebo tucked away beneath a couple of old cedar trees.

Ian and Ben both thanked her, Ben responding 'Max loves playing with older boys and Ian's lad is really good with him.'

Ian added 'And he loves to play with Mojo. We can't really get him a dog where we are at the moment, but any excuse to run around with animals and he's there.'

Joss was taking his seat again and chipped in 'You know you can teach him to ride at the yard if he's interested. We've a couple of very staid ponies he could get on and see what he thinks.'

'Thanks for the offer, but I believe my wife may have some reservations. She's not exactly one hundred percent behind me even owning a horse.'

'Even one that's going to Royal Ascot?' said Olivia in a shocked tone.

'Nope,' Ian replied, shaking his head. 'The gym, the swimming pool, and hockey are her passions. She plays hockey for a fairly serious ladies' team in London which has got a couple of the Olympic team members on its roster. She's there two evenings a week training and playing matches, and so I'm allowed to indulge in racing as the trade off.'

'Sound like the perfect match!' Duncan piped up.

'That's actually a good point,' Ben said to the table in general. 'If we are all at Ascot with a plan to find our blue eyed man then what happens to the extra people we'd usually bring along? Is everyone bringing someone?'

Demetri was the last person back in the room and again and he dimmed the lights from the door before heading back to his seat.

'Yes, Ben is right, we need to know exactly who will be there,' and he sat down, pen at the ready.

It turned out that there weren't as many extras as Ben had thought. Olivia, Janet, and Ian would all be there on their own. Joss and Marion would be there, along with Jake leading up and, of course, Raul as jockey. The Forties would be there, but just the three of them, there was no discussion of wives or partners and Ben realised he didn't know how any of them was fixed in that area of their lives and decided he needed to make an effort to find out. Duncan and Rob also confirmed they would be travelling to Ascot alone as the midweek fixture made finding cover difficult for Duncan's children and Rob's work.

'You're not bringing your Mother, Rob?' Olivia enquired.

Rob looked a little jaded when he looked up but forced a half smile

'Mum has gone downhill the last few weeks,' he admitted with sadness creeping into his voice. 'I'm pretty resigned to the fact that she's going to be completely housebound from now on.'

'Oh, I'm sorry to hear that,' Oliva said, stretching her hand across the table. He took it and thanked her, cupping Olivia's hand in both of his own.

Ben thought back to the day he'd last seen Rob at Joss's stables, how he hadn't stayed any longer than was absolutely necessary and he wondered what Rob's actual situation was with his mother. He was once again reminded that this season with The Ghost was affecting far more than just the horse's ability to compete.

A new set of slides was revealed and Demetri stood and walked around the table to be in front of the projection. What followed was a run-through of the two days at Ascot and specifically the build up to the race. From ensuring The Ghost was safe at home over the next fortnight, to his journey to Ascot the day before the race, and then an hour by hour breakdown of the race day, The Forties had seemingly thought of everything. The syndicate sat in shocked silence, boggling at the precision, audacity and in one case, impudence of their plan.

Everyone asked questions, especially Joss, who added certain critical amendments through his knowledge of the racecourse and its private areas just for horses, trainers, and stable staff. It was interesting to see how The Forties coped, with Ivan's intelligence underpinning their operation, Demetri bringing individuals into the conversation, and cleverly using subtle manipulation both with his own people and the rest of the syndicate to reach solutions. Armitage operated with practicality and a straightforward – get it done – efficiency. Ben couldn't help but be impressed.

Perhaps the most memorable section of the evening was when Ivan produced the technology the syndicate would be using for the two days at Ascot. He had been explaining how he would be acting as a controlling influence on all ten of them, being in constant touch with everyone, when Joss had pointed out that there could be three or four groups at different points on the racecourse at any one time.

'Not a problem!' Ivan said, producing a small box from a pocket of his leather case. The box was opened and inside sat twelve round silver and gold disks, three rows of four, embedded into black velvet. They were no more than a centimetre in diameter and shimmered in turn when the projector light caught them. Beside each disk was what appeared to be an even smaller glass button, no bigger than a one-penny piece.

'Ian, you might recognise these,' Ivan prompted sardonically, popping one of the silver disks out of the black velvet. It came away, with a two inch flesh coloured plastic loop trailing behind. He then carefully picked up the glass button which when removed from its velvet recess was revealed to have a pin and butterfly clasp.

It took a few seconds for Ian to catch on, but once Ivan planted the first device in his hand, recognition crept over his face.

'These are what you were using to communicate with Armitage and Demetri in the parade ring at Newbury,' he reported to the table. Ben didn't really get the buzz some people got from technology, but Ian was excitedly allowing Ivan to fit what turned out to be an earpiece and blazer button onto him. Together they produced their mobile phones and did something with an app which Ben didn't really understand, but had apparently been written by Ivan.

'Right. Now go and find your son outside,' Ivan instructed.

Ian, pressing the silvery gold disk to his ear so that it virtually vanished, did as he was told and left the room. Ivan tapped a few keys on his laptop and altered the projector slightly and immediately there was a video of someone walking through the back of the pub, and out into the garden. Ivan fiddled with something and the sound of bird song and children laughing and shouting came through the laptop's speakers.

Taking a headset from his briefcase, Ivan plugged the audio jack into the laptop and quietly said 'Hi Ian, can you hear me?'

There was a sudden jerk in the video as a hand flew up the frame then out of view and the word 'Ouch!' came through the laptop.

Ivan played with a few settings and asked 'Is this better?'

'Wow, er… Yes, much better. Can you hear me okay?'

'Loud and clear,' Ivan said in his mangled Scottish cum Polish accent.

They all watched as Ian approached Max, Mark and Mojo all playing in the stream at the bottom of the garden. The terrier's barks came over the small laptop speaker in staccato bursts. You could hear the boy's shouts getting louder as Ian crested a small rise and the video showed the two boys, one of them with legs shot out on a broad wooden plank swing attached to a substantial tree beside a shallow stream.

The video and sound was impressive, but it was when Ian started to speak with the boys that the technology really came alive. Ivan said a few more things to Ian and then started to hand out the rest of the ear buds, as he called them, and the glass buttons which he explained was where the video and sound was being picked up from. With the help of Demetri and Armitage, all ten people around the table managed to get the devices fitted and had the app downloaded to their phones. Janet's phone was unfortunately too old and basic for an app to be used, but instead Ivan patched both ladies into Olivia's mobile.

The next ten minutes was spent with the entire syndicate running around every room in the pub appearing to speak to themselves, each watched by a bemused set of early evening regulars. However, it then blew everyone away when Ivan started to switch people into one to one, three-way and then finally the entire ten people sharing the communication line. At this point he instructed everyone to push a button on their app and suddenly the screen divided into two, then five and finally ten small video boxes allowing you to watch each syndicate member individually, but all on their small phone screens. Admittedly, it started to get a bit confusing when everyone started to talk over each other, but Ivan seemed to be adept at maintaining the sound levels to acceptable tolerances.

He then got them all to start switching between videos, so a single tap would show that person's own view bigger than the other windows, and allow you to speak just to them. Double clicking the video got rid of everyone, apart from who you wanted to speak with. On the app was also a 'Controller' button which was just a grey ghost in the bottom right of every video screen. This allowed you to speak with Ivan, but watch what other people were doing. Rob and Olivia needed a bit of help with the app, as they weren't quite as savvy with their phones, but a couple of minutes tapping the screen got them proficient.

Finally Ivan did something at his end and the app cut everyone off and showed a 'Game Over' symbol and he announced through everyone's earpieces 'That's it people, we're all sorted now, please return to the room.'

By the time they all returned to the events room the entire syndicate was buzzing.

As each member of the syndicate came back to the table Demetri collected in all the earpieces and glass buttons, replacing them carefully and snugly into their places in the velvet. It then disappeared into Ivan's briefcase.

Ivan waited for everyone to be seated again and then finished his presentation.

'As you have discovered, the system is easy to use and extremely powerful. We've been using the local broadband connection today, but at Ascot we will have to ensure we have plenty of bandwidth because the public phone network will probably be unable to cope. The app will automatically connect you to a satellite link we will be installing in the stands, so you should suffer no outages.'

Janet turned to her daughter and gave her a bemused look. Olivia quietly promised to explain to her later, upon which the old lady stated loudly 'I'll be getting one of those proper mo-billy things Olivia, before we go to Ascot, I'm not being left out of all the fun!'

Amid general giggling and snorting Ivan piped up 'It is important that you all arrive at Ascot at the proper time, with your phone charged to maximum and the app ready to use. Janet, you'll need to get a smartphone sorted and then contact me so I can get it operating.'

Olivia and Janet both nodded, the latter with a big young girl's grin on her face.

Ivan went on to explain that he would be controlling everything from a private suite in the stands at Ascot. The Forties had apparently booked this some time ago, in preparation for The Ghost being able to race in the St James' Palace Stakes. Ben thought this was astounding in terms of pre-planning.

'One of the other benefits of the system is that I can know exactly where everyone will be on the racecourse, down to the metre,' Ivan told the group.

Joss was staring hard at a spot on the table but then flicked his eyes up 'Could you put one of these things on Raul during a race?'

Ivan thought for a few seconds. 'I'm sure we could put one of these on him and I'm certain it would work, but I don't think it would be worth flouting the rules of racing just to be able to give him in-race riding instructions.'

Joss rubbed his chin and gave up on the idea. 'Yeah, I forgot about the no contact rules. I guess it's easy to get carried away with what a new gismo can do. But it could be useful on the gallops.'

'Let's just get it working correctly for us all at Ascot for now,' suggested Demetri. He went over to the curtains and pulled them open, revealing the start of a fine sunset which bathed the floor with a reddish tinge.

He walked back to the table 'We can look at other applications after The Ghost has run his race. But remember that this is a covert operation, so please, no talking or sharing these plans or the technology with anyone.' He went around the table to elicit acceptance from everyone through a succession of smiles, nods, and thumbs up.

'The security of this plan is that we are the only ones who know about it. If you start sharing it with people outside this group, it could have dire consequences for the horse and ruin our chances of catching our blue eyed man.'

The meeting broke up in good spirits with jokes, handshakes, good wishes and calls of 'See you in a fortnight' and comments on the general excitement surrounding The Ghost's run at Royal Ascot and the plan to foil any attempt by the blue eyed man to stop the horse running.

Rob reminded everyone that they were welcome to stay and eat at the pub. The Forties declined, with Armitage heading back to the yard with Joss and Marion, who had to get back to prepare a couple of horses for racing the next day. Ivan and Demetri also departed straight after their presentation, citing other work they had to attend to, but the remaining syndicate members stayed.

Rob had reserved a large table out in the garden, close to a cluster of apple trees which still had the remnants of blossom colouring their branches. The six syndicate members, plus the two boys Max and Mark, enjoyed a 'grand buffet' as Rob called it, which consisted of pretty much everything on his menu with people picking the food of their choice and as much as they wanted. The conversation tended to centre upon The Ghost and whether he was good enough to win the St James' Palace stakes, and didn't stray onto the topic of the blue-eyed man. Demetri's warning about involving other people was still fresh in minds.

The two boys finished their meal in double-quick time and headed back down to the bottom of the garden to play on the swing again. Ben was thankful the sun was still out, as Max had managed to get the wetter of the two of them, but had at least started to dry naturally. He and Duncan followed the boys to the stream, leaving Ian, Rob and the Scottish ladies discussing where the colt could go racing after Ascot.

The two men said nothing as they walked, both quite comfortable with the silence. On reaching the stream bank they stood watching the boys playing on the makeshift swing, taking turns to push each other over the water. Ben was aware of a light breeze which was fanning his forehead and he closed his eyes, allowing the last dashes of sunlight to warm his skin

189

where they pierced through the branches of the trees.

Duncan held a beer bottle in his hand and took a draft.

Ben opened his eyes and still watching the boys playing said 'How much do you trust The Forties?'

Duncan took a sidelong glance at Ben and took another swig of his beer before answering.

'Until you just asked me, I was starting to like them a bit. But now I'm less certain. What's up?'

Ben sucked his teeth and with both hands in his trouser pockets, shrugged his shoulders.

'It was just a couple of things which have really only struck me now,' he said, turning to his friend and lowered his voice to be certain the boys couldn't hear.

'It was what Ivan said about most of the time it being the family, or in this instance, the syndicate that are usually the culprits in this sort of situation. What if the person making all these horrible things happen is part of the syndicate?' he said quietly.

Holding his beer bottle to his chest, Duncan considered this, but quickly dismissed it. 'No, you're... *they're* wrong. It can't be anyone in the syndicate or even around us. What have any of these people got to gain?' he indicated the table they'd left behind them with a jerk of his thumb.

'I just can't see it. Now, Billy Bentham does have a lot to gain from his horse winning all the major prizes for three year old colts this season and it makes a lot more sense,' he added.

'I know, it's just worrying me I guess,' Ben said resignedly.

'I wouldn't let it bother you. In two weeks time we'll have caught him in the act with a bit of luck and this whole sorry affair will be over.'

'It's not just the chance that it could be someone close to us,' Ben said, his voice no more than a whisper now. 'It's those space age communicators.'

'Why are they bothering you? I think they're brilliant,' said Duncan, his brow furrowing.

'Well look at it this way. Imagine you're The Forties, and you think the person trying to harm your investment – which is now potentially worth millions – is among the people closest to the horse. Yes, you want to catch this 'blue eyed man' but they seem certain he's just hired muscle. So how do you flush that main man out?'

Duncan looked confused and then skeptical and then confused again.

'You make it common knowledge that you think you've found the culprit. That reduces the pressure on the real crook who they then fool into making a mistake.' Ben hissed quietly, looking for a dawning of understanding in Duncan's face.

Duncan sipped at his beer thoughtfully for a few seconds. 'Okay,

190

so the Billy Bentham story is just a ruse?'

'Yes.., well, it might be.'

'And The Forties are now waiting for someone linked to the syndicate to make a mistake which proves they are the blue eyed man, or at least controlling him?'

'Yes.' said Ben, dropping his voice even further. 'And they now have the perfect way to do that… with this.'

He produced his mobile phone from his trouser pocket and waggled it between two fingers.

'The Forties and their app are going to be monitoring everyone in the syndicate. Every step you make at Ascot will have them watching and listening to what you say and do.'

Duncan took another sip of his beer and considered his response.

'It seems to me that whoever's responsible, even if it's a close friend, has to be stopped. If The Forties can make that happen, I'm still behind them and their plan.'

Ben let out a sigh which was a lot louder than he intended. 'I know, you're right of course. I guess there is nothing I can do if the person behind all this belongs to my syndicate.'

'Well it certainly isn't me, and I know it's not you or Joss, so we're almost half way there! I could be wrong, but I can't see any of the others being the types either.'

Ben nodded acceptingly at Duncan, who placed a hand on Ben's shoulder and gave him a squeeze.

The two of them turned back to the boys who were now both in the streambed, up to their knees in crystal clear water, kicking it at each other and squealing.

Duncan finished off the last of his beer and wiped the back of his hand across his mouth. 'We should hopefully get the answers at Ascot, one way or another.'

Ben forced a smile. 'Yes… one way or another,' he repeated, unconvincingly.

Twenty-Four

As the final declarations for The Ghost's Royal Ascot race refreshed and displayed on his monitor, Ben was still feeling ill. He had been feeling rough on Saturday morning, and then become so dizzy he'd had to miss going racing to watch one of his decent handicappers running at York that afternoon. Sunday had seen him feeling a little bit better but the thought of driving around with his head still pounding had led him to apologise to some owners he should have been showing around Joss's yard that morning. This was the third weekend on the trot he'd felt like this and the week before had been so bad he'd gone to his local doctor's surgery, a place he'd taken Max to a few times, but never attended on his own behalf. He had always been in good physical health and rarely needed to see a GP. Anna had insisted he register himself years ago, but Ben couldn't ever remember having attended because of his own poor health.

He'd managed to get an appointment the same day and had seen an amiable Indian chap who had given Vertigo as the diagnosis, which he'd gone on to explain could be caused by all manner of things. So Ben had been given a series of blood tests, provided swabs and produced samples. Combined with his regular visit to the psychologist in Leeds every other Wednesday, Ben was heartily sick of being sick.

Thank goodness, Helen was around to help out. She'd stayed over on the Friday lasagne night as normal, but then remained at the cottage all weekend to take Max to play for his football team on Saturday morning and had then kept both of them amused for the rest of the weekend. Queasy and totally useless in terms of running the house, he'd been really grateful she had offered to stay.

The final declarations were announced at around 10-15am on Monday for the St James's Palace Stakes, with the race being run on Wednesday 21st June. Not for the first time, Ben was thankful that Royal Ascot was towards the end of June and not in July, otherwise Joss's month long runners ban would have ruled The Ghost out of the biggest race of his career. The five day meeting started on Tuesday and ran to the Saturday, with Group One races being run every afternoon. A total of over three hundred thousand people would attend the meeting, placing it among the premier race meetings in the world.

The Ghost's race was one of the highlights on the Wednesday, as the St James's Palace Stakes was rated one of the most important three year old races for colts in the World. Classed as a Group One race, it offered total prizemoney of over half a million pounds. The plan was to travel down on Tuesday, ensure everything was set, stay overnight at a hotel nearby before heading to the track on Wednesday morning.

Ben was staring at the final list of runners when Helen came into his office with a laundry basket in her hands. It did feel a little weird having his mother in law doing the washing for him, but Ben had come to terms with the fact that he needed the help. She buzzed around the room, picking up discarded t-shirts and socks, pushing drawers in, straightening books, and matching shoes which had been kicked off in different directions by Max.

'It's a big field on Wednesday,' Ben commented, not lifting his eyes from the monitor of his computer. 'Sixteen runners and there are plenty with only a run or two, so a lot of unknowns in there.'

Helen made a positive humming noise in the background. Ben knew that she wasn't too interested in his chosen line of work, and the fact it had inadvertently led to the death of her daughter hadn't endeared Helen any further to the sport. However, she still openly supported Ben and knew how important The Ghost was to her grandson's future.

She came up and stood behind Ben's chair. 'Is that good one in this race?'

'Panama. Yes, he's in there and will almost certainly be a short priced favourite I would think.'

Ben considered reminding her that Panama was the horse who had accidentally kicked Anna, but decided against it. She probably wasn't aware, as the horse's name hadn't been too widely reported afterwards. The colt had been referred to as one of the other placed horses in the winners enclosure.'

'So does The Ghost have a chance of beating him?

'We're all hoping so,' replied Ben, swivelling his chair around.

'You know you could have come with us if you'd wanted.'

'Oh gosh no, I'd only be getting in the way. I'll look after Max and make sure he gets to school for the next few days. I'll record the race for him though, unless you don't want him to see it?'

'Yes, of course. I'll set things up on the television to record the race. He's disappointed he's not coming, but what with everything that's been going on, I think its best he stays at home and has a normal day. Besides, I'll be busy enough coping with the syndicate.'

Ben hadn't gone into much detail about the issues surrounding this race with Helen. She knew the horse was important, classy and the syndicate was difficult to manage, but he'd thought it best not to get her worried with the attempts to curtail the horse's career.

Helen murmured an 'Okay then…,' turned and sauntered off with her clothes basket, assuming Ben was engrossed in his work again, but he called her back.

'You know how much I appreciate your help, Helen,' he said standing up when she reentered his makeshift office. 'Max loves having you around and I'm really grateful for that.'

'What are you after?' replied Helen smiling, her eyes twinkling.

He returned an impudent smile. 'I'm positively opaque aren't I?

You and Anna always could work me out immediately.'

'Come on, out with it,' she prompted.

'Well, Duncan will be taking me down tomorrow morning so that I don't have to drive, just in case I get dizzy again. We stay over on Tuesday night, race on Wednesday and he wanted to stay for one more day's racing before driving back on Thursday evening and…'

'Yes, no problem,' she cut in. 'I'll stay and look after Max until Thursday evening. Just do me a favour and come back in one piece. Don't drive, don't drink, don't over exert yourself and if he wins, try not to get too excited.' She tapped his stomach with the rim of her clothesbasket a couple of times as she gave her instructions before leaving the room on her hunt for further items to wash.

Ben smiled and sat back down at his computer but soon lost his good mood when he scanned down his email inbox to find a message from Graham P Loote lying there. The title of the message had been written in capitals, which always meant it was yet another complaint.

****

That evening he was feeling much better and, after convincing Helen he would be fine, he picked up Max and Duncan's girls from school and after dropping the girls off, he and Max drove over to Joss's stables. After making it into the yard through the new security The Forties had overseen, the two of them went to see a couple of his two year olds and the broodmare, but most of their time at the stables was taken up with feeding The Ghost a few carrots.

Ben gave the grey a final pat on his neck, whispering 'Good luck, pal,' in his ear. Max gave the colt a hug, being lifted by Ben and trying to stretch his arms right around The Ghost's neck. Then the two of them headed home.

Half an hour later a large unmarked horsebox pulled into the back of the yard and, under the constant gaze of Armitage and Joss, The Ghost was loaded up.

Twenty-Five

The first day of the Royal meeting was well underway when Duncan and Ben walked across Ascot High Street towards the racecourse stables. The sound of the fifty-five thousand strong race-goers was to their backs, providing a constant drone of conversation intermingled with public announcements. However, the road right outside the racecourse was eerily quiet, the only movement being the odd passing car and a few members of Ascot staff. The race day staff ensured any racehorse coming from the racecourse stables for an upcoming race, or from the racecourse itself could trot straight across the road without being held up by the traffic. The two men watched a young horse come up from the stabling area, pass through the gate, and then trot over the road, staff waving him through and into the racecourse.

A hot, sticky day had made the car journey seem longer than Ben had remembered from previous visits to the racecourse. Even with air conditioning it had been an uncomfortable drive down the country. There was only a breath of a breeze which whipped up tiny pieces of dust from the road as they walked over the crossing. Ben was pleased The Ghost wasn't running today. He imagined the race-goers inside the course would be being slowly poached in their top hat and tails as the twenty five degrees of heat grew in intensity as the afternoon wore on. The Royal Enclosure was where the traditional outfit was strictly adhered to, regardless of the temperature. It was only in circumstances where people were in danger of passing out that the dress code was relaxed. Luckily, the weather forecast predicted overnight rain and a cloudy day with temperatures dropping to the mid-teens for Wednesday. That would be far better, for both horses and humans.

Joss was waiting at the stabling gate as Duncan and Ben approached and he had a word with the gate steward as they drew closer. Dressed in jeans and shirts, the two of them were given a long look up and down by the gate man, but were granted access after signing the relevant paperwork and Joss vouching and co-signing for them.

'At least the security is tight,' Duncan pointed out as the three of them walked away from the gate and down the single-track lane.

Joss said 'That's not the end of it either; Ascot is dead serious about security. There are people all over the place day and night. I think our blue-eyed man will need to be invisible to get close to The Ghost this time. There's CCTV around most of stables, night staff and the horses are booked in and out of practically everything they do while they're here.'

Ben noticed Joss was talking slightly quicker than normal, something he tended to do when he was excited.

'He's worked on the course this morning,' Joss continued. 'We got him onto the track just after eight o'clock, you know, before the day got too hot and he did a swinging canter up the home straight.'

'How did it go?' Ben asked.

'Oh, the work was fine; he went well. He'll be in great shape for tomorrow. Demetri and Ivan caused a bit of a stir though, as they were there too, ordering the security staff up and down the course to make sure no one got near to the horse. They also insisted he worked closely with the other two, but that wasn't too much of a problem.'

'So the two decoys were accepted by Ascot?' asked Duncan.

'Yeah, they didn't have a problem with them. To be honest, they couldn't really turn our request down as we made a really strong case for having lead horses for The Ghost.'

'So Ascot haven't noticed that The Ghost's two companion horses happen to be the same size, shape and colour?' said Ben with a smile.

'Not yet. I think it might be a bit obvious when three identical horses turn up at the saddling boxes tomorrow but it will be too late by then.'

The single-track lane opened up now, with the first few stabling barns coming into view in front of them. A stiff, serious looking wire fence topped with barbed wire ran right around the barns. To the left the landscapers had created a false hill which was relatively steep, sheltering a building behind it. As they continued around a tight corner, the lane petered out and suddenly there was far more going on. They walked into a large open area with horses walking around a large ring, some having post run warm downs, others jig-jogging in anticipation of their races later in the day. More horses, stable lads and also a smattering of Ascot staff continued to emerge and disappear from sight as they walked between the seven huge barns set back against the backdrop of a thick wood.

Opposite the stables was an industrial sized horse walker and various buildings which Ben couldn't determine their purpose immediately, although a stable staff café appeared to be doing a fair trade. Beyond the buildings was an almost flat forty or fifty acre field, most of which was populated with hundreds of rows of parked cars. Ben and Duncan had to shade their eyes when looking down at the car park from their slightly elevated position. The sun's rays bounced off the windows and polished bonnets, producing a dazzling effect from the sea of vehicles.

Joss beckoned to the two of them, and they followed him up to the line of seven identical barns. There was another checkpoint type arrangement in order to enter the barns enclosure and again, Joss had to organise entrance for his owners. As they signed in, Ben noticed Armitage sat in a small chair, his back to the nearest of the barns.

'He's been sat like that since ten o'clock.' Joss said quietly when he realised Ben had spotted the man. 'But I have to hand it to him; no bugger has got within ten yards of the Ghost since we got here!'

'I get the impression you're a fan of Armitage now?' Duncan

enquired, eyebrows raised.

'He'd never even touched a horse before he came to look after the security at the yard you know.' Joss explained. 'I've seen people who are naturals around horses, but this lad's got more than just a good way of dealing with them. He's like a horse whisperer who doesn't need to whisper. That's what Marion has said, and I think she's right. He's developed a real rapport with The Ghost and I really don't know when he sleeps, he seems to always be there when you need him.'

As they approached the stable Armitage got up from his chair and cast a glance over the stable door before meeting Ben and Duncan with a nod and a handshake. Ben had noted that since he wasn't fronting the purchase of The Ghost any more, Armitage seemed to be a man of far fewer words and far more action. The words he did speak seemed to be in a lot lower register as well.

Jake emerged from the box beside Armitage's and waved a hello, pitchfork, and bucket in hand.

Duncan looked over the stable door to the nearest box and peered into the dark recesses. A grey horse was lying down on a thick bed of shavings, apparently asleep.

'Decoy number one. He's called Bobby,' said Joss under his breath. 'This one is a four year old I picked up at the sales a few weeks ago. I bought him because The Forties said they needed a horse that could be made to look like The Ghost. Luckily he was fairly cheap. You see… his head and mane are incredibly similar.'

'That's also why I'm guarding this door,' said Amitage, a knowing look on his face.

Ben considered this and thought he knew what Armitage, in his role as equine security guard was suggesting. If he sat outside The Ghost's stable it was a great advert for where the colt was, but sit outside a different grey horse's box and it might confuse any would-be assailant. He was still close enough to the actual stable holding The Ghost if he needed to be on his feet quickly.

Duncan scratched his head and moved to the next stable where another grey horse had just popped its head over the stable door to see what was going on.

'That's not him either!' he exclaimed. His outburst immediately received a 'zip it' mime from Armitage and a shushing from Joss. He mouthed 'sorry' and put a couple of fingers to his lips.

In a whisper, Ben stated 'Isn't that Silvery Sun?'

Joss nodded and Armitage said in a low voice. 'Our man got him mixed up with The Ghost once before, so that booked his place on the trip down here. We got his owners a few badges for today's racing, so they're happy enough.'

Armitage moved up to the next door and The Ghost turned from the back of the stable, shook himself and walked over, bending his broad head down and poking his nose under Armitage's right arm. The colt then shuffled his nose up until almost his entire head was being held under the small man's armpit.

Joss touched Ben's elbow and jerked his head towards Armitage 'See what I mean?' he said under his breath.

Armitage rubbed the bottom of the colt's head and at the same time appeared to be speaking to the horse. Ben caught the tiniest hint of a smile on his face. It was almost imperceptible, but a faint smile line around Armitage's eyes seemed to have come alive. His pasty pallor returned as soon as he disengaged from The Ghost and turned back to Joss and the two owners.

'Demetri and Ivan around?' asked Ben.

Armitage rubbed his chin which rasped under a couple of days stubble. 'They've been here since yesterday morning, but I've not seen them more than once, last night. I'm sleeping with The Ghost at the minute.'

Duncan couldn't help himself, letting out a guffaw. However, once he caught sight of the look that Armitage and Joss gave him, he quickly straightened his face.

'They needed to case the entire course and also set up one or two things for tomorrow. But they are taking shifts tonight as well,' Armitage added, eying Duncan solemnly.

Duncan and Ben shifted uneasily, as they were not expected to be called upon to look after the horses during the night as The Forties, Jake and Joss were. Ivan had made it clear to everyone in the syndicate that the most likely source of another action against The Ghost would be during the night before the race. With woods and rough ground surrounding the racecourse barns it had been explained that their best chance of catching the blue-eyed man was if he made a move during the nights before the race.

'No sign of anyone last night?' Ben enquired.

Armitage shook his head.

Joss put a hand to his forehead and wiped away some sweat with his palm, leaving a muddy smear. 'Not even a single rustle of a leaf. We've got cameras all over the back of the barns, in the barns and in some of the trees and all we caught sight of last night were a few rabbits.'

'We're all set up. If he comes sneaking around or tries using a drone again we'll catch him. Everything is in place should we have a visitor,' Armitage assured them.

'Let's hope he's daft enough to try something,' said Duncan looking towards the trees and bushes standing behind the barns. The eight-foot wire fence ringing the barns looked solid enough and the razor wire running along the top would make entry from that direction which was challenging even for the most persistent burglar.

'So I think it's probably time you left then.'

Duncan looked a little hurt, but then caught Armitage's drift. To appear vulnerable to the enemy, it didn't do to have owners standing outside The Ghost's stable all day long. The point was that The Forties *wanted* the blue-eyed man to attempt to get to The Ghost in this environment because they had all manner of defences and traps enabled in order to protect the horse, but also to catch their man. It was a controlled zone and the trap was set.

'Err... yes,' Duncan managed and he and Ben thanked Armitage and Jake before walking back out of the barns enclosure and towards the racecourse again. Joss joined them, on his way to the racecourse to meet some owners.

When the three of them were well out of earshot of any stable lad or roving owner, Ben spoke again.

'I hope he makes his move tonight. It would be so much better to know everything was sorted before the race goes off tomorrow.'

'I'm not so sure he will,' Joss admitted. 'I'm not sure he will even try this time. There's so much security around because of the royal status of the meeting, I wonder if he'll admit defeat and allow us to run. Armitage and Ivan are convinced he will make some sort of attempt, and by god, they are prepared.'

Ben thought back to their presentation of how they were going to set up the three horses and their painstaking protection of The Ghost. Most of their plans to catch their man were based on an attack at the stabling area. They appeared to have the stables well staked out and Ben knew all sorts of recording and protection equipment were secreted around the stables, ready for the blue-eyed man to strike. It became far more complex when the horses were on the move and within the racecourse. Not for the first time, Ben felt relieved that The Forties were involved. This sort of counter espionage appeared to be second nature to the three of them whereas he was well out of his depth.

'I know you're not dressed for it, but are you coming into the course?' Joss offered once they had signed out of the last checkpoint.

Ben checked with Duncan, but it seemed that both of them were happy enough to return to their hotel and prepare for the coming day, so they thanked Joss and set off to the hotel, about a fifteen minute walk. Joss crossed the road and after being processed through the gate with another check of his trainer's metal badge he disappeared into the saddling and pre-parade ring. He was on his way to catch the last four races of the day and meet up with a number of his owners who were there to enjoy the top class racing.

Back at the hotel, a mid-sized budget affair which raised its prices to central London levels for the Ascot meeting, Ben and Duncan watched the last few races of the day and, as instructed, kept their mobiles on full charge and within easy reach at all times. There had still been no calls or messages from the Ascot barns by the late evening, which meant there had been no issues. Whether it was the wait for something to happen, or the gravity of the run the next day, they endured a nervy, distracted meal at a local Chinese restaurant in the evening and then headed to their bedrooms early, both men desperately hoping something would happen at the stables during the night in order to release some of the tension.

Twenty-Six

Ben rolled over and picked up his phone from his bedside table. The screen glared brightly into the dim room but displayed no missed calls or messages. It was 5:47 am and he had slept badly, waking intermittently throughout the night. Lying on his back, he stared up at the dusty grey stippled ceiling and felt the knot of tension in his stomach tighten as he ran through what lay ahead.

All the syndicate members would be meeting at 11:00 am at the Ascot barns to attend a final run-through of the day and also to pick up their earpieces and glass buttons. Each member had their own instructions and, in most cases, tasks which they needed to fulfill before the race. Then it was the race itself and, finally, getting the colt back to the barns again fit and well.

He rubbed his eyes and gave up trying to sleep any further, flicking the television on for company. Checking his mobile phone again, Ben looked up The Ghost's race online. Panama was a warm favourite following his 2,000 Guineas success, with a price of evens, which was predicted to go odds on by a couple of the racing pundits in their morning columns. The runner up in the Guineas was 5/1 along with a colt which had run and won once, only a few weeks previously. Following his facile success in Germany The Ghost was 12/1, the overseas form being regarded by many as inferior to any English performance. Along with The Ghost there was a group of about a dozen horses with prices between 8/1 and 20/1, which included a few lightly raced types and a trio who had finished behind the Ghost in the Greenham. A further handful of runners were being offered at even longer odds.

Several online racing websites made the point that this year's race had attracted a big field with sixteen runners lining up. The race normally consisted of between seven to ten runners. The general consensus seemed to be that there were many horses in the race that wouldn't normally have been there, all competing in order to potentially pick up the place money and enhance their potential values as stallions. It seemed that beyond Panama is was regarded as an 'open' looking race. Wherever you went to read about the race, Panama was expected to win, bar a major upset.

Ben found one tipster who had stuck his neck out and tipped The Ghost. A Northern based hack, he reasoned that the race at Newbury would have been a much closer affair if The Ghost had managed to get away from the stalls, but also pointed out that the colt was perhaps not too reliable. If only he knew the truth thought Ben.

He spent the next hour willing his phone to ring and for the news that The Forties had captured a suspect to be delivered. It did ring once: Max calling to wish Ben and The Ghost good luck before he went to school for the day. His heart had jumped when the phone started to vibrate, but it was a nice call and when he rang off there was a smile playing on his face.

Breakfast was a torrid affair for Ben, whose nervousness wasn't helped by having to watch Duncan pile drive his way through a truly enormous cooked breakfast. The 'all you can eat' breakfast was given a sound thrashing by the Welshman who appeared to be not in the least affected by nerves and had apparently slept soundly all night. Ben had pushed a rather sad looking croissant around his plate for ten minutes before setting it aside and settling for a sipped black coffee. Meanwhile, Duncan ploughed on regardless, hale and hearty, chatting about the day, with Ben giving one and two word answers and feeling a little sick as yet another rasher of bacon disappeared down his friend's gullet.

An hour later they met in the hotel foyer in their full Royal Ascot regalia. They had ordered their suits well in advance of the day, as Nancy had warned that renting traditional morning suits and top hats wasn't something which could be picked up at your average clothes rental outfitters. Duncan had gone for a dark grey while Ben was more traditional in pure black. They both had waistcoats with dark ties tucked into them over wing-collared shirts.

'Don't we look a right pair of Charlie's,' Duncan observed, balancing his top hat precariously on one ear.

Ben laughed nervously, but was glad for any release. Duncan was good at this. He could defuse pretty much any situation with his disarming Welsh charm. Checking his watch, Ben gestured towards the door and in his standard upper-class twit voice stated 'After you, Sir. Your carriage awaits.'

In fact, it was a seven year old Toyota Corolla which carried them to the racecourse, complete with faded seats holding questionable stains. The taxi driver never cracked a smile throughout the ten minute crawl to the course and they were delighted when he drove off in a cough inducing cloud of diesel smoke.

Ben checked his watch again and his mobile, receiving a shake of Duncan's head in response.

'For heaven's sake, just calm it. Take a breath,' Duncan advised.

They retraced their steps to the Ascot stables, went through the checks, and found The Forties plus Jake, Joss and Marion already there in a little ring outside the stables. The three grey horses, each with their heads looking over their doors, greeted the humans who to a man and woman looked pensive at best and in Ben's case, downright worried.

It took another fifteen minutes for everyone to arrive, but by five minutes to eleven the entire syndicate was there. Olivia and Janet completed the group, Janet approaching the knot of owners proudly brandishing her brand new smartphone.

Demetri updated everyone individually as they arrived, quietly passing on the news that there had been no sign of the blue eyed man for the last two nights. Although this was arguably a positive there was a palpable sense of disappointment among The Forties that an early opportunity to snare their prey hadn't presented itself. Demetri was keen to impress upon everyone that this lack of nighttime activity placed greater emphasis on the tasks everyone was assigned today.

All the men except for Armitage, Joss, and Jake wore full morning suits whilst the ladies outshone them completely with vibrant summer dresses. However, as instructed by The Forties, all of the ladies wore flat shoes and sensible, small hats. Jake and Joss were smart, but as they would be leading up the horses, they wore lounge suits instead of the full Ascot tails. Armitage was clean-shaven and as his role as a lead up man demanded, he wore a shirt and tie, dark trousers and a pair of robust looking boots.

With Armitage standing at the corner of the barn acting as a lookout, Ivan produced the small black velvet box once again and took one phone after another from each member of the syndicate, ensuring every device was responding to commands and the glass button was firmly attached to the user's lapel. He also made sure the earpiece was both secure and largely invisible on each user, testing each one and reminding everyone individually the basics of the technology's use.

Then Ivan looked to address specific groups of the syndicate.

'Janet, Olivia, Marion,' he stated abruptly. It seemed to Ben that Ivan was suppressing considerable agitation, speaking in staccato bursts and his eyes darted around more than usual. Ben considered the size of the crowd today, the general hubbub around the barns with horses arriving, moving around and departing to the track, and wondered if this was the reason for Ivan's tetchiness this morning. Facing sixty thousand people with his fear of crowds couldn't be something he was looking forward to. Ben looked up to Demetri with a concerned expression and immediately received a reassuring nod in response. He must have already sensed Ivan's anxiety and the effect it would have on the people around him and Ben relaxed a little.

Ivan continued at a breakneck pace 'Pre-race. Eyes around the Owners bar and restaurant. Get seen, see as many people as you can. If Bentham is there stay close and follow. Armitage, Ben, Duncan, Jake, Joss are The Ghost's entourage until in the parade ring. Before he moves, Duncan and Joss, pre-parade lookout...'

He was forced to stop speaking having appeared to have spoken the entire set of instructions without breathing. He panted a little and made to start speaking again but Demetri intervened.

'Ivan, it's time for you to get to HQ before the crowds start to build. Armitage, can you..?'

203

Armitage was at Ivan's side with alacrity and he gingerly took hold of Ivan's arm. Ivan appeared to consider contesting his partner's actions, eyes bulging slightly as he peered upwards at Demetri, but soon allowed himself to be whisked away by Armitage.

After the two of them were on their way Demetri took up the briefing without reference to what had just happened.

'Rob and I will be in our roving roles until The Ghost hits the parade ring. Don't forget that The Ghost will only be in the parade ring for a short time before we take him down to the starting stalls. Jake, Armitage and Joss will walk the horse to the start with the companion horse.'

'Do we have the permission to go to the post early?' Ben asked.

'Yes, we have to make one circuit of the parade ring and then Raul can get mounted and head to the start. The stewards are aware and have allowed us to leave ten minutes ahead of the rest of the field,' Joss answered.

Demetri looked down at Ivan's notes reading the next set of instructions 'The walk to the pre-parade ring starts at three o'clock, we're out of the pre-parade and into the parade ring for less than a minute. Then down the walkway to meet Silvery Sun and Jake, Armitage and Joss walk both horses to the start. Race off at three thirty-five.'

He paused and looked up at the semi-circle of people around him, all of whom were concentrating and had serious faces.

'And don't forget that we have a racehorse running in a Group One contest and we're supposed to be having fun as owners. Try to relax and enjoy the experience!'

This broke the tension somewhat. Oliva turned to Ben, clasping her hands together 'I feel like at little girl on her first day at school. It's exciting but so nerve wracking.'

Ben assured her and Janet that everything would run smoothly, and the likelihood was that nothing at all out of the ordinary would happen. However his own heart started to thump in his chest when they set off walking to the owners and trainers entrance, so much so he slowed his pace to make sure a dizzy spell wasn't coming on. A few short, regulated breaths seemed to put things right, but by the time he reached the entrance he was mopping a few beads of sweat from his forehead despite the day being on the cool side.

At eleven thirty the syndicate had made it through the turnstiles and stood in front of the pre-parade ring. Despite there being another two hours until the first race of the day the scene behind the stands was one of people milling, interspersed with Ascot staff zipping around in the act of preparing for the afternoon's onslaught of race-goers demanding food and beverages.

The syndicate split up into their groups and headed to different areas of the enclosure. As soon as Ben had walked twenty paces there was a quiet electronic buzz in his right ear and Ivan's voice was there, as if he was whispering from only a few inches away.

'Ben. Ivan here. We're set. I have your visual but it's too low. Can you adjust?'

Trying to remain casual, Ben altered his direction of walk slightly and came to rest against the white plastic railings outside the main parade ring.

He waited until a couple walked past and then replied 'Got you Ivan. Tell me when it's better.'

When he looked down to his chest he could see the glass button wasn't attached firmly and was drooping, its electronic eye pointing towards the floor. He removed it and reapplied the butterfly clasp.

Inside a locked private suite high up in the massive Ascot grandstand, Ivan sat in semi darkness behind an arc of ten flat screen monitors, two high and five wide. The top row of five screens each showed live video feeds, four per monitor. Every video feed displayed a syndicate member's view from their lapel. Some were almost static, such as Armitage's, sitting outside The Ghost's box back at the stabling barns. Other videos bounced around more energetically such as Marion's as she bounded up the stairs to the Owners and Trainers Bar. Each screen had a moving digital red box which constantly dashed frenetically around the screen, attempting to zero in on all the race-goer faces it could locate. Every now and again the red box would find a face, turn green, and track that person across the screen. For some of the faces, text appeared above the box. Olivia, Janet, and Marion's screens were currently lit up with a huge number of red and green boxes as they moved through a packed Owners and Trainer Bar area.

Ivan flicked his eyes from screen to screen, switching momentarily to look down at his laptop which sat open on the large table placed in the middle of the suite to hold all his equipment. The laptop's screen was different to the others, filled with scrolling data which filled the device and then emptied every few seconds. He wore a set of serious looking headphones complete with a microphone and tapped on the keyboard now and again, speaking softly as he worked.

'That's fine now, Ben. All good here. Continue,' Ivan instructed before tapping another few keys.

'Olivia. It's Ivan. Don't hold your hands to your chest. You're obscuring the view.'

A previously blurred screen leapt back to life in front of Ivan and he provided positive feedback into his headset.

Ben set off walking again. He was feeling much better now, had stopped sweating and although the knot in his stomach still twirled around, he felt sure it was the excitement of the day, rather than anything more sinister. Although it was a cool, overcast day, the sun was trying its best to burn through the grey clouds and the odd burst of sunlight made the day feel spring-like.

Ben had a circuit to follow which had been mapped out for him for this period of time before the race. He had committed it to memory, although it wasn't too complicated anyway. The key to everything the syndicate was doing for the next few hours was to cover ground and meet people. 'See and be seen.' was the way Ivan had described it.

The Forties hit list of people ran to over seven hundred people, of which Billy Bentham was number one. Ivan's technology wasn't just interested in Billy, it was attempting to identify all seven hundred suspects through face recognition and then tracking them as they went about their afternoon at the races. Ben had been stunned by this when Ivan had run through the plan. As soon as his system found a match to one of the seven hundred names and faces it would confirm they were at Ascot and start tracking them. The faces had been primarily attained from websites, blogs, and social media. For the few in the top one hundred which hadn't been available, Demetri and some of his hired help had spent a few days on the road 'acquiring' them. The advent of 'selfies' had made this task much easier as it meant Demetri could take photos wherever and whenever he wished without raising any suspicion in his targets.

During the evening at Rob's pub, Ben had been left confused by the weird technical things Ivan was doing to make all of this possible, but it had been explained that once a target person has been identified by the software, Ivan could effectively track them around the racecourse. Ivan had started to explain that by intercepting mobile phone data, using various 'networks', 'intelligent imaging' and looking for key words in phone, email and text messages from the course he could be pre-emptive should any of them show signs of striking. Pretty much everyone around the table outside The Forties had been completely lost at this stage, but Ian had seemed to understand most of what Ivan was explaining and apart from thinking it was 'pretty neat' he agreed it could work.

All that the syndicate had to do was try and get around the course as much as possible before the race so that Ivan could identify and track all the suspects. It had sounded like a tall order to Ben, but The Forties had been quite positive about the system and its abilities. If walking about the pre-parade and parade ring for three races, as well as dips into a couple of bookmakers and the odd corridor of private boxes would help to catch whoever was trying to hurt The Ghost, it would be worth it. Being able to walk freely around the Royal Enclosure was a big plus, something being an owner for the day allowed you to do, and The Forties were convinced either the blue eyed man or his boss would be in that enclosure at some stage during the afternoon.

It took two hours of wandering around, but by the time the horses were parading for the first race of the day, Ivan's top ten suspects had all received hits on his software. The three ladies had done wonderfully well and Ben's earpiece had been alive with Ivan reporting how they had managed to grab dozens of successful identifications by blagging their way into restaurants and private suites. It turned out that having an octogenarian with you, especially a wily Scottish one, provided all the excuse you needed to access all areas of a racecourse.

Ben had rarely attended Royal Ascot, having only once fielded a runner at the meeting. Given this lack of attendance he was astonished at how many people he recognised and in a lot of cases, knew well, as he made his circuits around the enclosures. Several of his owners in other syndicates had unexpectedly popped up, including Graham P. Loote, who had buttonholed him for several long minutes before he'd been able to conjure up an excuse. He'd met at least a dozen owners of horses from Joss's yard, there to cheer The Ghost on, including the owners of Silvery Sun and the other grey Joss had brought with him. Both had separately joked with Ben that despite not actually running, their horse was 'at Royal Ascot', and they weren't going to miss it!

There were past syndicate members who shook his hand and wished him well, along with a number of people Ben had never met before. The coverage of The Ghost and the link to the accident at York had been widely reported in the morning daily papers along with an old stock photo of him. That had helped his identification and Ben was touched by the half a dozen strangers who came up to offer their support. A little like Newbury, Eleanor Hart popped up with a small entourage, full of the day and brimming with excited anticipation. She had spent the previous afternoon with Joss and several other owners who were enjoying their association with the yard. Sheik Kamsun, whose colt re-opposed The Ghost, also stopped for a conversation with Ben, primarily about The Ghost's win in Germany. Flanked by his two minders, he had left them behind by cutting across a walkway to hold out his hand for Ben to shake before wishing him the best of luck. Clearly agitated, his men in black arrived thirty seconds later, having ungallantly pushed their way through the crowd. Ben shook the Prince's hand and, as their discussion about Germany developed, he pointed out a similar anomaly in the bloodlines of both horses which the Sheik seemed to enjoy, bowing his head towards Ben as they spoke. The two of them parted very amicably, with the Sheik leaving his business card with Ben before he departed, urging him to get in touch ahead of the October sales.

Best of all, Ben had been the one to manufacture a few words with Panama's connections: Billy Bentham and James Corrigan. Ivan had sounded like he was having a seizure in his earpiece when the software picked up Billy, and the first thirty seconds of Ben's conversation with the trainer had been drowned out with Ivan insisting Ben stayed with him for as long as possible. Ben had exchanged pleasantries with both men, commented on the draw they had received (right beside The Ghost in stall three) and wished them the best of luck. He had looked for any telltale signs of ulterior motives in both faces, but found nothing to indicate they were anything other than a normal trainer and owner enjoying a big day out.

There were even two of the ex-Ghost owners who turned up, much to Ben's surprise. Both Harry Maxwell (more than happy with his new car) and Rory Dent (still not letting on about why he sold his share) made a beeline for Ben when he picked them out of the crowd. Rory had wished him the best of luck with the colt and was keen to join another syndicate with him next season. After that ten minute conversation Ben wondered if he should do more of this wandering around at major racecourses, it seemed it could be good for business.

As the crowd started to swell ahead of the Queen's entrance down the track and into the Royal Enclosure, Ben spotted Courtney with two colleagues. The three of them were pushing up close to the walkway fence under the stands. Ben reasoned she was trying to get a decent vantage point for when the Queen's carriage rolled through under the stands ahead of the first race. It looked like it was working day for her and her pals, as they all wore an all red dress, red shoes and a wide brimmed red hat. The name of a bookmaker was emblazoned on the back of the dress and also on her hat in large, ugly letters. Ivan had spotted her too and encouraged Ben to get a little closer to confirm, as she was on the list, despite being a low probability suspect. So, he pushed into the ten deep crowd.

Once the Queen's carriage had whisked past Courtney and her two colleagues, all three of them turned around suddenly. Ben was caught far too close to his target and to his internal horror he found himself standing face-to-face with her, jammed into the crowd with the brim of her hat almost touching his nose.

He could see why she was able to maintain regular work on the racecourses. Her feminity shone through, even though the dress was a stock, off-the-peg garment. She made it look far more stylish than it deserved.

With nowhere to go, he locked eyes with Courtney. She looked into his face and then instantly looked away. Given her body language, Ben thought she was going to push past him, but as she raised a hand to push between two people she hesitated and rocked back to be in front of him again.

'It's Ben isn't it?' she asked in her Liverpudlian accent, a tight smile lighting up her face.

Ben stood rigid, feeling slightly intimidated; he was far too close to the woman for it to be a comfortable meeting. People were pushing past the two of them, including her cloned colleagues and the two of them found themselves being shuffled together and almost dancing to maintain their positions.

'Er. Yes, that's right,' he managed to stammer, feeling an embarrassed heat starting to build in his cheeks.

'Didn't she look wonderful?' Courtney continued, apparently unworried by Ben's proximity or his failure to produce more than a few words in reply.

Once again he was stumped, and it must have shown in his face as Courtney's smile started to fade before returning in a bigger, tooth filled replacement.

'I meant the Queen you dope!' she laughed.

'Yes, of course. She looked... radiant,' he offered uncertainly.

She examined him and shook her head. 'Men never understand Royalty. Come on, let's get out of this crush.' she said to Ben and her friends. He was shocked to find his hand being clenched by her as she led him through the packed causeway.

Ivan stated something about having successfully tracked something in his ear, but he wasn't really concentrating as he picked his way after the red-frocked ladies.

'That's better,' she said, releasing Ben's hand as they reached a small area of grass which was thankfully devoid of race-goers.

Ben began to apologise for being so close-up to her, but she waved it aside, insisting she introduce her two companions in red. Introductions over, Courtney explained to them who Ben was, their rather bored demeanour changed somewhat when she mentioned he owned one of the horses running today. Ben marvelled at how being identified as a racehorse owner elevated his status in some people's eyes. He neglected to inform his newfound audience that he only owned ten percent of the horse concerned.

He spent a pleasant few minutes chatting with Courtney, including a discussion on which race she was aiding the presentation (the second race) and if she'd seen the blue eyed man (a name she thought was suitable for him, but no, she hadn't). When she asked after Mojo the other two girls soon became glassy eyed again and made their excuses, promising to meet up with her later.

Far too soon, Ivan was bleating in Ben's ear about focus and he had to make an excuse to leave. Courtney seemed genuinely pleased to speak with him again and she pecked his cheek as he departed. He found himself walking with a spring in his step for the next few minutes and couldn't stem an audible chuckle at his own pumped up self-confidence. He pricked that bubble straight away, telling himself that his life was already far too complicated for another woman to enter it successfully. Besides, Courtney was probably twelve years his junior. Probably...

By the time the horses for the first race were parading, the soles of Ben's feet were starting to ache, so he stopped and found a space at the edge of the parade ring to watch for a minute. He was thankful it was an overcast day, as the past three hours of meeting and greeting would have been far more arduous in any serious heat or humidity, especially wearing his top hat and tails. He had met so many people he was a little boggled when trying to think back. Instead, he allowed himself to switch into syndicate manager mode and started critiquing the equine youngsters circling the ring.

As the jockeys started to part company from their owners and trainers in order to mount for the two o'clock race, Ben's earpiece buzzed a familiar chime and Ivan spoke.

'Almost two o'clock and we have four hundred confirmed trackers in place Ben. Time to head back to the stables.'

'Can't I watch this race. I don't need to be there until two forty five do I?' he asked, but immediately wished he hadn't spoken. He pulled himself back into the moment and what the objectives were.

'No Ben. We need you at the stables,' Ivan returned curtly. With a renewed focus he answered 'Understood. On my way,' and looked around for the nearest exit.

Twenty-Seven

Ben listened to the commentary of the first race over the public address as he walked away from the racetrack, down the single lane road to the stables. He couldn't help finding the two year old races anything other than fascinating, as they were the babies of the sport and carried the hopes of not only their owners, but bloodstock agents, studs and generations of breeding. Stallions could have their success on the track, but then their progeny would fight another battle for them on the same ground their own hooves had passed over only a few seasons before. It was a romantic cyclical dance played out by generation after generation of thoroughbred racehorses.

Rob caught up with Ben a few hundred yards from the barns and they swapped their experiences over the last few hours. Ben smiled to himself as Rob looked full of life, his eyes ablaze with excitement and he spoke quickly and at times, breathlessly. Ben decided not to admit to anyone he'd found the few hours around the Royal Enclosure exhausting and he noted with some discomfort that the soles of his feet were now humming in his dress shoes.

When they reached the barns the rest of the syndicate involved with the pre-race parade, and ensuring The Ghost arrived safely at the starting stalls, were already ready and waiting. Rob and Ben joined Demetri, Armitage, Joss, and Jake exchanging serious glances, rather than words, as they approached.

'Armitage is the lead on this,' Demetri told the group of men. He nodded towards his colleague 'Okay Andrew, over to you now.' Armitage beckoned with both hands for the small group to huddle a little closer and he ran through the commands one last time. Now that his unnaturally high-pitched voice had been dispensed with he managed to lace his words with such a serious thread, there could be no doubting their importance.

'Joss, you're leading up Silvery Sun. Jake, you're with Bobby. I lead up The Ghost until we are in the saddling boxes then Joss takes over. Understood?' Three heads nodded their acceptance.

'Until we reach the saddling area inside the course The Ghost stays on the outside of the three, on the left, as any attacker will automatically assume he is in the centre. Bobby goes in the middle, Silvery Sun on the right-hand side.'

Unbidden, the three men nodded again and mouthed silent positive responses.

'Demetri walks three yards ahead; he's our point man. Any trouble, he will call it.'

Everyone voiced their agreement to this instruction. A few of them looked nervously at Demetri, but he remained serious, fierce concentration written across his face.

'Only two horses enter the course proper. Bobby will return to the stables once we reach the saddling gate. Silvery Sun is the nominated companion horse for The Ghost.'

Armitage turned to Rob and Ben. 'You are our owners on lookout. You walk alongside the three horses, Rob left, Ben right. You do not look at the horses, you look out for any, and I mean *any* sort of danger. You stay with the horses throughout the walk, into the saddling boxes, round the paddock once and to the edge of the track. Look at peoples' faces, look at any reflection of glass, listen for noises you would not expect and discover where they are coming from. Keep your senses keen. Are you with me?' Ben and Rob gave positive answers under their breath.

Armitage continued 'We have permission to go to the start early and we have briefed Raul, he knows his role and what to expect. So, one lap of the parade ring and out. The Ghost will already be saddled before we leave here, so we are in and out of the saddling boxes as soon as we have permission to enter the parade ring. Demetri and I will join Ben and Rob down the walkway under the stands as this is the closest we will get to the public and is the primary attack zone.'

He paused, looking around the men's faces once again. 'Once on the track, Silvery Sun stays on the left of The Ghost, Rob and Ben leave and return to the parade ring and Joss, Jake, Demetri, Silvery Sun and myself walk the colt to the mile start on the round course and see him successfully loaded into the starting stalls and away.'

Armitage pushed up the sleeve of his jacket. 'It's now 2-20pm, we go at 2-45pm.'

Ben sensed the military atmosphere and almost responded with a 'Yes, Sir!' His forehead was starting to bead with sweat again and his palms were quickly following suit.

But Armitage had not finished. He drew himself up to his full height, breathing in deeply, expelling the contents of his lungs slowly before speaking.

'Remember, Ivan is monitoring all movements. If The Ghost is under threat, we get the colt out of there and to the next staging point. We don't engage with anyone unless we absolutely have to. If any of you get into trouble, Ivan will be with you along with the rest of the syndicate via your Smartphone if you need them.'

When Armitage had finally finished his briefing, he looked up and noticed the men, one by one, were staring over his shoulder. He spun around to look too. All three grey horses stood, unmoving, heads out of their boxes in a line watching the men intently. The magic only lasted a few precious seconds but was almost theatrical. Ben couldn't decide whether it was a serious drama or comedy as the three horses stared dolefully at the six men, identical heads appearing to be questioning the sanity of the humans in front of them.

Ben looked sideways to Joss. 'Seriously? You've painted a diamond on the heads of the other two horses?'

Joss smiled, nodding vigorously. Marion had made a valiant attempt to tame his wedge of unruly brown hair for today by combing it back over his ears, but this action sent it cascading back over his face.

'Not painted,' he announced proudly.

'Jake and I have been learning the delicate art of hair colouring. A very nice lady at Marion's hair salon in Bedale was most helpful. We even did skin tests and colour matches,' he added.

Ben examined his friends' excited face and then looked to Jake who shrugged. The trio of greys continued to peer at the knot of men outside their stables, the two with their foreheads brandishing a brand new browny black diamond were certainly striking. On closer inspection, Ben thought the additions between their eyes glinted, ever so slightly.

The absurdity of the situation soon struck home and a few choked laughs reverberated around the barns. Ben thought he even caught sight of Armitage with a smile on his thin lips, although it was so fleeting he dismissed the possibility. Joss seemed a little hurt by the giggling at first, but after looking back at the three horses again his hand went to his mouth and tried to stifle a chortle.

Ivan watched the scene from his perch up in the stands and sighed. He checked his monitors again and saw that Marion and Olivia had reached their agreed vantage points. Janet was still making her way to the causeway under the stands and Duncan and Ian were together outside the parade ring, ready to represent the syndicate inside the ring, but also keeping an eye on Billy Bentham and James Corrigan.

Despite being pleased The Ghost hadn't been the subject of a show of aggression, Ivan remained unsatisfied with his morning's work. As the terabytes of data came in and had been processed, compared, and analysed he'd hoped for the telltale signs of a potential aggressor to emerge. But the entire system and all the people within it had started and remained in the green. It was fifteen minutes to the start of activity over at the barns and he had nothing of any significance to show for his eight weeks of preparation.

He switched his focus to his laptop and the scores which constantly altered as the targets moved around the racecourse. He was searching for that call, message, app submission or movement which singled them out, that brought them to the surface. Anything out of the ordinary would do. He scowled at the laptop and scrolled through a few hundred names, the percentages, and scores against each name blurring. There had been no movement of any significance. He'd hoped for a movement towards a suspect before the race preliminaries because it was far more controllable at the stables. The technology over at the stables had captured hours of white sound and banal conversations between stable staff, and nothing more. Now his tracking system was delivering the same results.

All his models expected another assault on The Ghost. It would fit perfectly. The psychological models told him so.

Ivan gritted his teeth, snatched a glimpse at the clock in the corner of his laptop screen, cracked his knuckles, and limbered up. It hadn't happened in the last two days. There was now two minutes before The Ghost would set off. It would happen in the next thirty minutes if it was going to happen at all.

Armitage checked his watch one last time, nodded at Jake and Joss standing outside their allocated stables, and announced: 'Ghost is on the move.'

In unison the three of them unbolted their stable doors, entered and then emerged a few seconds later leading a horse. Each horse had an identical head collar. Each horse was saddled but you wouldn't know it to look at them as all three horses wore an all over coat which stretched from the top of their necks down and under their stomach. They each had a set of blinkers on and a hood over their ears. Their legs were strapped up and they wore rubber boots on each foot.

Ben looked at the animals in awe, his jaw dropping open. Virtually every single inch of their bodies was protected in some way. The three of them looked more like jousting mounts than racehorses. He was once again thankful that today was cool; otherwise all three of these horses would surely overheat.

Joss saw the look on Rob and Ben's faces and wanted to explain, but the three horses were now catching the attention of a few of the passing stable lads and trainers. There were a few comments made behind hands and some surreptitious pointing towards the trio had already started. Joss groaned inwardly. It was bad enough that all three of them had slept with the horses for the last two days, two of them always on guard day and night – that was considered over the top – but this made the horses look pretty stupid. Stupid but necessary, he reminded himself. He remained silent.

The horses were not the only ones sporting new apparel. Joss, Jake and Armitage were now each wearing dark grey Fedoras with what looked like a silver fleck running around the brim. Demetri entered one of the stables and returned with three expensive looking umbrellas, handing one each to Rob and Ben.

Ben took hold of the large umbrella by its traditional hooked handle. It felt substantial, well made, and it fit nicely into his grip. He automatically leant on it, already well aware of its capabilities as Demetri had already introduced himself and Rob to this implement the week before. The Forties warned the syndicate they would be providing 'extras' to certain members as needed and saw no reason to share this information between everyone. There was one exception: The Forties had supplied every single person in the syndicate, ladies included, with a long vest with short sleeves and made of some weird sort of material which Demetri had described as 'A garment which could save your life so I advise you wear it.'

Armitage said something unintelligible, presumably to Ivan and then drew The Ghost up to stand on the outside of Silvery Sun, then Jake brought Bobby up between the two and the three of them set off, three abreast, Demetri two paces in front. Ben and Rob fell in on the right and left of the three horses and the strange group of horses and men set off down the stables lane.

There were no horses or lads coming back along the lane or leaving; it was deserted. The timing of their departure meant they hit the lull in equine traffic between races. Soon this walkway would be thick with runners from the third race returning and the other competitors in The Ghost's race heading to the saddling boxes and the pre-parade ring. Ben and Rob traded glances as they travelled towards the white stand which dominated the skyline about three hundred yards in the distance. There was nothing out of the ordinary, and the three horses hooves on the tarmac were the only sound for the first hundred yards. The sound of the crowd and the public address started soon after, and by the time they had reached the stables gate the third race was underway and the commentary came at them in waves as the breeze altered direction.

Through the stables gate the assembly moved forward another twenty yards and halted. An Ascot official stood at the road crossing and waved them on and Demetri set off over Ascot High Street, the three horses following obediently in line with their lads walking alongside. Rob and Ben had to hold back slightly, as the crossing wasn't quite wide enough for them to maintain their positions on the wide outside, so they dropped in behind the horses as they crossed the road.

There was a line of cars waiting patiently on both sides of the road as they crossed so when the roar of a high-pitched engine pierced the air, it was to this line of traffic that all heads were turned, except for Demetri and Armitage. They tried to move forward but the Ascot official at the other side of the road wasn't ready for them and the three horses and six men ground to a shambling halt.

The commentary from the track was now louder and more frenetic than before. As the race sped towards its climax, the combined noise of a huge cheer from the crowd and public address description of the action suddenly drowned out the engine. Ben gripped his umbrella tightly and standing on his toes, tried to see over the line of cars and vans in front of him and spot where the throaty engine noise had come from.

A lull from the commentator inside the racecourse brought the squealing engine noise back. Ben realised the note of the engine was far too high for a car and as he did, a powerful looking motorbike swerved from behind cars and into view about thirty yards away, driving on the side of the road clear of traffic. The rider corrected, straightened, accelerated and headed straight towards the three horses. For one horrifying moment Ben thought the rider, decked in all black leathers and a blacked out helmet visor, wasn't going to stop and simply plough headlong into the horses, but twenty yards away the biker slammed his brakes on, wheels squealing and smoking.

Ben's hands went to his umbrella just before Demetri screamed. As the bike drew to a stop he'd seen the rider reach down to the bikes' petrol tank, grab something and raise a black object in his hand. Ben ran forward three paces to the flanks of the horses, flicking the switch which was neatly hidden in the handle of his umbrella.

'Acid!' bellowed Demetri, stretching the word in a scream of combined frustration and anger. He too was taking giant strides towards the man on the machine.

Even before the bike had come to a stop the black rider was reaching back with his arm in order to toss the black object towards the horses. He came to a side on halt ten yards away from the horses who jig-jogged nervously somehow aware something was wrong. The rider released his grip on the object, hurling it underarm towards the crossing and the three horses.

Simultaneously, Ben flicked the switch on his umbrella and a split second later Demetri did the same.

The crowd noise suddenly swelled again and the commentary fizzed as the race entered its final furlong. But above that wall of sound there were two pops. Something apple-sized, black, and puck-shaped leapt from the rider's right fist, bounced once and then skittered across the tarmac.

Ben reeled a little from the noise when his shield activated. He could feel the gas in the umbrella push him backwards slightly as it forced its way into the metallic sheeted membrane in order to expand rapidly. A rosette of diamond shaped panels burst from the umbrella. Teeth clenched, he fought the rapidly expanding sail, angling it down into the road surface.

The puck's trajectory bisected himself and Demetri, whose own umbrella was also in the latter stages of expansion. Five yards in front of Ben the puck's bounce brought it closer to him and he dived towards it, throwing himself to the tarmac, arms outstretched, thrusting his shield, now three yards wide, at the incoming black object. The puck made a whapping noise as it struck one of the top panels on Ben's shield and for what seemed an age; it bounced back and upwards in a flat arc before landing back on the road, rolling in a circle on its edge. Demetri inverted his shield and thrust it down at the puck, shouting 'Heads d...,' at the top of his lungs. He only got his first word out before the puck fizzed and exploded with a dull crack.

Despite Demetri's inverted shield being over three yards wide, the watery lime green liquid still managed to squirt out from several branches of his umbrella in yard long thin streaks across the road. Ben gingerly picked himself up off the road, pain in his elbows and his left hand. The latter was smudged with blood and pricked with tiny stones and debris from the tarmac surface. He peered over the brim of his own shield to see Demetri on a dead charge towards the motorbike rider. But before he could close the ground between him and the rider, the bike engine emitted a high-pitched squeal once again. The rider shot off to his left, this time darting between cars on the opposite side of the road.

The combined noise from the crowd inside the racecourse and the excited torrent of words from the race commentary reached its zenith as the race climaxed.

Demetri slid to a halt, his charge now thwarted. He twisted backwards, hands to his mouth and screamed 'Rob! Shield!'

Still prone on the ground Ben could make out Demetri's words but only just; he looked back to where he imagined Rob to be and relayed the message. But Rob's shield was already inflated and he was guarding the back of the horses, legs planted apart, both hands grasping the shaft of his umbrella-cum-shield. Ben followed Rob's gaze and a black slur whipped past his view, followed by a motorcycle roar.

The rider raised his right fist from his bike's handlebars and then his left, riding no handed, but at speed he appeared to be having trouble locating his next acid puck and was behind his target by the time he found it. He aborted this drive by attempt, then slowly, almost lazily, he dropped his speed and turned his bike back to face his opponents like one of those cowboy street shootout clichés. Then Ben noticed Armitage. He wasn't with The Ghost. That lead rein was now in Joss's hand. Armitage had fallen back off the group and was now on his own headlong charge towards the motorcyclist with his Fedora hat in his hand. Ben couldn't quite make sense of what he was seeing.

Now at a crawl, the rider took more time, drawing back an arm in an under-hand motion. Rob tracked the biker with his shield, moving across to place the horses at his back. The rider tossed his second puck high, trying to loop over Rob's guard and the acid puck wobbled out of his fingers like a lightly thrown Frisbee. It was a poor throw, nowhere near enough velocity to reach its intended target. It landed with no pace a few yards in front of Rob and lethargically rolled towards him.

Ben was still confused with what Armitage was up to, but the way the biker had thrown this puck twanged at a memory. It was something about the action...

Rob leapt on the second puck-shaped object, inverting his shield exactly as Demetri had done moments before. Even before it exploded, the rider had gunned his throttle, spun the bike, and, in a fan of tyre smoke, started to depart. Armitage continued to close on him, his right hand grasping his Fedora was now raised. The rider's back wheel found its grip and pulled away a split second before Armitage reached him but he still brought his Fedora down in an attempt at a sideswipe.

To Ben's amazement, the leather on the rider's shoulder split open along the same line of Armitage's hat swipe. A fluffy white lining now shone out of a three-inch long slice in the black leather. Armitage himself tumbled onto the road as a result of his exertions, still clutching the brim of his Fedora. He sat up and watched intently as the rider sped away before getting back to his feet, dusting himself down, reshaping his Fedora and replacing it at a jaunty angle on his bald head. As he did, the official result of the race inside the racecourse crackled over the air.

Ben tried to steady his breathing, looking around and checking everyone at the same time. The three horses had coped admirably with the sound of the motorbike, the popping of the umbrellas and the general hubbub from inside the racecourse. However they chose this time to get a little anxious at having been stood stock still for about forty seconds. They still looked vaguely ridiculous in their full body protection, but clearly wanting to get off the road; Bobby in particular was snorting and gave a little disconcerted kick to the tarmac from a single back leg.

Once the motorbike rider had disappeared down Ascot High Street a few people started to leave their cars and approach the crossing. The Ascot racecourse stewards also came up to investigate, although they kept their distance from the two prostrated umbrellas-cum-shields. The entire stand-off had only taken forty seconds and most people seemed confused as to what had gone on, mistakenly thinking it was just an irate motorist who had thrown something at the group crossing the road and then been fended off.

Ben's heart was still thumping loudly in his chest as Demetri passed and landed a large hand on his shoulder on his way to the horses. 'Well done Ben, good catch. Get the horses moving. We have to get them away from here.' Demetri had a similar one-line conversation with each member of the group and soon had everyone focused and organised again. As everyone got busy Demetri went back to where his umbrella, looking more like a very large upturned beetle, lay inverted on the road. Lifting the umbrella up a few inches he squatted to inspect the mess underneath, poking at this and that and sniffing the air. He produced a small plastic bottle of water from his jacket pocket and poured a little over the lime green fluid on the road. Then he followed a thin green streak of the substance for a yard or two towards the crossing and inspected Bobby, who had been the closest to the first puck.

'Jake, it may be sensible to get Bobby back to the barns and check his feet. I think he might have stood in some of this,' Demetri instructed, turning to Joss for his support. Joss handed his reins to Armitage and took one of the colt's feet in his hands 'I think it will be okay, but we can't be too careful. Get plenty of water onto his legs and feet and stay with him.' Jake nodded smartly at his boss and started to lead the colt back the way he'd come.

Demetri directed his next words to Joss 'Can you organise getting The Ghost and Silvery Sun into the saddling boxes without Jake and myself? I have things to do.'

'Sure,' Joss answered, collecting the reins of Silvery Sun once again.

'Continue on plan without me,' Demetri announced to the others.

Rob and Ben straightened, brushed off their suits as best they could with their hands, and recovered their top hats from the road. Helping to check each other over, Ben saw similar minor cuts and scrapes on Rob's hands, but neither mentioned them. Then they took up positions in front and rear of The Ghost and Silvery Sun and with one final quick look behind him, Rob led Joss, Armitage, the two racehorses, and finally Ben through Ascot's ornate metal saddling gate and into the racecourse. Jake went in the opposite direction, back to the stables with the third grey.

Demetri watched the horses disappear in both directions and then checked his watch. He squared things with the people on the gate, asking them to put a hose or bucket of water on the two mangled umbrellas if they could spare the time. He feigned knowledge of exactly what had happened, suggesting it was simply a joker with stink bombs. Then he moved away and had a conversation with Ivan over his earpiece.

'You catch it all?'

'Yes, most of it. Homemade acid?' Ivan queried.

'Almost certainly. Very low level stuff though, household grade hydrochloric inside an internet bought firecracker I'd say. It might have stopped The Ghost running if it had struck an eye or another sensitive area, but it was a half-hearted effort if you ask me. He also tried to be too nonchalant with his second one. He'd have been better off really giving it some power.'

'Just as well he couldn't throw properly,' Ivan returned.

'Any target movements of note to report?' asked Demetri.

'None. Could he be working alone?'

'Let's hope so, but I doubt it.'

Ivan continued 'The blue-eyed man?'

'Can't be sure. The height was correct. Armitage got closest and almost caught him, but there was no way to identify him through the blacked out helmet. However he may now have a minor cut on his back where Andrew caught him. Those sharpened steel brimmed Fedora's were a good idea of his.'

The conversation died for a few seconds, then Demetri spoke slower, as if realising a truth. 'Our blue eyed man is like a kid, playing with toys he thinks are grownup, but aren't.'

Silence again for a few seconds. Then Ivan asked 'You think he's military trained?'

'Absolutely not. Territorial's or Cadets. If that.'

'I'll reprocess that possibility in my models,' Ivan responded.

Demetri took a long look up and down Ascot High Street and saw no sign of any motorcyclists. The horses from the race which had just run were now starting to leave the course and crossing Ascot High Street. A little way off the two impaled umbrellas were being dowsed with buckets of water and brushed from the road into the gutter. They were looking more like broken umbrellas now, rather than high-tech shields. The Ascot Stewards were spot on though, thought Demetri. The traffic was flowing again and the High Street was returning to normal.

Demetri spoke again. 'We have our target assailant mobile outside the racecourse, so I'm going to stay outside until after the race. Agreed?' Ivan took a few seconds to respond. 'Agreed. But get yourself a vehicle.' Demetri confirmed, checked the traffic, heading back over the road and down the stables lane.

Inside the racecourse Rob led the horses straight to a couple of empty saddling boxes which could be completely closed if required. The Ghost took the first with Armitage and Joss led Silvery Sun into the adjoining stable. Ben joined Armitage and Rob went in next door to give Joss a hand.

'He can't parade with the protection on, so help me get it all off and let's check him over to make sure he's okay,' Armitage instructed Ben, already busy with buckles and straps. 'We've lost Jake and Demetri so we'll have to parade him ourselves.'

'Will Silvery Sun be parading?'

'No. He'll join us down the walkway to the track. Joss will ride him down to the start tethered to The Ghost.'

The familiar chord buzzed in Ben's ear and Ivan started speaking

'I'm with both you and Armitage. Ian and Duncan have just entered the parade ring, there's no one else there yet. Raul should be coming out in the next few minutes from the weighing room. Marion, Janet and Olivia are in position down the stands walkway.'

Ben and Armitage didn't bother answering as they were too busy pulling the layers of protection away from The Ghost. The colt was well behaved, although he wasn't too pleased with his ears being pulled when the hood came off.

As Armitage took the last rug off the colt, which Ben could have sworn was made of the same material as his vest, a saddle and number cloth was revealed along with the grey's wonderful summer coat which even in the relative darkness of the stable seemed to shimmer in the half-light.

220

Ben walked around the horse, looking for any obvious problems with him, but was relieved to find nothing out of the ordinary.

'Let's get him into a better light and make sure,' suggested Ben, but Armitage, holding onto the colt's lead rein shook his head.

'No, when we go, we go. It's once around the parade ring and then out under the stands.'

'But surely there won't be any problems now. We've seen off the biker and he was outside the racecourse,' Ben reasoned.

'We don't even know if it was the same man. There could be multiple people involved and we still haven't any solid leads on who keeps attacking the horse.' Armitage's voice was bordering on scornful and he was clearly irritated. That said, he was treating The Ghost with every kindness and Ben decided silence was the best option for now.

'We need a prompt to parade,' Armitage said to The Ghost's neck, as he tested and then straightened the colt's saddle. Ben was about to answer, but was relieved when he realised Ivan was the recipient of the demand. He determined to try harder to interpret these conversations despite the unseen third man listening and contributing in an ad-hoc manner.

'Patience. Thirty seconds, a minute maximum,' came the reply.

Armitage grumbled something under his breath and Ben looked over at the man, who was sweating profusely from his forehead and around his neck. The exertions he had made on the road and in this claustrophobic box were taking their toll.

Ben was shaken out of his observations by Ivan's voice in his ear once more.

'You should be walking The Ghost with Jake. The stewards will expect to see two stable hands taking him around, that's our reason to have the lead horse. He's supposed to be a difficult horse to take to the start.'

Armitage's turned to face Ben and scowled again, but this time it was an inward emotion. He was frustrated at having missed this obvious issue.

'We'll walk him together,' said Ben, removing his top hat and throwing it into the corner of the stable.

By the time Armitage had thought about this and considered the options, Ben had already stripped to his shirt. He took off his cufflinks and turned up the sleeves and undid the top button and took hold of the Ghost's head collar.

Armitage nodded approval and a few seconds later Ivan gave them the signal to go.

Out in the parade ring Ian and Duncan looked around the large deserted circular expanse of manicured grass. The crowd was still sparse with the last race having just run and the public address system was relaying the prize giving ceremony in another area of the racecourse. The two of them stood, legs apart, arms crossed and were not speaking or looking at each other. Instead, they were systematically scanning the people around the ring. Duncan kept holding a finger up to his ear in response to Ivan's words but was soon reprimanded and shoved the offending hand into a trouser pocket.

Raul appeared and trotted into the parade ring wearing the starred blue and yellow silks, twirling his whip in his right hand.

'Not many of you here?' he queried as he was shaking the two men's hands.

Duncan rolled his eyes, but under strict instructions from Ivan not to mention the fracas outside the course he replied 'We're all here, but with the er… issues at Newbury, we're making sure you don't get shot again!' Raul winked and provided the two Owners with a cheeky grin. 'Yeah, that was pretty rough. I've got a little chunk out of my ear, but I'll be drinking out on that story for years once we've won this and the Ghost is champion in Europe!'

Ian and Duncan continued to scan the ring but independently turned back to the jockey long enough to acknowledge Raul's comment.

'On lookout, eh?' he ventured.

'Something like that. At the moment we're looking for the blessed horse,' Ian said, trying hard to mask his agitation. He walked a few steps forward to gain a better view of the saddling boxes and when still nothing appeared stood with pursed lips, looking down at his watch.

The next moment he became visibly relieved and he announced. 'Ah, he's on his way.'

Confused, Raul knew better than to challenge an owner so he joined the two of them in looking over in the direction of the saddling boxes and the pre-parade ring. A couple of other horses for the St James's Palace Stakes were already milling around at the saddling boxes now, but walking through them and standing out like a sore thumb was a large grey horse with an almighty brown black diamond on his forehead, a voluptuous creamy mane and bristling with muscle. He floated across the ground in a fluid movement. The Ghost had been turned out close to perfection.

As the colt approached the parade ring Raul realised that Ben and Armitage were leading the horse up and Jake was nowhere to be seen. When he voiced this, Ian quickly explained there had been an issue which meant Jake was back at the overnight stables, looking after a horse.

The Ghost certainly appeared ready for the contest ahead of him, striding around the parade ring like he owned it. The same could not be said for the two lads leading him up. Both Armitage and Ben were sweating freely which made them appear harassed and they walked a little awkwardly with the horse between them. Armitage wore his crumpled Fedora and had dust smears running down the back of his trousers. Beside him Ben's attire was also looking tired. Having thrown himself onto Ascot

High Street, there was now a hole in one knee of his trousers along with scuffmarks and his right hand had rivulets of blood which had dried in place on his hand and up one arm. He had attempted to flatten his hair down, but it was now looking ruffled.

Checking that everyone was in place, Ivan opened up the communications to all four of the syndicate in the parade ring and gave them the instruction to get Raul on the horse. Ian and Duncan, continuing to scan the crowd around the ring, wished Raul good luck and went over to the colt to watch over the young lad getting the leg up from Armitage. Ian leant over to Duncan. 'He doesn't look nervous at all.'

'He's young. He still thinks he's invincible,' replied Duncan with a touch of regret in his tone.

Raul made a few adjustments to his stirrups and bobbed up and down a few times to ensure his tack was solid before he was led straight out of the parade ring to where Silvery Sun was waiting with Joss already on his back and Rob holding his lead rein. The Ghost stopped momentarily so a lead rope could be passed between the two horses and then they stepped a few paces forward before halting again.

Up in his suite in the grandstand Ivan was furiously switching between screen views. The walk through the public areas was always going to be a good opportunity for someone to get close to The Ghost and the next minute rated the highest probability of attack according to his predictions.

'Janet, Olivia? Can you look out for anything irregular, but *do not* get involved. If you see anything, just describe it to me. Please remember, you're worth more than any horse.'

Olivia stifled a laugh, surprised but also touched at how human Ivan had revealed himself to be. If Ivan heard it, he didn't react, instead speaking with Marion. She was down at the apex of the walkway, where the horses would step onto the racecourse proper.

'You should see them passing your position in about forty seconds. Be alert and report if there is anything not as it should be,' said Ivan.

'No problem. All quiet here at the moment,' she replied.

Ivan pushed a few keys on his keyboard and first Joss and then Raul urged their mounts into a determined walk under the stands. Ian and Duncan watched them disappear into the distance, their roles now complete.

Ben took up a position behind the two horses as they set off down the walkway. The colts walked side by side and Rob was once again in front. Both had been reminded of what and who to look for by Ivan. Ben stared into each face at the rails and assessed them, turning every few strides to look behind him. They passed Janet, who stood surveying everything from an elevated position on a staircase. She gave them a thumbs-up signal as they passed and Ben returned the gesture.

Armitage was on the right-hand side of The Ghost, effectively making sure the horse was protected on each flank. They passed Olivia, again viewing the procession from a height, and slowly but surely they closed in on the lush green grass of the track which was only five to six yards away.

Joss saw him first. He was already making people open up a gap in front of him as he headed for the rails at a run.

'Man in morning suit far right...,' he called to everyone around him. '...coming over the rails.'

Rob reacted first, looking to his right and immediately jumping forward to meet the man as he got an arm and one leg over the white rails. With the flat of his palm he planted it firmly into the face that was following the limbs and the young, drunk, and now surprised interloper fell backwards and landed with a thump on the concrete the other side of the rail.

Rob examined the man scrabbling to get to his feet, turned, and reported 'Just a daft young lad showing off. That was not the blue eyed man.' He went on to repeat his words, just to be sure that anyone listening would be standing down from any further action.

The two horses continued, passing a relieved Marion to their left and they broke onto the racecourse together and started to jig-jog. Joss held onto the reins of Silvery Sun tightly and told Armitage to release the Ghost and with a little kick the two horses wheeled to the right and started to canter past the royal enclosure and then the Tattersalls enclosure. It was awkward at first, but Joss and Raul seemed to find a rhythm after five or six strides and settled their mounts for the five minute hack to the round mile start.

Armitage followed the horses for the first ten yards then ran back and grabbed Ben's arm.

'Come on, you're with me. Jake was supposed to be helping but he's still with Bobby.'

He dragged Ben a few yards across the track. 'We need to be the eyes at the start!' he exclaimed between puffs of breath. Ben simply responded with an 'Okay,' and the two of them jogged across the flat track, bobbed underneath the running rails and then traversed the National Hunt track, which would lie unused for the summer.

Ben followed Armitage under another set of rails and for a moment he thought the bobbing Fedora wearer was going to have him run the full mile down to the start. However, a large quad bike was revealed behind an advertising hoarding and Armitage jumped on and twisted the keys that were already in the starting position. Ben jumped, rather ungainly, onto the secondary seat behind Armitage and grabbed his companion's waist. With no further comment, the engine caught and seconds later they were whizzing down the emergency road on the inside of the course.

Four furlong markers whistled by before the thin road banked to the left. Ben spied the two horses in front of them, still going down the course at a slow canter. They slowed as they approached the two animals and then passed them.

'They should be safe here. No cover for a shot or approach,' Armitage shouted over the wind and engine noise.

'We'll get to the start and make sure they go in safely. It'll be a twenty minute wait down there.'

Ben hollered his agreement and hunkered down behind Armitage's back as the speed of the vehicle increased. The rushing wind had him feeling cold now, but there was the huge rush of adrenaline which more than compensated. They passed a couple of chase fences and then on the left the road fell away to a large circular lake on the inside of the track. Once again, they followed the road round to the left before Armitage started to slow.

'We're going over the track and then you'll have to hang on for the last few hundred yards. It's a bit rough,' he announced.

Armitage turned a sharp right and soon they reached a racecourse gate which was opened for them as they approached. Then they were bouncing on the turf as they crossed the flat and jumps racetrack once again. The going didn't improve once they got to the other side, as the road deteriorated into nothing more than a grass and mud track. The quad bike pitched and rolled and Ben had all on to stay in contact with Armitage, his arms jumping around the younger mans waist with every bump and pitch.

A minute later the rails of the round course appeared once again and after following the track for another hundred yards, Armitage pulled the quad bike off the track and turned the engine off.

Ben dismounted stiffly, followed by Armitage and the two of them surveyed the scene. The Round Course at Ascot is so named because it's a circuit. However, when horses run over a mile on the round course they start on a spur of track which runs straight for a furlong before the horses reach the circular track. The 'round mile' is something of a misnomer as it consists of a straight run for four furlongs, a right-hand bend and then another straight four furlongs to the finish.

Rubbing the base of his back, Ben followed Armitage to the rails, ducked under them and tried to catch his breath. Panting, he looked up and down the course. They were standing halfway down the straight spur. A hundred yards to their left the starting stalls were already in position, with about half a dozen stalls handlers standing beside or leaning on the open gates. Fifty yards in front of the stalls, to the inside of the track, a lone cameraman stood on a small platform, pointing his camera up the racecourse. To the right Ben could just pick out Silvery Sun and The Ghost about a furlong away, lobbing along the middle of the racetrack. With nothing but grasses and small hillocks behind them, they had no worries from that direction, but on the opposite side of the racetrack a natural backdrop of mature woodland fringed the entire furlong.

Armitage nodded at the other side of the racetrack. 'That's where we need to be,' and he stalked away over the track. Ben groaned and following in his wake. As they strode through the pristine three-inch long turf Ivan spoke to the two of them.

'There's a main road behind those trees, and then a golf course. Plenty of places to hide or disappear into. Demetri has been around the area but there's no sign of our biker.'

'How are Joss and Raul doing with the horses?' asked Armitage.

'All good.'

'Any alerts from the hit list?'

'I would have informed you,' Ivan replied testily.

Armitage looked over at Ben who returned a couple of raised eyebrows, but the seriousness written on Armitage's face didn't alter one iota.

They reached the other side of the track and, before they disappeared into the tree line, Ivan came through again. 'I've switched all the other syndicate members to watch mode on your two feeds and Joss's. We're all with you.'

The wood turned out to be quite easy to navigate. The trees had boughs down to the ground, but once you walked under them, it was easy to pick your way through. It was also only twenty yards until the main road provided a natural break in the cover. Armitage sent Ben to the far side and he stayed a few yards into the wood, keeping an eye on where the two horses were on the racetrack.

'Don't forget to look up as well as through,' he shouted over to Ben as they started to scan their way through the trees towards the starting stalls. 'He could be up in the trees.'

Ben immediately strained to look up into a large sycamore he was under and promptly walked into a low hanging branch, cursing as it scraped along his trousers. The suit rental company would definitely need to claim on their insurance for these trousers he thought, pushing his way through the next set of waist high whippy branches, and depositing another swathe of green algae onto himself.

They had managed to cover about fifty yards when The Ghost and Silvery Sun trotted past. Armitage emerged from the tree line and shouted 'Walk the rest,' at the two riders, who immediately slowed their mounts. Then he disappeared underneath a large ash tree to resume his search.

Two minutes later the horses and the woodland search party had reached the bottom of the track. Joss and Raul uncoupled their horses and got off their backs, leading them around in front of the stalls. Ben and Armitage appeared from the wood and walked over to meet them looking like a couple of tramps. Two stalls handlers started to walk towards

Armitage, who to be fair, didn't look too savory, but a couple of words from Joss saw them placated and they retraced their steps back to the line of starting stalls.

Armitage was first to reach the horses and immediately gave The Ghost a slap on his neck.

'Nothing in there,' he reported. 'Ten minutes to the off and we're looking good.'

Ben arrived and received a big grin from Joss. 'You look like you've been dragged through a hedge backwards.'

'That's because I have,' Ben replied without a hint of irony.

Raul joined in. 'You going to accept the winners prize looking like that then? You'll never get back in the Royal Enclosure, they'll kick you out!'

Armitage looked Ben up and down and maintaining his deadpan look said. 'He has a point.'

Joss and Raul laughed out loud, which seemed somewhat odd, in this quiet backwater. Their laughter seemed to reverberate around the little amphitheatre created by the trees. A few of the handlers even poked their heads around the side of the stalls to see what was happening.

'Have you seen *yourself* lately?' Ben retorted, fascinated by being the source of Armitage's stab at humour.

Armitage's neck wobbled as he craned to take in his current state of dress. He too was filthy with holes at his elbows and he discovered a rip in the back pocket of his trousers. Like Ben he was encrusted with dust, leaf debris, and green tree algae. His Fedora was stained with sweat around its rim, but remained stubbornly pointed at a jaunty angle on his head.

'I can carry this look off, whereas you...'

'Can we please do the final checks before the rest of the field get to the start,' interrupted Ivan in everyone's ear apart from Raul. 'Don't lose focus now.'

Armitage clicked into serious mode once again and sent Ben off to check some of the hillocks to the left of the stalls whilst he went through the very sparse area of trees at the end of the spur. He could see right through the trees here to the road beyond, but found nothing. Finally he called Ben over.

'That corner has some large trees. I think there's a house behind it. Have a good look, just in case. I'll stay here and look for any movement.'

Unquestioningly, Ben set off into the woods again, but after two more minutes of peering up into tree after tree and through all the branches he returned to where Armitage was standing, scanning the trees.

'Okay, we're done. The rest of the horses are starting to arrive.' Armitage said, pointing a thumb over his shoulder. Beyond the stalls The Ghost had been joined by two other runners and there was an array of horses and their riders at different distances heading down the spur.

'One last job,' Armitage said quietly to Ben and turned on his heel, striding towards the stalls handlers. 'Come on, two sets of eyes and all that,' he added, and Ben set off after the small figure.

'What are we doing?'

'The stalls. We need to check them and the handlers for six foot blue eyed men.' replied Armitage plainly.

Two sets of starting stalls had been linked together across the track to allow for the sixteen runners. Armitage made a beeline for the very end of the line and walked down them, examining each bay as he went. Ben followed, looking over the green and white metal. For what, he had no idea. They all looked the same.

The two of them managed to make it down to the last five bays before they were accosted by a stalls handler. He definitely wasn't the blue-eyed-man, as his eyes were hazel and he was only five feet tall.

'You have to move back gents. We load in two minutes. I know Mr O'Hoole has vouched for you, but we've a job to do.'

Another two handlers appeared through the stalls gates and Armitage nodded, smiled broadly, and appeared to accept he wasn't going to finish his inspection of the stalls. He started to turn away, but then asked

'Ben... What stall is The Ghost drawn in?'

'Three.'

Armitage swung back around and looked for the stall numbers. But there was nothing to see. The numbers were facing up the course. Ben understood and said 'It's that one there.' and pointed to the third stall in from rails. Armitage hadn't been able to check that one out yet.

The handler who had instructed them to leave was still standing watching the pair of them.

'Could we possibly just have a quick look?' asked Ben. 'Ten seconds, that's all.'

The small man, who Ben half recognised as a retired jockey, checked his watch and said 'Make it quick,' and turned his back on them. Ben followed Armitage to the third stall and looked around, meanwhile Armitage finished looking at all the last five stalls, running his hands down the metal struts as he went. He completed the last of them and then came back to Ben, who was stood outside stall three.

'Come on Armitage, we really are done. They are going to start loading.'

Ben moved off a few paces, set to walk to the back of the spur, but Armitage stood still, looking at the grass inside the third stall. He stalked into the stall and bent over, disappearing from Ben's sight for a moment. Armitage looked down at an area of the turf that seemed to be flattened at the front end of The Ghost's stall. There was a small, tuppence piece sized disc of mud in its centre. He bent down for a closer look, brushing the perfectly round disc of dried mud away with the back of his hand,

228

revealing a ring of black plastic pipe. There was a quiet buzz.

Armitage gasped as the crossbow bolt ripped through his forearm and embedded itself in his chest. Air was immediately squeezed from his lungs and he toppled forward. He tried to cry out, but only a rasp issued from the base of his throat. Then a white-hot heat moved through his body and a searing pain hotwired itself through every single nerve in the top half of his torso.

He stayed there, on his knees, wincing with every tiny intake of breath. His Fedora parted company with his head and fell beneath the next stall. He stooped, strangely in that moment, his brain wished him to pick it up, but he ended up crumpling on the floor on his back, a hand to the last two inches of the bolt that hadn't penetrated.

Ben rounded the end of stall three to find Armitage lying face up with the shaft of a crossbow bolt sticking into the right-hand side of his chest and a quantity of blood smeared to his face. Despite all of this, Armitage was apparently concentrating hard in order to hold an index finger to his lips, his eyes imploring Ben to remain silent.
Ivan started screaming in Ben's ear, but he didn't hear any of it. He rushed forward and down to the stricken man.

'Be... quiet,' Armitage gurgled in Ben's ear. 'Get Joss.'

'But you need help, I...'

'Nnn,' He spat some phlegm up and tried again. 'Nn...ot yet. Get Joss.'

Ben looked down at the carbon fibre tipped hole in Armitage's chest, then the bone and flaps of flesh handing off his arm and fought down the urge to scream for help. He took a breath and then ran out of the stall, spinning around to try and locate Joss.

Joss was already running towards the stalls under Ivan's instructions. A few seconds later he and Ben were inside stall three. Armitage was still attempting to shush the two of them when they bobbed down.

'Look... up,' he pleaded when they were close to him. 'He... is...' Armitage groaned slighted but finished with 'H... here.'

Both Ben and Joss screwed their faces up, not comprehending the meaning in the hissed words.

Ivan's voice was icy when he spoke. 'He means the blue eyed man must to watching you now!'

Ben shot a look to the sky and then to the large trees on the far side of the track.

'He had to be close to see Armitage enter the stall to activate the trap,' continued Ivan. 'And he probably needed height too. Look to the tallest trees or buildings.'

Ben felt a shaft of pure anger run through him, and he stood upright, fists clenched, staring at the four or five tall trees in the bottom corner of the spur. Joss brought him back down though, taking one of Ben's wrists.

'Is Armitage able to move safely?' Ivan said to all three of them. Armitage nodded. His breathing was poor, but regular and he seemed lucid to Joss.

'He says yes,' Joss relayed.

'Okay, get him out of there and to the back of the track.'

'Really?' asked Ben, horrified at not immediately getting the ambulance over to Armitage. After all, it was stood there, only forty yards away.

'Yes, really,' Ivan insisted. 'Get him out of there now. He is only wounded and will live. If we call the ambulance crew the race will be delayed. If they see the pipe it will be cancelled. If they find Armitage...'

'Okay, okay!' Ben hissed to the man in his ear.

Ben took a look under the front of the stalls and saw that the horses were all still milling around. However one or two horses had started to walk behind, ready for loading to begin.

After taking a calming gasp of air Ben said 'Okay, let's make this quick.' He looked Armitage in the eye and added 'Get ready for some pain.'

Joss took one arm and Ben the other and they dragged Armitage up to his feet, supporting him as he tenderly took a few steps, the bolt still sticking out of his chest just above his right breast. Joss took note of this, spied the Fedora on the ground and scooped it up. He placed it over the bolt and moved Armitage's good hand so he could hold the hat to himself, hiding the bolt.

'Here. Keep that there until we're out of sight.'

'And bloody tell us if you're going to die. This is crazy,' spat Ben angrily to anyone who would listen.

'I'll be okay...,' Armitage managed as they half dragged, half lifted the small man out of stall three and over the thirty yards to the very back of the racetrack.

A stalls handler stopped to watch the three of them stumble away from the stalls and Joss called over 'A bit too much to drink... all the excitement. Too much for him,' and the handler clucked and turned away.

'It's a good job you're a half pint,' Ben wheezed as he carefully helped lay Armitage down in the longer grass at the back edge of the track. Armitage tried to stifle an agonised groan as his back touched the grass and then proceeded to cough as if he was gargling black treacle. Ben tried not to think of what was causing the slurping sound in the man's throat.

Ivan's voice buzzed into Joss's and Ben's ears and a worried voice said 'We have to make sure that pipe is blocked before The Ghost goes in.'

Switching off Ben's earpiece Ivan gave an instruction just to Joss. The trainer remained stock still, kneeling over Armitage, but not really

230

looking, concentrating instead. Then he glanced quickly around. One or two horses were behind the stalls now, including The Ghost and Raul. Silvery Sun was still tied to the back rail a few yards away, where he had left him per Ivan's earlier instructions. The colt was munching happily on the lush racetrack grass.

Joss got to his feet, quickly glanced down at Ben and Armitage then turned and ran back to the starting stalls. Stalls handlers shrugged at him as he dodged past them, but he waved them away. Once in stall three he pulled a shoe off without undoing the laces and removed his sock, frenetically pushing it into the barrel of the plastic pipe as far as it would go.

'Is there any blood around?' Ivan asked. 'Mop it with your other sock. It will also help it block the pipe.'

Joss pulled off his other shoe and used it to wipe a splatter of blood away from the padded sides of the stall. He also rubbed a small pool of Armitage's fluids into the grass.

'It's almost certainly a single shooter mechanism, but we can't be too careful,' Ivan opined in Joss's ear as Joss stuck his fingers down the deadly tube once again.

The words 'It better bloody be,' went through his head, but he didn't vocalise them.

'Pack it in good and solid,' Ivan added as he watched Joss working the second thick cotton sock into the inch wide neck of the pipe.

Joss became aware of someone standing behind him. Before he could turn a voice said 'You need to get out of here. Now!' Joss screwed his head back to see the lead stalls man standing, hands on hips, looking down on him. He pushed the last of the sock into the tube and got up.

'What you doing in there anyway?'

'Just checking the ground,' Joss replied weakly. 'My horse likes to stand on even ground in the stalls,' he added.

The stalls handler looked down at the incredibly level turf unconvinced, but with horses and jockeys started to make the back of the stalls busier by the second and shouts for help being traded between the handlers, he hadn't the time to argue with an overzealous trainer…

'Just get out of the way. You'll get in trouble,' he said, moving from the stall entrance.

Relieved, Joss offered 'No problem!' and jogged away from the starting stalls, amazed that the handler hadn't noticed he was bare footed.

About ten yards away he overheard the handler curse and mumble 'Trainers!' to his back and Joss allowed a grin to creep onto his face.

He got back to Armitage and Ben to find the younger man looking grey in the face and extremely uncomfortable. He was panting in short, staccato breaths. Ben was bent over him, apparently trying to make sense of what the prone man was saying.

'Look... up,' Armitage gurgled painfully, swiveling his bloodshot eyes several times in an upward direction.

Ben turned and judged where Armitage was looking. Then he saw him. Someone was in one of the tallest trees. They appeared to be seated, dangled from a rope which swayed slightly in the light breeze. Ben strained his eyes and picked out a harness and realised the figure was winching themselves downwards.

'You seeing this Ivan?' Ben demanded.

There was no reply.

'Oh great! Just when I need him,' he spluttered. Ben locked eyes with Armitage, who kept directing his eyes to the trees and then returning to Ben. He felt the same anger from a few minutes earlier start to rise through him and one after the other, his fists clenched.

'Joss, look after him. I'm going to get the blue-eyed man,' he said, backing away. Then he turned and headed directly for the largest tree in the corner of the grove at a run. He ran, then jogged, switching his view to avoid what was in front of him, back to the dangling silhouetted figure who was now inching towards the lower branches of the surrounding trees.

Ben hopped between the rails and then had to clamber over the advertising hoardings, turning to look up again. In that moment the figure froze, facing Ben. He stopped, breathing heavily, and squinted directly at the gently swinging figure who was no more than thirty yards away from him. Suddenly the winching became frenetic and Ben set off again, diving under the first couple of branches he encountered. Gathering his bearings, he forced his way between a group of saplings. He must be almost under the right tree now.

'Stop Ben!' shouted a commanding voice to his left.

Shocked, Ben came to a halt, but with his body tensed, ready for an attack he circled around on the spot seeking out the source of the instruction. He didn't have time to work it out as at that moment a man fell out of the sky a yard in front of him. He landed with a hollow thump and a sickening crack of bone onto silky black compacted leaf litter.

The fallen man let out a howl of pain and Ben jumped back in fright, his heart dropping to his feet. A cascade of fresh green leaves fluttered down around the figure for a few seconds and he tightened into a ball on the floor, hugging his knees and cursing.

'Watch out, he's cut himself down, he'll have a knife.'

Ben looked in the direction of the speaker and with huge relief realised it was Demetri. The anger in him started to dissipate and he found himself smiling stupidly up at the Scotsman. He was standing, hands on hips, on what looked like a telephone box, casually looking down at the scene. The main road was in fact only ten yards away from the tree and Ben could now see Joss's Land Rover parked up against the fence a little way down the road.

Demetri sprang off the large square box and into the wood, landing surprisingly lightly for a large man, and picked his way through the nettles on his way over to Ben.

'You lost your earpiece I guess,' he said, pointing at Ben's head. Ben's probing fingers confirmed that the earpiece was no longer attached to the inside of his ear.

'It must have dropped out when I was helping get Armitage out of the stalls.'

Demetri flashed a wide grin at him. 'Ivan is doing his nut. He was trying to tell you about where I was but you just ran over here like a madman. His words, not mine,' he added with a chuckle.

'I've been here five minutes, waiting for our friend here to land.' Demetri aimed a light kick at the bunched up man who appeared to be holding both his legs and moaning.

'Knife!' Demetri demanded. 'Toss it away now and you'll get treatment for your stupidity.'

The squirming ball was dressed in ill-fitting army fatigues and a black ski mask.

'Rob would have a field day with this chap,' said Demetri conversationally. 'He'd not last a day in the army. Look at the state of him.' He prodded the man leg with a booted foot.

This time the man reacted, unfurling and attempting to sideswipe Demetri's foot with a blade in his right hand. Without any fuss, Demetri allowed the man's arm to spin around its parabola and then neatly stamped hard on the man's forearm, resulting in his knife being ejected from his grasp. It was then that Ben noticed the shinbone poking through the man's trousers, along with a trail of oily blood splashed over leaves and dirt. He flicked his view up to the ski mask and met a pair of cobalt blue eyes staring hatefully back at him.

Demetri picked up the knife, tutting to himself as he inspected it.

'Low quality steel my friend. That's why it took so long for you to cut through your rope. Now, let's make sure we have our man.'

He circled the figure and then wrenched off the mask from behind in one quick motion. It revealed the blue-eyed man. The fake policeman, the shooter, the acid attacker. The man's eyes warily followed the Scotsman as he continued to circumnavigate his prey.

'Is that enough?' Demetri asked.

The blue-eyed man looked confused, but Ben realised Demetri must be speaking with Ivan. Ben guessed he was providing Ivan with the ability to identify the blue-eyed man.

There appeared to be a short conversation and then Demetri produced his phone from his pocket. He tapped the Smartphone a few times and it sprang to life, lighting his face up in the gloom under the trees.

'Now then friend,' Demetri whispered with enough malice that even Ben started to become uncomfortable. He aimed a toe of his boot at the blue-eyed man's leg once again and gave it a prod, eliciting a scream followed by whimpering.

Demetri continued 'The St James's Palace Stakes is under starters orders. Let's find out whether all of this…,' he waved a hand theatrically over the man '… two broken legs and a stretch in prison will prove to be worth it, or alternatively, you've made an error of judgment *on a monumental scale.*'

Twenty-Eight

Raul walked The Ghost towards Joss and Armitage, raised his hand to his cap, and saluted towards them. He was a little surprised to see the trainer and owner lying arm in arm on the grass, but then he reasoned there was nothing normal about this syndicate. He was about to race on the best horse he'd ever sat on, in a race which determined the best from the best. He dismissed everything else from his mind and concentrated on the race. The handlers called number thirteen and he walked the colt forward towards the right-hand side of the stalls.

Joss slid his arm underneath Armitage and helped him up onto his elbow so he could watch The Ghost enter the starting stalls. He started to cough, but waved Joss away when he tried to help. The tourniquet they had fashioned out of Armitage's socks bit into his arm, but did seem to be halting the loss of any more blood. His chest heaved in quick order, and he could feel his heart pumping. The Ghost was the third last to load and walked forward quickly and quietly. Joss held his breath and Armitage, not having too much breath to hold, just kept breathing.

On the steps of the Royal Enclosure grandstand Ian, Janet, Olivia, Marion and Rob stood clustered together. They watched the feed from Joss's glass button and kept glancing at the big screen in the centre of the racecourse.

When The Ghost was safely enclosed in stall three, Joss's heart missed a few beats. He waited for a twanging noise and the colt to fall to his knees, but nothing out of the ordinary happened. He stood steady, rocking his weight back, ready to kick out.

A shout of 'Jockeys!' went up from the starter and the starting gates clanged open as one and The Ghost jumped smoothly out the front of his stall and quickly disappeared out of view of the two men on the grass.

'Job... done,' croaked Armitage and eased himself back onto the grass, gritting his teeth as his spine touched the turf.

'Ivan, can you...,' Joss began.

'It's already on its way,' Ivan broke in. 'Look down the racetrack, an ambulance should be arriving within a minute. I've patched the television coverage through to your mobile app, if either of you can stand to watch what happens in the race. Oh, and well done both of you.'

As Joss patted his trousers in search of his phone, the sound of a vehicle reached him from the direction the horses had run. A white roof appeared and then the rest of the ambulance bobbed into view as it raced over the undulations in the track.

Raul had been disconcerted when he looked down in the stalls. A quantity of blood had been inexpertly wiped, or to be accurate, smudged across the side panels. It struck him that it might have something to do with the owner lying in the long grass but he soon dispelled the thought.

This was the most important ride of his life.

The Ghost had managed to get away cleanly and after a dozen strides Raul found himself in a prominent position, travelling behind the front rank of horses. The runners had immediately grouped to the inside rail and a single horse was a good two lengths clear of the chasing pack already, setting a very decent pace.

The first furlong was over in a flash and when the rail disappeared and the field joined the round course Raul steeled himself, remembering Joss's instructions, and let an inch of his reins out. The Ghost seemed a little fresh and pulled ever so slightly, wanting to get on with things, but he knew that was just the way the colt raced. The Ghost wanted to go forward and he felt strong but his speed was still contained. That extra inch of reins provided room for him to gallop and it took him closer to the front of the field. The flanks of Panama jostled for space in the line of three horses Raul was tracking, and he considered switching to the outside. Not on this horse. Not yet. The Ghost was in need of competitors to pass.

Another furlong marker disappeared behind them and the lead horse continued to bowl along, but now Panama made a move, going up to gallop alongside the leader as the third furlong slipped by. He was going to try and boss the race from the front. Raul couldn't help the rush of excitement that coursed through his body as he saw Panama make its move. He had ridden this race in his head hundreds of times, lying awake at night, imagining the conditions, moves and switches. Panama was the horse to beat and Raul's split second decisions could be the difference between victory, or being a part player in another jockey's place in the history books.

With two hundred yards to travel before the long sweeping turn into the home straight, Raul gave The Ghost another inch and a half of rein and he felt the engine beneath him change gear. He knew this was early in the race to be using so much energy, but he and Joss were sure. They were sure the Ghost had the qualities required to win a Group One race. *This* Group One race.

The Ghost's ears twitched, flicked forward and then went back again as Raul asked him to go forward. It was as if the horse was receiving the request, considering its merits and then making his agreement known through action. The Ghost lengthened his stride and cruised up to sit on the outside, three abreast off the rail in a share of the lead. Panama's jockey glanced sideways, saw who it was, grimaced and took Panama into the lead. The colt still travelled well within himself. A significant increase in the volume of sound from the watching crowd was met with a new pitch of excitement from the course commentator.

The single right-handed bend started to take the horses into the three furlong home straight and Raul asked The Ghost for a little more again, and they left the horse on his inside and moved in front and then onto the rail, tracking Panama in Indian file.

Several jockeys sat in behind the front rank were caught out by this move. The pace was already too punishing for many. Every rider knew the consequences of using too much too soon: not having the strength to see out the one mile trip. Six jockeys let their mounts down and they moved forward as the turn reached its apex. There was scrimmaging, and two rows of three runners went wide into the bend, bumping each other in the process.

Raul only cared about one horse. His race was now a duel. Panama, only a half width off the running rail, started to straighten up for the three furlong straight run-in to the winning line in front of the Royal Enclosure. The Ghost was on Panama's heels, bang up against the rails. Raul waited. He waited for the horse and jockey in front of him to revert to type. The bend continued to flatten out and Panama hugged the rail, his jockey still not moving. The stands to the left suddenly filled Raul's view and he held his breath, tugging faintly on The Ghost's reins to keep him safely away from Panama's thrusting hooves. It needed to happen now and he steeled himself, poised. The Ghost seemed to sense his rider's heightened awareness, changing his lead leg.

Panama edged out, one, then two yards. As the running rail became straight once again, the move Raul was now screaming for in his head was on. He and Joss had spent days watching video of Panama and noticed the colt would tend to run away from the rail on right turns, only slightly, but enough. He'd done it twice as a two year old and subsequently stayed on straight tracks. Raul was banking on Panama retaining the trait as a three year old. And he did. Panama needed the rail and Raul was about to pinch it from him. He shot The Ghost up the inside of Panama, pushing for only two strides, and suddenly there was a clear, straight track ahead of him, with Panama's rider looking over at Raul, bewildered by what had just happened.

In behind came the sounds of jockeys urging their mounts along with shouts and whip cracks. Raul became aware of a horse on his own heels, another out much wider on the track, both with animated riders. He edged the Ghost into the lead, faintly pushing the colt, but nothing more. Panama's jockey responded, pushing his horse to be nose to nose, then into the lead by a head, a neck and more. The two furlong marker whipped past.

Raul remained in his same rhythm; he rode as if he was breezing the colt up the home gallops in summer, enjoying the breeze in his face and sun on his back. 'Fill yourself with confidence Panama,' he heard himself whisper. 'Fill yourself up.'

At a furlong and a half out, Raul shouted 'Come On Ghost!' and the colt's head visibly dipped in response and Raul felt the three year old accelerate up the rail like no other horse he had ever sat upon. In two strides the Ghost was level with Panama and at the furlong marker they were a length up. Panama's rider drew his whip and pushed his other hand down the horse's neck, asking for more length, more speed. The horse responded, but could only maintain the distance between them, he couldn't reduce it. The stands erupted with a wall of sound.

Raul again sensed horses out wide, but behind. He flicked his whip once at The Ghost and his heart jumped as the colt lengthened again, found more speed and started to pull away from Panama with every stride. Raul stole a glance round to his left with eighty yards to go and suddenly realised The Ghost had kicked five lengths clear of his nearest challenger.

The Ghost's audience lost its voice for a couple of seconds. Stunned by his turn of foot, a tingling ran down spines and enforced intakes of breath silenced tens of thousands. As The Ghost Machine crossed the line five lengths clear of his nearest competitor and pricked his ears the sound burst forth again, twice as loud. The course commentator's voice broke mid sentence and it took him a few seconds more to call the placed horses' home.

Twenty-Nine

Raul was numb. He crossed the line without a fist in the air, no waving of his whip, no showboating. He was in awe. He reflected on the life that had brought him to this moment and the life that may be ahead. He could hug the horse, this beast of a racehorse that had carried him to victory. This wasn't just a win, this was a victory. A victory against the odds.

He satisfied himself with a slap to the horse's neck and rubbing the colt between the ears. The Ghost responded by tossing his head in a circular motion as horse and rider slowed to a jog and then a walk at the bottom of the track. The colt was breathing in steady, strong snorts of air through his nose. There was no heaving of his chest; everything was as it should be. Raul tugged faintly on The Ghost's left rein and the two of them turned, cantering slowly back to the stands, and into a melee of reporters, stewards, stable hands and handlers attempting to reunite themselves with their horses.

The Ghost slowed to a walk once more and a reporter immediately stuck a microphone in front to Raul's face whilst he was still on the horse. The lady asked some sort of banal question and Raul, still in his own thoughts, missed the question completely and peered down at her, bemused. He attempted to say something when her eyes widened and she started nodding encouragingly a few seconds later, but his words caught in his throat and his eyes inexplicably began to water. The microphone continued to hover in front of Raul's face but he wasn't in any fit shape to speak and pushed it away with the back of his hand. It was then quickly retracted and the lady turned to face her cameraman and curtailed her interview with a short explanation to the camera.

Leaving the camera crew behind, The Ghost walked on and Raul scanned the scene, trying to pick out Jake or Joss, when Panama walked past. His jockey shouted a 'Hey!' and extended a hand. Raul's shook it uncertainly for a moment, but then managed a smile.

'Well ridden, lad,' the much older rider said, bowing his head slightly. 'You got me up the rail. But it won't happen again!'

Raul realised he didn't even know where Panama had finished. He had a feeling Lucky Landing, the horse he'd dead heated with at Newbury had been the challenger for second place in the closing stages. Before Raul could say anything in reply to Panama's rider, a stable lass ran up and grabbed the colt's head collar. She shot an extremely unhappy scowl at Raul and led her horse away leaving him curious to discover what he'd done to warrant such a cruel response to his win.

Raul was relieved when he spotted Rob dancing through the plethora of people scattered across the track, a lead rein in his hand. He was almost jumping with each step he took on his way to the colt and threw his arms around the horse's neck and then almost pulled Raul out of his saddle in the joy of the moment.

Eventually Rob looped the lead rein on, explaining: 'There's no one to lead him in. Joss and Jake aren't here and Armitage is…,' his words tailed off, but he recovered 'So I only realised a minute ago and grabbed a lead rein from one of the other lads and ran down here. Come on, we can't keep the Queen waiting!'

Raul smiled down, still in a hazy world of his own.

Rob proudly led Raul and the Ghost to the entrance of the walkway amid wildly enthusiastic crowds ten deep in places. A round of applause never abated all the way to the parade ring and finished with a roar in the half-moon winning horse area. They were met by Marion, Ian, Janet, Duncan, and Olivia who had been hugging each other before Raul got off The Ghost, and then proceeded to transfer their affection to their jockey and the horse. The Ghost Machine stood tall, with his head up, surveying the scene like a king observing his minions whilst Raul removed his saddle. Then he took the opportunity to bury his head in a large bucket of water offered by Rob, and managed to soak anyone within a few yards by spraying it through his teeth, all of which was greeted with even more enthusiastic clapping and slaps to the horse's neck.

More reporters and television cameras descended on Raul as soon as he managed to tear himself from the grasp of the syndicate, and this time he managed something more intelligible, commenting primarily on how much he owed to the horse. A couple of minutes later he was tugged by the elbow mid-interview by a steward insisting he weigh in, so he quickly apologised and headed off, accompanied by two stewards.

Ivan still sat behind his array of screens with a huge smile on his face. His systems continued to monitor all nine members of the syndicate and the several hundred targets, but he remained glued to three screens which showed the winners enclosure. The red and green targeting lines still flickered across the faces, but he ignored them for now, enjoying the moment. He hadn't spoken for three minutes. He didn't need to, there was nothing to say.

Ben and Demetri had carried the still silent - apart from his screams of pain – blue eyed man into the back of Joss's Land Rover and watched the race from the roadside before dropping a terribly excited Ben off at the stabling gates. Demetri had then driven a few hundred yards down the Ascot High Street and was now introducing the man to the Ascot police whose station was handily located directly over the road from the racecourse.

Before Demetri entered the police station Ivan asked after Ben. Demetri reported he last saw the syndicate manager vaulting over rails and pushing people aside in order to reach the winners enclosure before the horse departed. He noted that Ben's progress hadn't been assisted by the state of his attire and the fact his face was smudged with dirt and blood.

On another of Ivan's screens the roof of an ambulance had been visible, but was now in blackness as Armitage had been relieved of his upper body clothes. However, an audio feed still came through and the words 'Bloody lucky mate.' and 'Two inches the other way...' had been mentioned a number of times in the last few minutes. Ivan caught himself sighing heavily. Was this a feeling, relief or frustration? He decided it was both; relief Armitage would recover, frustration for the team having a man out of action for a number of weeks. He silently cursed his analytical brain and cast his feelings to the back of his mind.

The next screen was Joss's. He had been forced to leave Armitage with the ambulance crew in order to take Silvery Sun back to the stables, but only after they had confirmed the injuries sustained by the crossbow bolt were not life threatening. His feed showed him beside the colt, its head nodding in and out of the shot as they walked through the walkway under the stands. Joss was thanking well-wishers and doing his best to fend off interviews, citing his not inconsiderable partner as an excuse, who he insisted 'Needed to be placed in a stable.' Ivan patched himself into Joss's feed.

'If you are quick, you won't miss the presentations,' he advised.

'Thanks Ivan. How's Ben doing?'

'I imagine you're just about to bump into him,' Ivan responded. 'I can't contact him but he should be with you any minute.'

At the top of the walkway Joss heard his name shouted from the public area behind the rails and a waving arm identified Ben, negotiating heatedly with a race day steward in order to gain access to the walkway. Joss went over and placed a hand on the steward's shoulder.

He could understand the steward's reticence to allow Ben access to the royal enclosure. He looked a shadow of the man who had been walking around the paddock earlier in the day. His hair still had debris twisted through it from walking through the trees and his face was several colours it should not have been and was dotted with several small cuts. He had streaks of dried blood up one arm and he was trying to hide rips in both his dress shirt and trousers.

'I know it will be hard to believe but this chap owns the winner of the last race,' Joss told the steward patiently. The steward spun round to find Joss smiling pleasantly and Silvery Sun's head bearing down on him. The man's eyes bulged and the gate to the walkway magically opened.

Ben immediately gave his trainer a bear hug, lifting him off the ground. The two of then broke into uncontrollable laughter, to the amusement of the race-goers pushing up against the rails beside them.

'Come on, I'll put this one into a pre-parade stable for a few minutes and then we'll need to get across there,' Joss said, lofting a thumb over his shoulder towards the parade ring.

A minute later Joss and Ben joined the rest of the syndicate in the winners enclosure where the handshakes, hugging and tears restarted for a couple of minutes. Ben quickly relayed what happened in the wood and Joss re-assured everyone that despite the truly awful sight of a man with an arrow sticking out of his chest, he had been assured that Armitage would live.

The 'Horses away!' announcement was made over the public address and Joss and Marion made moves to lead Silvery Son and The Ghost to get washed down and then back to the racecourse stables.
Ben was straight over to them.

'Forget that, you're going to collect the trainer's prize and revel in your achievement,' he ordered. 'And you...' he looked to Marion and indicated the podium. 'You are going to make sure he gets up there, smiles and the two of you are going to celebrate your husband's first Group One winner.'

Joss shook his head but a chorus of syndicate voices behind him made it clear he wasn't going to be allowed to get away from them.

'Besides,' Duncan pointed out. 'We can't have Ben going up to the winners podium to accept a prize from The Queen looking like that!'

Rob, who had thoroughly enjoyed leading The Ghost in after his win, nodded to Joss saying 'We'll be fine. We'll get them both washed down and back to their stables. There will be nothing to worry about. You and Marion enjoy your big day.'

Rob and Ben set off with The Ghost and the syndicate faded into the mass of people behind them. The two of them made their way over to the pre-parade ring where Ben was reunited with Silvery Sun. They washed both horses, took the sweat off their backs and cleaned off, gave them another drink of water and then set off walking the horses across the Ascot High Street and back to the racecourse stables.

Rob could hardly contain his excitement and managed to run through every stride of the race as he walked his hero back. Ben listened indulgently, adding the odd comment and sharing the highlights of the race with his enthused owner. They crossed the road and ambled happily down to the stable gate and then up to the same boxes they had reserved for the three horses.

Bobby's head was poking out of his box when they arrived, Jake sat outside on a small foldable chair. He jumped to his feet when the two horses arrived, running over and making a fuss of The Ghost.

'Did you see the race?' Ben asked.

'Oh yes! I watched it on my phone. It was just... epic,' he managed.

Ben saw sadness cross Jake's face, but the lad soon brightened as he gave the colt a rub between the ears and a scratch down his neck.

Rob must have caught the same look. He said 'I'm sorry you didn't get to lead him in Jake. He's your horse after all.'

Jake looked up at Rob, a tinge of regret written across his face once again. 'That's okay, I'm just pleased for the boss and the horse. He really deserved that win after everything that's gone on.'

Ben and Rob traded a quick glance and in doing so, passed a silent understanding to each other.

Ben said 'Jake, get yourself away to the parade ring. They will be doing the presentation ceremony now, but you'll still be able to catch everyone and go for a glass of champagne. Here, take my owner's pass and you'll not get stopped.'

Jake's mouth broke into a grin which expanded right across his face. Thirty seconds later he was half running, half skipping up the stable path. They watched him disappear around the corner and shared a few comments regarding the exuberance of youth.

Bobby looked well enough, his head bobbing up and down over the stable door. Rob opened the stable next door and Silvery Sun obligingly walked straight in after him. Ben tried the same thing with The Ghost, but the colt was far more interested in standing outside in the sun. Ben was started to coax him inch by inch into his stable when a male voice behind him said 'Want a hand there, Mr Ramsden?'

Ben looked around and found Billy Bentham and James Corrigan standing a couple of yards behind him. He shuddered and suddenly a feeling of vulnerability washed over him. His face must have telegraphed this to Billy, as he held up a hand. 'Just wondered if you wanted help getting this lad tucked up?'

Ben looked over to Silvery Sun's box which still had its door closed. 'Umm. Yes,' Ben ventured hesitantly.

Billy came up behind the colt and whistled a little and waved one hand. The Ghost immediately obliged and walked nonchalantly into his box as if that was what he had been aiming to accomplish all along. Ben took no chances, and tried not to turn his back on the two men, immediately taking The Ghost's head collar off and exiting the stable, pulling the stable door shut behind him and bolting it.

'He beat us fair and square today. He's some horse,' observed Corrigan, in a genuinely interested tone.

A little taken aback, Ben tried to find something intelligent to say but only managed 'Er... well, yes, he's a bit special.'

Billy added 'We thought we had the best horse this year, but it looks like we have some serious competition now.' And then to his surprise, Billy produced a broad, generous smile. Ben was disarmed and totally at a loss as to what to say.

'It's good to see someone like yourself winning a Group One,' Billy continued. 'Like you, we've not got millions to spend on our horses, so when you get a nice one on a budget and can beat the big boys it's good for the sport.'

Ben nodded his agreement, but then shrugged, 'I think there was a fair bit of luck as well.'

'Ah well!' Corrigan exclaimed. 'We all need that!' and broke into a laugh laced with gravel.

Behind them, Panama appeared. He was bare backed, having been washed down and he clicked past, led up by his stable lass. Billy and Corrigan offered a handshake, thanked Ben again, and then followed their horse to the next line of barns.

Ben only then realised that Rob was beside him.

'It looks like Ivan was wrong about those two,' Rob said quietly.

'It certainly seems that way,' he replied thoughtfully.

Ben looked around and saw there was only the one single, small chair up against Bobby's stable door.

'Look, there's no need for you to stay here. Why don't you get back to where the fun is? I can look after these three and I would guess that most of the syndicate will be back here before too long. Maybe you can grab me a glass of champagne before they're all gone?'

Rob didn't need any further persuasion. He may have been over sixty, but the way he power walked up the stable road back to the racecourse amused Ben hugely.

He checked on the three horses again, making sure they all had water and then pulled the rickety wooden chair over to The Ghost's box, setting its back against the door and carefully easing himself onto the seat. The joy of being able to relax his body wasn't diminished in the slightest by the fact the chair had a hard wooden seat. There were few people around the racecourse stables now. A lone horse walked around the parade area with its handler and most of the lads appeared to be either in the staff canteen on the other side of the compound or at the track. It was still overcast, but warm enough in his shirt and Ben took a long, deep breath, his hands lying limp on his lap.

Looking out over the stables parade area, horse walker and then further still to the expansive car park beyond, Ben finally allowed himself to close his eyes, reliving the final few furlongs of the race in his own private theatre. He spent a glorious few minutes reviewing the race in his mind and he considered everything else that the day had delivered for both himself and his syndicate. He concluded that both parties had emerged victorious in more ways than one.

This halcyon moment was broken by the sound of raised voices behind him, one or two barns away. Ben listened for a few more seconds and then jumped to his feet, grimacing when his tired muscles protested at their sudden use once again. There was real anger being vented by someone, a woman by the sound of it, and he recognised the voice of the man who was remonstrating with her. It was James Corrigan.

He couldn't make out every word, but it sounded like the woman was getting the best of the argument. He made out words like 'spineless', 'decrepit' and 'champion sire' among many expletives, but couldn't piece them together. Billy's voice also broke in, a softer, calming tone to it, but if anything the woman's response was even more vitriolic. Then the exchange stopped abruptly.

A few seconds later Billy and James Corrigan walked swiftly past the end of Ben's barn and headed down the stable path together. At one point they stopped and had an animated conversation, Corrigan flinging his hands out and pushing the hair back on his head in apparent frustration. Ben couldn't see their faces, but their body language confirmed to Ben that whoever they had been speaking with had seriously screwed up their day.

Another set of footsteps crackled on the pea gravel from the corner of the line of barns and Ben remained standing, unashamedly staring to see who would come into view. It turned out to the blonde stable lass who always led up Panama. She had a tear stained face and Ben thought of saying something, but realised he didn't know her name.

Instead of turning towards the canteen or the racecourse she unexpectedly whipped around and came towards Ben, stomping down the row of stables towards him. She called out before she reached him.

'Are you Ben Ramsden?'

Ben looked her up and down. She was tall and slim, maybe twenty-two or three. Her blonde hair was tied back in a tight ponytail and she wore a smart, tight polo shirt, the short sleeves revealing sizeable muscles to go with quite a boyish face.

'Yes, I'm Ben. I think you're with Panama, aren't you?' he asked in as amiable a voice as he could muster, uncertain how to play the young girl.

'Yeah, that's right,' she said, cocking her head towards the stable with The Ghost inside. 'That little bugger cost me dearly today.'

Ben stood motionless watching the girl, expecting her to continue, but instead she went up to the stable door and peered inside. He moved a little closer to the stable, not knowing what to expect. It seemed the girl had plenty of emotions going on, but he sensed she wasn't a danger to The Ghost. Sometimes stable lads or lasses could build up an unbreakable bond with the animals they spent all their working life with, and it had been known to cause issues when owners wanted to sell them or take them to another trainer. Perhaps that's what the argument had been about.

'Why would losing a race cost you your job?' he ventured.

She turned to face him, hands in the back pockets of her black jeans. 'Oh it's not my job I'll be losing, it's *my brother*.' The girl hurled the last few words at Ben, tiny bubbles of spittle looping out of her mouth.

Ben suddenly felt weak and pain shot down his legs and up his back. Then a ball of excruciating pain burst from just below his stomach.

His knees buckled and throat constricted and he fell to his knees.

The girl retracted her foot from Ben's groin, a curl of satisfaction on her lips. Then she took out the two steel horseshoes she had been fingering in her back pocket, gripped them tightly, held her weapons high, and brought them down on the back of Ben's head. Ben looked up quickly enough to see the first blow coming, but could do nothing about it. Before the second came Ben recognised the arc of her arm; she had thrown the acid bombs.

Thirty

He is aware of the warm, musty smell of a horse close to him, a woman speaking... and then, a huge spear of pain at the top of his head. The agony travels to the back of his skull and sends fire down his spine. He gasps for breath and opens his eyes but sees nothing. He lifts his head and stars shine brightly everywhere, so brightly it hurts. He slips back into glorious pain free blackness again.

Seconds or hours may have passed before Ben next woke he had no way of telling. This time he was careful to wait until his body was able to cope with movement. For what seemed an immense amount of time he explored his body and environment, moving every muscle and joint as slowly as possible.

With his head lolling forward almost to his lap, he tried to open his eyes. One opened with watery blurriness, but the other refused, producing a fuzzy, dark red haze instead. His left eye took several seconds to adjust to the low light, but rapid blinking eventually allowed him to spy wood shavings, horse dung, and wisps of dry hay on the concrete floor.

His jaw ached, but trying to close it rewarded him with nothing but pain. It was being held open by some foul tasting substance stuffed into his mouth. He could just see out of the corner of his good eye some sort of string or twine wrapped tightly around his head several times. On closer inspection he was sure it was blue baling twine. It was tied so tight it burnt the corners of his mouth. He tried to move his tongue to investigate, but he couldn't get it past the packing. Ben breathed heavily through his nose, but when he took a few seconds to check his heart it was beating solidly and regularly. His body felt like it was in meltdown, although inside his head he was surprisingly calm given the situation. Perhaps this is what happened just before your physical body shut down for good...

Ben was sitting, right leg straight out, the other folded awkwardly, his left foot placed under the opposite thigh. He decided not to try and alter this position for now. He was propped up against a soft surface, but he realised it was his own arms, folded behind his back and probably tied. His hands and wrists ached and something was cutting into them, so much so, even the slightest movement produced pain, although worryingly his arms themselves appeared to be numb. A slight twist of each wrist signaled he wasn't going to be capable of moving them.

At first Ben thought he was sitting in silence, although there was a distant ringing; was it from his ears or inside his head? But when he listened harder there was also warm, wet breath being sprayed over him. He tried lifting his head, fighting back the pain which seemed to swirl from one side of his head to the other. Muscles in the back of his neck clicked into spasm sending a thump of pain behind his eyes, but he managed to put his head to one side and focus his good eye across the room. No, it wasn't a room, it was a… stable. Was he still at Ascot racecourse stables?

He suddenly thought of Ivan, then realised he had no earpiece. His phone had been in his trouser pocket, but that was gone too.

A large black mass moved right in front of him, shifting in the darkness, and moving the darkness around. Ben blinked to clear the fluid which continued to collect in his eye, expecting more pain to rain down on him. Instead, a horse, definitely a horse, snorted close to the top of his head and tapped its muzzle onto the back of his head.

Ben looked again, trying to increase his angle of view and his eye now caught several small shafts of light slicing through the darkness, motes of dust sparkling when they hit the narrow channel. The thin spears of light painted long horizontal and vertical lines onto the far wall and down onto the floor.

A rustle of wood shavings directly opposite him caught his attention and he risked lifting his head a little higher, trying to focus his good eye on the far wall of the stable. There didn't appear to be anything moving in the darkness and the light from the cracks in the stable door revealed nothing. He scanned the wall once more but frustratingly found nothing.

'Hello Ben!' said a female voice in what seemed a wholly inappropriate upbeat manner. 'Ah, you're awake,' the female voice added officiously.

Ben started to voice a reply but the attempt resolved into a crackled cough and the flowering of pain from his trachea up into his lungs.

'You couldn't leave well alone could you?' she stated sharply when Ben's spasms and coughing had subsided, then proceeded to answer her question. 'No. You and your syndicate have been intensely persistent and now I've been forced to put things right myself.'

Ben concentrated hard on where the voice was coming from, cocking an ear towards the wall. It was definitely female, but he couldn't place it. There was a small rustle of wood shavings grating against each other and he whipped around and caught a glimpse of her, mostly in blackness, but she must have shifted her position slightly, as a vertical shaft of light cut across an inch of her face from the corner of one eye down to her chin and breast. She was also sitting, her back against the far wall. Then frustratingly, she moved into the blackness again.

It didn't make much sense, her skin had looked… well, wrinkled. It couldn't be the young stable lass, unless she was wearing some sort of mask. If it wasn't, then why would an old lady be sitting opposite him, in the dark, spitting venom at him? This was lunacy.

The figure took a deep breath, girded herself and struggled to her feet with a small groan, using the wall to support her. 'Well, we best get further on with this,' she stated as if calling time on a tea break. 'Mind you,

I can do this at my leisure because your bloody syndicate will be busy clinking their crystal glasses and quaffing champagne…'

Realisation suddenly struck Ben. It was the words 'We must get further on…' he'd heard it before. Perhaps even today? He said the name, but instead of his lips moving, he gagged on the padding in his mouth, bringing on another coughing episode. The name bounced around his brain as his retching wreaked havoc on his lungs. Still it made no sense. It was Eleanor Hart. Eleanor bloody Hart.

She was continuing to chatter in the darkness, just as she always did around Joss's kitchen table, and now Ben had the name in his head he started to see the woman clearly from the odd flashes of her face and body in the cracks of light. Then she stopped talking to herself and she was coming forward and tugging on a lead rein. The horse lifted its head and turned towards her, going a few steps forward so that his back legs were about three yards in front of Ben.

'…and it all started at my stud, of course,' Eleanor said as she messed with the horse's head collar. 'I don't suppose you know that I bred this chap.'

Ben could imagine the woman smiling as she said this, she spoke proudly, with pleasure in her voice.

'Yes, that bastard Corrigan insisted his name went down as the breeder with Weatherby's, but it was me who brought his mare together with the right sire to produce this lad. I foaled him and I nursed him back to health when he got colic as a yearling…'

Ben's mind whirled. She was referring to James Corrigan, the owner of… Oh Jesus, he couldn't be sat behind Panama could he?

Eleanor fiddled a little more with the horse's mouth then let out a loop of rein. Ben could hear it flopping onto the pile of shavings Panama stood on. That made no sense, what the hell was she doing?

Eleanor's chatty tone hardened 'When you spend so much time with a young horse, you get used to every habit, every little nuance they have. That's why I can make him do this…'

She reached her right hand down to Panama's front leg. Vertical and horizontal shafts of light bisected each other, bouncing off the three year old's flanks. Ben could see her moving her palm around until it was between the colt's chest and under his front leg. Then she opened her fingers to create a claw and raked her fingernails from the inside of the colt's leg up towards his chest.

Panama immediately let out a whine, jigging forward slightly. He went up on his front two legs and bucked. Two thick back legs which a few seconds ago had been benignly planted in the shavings now struck out like rods of death. They struck out at Ben.

He tried to make himself small, as small as he could, wincing, waiting for the contact to be made. The hooves only partially struck their

249

intended target; the left shoe ricocheting off Ben's right shoulder, almost certainly breaking it, but the right missed completely, whistling past Ben's right ear. He tried to cry out when the pain arrived, but nothing came from his vocal chords. Now his heart was thumping and beating an uneven song of terror in his throat.

The colt's feet returned to the wood shavings strewn floor and he snorted again uneasily, whinnying. Eleanor held his head collar, speaking softly to him. Then she immediately repeated the same movement and this time the colt's feet splayed apart, catching Ben full in the chest with a single aluminum shoed foot that flashed silver before it connected. He felt dizzy and the room swam for a few moments, then the new pain in his chest exploded, wrenching him forward. The sides of his nose expanded and contracted as he fought for air and a way of breaching the pain. Water, blood and a few other fluids flowed freely from his nostrils. He started to convulse.

'You know, about one in a hundred horses respond this way to being touched in the right way,' she said conversationally, ignoring the sound of Ben choking on his own blood. He concentrated on his breathing, counting the thousands as he'd been told to do by his counsellor on the occasions his breathing tightened or he became dizzy. The stable went quiet again and Ben caught his breath. She appeared to be waiting for him. When he'd steadied himself, Eleanor spoke again, continuing as if there had been no interruption

'It's a game we would play with him out in the paddocks, stroke him here and he kicks high, stroke him there and he kicks low.'

She could have been at a garden party, telling the village vicar a story. She sounded completely alien to Ben.

'Once your colt beat us last year I knew I had to do something,' she added breezily. 'I said to Stephanie, we can't have this, not when Panama will be coming back to my stud to stand as a stallion. It's just not on, he's the best horse in training, we know that. Of course she knew how to make him buck because I'd shown her. She loves Panama, and so I got her to take The Ghost Machine out after the race. She missed of course, but Panama wasn't to blame for what happened. Now, where did I put that last carrot...?'

The truth slammed into Ben's brain.

He was stupefied for a few seconds. His heart didn't beat. Images of Anna, the day at York, that pristine parade ring turf with her dark red blood oozing from the smashed remnants of her head. It had been awful, it had been... done on purpose...

He managed to stem the sudden urge to throw up, swallowing down the bile that had started to rise. He wanted to scream at the old lady but instead his mind was screaming, screaming obscenely. Ben's heart banged away in his throat again and it seemed every bone, muscle and sinew was singing with pain.

All at once, as if the on off button had been pushed, his body switched off the pain. Ben entered a serene moment. It felt extraordinarily dangerous, but he allowed it, he determined that he mustn't drift off into sleep though, he had to return. Down that route lay oblivion if he allowed it.

His rage was brought back a few notches by Eleanor, who started to babble once more.

'It was unfortunate about your wife, it really was. It... changed my perspective you see...'

Ben went rigid. This... monster thought it was unfortunate. His anger mushroomed once again.

'...it made me realise we simply had to stop your horse. Your wife took the punishment that time and The Ghost Machine will have to take his. Panama deserved to be the winner and his wrath will fall where he determines.'

She delivered this in a manner which left Ben befuddled. Eleanor spoke as if she was telling a small child some edifying truth about the way the world worked. He imagined her scolding voice telling him 'Don't get in the way of my Panama, or you'll be punished.'

Ben marveled at the crookedness of the woman's mindset for a moment. Her ethics were so warped she had apparently granted a racehorse the divine rights to punish people.

Eleanor's monologue continued. 'Stephanie knew it was only right and her brother... well, Richard is a bit scary isn't he, and he's not a horseman. You have to laugh, a huge grey horse with a big diamond on his face and he still couldn't get the right one, bless him.'

Eleanor shook her head and put her hands on her hips, a genuine smile on her lips.

'Oh, the joy when you didn't run in the Guineas,' Eleanor said, hugging herself. 'I thought you and Joss had got the message, but no... such a shame.'

She dropped her arms to her sides and with a sharp intake of breath through her nose seemed to shake herself out of her reminiscences. She wagged a bony index finger at Ben and asked accusingly: 'Now where have you put that carrot you naughty boy?'

Ben stared bewildered at her dark figure through his one good eye. She was crisscrossed with the lines of light, which illuminated her waggling digit as it berated him like a schoolchild. His anger had been momentarily diluted by this sudden change in direction. Now he tried pushing those thoughts aside. He must concentrate.

Eleanor was still talking but Ben ignored her. For some reason Esme in Leeds, his counsellor, floated into Ben's mind and she spoke to him: 'Isolate the physical symptoms and beat them. Take your anger and try to channel it for use in other ways. Release its power for good,' she said smoothly. Ben considered this. Then he considered Anna and Max. Max. He had to do this for his son. He had to release the anger and use it for... violence.

Ben allowed the pain to return, but only enough so he could harness some of it. He tugged at his arms, a white heat emanating from his shoulder. He was tied to something, but it did move, ever so slightly. Eleanor was now wandering to and fro at the other side of the stable, her frame being captured by the thin lines of light every few seconds. Ben pulled some more. It felt like his shoulder had come apart from his body, he couldn't feel anything that side, but he wrenched some more and something gave an inch.

He needed to know what he was attached to. He thought hard about the inside of The Ghosts stable. If he was still at Ascot every stable would be the same wouldn't they? What could he be tied to? A wooden stanchion, or a feed box, or a... He remembered a water pipe in The Ghost's stable, running down the inside of the box, feeding the manger. He had to see. Dizziness threatened to engulf him as Ben turned his head over sideways to give his left eye a view above him. He fought the nausea back, blinked the water from his pupil and his heart leapt when the thin, rusty one inch wide pipe finally came into focus. He liked thin, he liked rusty.

Eleanor was bent over at the other side of the stable, still talking to herself and wafting hay and wood shavings aside.

'Come on little carrot, where are you...?' she called in a little girls voice.

She looked over at Ben and stood up straight again. 'And don't be thinking that I will be letting you go Mr Ramsden. Oh no, no, no! You're a thorn in our side.'

Then she gestured to Panama. 'My little deception is perfect you see. I'm afraid your precious Ghost is going to kill you Ben. He's going to turn you into a ghost!'

There was something wrong with Eleanor. Ben could now make sense of the woman. She had come to a halt with a band of light running straight down her face, down her Ascot dress and to her expensive looking shoes. It was her eye, it didn't look right. She continued to speak, but Ben was morbidly fascinated by how the one eye he could see danced with madness, pure unadulterated, madness.

'You're almost dead now. One more kick from Panama should do it I think. Then we'll take you back to The Ghost's stable, where we'll pierce his tendons and leave you there with him. All terribly sad you see – horse has to be put down after going wild in his stable and kicking his owner to death. One hoof looks like another, what a shame, all dead and my Panama is European horse of the year and retires to stud the star he richly deserves to be.'

Ben looked Eleanor in the eye and then flicked his down to the floor in front of her. She returned a quizzical stare. He did the same again. Her wrinkled face ironed itself out a little as she frowned down at Ben. Again, he locked his eye with hers and theatrically, fractionally using his head this time he indicated the spot on the floor.

She looked down. Then she smiled. 'Panama's carrot!' she exclaimed delightedly and bent forward to scoop up the vegetable which was lying half buried in the wood shavings, hay and other detritus on the stable floor.

Ben had been holding onto his anger. He'd balled it up and pushed it down for the last ten months. The funeral slipped into his mind, the sadness, the heart ripping sadness. Their friends in mourning, all faces, faces that didn't know what to say or how to help. He saw Helen making the best of things. Then Max filled him. His little boy was without a mother, trying so hard to be strong, but terribly bereft. His Anna was gone. His wife, his wonderful soul mate had been taken from him, and for what?

To win a horse race.

Ben sensed the anger was almost ready, it was filling him. The walls of his being were breaking down and he was going to produce a final effort, a last burst of brilliance and harness all the hate and loathing which was now reaching its zenith.

Ben uncorked his anger and felt his pain vanish and his strength return. In one movement he lurched upwards and forwards, ripping the water pipe from its aged clasps. There was a wrenching noise as screws popped from the wall but Ben was oblivious. He took three strides to reach the woman who was straightening up with a carrot in her hand. With his last step Ben launched himself head first into Eleanor Hart's eyes. At the last moment Eleanor looked up. Those wicked, madness riddled eyes widened, and Ben rushed headlong into them.

Thirty-One

Race winners tend to receive polite applause. Ivan noted this wasn't the case with The Ghost Machine. Probably due to the press reports on the colt and his link to the accidental death at York last year, plus the fact he was the diamond marked grey underdog from the North, the crowd in front of the presentation stage bellowed their appreciation when Olivia, Janet, and Marion accepted the prize for winning the race. Rob, Joss, Ian, Duncan, and Jake watched on from just beside the stage, each of them unable to remove the smile from their faces.

It was an absorbing scene, but Ivan shuddered as he watched a feed which panned over a sea of faces in front of the parade ring. The crowd appeared to him to be a seething mass of human bodies, squeezed together in an unnatural clod in which moving and breathing became impossible. He turned his attention to another monitor to shift the coldness he now felt down his back.

Flicking through the syndicate members, he came across Ian looking and speaking with Rob and questioned why Rob, and for that matter, Jake, who appeared in the background, were there at the presentations. They should have been at the racecourse stables. But with no alerts, and the danger of attack over, it perhaps was understandable, given the result of the race.

His monitors shimmered, sending out a steady glow into his darkened room up in the Ascot stand. He was the only user of a private box to have his curtains closed for the entire afternoon of racing. Watching the aftermath of the win from the various devices on the syndicate member's lapels he stuck to the one-to-one conversations and delighted in getting a close up of the Royal representative as Marion went up to collect the primary prize.

His one-on-one contact with Armitage had broken off completely as soon as he'd reached Heatherwood hospital, even though it was only a quarter of a mile away from the racecourse. The visuals had gone in the ambulance and the audio disappeared when they arrived and were booking him in. However, he'd maintained contact with his colleague via his mobile phone. Everything looked okay on that front although he was going to be out of action for the foreseeable future.

He'd also been following Demetri's progress as he went through the process of handing in the blue-eyed man to the authorities, and explaining what he was doing carrying a man with two broken legs into the police station – a man who refused to say anything, including his name. The man himself had been sent straight off to Heatherwood too. Unlike Armitage, he went with a significant police escort.

Ivan had already informed the Ascot racing authorities about the device secreted under the ground at the round mile start. He'd seen an official Ascot vehicle down there already and was pleased at how proficient the course was when it came to safety. Luckily, there wasn't another mile race due to be run on the round course today. The involvement of police and racecourse officials did mean that the story of the day would start to come out in the media and online. Ivan was monitoring the social networks and news websites, but nothing had bubbled up yet. He reflected sadly that The Ghost's win would be more likely remembered not for its excellence, but the attempts on his life.

The alarm cancelled every other sound and Ivan's focus was immediately elsewhere. He checked the alarm result on his laptop and before he could make sense of it another positive target was found, and then another. They were all emanating from a social media app which allowed closed groups to share a text conversation. He checked locations and then tried to contact Ben by phone. It was switched off, his last geographic position being the racecourse stables, the same location as the alarm.

For the second time that day, Ivan made a call to order an ambulance. Then he spoke with Demetri one to one, followed by a contact with Rob, Duncan, and Ian all at the same time with the same message: 'Get to the racecourse stables. Now! We have confirmed targets potentially within yards of The Ghost and Ben.'

Once the ladies had exited the presentation stage, he relayed the same message to them.

****

Panama stood, his head bent over the inert human body, breathing, sniffing and poking at the mass of unmoving, jumbled limbs with his nose. When a guttural cough came from the pile, the colt shook his head and picked his way over to the small water tough in the corner of the box and drank loudly.

The slurping noise was the first thing Ben heard when he came round, which really freaked him out, as he couldn't feel much of his body and he had his head on the floor, his good eye facing the wood shavings. For one awful moment he imagined himself being eaten by something, and the terror it induced caused him to quickly spin over and sit up. Pain bombarded his senses and made his head spin, but once he could focus on Panama it at least allowed him to dispel the outrageous thoughts of being eaten alive. The sudden movement made the colt stop drinking and look dolefully back at him. His white blaze was quite striking, even in this light.

Then he realised Eleanor was gone and the panic resumed. He was still gagged and he could see now that his arms still disappeared behind his back, although he couldn't feel them, or his hands, which he couldn't decide was good or bad. At least he didn't have the pain. That said, he had

255

quite enough of that in his upper body and in his head. Some of the wood shavings had stuck to the side of his cheek, and he could feel them pinching his skin. He could see them vaguely and wished he could remove them, then caught himself. What a crazy thing to be worried about in this situation.

Ben examined the stable through his left eye. There were significant blood spots on the colt's bedding and he surmised, somewhat gleefully, it couldn't all be his own – or could it? He tried to bring his thoughts into shape, concentrated exclusively on the stable door and had to look intently, blinking rapidly to clear his double vision, before he could allow himself to believe what he was seeing. The stable door was ajar, only a crack, but the bolt wasn't in place because there was an unbroken vertical shaft of light running from the floor to the ceiling. Eleanor must have left in a hurry and not closed it behind her. That could also mean she was just on the other side.

Ben tried to get to his feet but failed miserably, rolling onto his side in agony as the external and internal injuries worked together to send all the wrong messages to his pain receptors. He lay on his side convulsing for half a minute, praying for it to stop or to pass out once again. As he lay on his bed of shavings, spasms wrenching at his back and chest, fatigue biting at his sanity, he concluded one sure fire certainty: he wasn't going to get out of this stable under his own power.

He finally relaxed into a pain-riddled stupor, lying on his side, arms still tied behind his back, baler twine wrapped around his head, taking small, short snorts of breath. He was sweating so much the salty fluid had matted his hair and now formed a steady stream down the side of his head and into his eye socket, providing yet another irritant he desperately tried to blink away. An involuntarily shudder issued from his battered body and the movement prompted Panama to cast another doubtful look towards him from the other side of the stable, then padded over to him.

Ben looked up at the huge, muscular colt as it stepped close to him and then stood, unmoving over him. The weapon used against Anna and himself bent its head down and snuffled at the glistening sweat around his hairline, blowing hot, musty hay breath into his ear. The crack in the stable door was four yards away, but it may as well have been four miles away Ben thought bitterly.

The colt continued to nibble tenderly at his ear and cheek. Then a childhood memory took hold. Ben wondered at how far addled his brain must be for 'Lassie Come Home' to be bothering his synapses at this particular time, but there it was: send the animal for help. He raised his head an inch and Panama moved back slightly, he forced his head up further, his brain sending instructions to arms he couldn't feel against what he thought had to be the horse's left front leg. Every movement sent lightening strikes of pain up through his chest and legs, but he managed to edge his head slowly up the colt's right leg until he was exactly where he wanted to be.

Taking three snorts of air in through his nose he violently thrashed his head, rubbing the baler twine as hard as he could into the same area he'd seen Eleanor scratch the colt. Panama immediately backed away from him, sending Ben in freefall to the wood shavings once more. There was no launching of a full buck, but one back left leg shot out involuntarily and landed a sharp blow on the stable door.

Ben lay prone on the floor of the stable, twitching. The colt's reaction to being scratched had sent him tumbling back to the floor of the stable with his good eye flat to the wood shavings. Fighting the drowsiness which started to fill him, he forced his head to turn through the carpet of woodchip to face the stable door and a wonderful pupil clenching light filled his retina. Ben closed his eye and allowed the blackness to take him.

Thirty-Two

A cool evening breeze had started to whip up into the trees at the back of the stables and the sound of fresh new green leaves fluttering added to the soundtrack of stable lads calling to each other and the crunch of gravel under horse's hooves. The last race of the day was twenty-five minutes away and the last of the runners were leaving for the racetrack.

Eleanor Hart wasn't feeling well. To be fair, she hadn't considered herself too well for some time, but nothing like this. Ben's head butt had knocked her out for... well, it must have been a few seconds, or could it have been a minute. She winced at the globe of pain which was growing in her head. It was after she'd rolled his horrible, sweating dead body off her that she'd started to feel peculiar. She probably had a broken nose, her head was thumping with a headache, and her vision kept jumping around. She'd stumbled outside the stable, found that stupid girl on that app she always used and then sent her off to get the barrow back again. She and her brother had ended up screwing everything up.

She felt a wave of nausea and light-headedness wash over her and steadied herself against the wire fence. She was determined that once that girl got back they'd finish this today. Stick that bloody idiot's body in The Ghost Machine's stable then stick a pitchfork in the horse's tendon. Yes, that would tie things up nicely.

Stephanie pushed an empty wheelbarrow round the corner of the last line of barns, the least occupied in the entire stabling block. She glanced back over her shoulder pensively to see if anyone was following her. It was getting chilly; she was tired and worried about Richard and wanted to go see him. And she really wasn't sure about this whole thing anymore. Even the money was starting to look less important now Richard was in hospital. His call had come from a phone she didn't recognise and he'd only spoken for a few seconds, but he'd been really angry and sworn at her. He never did that. Mrs Hart had been angry too, and taken it out on that man, the one with The Ghost Machine. She hadn't meant to hit him that hard with the shoes. But she didn't kill him, Mrs Hart had done that, so that was alright.

She looked up when her name was called and saw Mrs Hart standing against the back fence, holding it tightly, as if for support. She was calling her name over and over now and not in a nice voice. As she trundled the barrow up to her, she noticed Mrs Hart's nose and one of her eyes was now coming out black and purple. She didn't look right.

'What took you so long?' demanded Eleanor in an irritated half scream.

'You can't leave the barrows. They have to be returned each time you use them. I told you,' Stephanie replied patiently.

Eleanor held one hand to her face and looked to be in pain.

Stephanie took the chance to grab her jacket from a nearby fence post and pulled it on.

Still holding the palm of her hand to the top of her face and gripping the wire mesh fence with the other, Eleanor swayed a little.

'Just get that bastard back to The Ghost's stable. He'll not give you any problems now.'

'And then we can leave?' asked Stephanie hopefully.

'Yes, yes. You can leave and go and see that fool brother of yours,' Eleanor spat. 'So get him back round there. Now!'

Pleased with her new instructions, but angry with Mrs Hart's tone, Stephanie stayed motionless and took a long look at the rotund, wrinkled and disheveled woman in front of her.

'You shouldn't talk about Richard like that.'

Eleanor dropped her hand and her eyes bore into the girl 'And *he* shouldn't have screwed up...'

Neither woman got the opportunity to continue the conversation as a loud thunderclap of hoof on wood cracked behind them and Panama's stable door flew open. Both of them stared.'

'You said he was dead,' Stephanie said accusingly.

Panama's head and shoulders appeared at the door and Stephanie stepped towards the colt, cooing to him to remain in the stable. He looked at the two woman and then trotted directly out of the open door, turned left and set off at a trot down the line of boxes, leaving his lass to chase after him, shouting his name.

Eleanor released her grip on the fence and took two steps to follow the younger woman and then wished she hadn't. Her knees buckled and she fell like a dead weight to the ground, her ample body making the pea gravel crackle as it settled.

Jake and Duncan, being the youngest and fittest, reached the stables first, having run all the way from the racecourse. Duncan had thrown off his top hat and tails, and both men were being pursued by two sets of gate officials (which Duncan saw as a positive), because they hadn't stopped to show any identification. They arrived at The Ghost's stable to find there was no one there. They opened the stable doors, shouting for Ben. To Jake's relief all three of the grey horses appeared to be in good health, although with feeding time approaching, they were nudging him for dinner. He had no time for that just yet. Ivan had been explicit: find Ben, his life may depend on you reaching him quickly.

When he emerged from the boxes a duo of red-faced gate attendants had started to get agitated with Duncan, demanding to see his stable passes. Jake took the two them in hand while Duncan went from stable to stable, shouting Ben's name, banging on closed doors and asking anyone he could find if they had seen a man of his description. With close to two-hundred boxes in the complex Duncan was becoming more frustrated with every stable door which was bolted and every blank face and shaken head. Jake was trying to explain to the officials why he and Duncan needed to inspect the contents of every stable when there was the sound of a horse cantering close by.

A horse cantering on pea gravel makes a noise from some distance away, and Jake immediately pricked his ears up, as every horse always walks around shared stables. A cantering or galloping horse doesn't go unnoticed in racecourse stables as it means it is a loose horse; dangerous for the horse, very dangerous for humans who get in the way. All four men turned towards the sound of hooves as it intensified and automatically started to move back towards the nearest wall. The shrieks of a young woman also started to pierce the early evening air.

A few seconds later Panama cantered past them, easily identifiable by the white lightening strike down his forehead offset by his jet-black coat. The colt seemed to be maintaining a distance between himself and his handler, who flew past the four men in pursuit, panting with the exertion. As the blonde girl went past them, Duncan noticed she was wearing a black leather jacket. When she passed him he was able to confirm there was a three inch rip from the shoulder. Without explaining he set off running after the girl, leaving Jake bemused, and the two officials shaking their heads and remonstrating with him.

Ivan was watching both Jake and Duncan's feeds. He switched immediately to Demetri's once Duncan set off, and said a few words. At the bottom of the stabling block, Demetri waited. The colt flew past and then mounted a grass verge and headed down to the large exercise area. Ivan said a single word and Demetri shot out of the cover of the end of the barn and ran the opposite way to the colt. Stephanie saw the large man coming and tried to avoid him, assuming he was going to run past her. Instead Demetri threw himself to the ground horizontally just in front of her and took her legs out from under her. By the time she had come to a dusty heap in the gravel Demetri was pulling her to her feet and shouting in her face.

'Where is he?' Demetri demanded with menace, his large hands holding her by the shoulders at arms length.

The girl looked shocked but then tried to aim a kick at Demetri, only to see it deflected by his knee. He repeated the demand, shaking her shoulders. A few other stable lads started to approach the two of them, having witnessed the way Demetri had brought the girl down. She was clearly one of them, and needed protecting.

Demetri continued 'Where is the stable? Ben Ramsden. Where is he?'

Still the girl said nothing, a hateful scowl the only reaction she was able to pass to the big man. Duncan arrived a moment later and quickly took in the scene. Three stable lads were circling Demetri, less than impressed with the big man shaking one of their own. Duncan immediately started to relate the true reality of the situation.

'Look lads, we need your help. A man may have been killed or be in serious danger. He is in one of these stables and this girl knows which one. We have to find him.'

Stephanie screamed 'Get off me!' and struggled to free herself from Demetri's grasp, desperately looking for signs of Panama or Mrs Hart.

Casting her eyes down the hill, she realised her horse had come to a halt down by the horse walker. Panama's muzzle was touching the ground as he took a pick of grass, then he straightened and looked back up the hill as he ground his mouthful between his teeth. There was no sign of Mrs Hart, and the girl's anger started to transfer to the old woman who couldn't be bothered to help catch such a wonderful and important horse.

Stephanie looked straight up into Demetri's bulging eyes. She crossed her arms like a spoilt little girl, looked to the sky and coldly informed her audience 'You're too late. He's already dead.'

Demetri's eyes fizzed with rage and he raised a flat hand as if he was about to slap her. Ivan's voice pleaded in his ear and Duncan made a grab for Demetri's arm. As he was about to start his flat palm on a trajectory to land a blow to the girl's cheek she flinched back and then burst out with 'Top Barns. He's in the top barns, the very last box but one...'

By the time the word 'box' had left her mouth both Demetri and Duncan were running up to the top of the seven lines of stabling barns.

They rounded the final corner and pelted down the avenue of stables, horses' heads poking out above stable doors to see what all the commotion was about. Demetri got there first. He hardly glanced at the woman lying outside the stable as he charged up.

Skidding to a stop on the gravel, Demetri found the stable just as the girl had described. The door was half open. He peered into the darkness and tentatively pulled the stable door wide until he could see what lay inside.

Thirty-Three

Marion opened the front door and smiled briefly at the two men stood on her front porch. Ivan and Demetri looked up at her a little awkwardly, but relaxed when she waved them both into the house. 'Be quiet for heaven's sake, Joss,' she called down the hall to the kitchen as she closed the front door. A number of both female and male voices could be heard arguing in the distance, but they subsided once Marion's warning was sounded.

The men waited just inside the hallway and Marion bustled past them, reaching the kitchen first, and held the door open for the two owners.

'You must have seen this?' Ivan queried, holding up a copy of The Racing Post before he entered the large kitchen. His index finger tapped the headline which read 'O'Hoole Exonerated Following Royal Ascot Affair.'

'Has he seen it?' Marion replied ironically, winking at Ivan as he stepped into the kitchen. 'He must have five copies of that report and has already read it to me three times today.'

'Make that six copies,' said Ivan slapping the paper down on the kitchen table which received a round of friendly agreement from the room.

Joss stood behind the door and energetically pumped the hands of both men once they entered, sharing smiles and greetings with them. Ivan looked round once Joss had done grappling with his hand and found the rest of the syndicate either seated around the vast kitchen table or leaning up against walls, the fireplace or window ledges. Ian, Duncan and Rob raised hands or nodded, while Janet and Olivia sat at the table and beamed up at him.

Demetri moved into the room, sharing an easy few words with each person as he met them. Ivan followed in the wake of the big man in terms of social interaction, as he had for fifteen years, eventually pegging a seat beside Janet. As a rule he found women more interesting than men, and older women far more direct and easy to deal with. Janet was also Scottish, which also seemed to help. After working his way around the room, Demetri struck up a conversation with Joss and Marion, although eventually everyone was listening to what he had to say about Eleanor Hart. Five weeks had passed since Royal Ascot and every member of the syndicate had been interviewed and re-interviewed by the police.

The Forties had come in for heavy-duty treatment from the authorities, with their explanation for how they managed to attain private information and track private citizens coming under specific scrutiny. Ascot had been interested in how an acid attack could happen outside their front gate without their knowledge while the police were fascinated to know how Ivan could instruct the syndicate without any equipment being found at the track. After a fortnight of intense activity the pressure started to fall away, and due to the circumstances surrounding Eleanor Hart it seemed the whole episode was now in the hands of the Crown Prosecution Service.

Demetri started with the words 'Eleanor Hart...' and the kitchen fell silent. 'She's still in hospital, although she has been transferred to a secure specialist unit.'

'Do they know what's wrong with her? She really didn't look right before she was bundled into that ambulance at the stables,' asked Duncan, who had admitted at the time that he'd always 'Quite liked the old trout,' and how out of character her actions seemed.

'It's inconclusive at the moment, but we understand her doctors have recommended a period of psychological evaluation. They are suggesting early onset dementia or possibly schizophrenia. Either way, it's unlikely she will face trial any time soon,' Demetri reported.

He continued 'The doctors were looking for a major event which may have triggered the change in her character.'

'The attempt to aim a kick at The Ghost at York and Anna's subsequent death would seem to fit the bill perfectly,' suggested Ivan blandly.

Duncan looked perplexed and then challenged 'So she blames herself for Anna's death and as a result becomes even loopier?'

Ivan couldn't help himself, he answered 'I wouldn't have used that turn of phrase, but as ever Duncan, you have painted a wonderfully crude synopsis which underlines all the major themes with a loquacious veneer.'

Duncan's face went through several iterations of pleased, confused and umbrage at Ivan's reply, but in the end settled for a sheepish smile.

'I think Ian might have some inside information on the other two,' Demetri prompted, keen to move the conversation away from Ivan.

Ian, who was leaning on the fireplace, pushed his glasses up onto his nose at hearing his name and cleared his throat. 'Yes, indeed. I had a word with my Inspector friend in the force in London and he had a little off the record chat with the lead officer on the case in Ascot. Stephanie Austin provided the full story to the police. It appears she was a much better stable hand than budding master criminal. It's her brother who is the nasty piece of work.'

'I know some of you will know some of this, but for those of you who don't, I'll give you the full version,' said Ian, pulling a chair out from under the table. He slid into the seat, steepling his hands in front of him.

'Eleanor Hart bred Panama for his owner, James Corrigan. She suggested the mating with a decent mare Corrigan had owned. When the horse was just a yearling she must have realised he was a bit special and managed to get James to agree that should the horse end up being good enough to be a stallion, he would return to Eleanor's stud to stand in Berkshire. Her Father set up the stud eighty years ago, but business has been poor in the last decade. It looks like Eleanor's choices of broodmares and matings didn't work out for some time. So, when Panama won as a two year old and started to look very special indeed, it was all going swimmingly for her, until The Ghost Machine turned up and beat her big hope at York.'

Olivia raised her hand and Ian, smiling, nodded at her.

'So what's it worth to a stud to have a horse like Panama or The Ghost?' she asked in her sweet Scottish lilt.

Joss answered. 'Potentially it's tens of millions of pounds over the course of their career as a stallion.'

Ian picked up the story again. 'I imagine the decision to try and kick and injure The Ghost was made in haste, during the aftermath of the York race and driven by the bitter disappointment of being beaten. Stephanie told the police that Eleanor had promised her ten thousand pounds if she could injure The Ghost. All she had to do was stroke him in the right place after the race. When Stephanie missed The Ghost and Panama kicked Anna instead, the whole episode spiraled out of control. From what Demetri has said, it sounds like it probably affected Eleanor mentally as well.'

'Stephanie seems to be a deeply misguided young woman, but her brother Richard is well known to the police,' Ian said, pausing to take a piece of paper from a wallet he produced from his inside pocket.

'He answered 'no comment' to every single question the Police put to him. It seems Stephanie is very close to her brother. She asked him to help once Eleanor spoke to Joss in spring and discovered how well The Ghost was going on the gallops.'

Joss shook his head and shrugged. 'I still can't believe I sat at this table and gave her all the information she needed to try and hurt people. She started coming every week from autumn onwards, I thought it was just because she liked us and her two horses she had here.'

'I think all of us were taken in by her,' Marion said softly, placing a reassuring hand on her husband's back. 'Both her horses have gone elsewhere now anyway.'

Ian continued 'Richard was refused basic training after failing the medicals for both the RAF and the Army in his teens. He spent the next five years as a bouncer, getting a reputation for being rather heavy handed, and was charged twice with affray, finally being sent to prison for three years for beating up the manager of the club he was working for at the time. The last couple of years the police believe he was acting as a set of fists for hire, but I guess The Ghost gave him the opportunity to branch out.'

Ian referred to his piece of handwritten paper again. 'The two of them are going to be charged with various things, but the main one is manslaughter.'

'So who was on the motorbike?' Joss asked.

'Stephanie,' replied Ian. 'She told the police she waited until we left with the three greys and then jumped on her bike which was parked in the racecourse public car park. She got the acid bombs from her brother who told her they were firecrackers which would scare the horses and make them bolt. Then she rode straight back to the stables by cutting across the wood behind the barns. They found the motorbike in the trees. My inspector friend said she was really upset when the interviewing officer pointed out that there was some sort of acid in the bombs. Apparently she showed more compassion for the horses involved than the people.'

Olivia broke in. 'Her brother must be a really wicked person to happily fire acid and crossbow bolts into people and horses. How is Armit... Andrew?'

'He's like a bear with a sore head, desperate to be busy again, but we've got him under wraps just at the moment – so no work. However, he did threaten to turn up here later this evening,' Demetri answered.

'Oh good, I'd love to see him,' enthused Janet.

'I'd love to see what the doctors have made of his chest!' Duncan admitted. 'For example, did they pull the bolt out from his back, or did they...'

'Duncan!' Marion scolded.

'But seriously...,' Duncan continued, a little wounded. 'That was a serious fourteen inches of ...,' his voice tailed away as Marion's stare increased its intensity. Armitage had certainly fostered some staunch friends in the yard thought Duncan, and was silent once again.

Ian tried to curtail a smile and having done so, continued to finish off his report.

'Richard is a nasty piece of work by all accounts. But that said, he went to pretty extraordinary lengths. It seems the acid attack was staged to put us off our guard for the really serious one he had planned for The Ghost in the stalls.'

Rob interrupted. 'I've not worked out how he managed to get it into the ground and in the right place. That must have been really difficult.'

Ivan answered this query. 'Not really,' he said, with a slight hint of arrogance which made Demetri wince slightly.

'The stalls are always placed in the same place for every mile race on the round course. You can actually go and see where the rails are removed and the ten bay stalls are wheeled into place. Each stall is three quarters of a metre wide. All you need to do is measure across from the rail two and a quarter metres from where the wheel marks are.'

'But how did this Richard know which stall The Ghost would be in?' asked Janet.

Again Ivan replied. 'The stalls positions are known two days in advance. So he'd have known on the Monday morning The Ghost was in stall three. I assume he installed the crossbow on Tuesday night.'

Ivan continued 'It was actually quite ingenious given he used very crude implements. He put the crossbow into a metal cradle, pulled the bow back, and inserted the bolt so it would fire through a plastic tube to maintain accuracy. But he needed to get the bolt to fire remotely, so he placed a mobile phone beside the release mechanism and put it on silent ring and vibrate. The vibrations set the bolt off. That's what Armitage heard before he got shot. The blue eyed man sat in his tree all day, waiting for the race, and when it came to his big moment Armitage got in the way.'

'Instead of accepting it, the blue eyed man pulls the trigger, or calls the phone in this case, and gets the man instead of the horse. Without the protection of his vest Armitage could have died, and I think The Ghost would have certainly been very badly wounded,' Ivan concluded.

'I think we're all amazed Armitage found it before the race!' exclaimed Rob. 'It's great news that he's on the mend, but tell me, is that really what you call him – 'Armitage'?'

'We have called ourselves by our surnames since we were eight. His stuck, but Demetri wanted his first name used when we left school. I'm referred to as Mr Pod by the others.' Ivan stated matter-of-factly.

'Mr Pod?' Duncan sniggered.

Ivan looked up at Duncan and sighed. 'My name is Ivan Podogrocki. Even I have to admit it's a mouthful if you aren't Polish.'

'Moving on!' Ian exclaimed, keen to complete his update.

'My contact reckons it will come to court in about three months time and we may all need to provide evidence. Given the fact that Stephanie Austin has admitted all the offences and will be pleading guilty, her brother may eventually follow suit. He's offered no comment to everything so far but could be convinced to plead as well, in return for a lighter sentence.'

Ian looked up and around the room 'And that's it. That's all I have for you.'

'Thanks Ian,' said Demetri. 'That just about wraps everything up I think. We are certain it was Richard who made the attempt on The Ghost with the drone. It seems this was his style, and he was definitely the fake Policeman who came in here and doped the wrong horses. The police checked, and Eleanor ordered the antibiotics online ten days before he arrived here. We also believe Stephanie arranged the kids to lay the tacks in Lambourn before the Newbury race.'

'And I hope that's the end of the whole sorry affair!' Marion stated to the room.

Duncan chimed in with 'Hear, hear!'

'Mind you,' Janet said in her soft voice, a spark of naughtiness in there too. 'I quite enjoyed myself!'

One or two people allowed themselves a chuckle.

She continued 'I've got enough stories and anecdotes to keep me going at all my bridge evenings for the next six months!'

This brought about a proper round of laughing. When it had subsided Rob spoke up.

'Before we go and see The Ghost I wanted to tell you...,' his voice trailed off, but he swallowed and continued '... that I will be leaving the syndicate. Well, sort of.'

There were looks of astonishment around the table from the syndicate, but Demetri and Ivan looked stoically down towards the floor.

Rob explained: 'You'll all know that my Mum isn't too well, and it's getting harder to look after her at home as her condition, well.. becomes worse over time. Well the Forties have made me a really good offer for my share and I'm going to sell to them.'

Joss and Ian both looked as if they were about to say something but Rob held up a hand and went on. 'Given everything that happened at Ascot, I think we all know we can trust these guys to do the right thing by The Ghost. They've guaranteed he will stay with you Joss for the entirety of his racing career and I would imagine they will want to stand him as a stallion up in Scotland when he's done racing, but I think they will do right by the horse and the rest of you.'

'What this will mean to me is that my Mum will get the very best of care and I can afford to put a manager in at the pub so that I've got more time for her. They'll get a really super stallion to breed from and I'll still get to go racing with him, that's part of the arrangement,' Rob concluded.

'I think you're absolutely right,' said Duncan positively before anyone else could make a comment. 'You're doing the right thing Rob. And as for you Forties boys, I'm with Rob, I trust you'll look after the horse.'

Ivan and Demetri looked pleased but said nothing, waiting to see what response came from the rest of the syndicate.

Ian placed a hand on Ivan's shoulder, and even though the man seemed to shrink from his grip, he continued to smile. 'I think Duncan is probably speaking for all of us, and I for one would love to see The Ghost end up standing as a stallion for the newest stud in Scotland... but with one proviso... we get to send a really nice mare to him in his first year!'

Ian's words received universal approval and Rob's initial uncertainty turned quickly into relief and a broad smile.

'Okay, are we good to go then?' enquired Joss of everyone. A series of nods and people getting up from their seats indicated they were and the whole syndicate trooped outside. Once there, Joss sent several staff out into the yard to round up people. Duncan's wife Nancy and his girls appeared, as did Ian's son Mark, along with his mother and sister. Zippo was happily darting about between the owners and a number of other syndicate friends also appeared from the far end of the stable yard. Once together, the group of about forty people headed down to the bottom paddock, over into the meadow and to the river beyond.

It was a lovely warm summer evening with just the hint of a breeze and, as the group of adults strolled downhill, Joss's children's voices could be heard down at the boathouse, splashing each other in the shallows. A call went up for the yard staff and one by one, they appeared from all directions. Two stable hands joined the procession, both wheeling laden barrows covered with large checked tablecloths. Underneath the cloths was enough barbeque food and drink to satisfy a small army. Joss ordered people to move furniture, build fires, light-heating lamps and generally acted like a racehorse trainer. Soon the ten foot long barbeque was lit and Marion and the Scottish ladies laid the huge boathouse table.

The atmosphere was relaxed and joyful. Adults ran around after the various children or kicked footballs around, whilst others splashed in the water. Everyone waited for the coals on the barbeque to turn white and the cooking to start. Presently, there was a shout from up the hill and a man with a crutch under each armpit and a black Fedora tilted down just below the eye line on his bald head came tri-podding down the meadow.

'Armitage!' Duncan screamed in delight and went running up to the small man, attempting to lend a hand. He was summarily dismissed by Armitage and he rolled into the boathouse under his own steam to a smattering of applause and the obvious delight of everyone there. They knew his story and how he had been pivotal to the success at Ascot.

After the barrage of questions, a display of his chest wound (much to Duncan's approval) and many hugs, claps on the back and offers of drinks, Armitage settled into an old armchair in the front of the boathouse and took on the role of 'returning hero' to the best of his ability.

The coals were almost completely white when Joss checked his mobile phone and managed to elicit silence from everyone at the riverside. The only sound for a few moments was from the songbirds in the two huge trees which hung over the river and dipped their roots into the water. The lapping of the river against the bank seemed to increase in intensity and then, from around the bend in the river a small pleasure boat appeared with four people apparently enjoying an evening cruise. The engine in the small boat phutted its way up the opposite bank, but then as they drew closer to the boathouse the craft tacked over to the nearside bank and everyone could then make the positive identification.

Ben Ramsden sat in a wheelchair on the extremely small prow of the boat with a perplexed look on his face. The entire riverbank appeared to be bursting with people shouting and waving at his boat and at him. Soon the whole riverbank broke into a rendition of 'Happy Birthday.' Helen and Max sat behind Ben and he turned but couldn't speak for a few seconds, a single tear rolling down his cheek.

'You are so naughty!' he told Max playfully, tickling his son who jumped up to stand beside him, fingers in his mouth, watching the boathouse slowly draw nearer and holding onto his Dad's wheelchair.

Helen got up from her seat on the other side of the riverboat cruiser, aided by its skipper, and hugged Ben, tears also welling in her eyes.

'It was Duncan and Joss's idea really, but they got me to set it up for them. I hope you didn't guess?'

Ben looked at his mother-in-law in amusement. 'You really think I had any clue which river we were on or where it was going? I thought it was really a treat for Max!'

The boat's engine was cut and it coasted into the boathouse moorings. Max was first out along with Mojo, who skittered over the side of the boat, almost falling between the boat and the mooring boards, before pelting off with Zippo and all the children, Max following close behind.

Demetri and the skipper of the boat brought Ben ashore and the next fifteen minutes were spent with Ben relating the story of Ascot to a large group. He had just finished his explanation of what happened when the blue-eyed man dropped out of his tree, when Joss tapped on his shoulder and pointed up the meadow.

'Look. There are another couple of people here to wish you well.'

Jake stood with a lead rein on a grey colt which sported a large diamond of dark, brown black on its forehead. A small figure sat on top of the horse, waving enthusiastically from side to side. There was no tack on The Ghost, but Raul Garcia's outline was unmistakable, even without his jockey paraphernalia. He waved a few more seconds and then slipped off the horse when the children ran up to the colt.

Marion bobbed down beside Ben's wheelchair. 'I know you haven't seen him since Ascot, so we thought we'd bring him down for a walk out. Do you want to get up there and see him?'

'Do I? Get me up there now!' Ben responded loudly and positively.

Joss placed the first burgers and steaks onto the grill and soon the smell of sizzling barbecued food was wafting all over the riverbank. The children petted the big colt and Marion produced a few carrots for the youngsters to give to him. For his part, The Ghost stood stock still apart from whisking his tail at the flies, lapping up all the attention. Ben eventually reached the side of the magnificent colt in his chair and was delighted when the three year old dropped his head onto his lap to grab another carrot. He rubbed the colt's nose and head and the talk was of where he would run next, whether he would race as a four year old or go straight to stud and if he would figure as racehorse of the year.

A few hours, lots of food and drink and many tearful reunions with friends later, Ben sat in an armchair which was the twin to the one

Armitage had bagged, the two recovering heroes looking over the river as the sun dipped behind a line of trees in the mid-distance. Both men had drinks in their hands which hadn't been touched for many minutes, but the act of holding the unfinished alcohol seemed to allow the evening to extend.

'Did I tell you that I discovered why I was having those dizzy spells?' Ben blurted with a half laugh bubbling up after he had spoken. He noted that the mix of alcohol with his medications was starting to take effect.

Armitage admitted he hadn't been aware of this discovery as he'd been in hospital for the last three weeks, which he related with a certain hint of sarcasm in his voice.

'Ah, I know all about hospital,' retorted Ben, oblivious to any sort of hidden meaning in Armitage's words. 'No, I found out why I've been getting dizzy and falling about everywhere for all those weeks before Ascot. As a result of the hundreds of tests on me, the doctors found out something.'

Armitage sighed. 'So what did they find out Ben?' he asked in a child's voice.

'You do that children's voice really very well you know. I think I prefer your high-pitched one,' Ben pointed out with another laugh.

'No, no. The dizzy spells I was having everywhere were down to an allergic reaction to saffron.'

'Saffron?'

'Yes, you know, the herby, flowery thing you put in food,' Ben explained, the alcohol starting to fuddle his thoughts a little. 'Every Friday night my lovely mother-in-law, Helen.' he pointed her out stood over at the barbecue with a flick of his hand. 'She always comes over to cook a lasagne, which is just superb by the way, and she has a magic ingredient. I saw her adding it when Anna was alive. She adds a smidgen of saffron. Expensive stuff but it makes a big difference I guess.' He nodded to himself in agreement, rolled the whisky round in his glass making the ice cubes plink and took a small sip.

'So I was eating my way through a couple of pounds of lasagne every Friday night and loving it, and then falling over all weekend because it was doing weird and wonderful things to my brain! The doctors had a field day with that one, even got in touch with my counsellor because they thought it could have been bringing on the panic attacks.'

'Well that sounds like something positive that's come out of all of this then!' suggested Armitage, heaping sarcasm into the delivery of his words.

'Ah, well, it would be a wonderful breakthrough,' Ben admitted, the sarcasm lost on him. 'So tell me my dear Armitage, how do I tell my lovely mother-in-law she's been poisoning me with her lovingly created lasagne every week for the last ten months?'

'Do you *have* to tell her?'

Ben considered this, but quickly ruled it out. 'No, no, that's no good. No help at all,' he shook his head slowly and grimaced.

Armitage pressed the point. 'What's so wrong with keeping it to yourself and not eating the food?'

Ben produced a theatrical sigh. 'If I don't tell her, it will be lasagne again next Friday, and the Friday after that… What am I supposed to do, poke it around the plate every week? Besides, it's *really* lovely stuff.'

Armitage's nose twitched and then a broad grin spread over his face. 'Perhaps *I* could tell her for you! Oh go on, let me. You know I still haven't forgiven you for that *I'll sell my share… for a million* lark you pulled on me! He squeaked a little behind clenched teeth and then managed to control himself. '*Please* let me tell her!'

'Aha!' said Ben triumphantly. 'And I wasn't even trying. I've finally got you to smile. That's the first time since we've met… and all I needed was a bad news story about myself and to ply you with alcohol!' Ben paused before saying a little flatly. 'Besides, I do wonder whether the way the allergy affected my brain didn't actually help me get out of that stable alive…'

Armitage waited. When no further words came from Ben he cleared his throat. '*That's exactly* how you tell Helen.'

The two men fell back in their chairs, Armitage contemplating Ben's statement regarding his own lack of outwardly displayed joy. He dismissed it as an issue almost immediately. Ben made a decision to come clean to Helen on the way home. Armitage's suggestion had its merits. Also, it might be easier when he was slightly tipsy.

They were both silent for a while, watching the last remnants of the blood red sun disappear completely from view and the transition around them as the boathouse fairy lights and candles took over the job of maintaining the illumination as the natural light faded away.

Armitage broke the silence this time, asking 'So your dizzy spells were down to saffron poisoning, but how about… well, everything else? I was in hospital for three weeks so you've beaten me there by another ten days.'

'You're asking after my physical or my mental health?' Ben probed, poker faced.

'Either or. Up to you, hero boy,' answered Armitage, feeling he might have asked too stern a question. He was relieved when a response returned relatively quickly.

Ben took a couple of breaths 'Well, the ribs, shoulder and wrists will all fix in time, although they still hurt like billy-o at the moment. The skull fracture seems to be okay, but I've got plenty more tests on that to look forward to. The doctors have taken out lots of bits of my organs and sewn them back together which is fine, after all, who really needs all their spleen? But the bummer is I'm going to be partially sighted in my right eye. Ms Hart must have got one really good kick in at me and managed to pretty much blind me in my right eye. Apart from that, I'm fine and dandy…'

'So the dizziness was the lasagne. You're blaming the food for your panic attacks as well?' Armitage asked.

Ben cast an eye over to the other armchair and considered not answering but Armitage appeared to be genuinely interested.

'No, they are all my own making. I've already seen my counsellor this week,' Ben replied as if showing patience to a tiresome child. 'I'm hopeful that the lack of a mad woman trying to kill me will help me beat that one. I'm also going to get Max some time with me and the counsellor. I've arrogantly assumed I was the one affected by Anna's death but I want to make sure he's going to be okay as well.'

Armitage murmured a positive noise and after another short silence he asked 'And the wheelchair?'

'Oh, hopefully I'll be out of it and on my feet in a month or two.' Ben said brightly.

There was a short pause. Then Armitage said 'Well, that's nothing, I had fourteen inches of carbon fibre sticking out of my chest for twelve hours!'

Ben guffawed, trying desperately not to spill his drink. 'Yep, I guess out of the two of us yours is a far sexier story, and even better, it's far shorter.'

Ben caught Armitage grinning for a few seconds and was strangely pleased with that reaction from the man.

Again, they fell into a contented silence and Ben listened to the children calling to each other up in the meadow, playing a game with Duncan and Joss.

'You know the question I really don't like to answer about Ascot?' Ben said sleepily, slurring his words ever so slightly.

'No?' replied Armitage, his interest suddenly piqued.

'So Ben, how did you survive after being kicked countless times in the head by a horse?'

The two men hadn't been looking at each other, but at this Armitage shifted in his chair and peered into the syndicate manager's face.

'The reason I don't like the question is because I have to lie.' Ben admitted.

'What do you say?'

'Oh, something about not giving up, you know, focusing my mind on positives.'

'And that isn't how you survived?' asked Armitage, his continued interest starting to show in his tone.

'Nope,' Ben replied, smacking his lips as the finished the word. He then paused for another sip of his drink.

'You want to know how I survived?' Ben repeated, but didn't wait for an answer.

'I kept thinking of you... I thought to myself, there is no way I'm going to let that little jumped up bald chap get all the bloody sympathy!' said Ben before a fit of giggling took hold of him.

'If I could walk I'd... walk right out of here.' Armitage barked back, laughing too. When Ben's whisky fueled giggling wouldn't stop, Armitage removed his hat and unsuccessfully tried to whack Ben from the confines of his armchair. A couple of attempts later the steel brim of the Fedora buckled and bent against the arm of Ben's chair and Armitage gave up and plopped it back on his head. It now looked ridiculous and they both laughed some more.

Thirty-Four

Joss and Ben took a wide path through the bottom of the central oval of the primary yard and emerged into the bottom yard, where two modern stabling barns stood side by side, spaced wide apart between the well-trimmed hedges and manicured grass verges of Joss's Middleham yard. To the far right, a smaller path wound its way up a terraced row of five purpose built single story homes for staff accommodation, with a laundry-cum-tack room alongside.

The sun poked through from behind a slate grey sky and sent shards of light down, momentarily backlighting the scene. Ben started off down the right hand path toward the 'in-training' barn, but Joss set off down the left, saying 'No, no, this way…'

Then Ben understood. 'It's happened then?' he said, excitement in his voice.

'Late last night,' Joss replied with a big grin on his face. 'I knew Max would be in bed, so didn't want to bother you. She finally foaled at three o'clock in the morning and we have a brassy bay colt on the ground.' He paused, with his grin growing larger. 'And he has a rather interesting... well, I'll let you see for yourself.'

They walked towards the breeding barn, Ben feeling the pulse of excitement coursing through him with each step. The anticipation almost cancelled out the prickles of pain. He'd been walking unaided for a couple of months now and his physiotherapist was pleased with his progress, but he still experienced twangs of nerves jangling down his legs when he tried to pick up the pace. Joss led the way, past the first three foaling bays and then stopped in front of the fourth. Two or three staff busied themselves up and down the barn, but as Ben and Joss approached, a man in his twenties who had been unbinding bales of wood shavings looked up, pocketed his implement and joined them.

'Hiya Jake,' said Ben in greeting. 'Everything okay with the two of them?'

The stable lad gave a single, positive nod 'Mother and son doing well. Bertha needed a bit of time to get over the birth, but she was soon into the swing of things. The colt is… well, take a look, he's strong and correct, which is as much as you can ask for after only a few hours of life.'

Over towards the back of the specialist foaling bay a mare was lying. She looked up as the three men peered into her personal space, but she soon put her head back down and resumed licking the quivering lump which lay curled up at her chest. As if to order, the foal lifted its head and its rump rose uncertainly, followed by his front end and it shakily stood up, turned, and took a few uncertain looking steps to face, and then look up the men.

Ben's mouth opened but made no sound. Joss looked into Ben's face and then clapped a firm, friendly hand on his shoulder and shook him slightly. Then he looked back to the foal, which remained standing unsteadily, staring into the middle distance.

The foal was a grey and in the centre of its forehead was a large diamond of dark, brown black.

'I think we might have a bit of fun with this one,' whispered Joss.

Enjoyed this book?

I do hope you have enjoyed reading The Syndicate Manager. If you have, I'd *really* appreciate it if you would visit the Amazon website and leave a rating and perhaps a short review. If enough people like this story, I may be persuaded to write another… then again, something strange did happen at a trainer's yard the other day which has given me an idea…

Many thanks.

Richard Laws
August 12th 2018